THE HOUSE ON FOSTER HILL

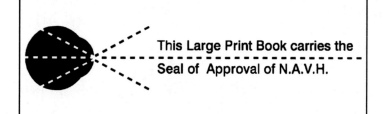

This Large Print Book carries the
Seal of Approval of N.A.V.H.

THE HOUSE ON
FOSTER HILL

JAIME JO WRIGHT

THORNDIKE PRESS
A part of Gale, a Cengage Company

Farmington Hills, Mich • San Francisco • New York • Waterville, Maine
Meriden, Conn • Mason, Ohio • Chicago

**LIBRARY OF CONGRESS CIP DATA ON FILE.
CATALOGUING IN PUBLICATION FOR THIS BOOK
IS AVAILABLE FROM THE LIBRARY OF CONGRESS**

ISBN-13: 978-1-4328-4630-5 (hardcover)
ISBN-10: 1-4328-4630-2 (hardcover)

Published in 2018 by arrangement with Bethany House Publishers, a division of Baker Publishing Group

Printed in the United States of America
1 2 3 4 5 6 7 22 21 20 19 18

To Nathan. My Cap'n Hook.
The pirate I despised, then tolerated,
then finally loved.
I don't need my heart back. You can
keep it.
Pirates treasure those types of things.

And to Daddy. We did it.

I washed the weather and the journey from my face and hands, and went out to the memorable old house that it would have been so much the better for me never to have entered, never to have seen. . . .

That was a memorable day to me, for it made great changes in me. But it is the same with any life. Imagine one selected day struck out of it, and think how different its course would have been. Pause you who read this, and think for a moment of the long chain of iron or gold, of thorns or flowers, that would never have bound you, but for the formation of the first link on one memorable day.

Charles Dickens, *Great Expectations*

CHAPTER 1

IVY

Oakwood, Wisconsin
March 1906

Death had a way of creeping up on a soul, and Ivy Thorpe was determined that when it visited her, she would not be surprised. Her story would be recorded and remembered. There was nothing worse than seeing the casing of a soul that had drifted into eternity, knowing the body would return to dust while the life lived became a tin-plated photograph with a forgotten name. Lives lost in the passage of time. Unremembered. Like Andrew.

Ivy averted her eyes from the path leading to the pond where her brother had died. A different soul needed her attention today. Shedding tears over Andrew would only waste time and leave her dehydrated.

"Where did they find her?" She posed her question to her father, whose long strides

9

were in rhythm with the medical bag swinging from his hand at his side.

He stepped over a tree root buried just under the surface of the dirt road. "In the hollowed oak tree."

Ivy hoisted the hemline of her green wool skirt. She frowned. The tree was ancient, and the memories it had witnessed fascinated Ivy's curiosity. Stories hidden in its leafless soul — if such a thing were possible.

"The oak that has no bark on its trunk?"

Her father gave a curt nod. He was as focused as she was but for different reasons. The mind of a doctor dubbing as medical examiner would be spinning with the questions about how the deceased died. Or what the method of death could tell them about her last moments? But for Ivy, separating the person from the science of her death was impossible. Who was she? Not just her name, or if she struck a familiar chord, or could be identified. But, what was her story? What memories did she leave behind, and what hearts were broken in the wake of her passing? Ivy blinked to shove away a surge of unwelcome sentiment. Grief was a high currency to pay for loving someone, and she paid her dues on a moment-by-moment basis.

Trees arched over the road, their scraggly

arms outstretched. Spring was on its way, though ice was still trapped in tree crevices, with patches of snow in the shaded pockets of the root base. As they rounded the corner, Foster Hill came into view, so named for the town's founding family. At the top, glaring down at them with empty eyes, was Foster Hill House. It had been abandoned before Ivy was born. The years had not been kind to the old house.

Ivy squinted into the sudden glare of sunlight as the bright orb escaped from behind gray clouds. Several men congregated at the bottom of Foster Hill, their backs to her and her father as they surrounded the base of the largest oak tree in Oakwood, Wisconsin. Three of the men she recognized: the sheriff, his deputy, and Mr. Foggerty, who liked to trap animals on the abandoned property — mostly raccoon and mink by the stream that ran into the pond, and . . .

"For all that's holy." Ivy froze, releasing her grip on her skirt and allowing the hemline to settle on the muddy earth.

"Ivy!" Her father should be used to her unorthodox exclamations by now.

"Joel." She knew the lifeless expression in her voice did nothing to represent the pounding of her heart in her ears. Her vision grazed the broad back encased in a black wool coat. The fedora that tilted on his head hid the majority of the familiar dark brown hair, but Ivy still narrowed her eyes at the strong column of his neck.

"Who?" Her father resumed his long strides, unwilling to allow Ivy's momentary shock to dissuade him from reaching the body discovered only an hour earlier.

Ivy matched his pace, yet this time she questioned whether uncovering the dead woman's story was as critical as avoiding Joel. The orphan. The childhood miscreant. Her best friend, who had abandoned her when she'd needed him most so many years before.

"Joel. Cunningham." She reminded her father. "Andrew's Joel." *My Joel.*

"Oh!" The name jolted her father's memory and earned her a sideways glance.

Yes. Him. Ivy's unspoken words to her father sparked a different light in his eyes. Would he defend her now, or did he still believe Joel had a reasonable explanation for his behavior that night? Her relationship with her father had never been quite the same since Andrew's death and Joel's subsequent actions.

The men turned as they neared. Joel's hands were deep in his trouser pockets. He twisted just enough so she could see his squared jaw, furrowed brows in that old familiar look of concentration, and his blue eyes. Blue eyes with a hint of gray. A flicker of recognition lighted in them, then vanished, as if he'd snuffed it out along with their past. Their friendship merely a speck on the timeline of their lives. Ivy avoided his gaze, stiffening her shoulders. He wasn't worth her consideration. She bit her bottom lip as a rush of memories threatened to overwhelm her. He really wasn't, she convinced herself.

"How old is she?" Ivy's father dispensed with formal greetings, and he brushed between the men to approach the tree.

"No idea." Sheriff Dunst's voice carried on a cold gust of March wind.

Ivy set her focus on the tree. It was long rumored that the Foster Hill oak tree was not only the largest but also the oldest tree in Oakwood. While its top rose to a marvelous height, it was still dead and its branches never blossomed. The trunk was very wide at the base and split open to reveal a hollow inside. Many a child had hidden there during a rambunctious game of hide-and-seek. They wouldn't hide there anymore. Not after today.

The petite body was curled into the position of a babe, inside the tree's womb. Blond hair hung free over her cold, bare shoulders and floated out on the wind. Her torso was covered in a paper-thin dress of gray calico. It was nowhere near enough to keep her warm, but it was more than the cold that tinted the young woman's skin blue. It was death.

Ivy watched as her father fingered the wrist. It was clearly too late. As Ivy tilted her head to see around his shoulder, she sensed a presence beside her. Joel. Their eyes met, locked, and then broke. The next breath Ivy took shuddered, and she hated herself for it. Years had passed. Joel should no longer affect her with such magnitude.

"What done her in?" Mr. Foggerty begged the question they all wondered.

"It's too soon to tell." Joel's answer for her father caused her to give him a questioning raise of her eyebrow. He had no right. No medical expertise.

But, one might argue, neither did she.

"No one knows who she is?" Joel's voice sent vibrations through Ivy's body. She edged away from him.

"None of us, anyway." The sheriff shrugged. "I'll start to investigate her. Maybe she's from a surrounding farm or part of a gypsy group passing through, what with the circus down south and all."

Dr. Thorpe grunted. Ivy saw what her father saw. The bruises on the body. Her wrists, her forearms, her neck. They told a frightening tale of abuse, whether long-term or suffered at the time of her death, they wouldn't know until they moved the body to the clinic. Ivy wrapped her arms around her torso, not from cold and certainly not from being squeamish. This had not been an accident. The girl had suffered and it seemed she had suffered alone, with no one to hear her cries and no one to care that she had gone missing. Already, in the early spring chill and the gray mist that rolled from the forest to the base of the tree, the girl was a mystery at risk of being lost for eternity.

Ivy squeezed the cloth over the porcelain washbasin. The drips from the rag into the water were the only sounds in the room. She draped the damp cloth over the edge of the bowl. It was ready to minister to the poor young woman who appeared shy of twenty years of age.

"Now?" Ivy met her father's eyes. He gave a short nod.

She reached for the top button of the girl's dress and paused. Fine cheekbones, pale in the pasty white of death, light blond brows, lips in the shape of a perfect rosebud minus color . . . she was beautiful. Even in death. It was moments like these that tugged at Ivy's empathy, even though Oakwood thought she was half crazy. Had the girl's last breaths been frantic, filled with terror and panic? Or had she passed in her sleep, and someone disposed of her body in a bewildered state of grief?

Ivy grimaced as she spread open the girl's threadbare garment. Not with the bruising. There was nothing peaceful in this death. Distinct markings curled around the base of her throat, and Ivy touched them with her fingertips as she raised her eyes to meet her father's.

"Strangulation?" Ivy murmured. The horror of suffocation stuck too close to another death that haunted her daily. An accidental one, but accidents never diminished trauma.

Her father pushed his spectacles up his nose and bent over to eye the markings. "Most likely." He folded the dead girl's dress off her shoulder to reveal more of her skin. "She's also been manhandled. We definitely need further examination."

Ivy ached for the girl in a way she couldn't explain to anyone. It wasn't sadness, it wasn't even grief. It was a throbbing fury

16

for what this young woman endured. This was why Ivy wrote the stories of the dead in her journal. Oakwood residents called her the "memory keeper" and referred to her book as her "death journal." They formed the assumption that Ivy had developed a morbid fascination with death since Andrew. What the citizens of Oakwood didn't understand was that no one, ever, deserved to be forgotten, and Ivy would do everything possible to preserve their stories beyond a factual obituary in the newspaper.

She smoothed away a lock of hair that lay across the girl's forehead. Ivy's eyes narrowed in focused determination. No one should die nameless.

"Ivy."

Dr. Thorpe's mouth was hidden by his full, white mustache. The wrinkles around his eyes were gentle, but her father's stern expression told her she needed to continue. Ivy was thankful he didn't have pity in his eyes. He understood what many didn't. She saw Andrew in every person who struggled and passed away in spite of her father's meticulous and caring practice. She saw Andrew in the face of the unremembered girl in front of her. Ivy fingered the empty locket that dangled around her own neck. Andrew had given it to her, and one day she would fill it with something precious. Something that promised life had a beginning, instead of an unending line of passages into eternity.

Ivy chose to ignore her thoughts. They would only distract her and take her to places in her grief that would result in nothing good. She pulled the tail of a stained ribbon that held the scooped neckline of the deceased's chemise together. More bruising peeked from beneath the soiled cotton, just above the girl's breasts. Fury mingled with Ivy's impassioned need to find justice for this victim. She unbuttoned a tiny white button on the chemise that rested between the young woman's cleavage.

"Stop."

Dr. Thorpe leaned forward to examine a small mole.

"It's not dirt," Ivy observed, and her father nodded. Turning, he made a note of the potential identifier in his medical journal.

"Keep going." He motioned with his hand. She did.

Ivy admired her father's hidden talent of postmortem examination. It wasn't something all doctors were schooled in, but with newer medical practices coming to the fore, her father wasn't one to be surpassed by the younger doctors. On occasion, a medical examination needed to be completed, and Oakwood boasted of a practitioner who was more than capable. Her father's immersion into the medical world after Andrew died was even more wholehearted than when Andrew was alive.

The clearing of a throat jerked both Ivy and her father from their intensive examination. Joel Cunningham lounged in the doorway, overflowing with the self-confidence Ivy so easily remembered. That confidence had once attracted her as a young woman of fourteen. She waited for his look of discrimination at the sight of a lady assisting with a postmortem medical examination. There was none. He looked beyond her. Ivy squelched the sting of being passed over.

"What have we found?"

Joel stepped into the room. He was all business, wasn't he? Ivy narrowed her eyes. Thank goodness her father wouldn't answer Joel. Just because he had been at the site of the body's discovery didn't mean they owed him any explanations.

"It appears she may have died of strangulation."

Well then. Maybe she was wrong.

Joel approached the table, and Ivy yanked

the sheet over the young woman's body. Indecent. The man had no propriety. He most definitely had not improved with age.

She gave him a hasty glance. Well, his *personality* hadn't improved with age. His lean form hinted at a chest that had matured from a young man's lanky frame into strength and breadth. The tailored suit coat he wore suggested he'd stepped up in the world from the orphan he once was. Why was he home in Oakwood? And why was her father handing over information as if Joel Cunningham was working for the sheriff?

"Anything you can tell about how she died might help with my investigation. The sheriff has engaged my assistance with this case, as his detective."

Oh goodness no. He *was* working for the law.

"There are many variables." Ivy couldn't hide the snap in her tone. Detective? Was that why Joel had finally returned, to take a job with Sheriff Dunst? Or was it for another reason? What Ivy knew, and what really mattered, was that for this moment the young woman was still theirs.

Protective, Ivy leveled a glare on Joel that hurt her eyes, but when he ignored her, Ivy looked away. The sweetness of the young woman's face, stilled in permanent sleep, increased Ivy's irritation. The girl wasn't a "case." She was a lost, nameless soul. She had been a person with a story, a *life.*

Ivy's hand hovered over the body before coming to rest on the shoulder with every ounce of possessiveness in her spirit. The cool skin of the young woman pressed beneath her palm.

"No one has identified her yet." Joel's statement ripped through the intimate connection of souls, and Ivy jerked her hand away from the body.

The woman had no identification yet. Even so, it dawned on Ivy with clarity, though she knew immediately it wasn't supernatural. The young woman had named herself and whispered it into Ivy's soul. Maybe this was why the town of Oakwood speculated as to whether Ivy Thorpe really was just an overcurious woman investigating the lives of the dead, or if she had some undefined connection to the afterlife. To Ivy, the dead were still alive.

She tried to control her breathing as she inhaled slowly. "Gabriella."

"What?" Joel tipped his head, his features sharpened with suspicion.

"Call her Gabriella."

"You know her?" Even her father was

surprised. Ivy avoided looking at him. It was poetic. Gabriel. He'd been an angel. And she was — Ivy couldn't help but transfer her gaze back onto the silent woman — she was an angel now too. She deserved a name.

Chapter 2

KAINE

Oakwood, Wisconsin
Present Day

Kaine checked her rearview mirror. She'd made a habit of it as she traversed the country from the ocean-side walkways of San Diego to the obscure midlands of Wisconsin. No one believed her. They probably never would. Danny's death two years ago still whispered its curses in her ear.

Your fault. Your fault.

She would never escape them, though no one else blamed her. Kaine was tired of violence touching every molecule in her body. Its ugly, poisonous fingers wrapped around her heart, squeezing until she couldn't live life this way anymore. Danny had begged her ages ago to relocate to his beloved Midwest in order to start over and shake the shadow of depression following her.

She had refused and he had died.

The shrill ring of her cellphone shattered the silence of the car. Kaine jumped at the sound. She glanced down at the pepper spray, always handy in the passenger seat, then in the mirror again. Shadows clung under her eyes.

God, please bring me hope here.

The repetitious, old-fashioned telephone ring clamored for her attention. Kaine reached for her phone and eyed the number while her left hand clasped the steering wheel tighter. Leah. She tapped the green answer button.

"Hey."

"Are you there yet?" Her sister's voice was a welcome peace calming her heart.

"Almost." Kaine ducked her head to get a better look beneath the visor that blocked the sun. "This place is really out of the way."

"Well, it's not San Diego." Leah's laugh soothed Kaine's frayed nerves. She missed her sister. Terribly. Just to hear her laugh brought a lightness to her soul, even if it would last only for a moment.

"Not at all." Kaine braked as a squirrel darted across the road in an erratic, nervous race against the car. "Stupid squirrel."

"Huh?"

"Nothing." Kaine readjusted her grip on

the phone. Her car was too old to have Bluetooth built in, and her headset had died somewhere in Illinois. Kaine glanced around at the wooded acres that flew by her on both sides of the road.

"We should video-chat when you get there. I want to see this place."

"It's just a house." An empty dream, Kaine didn't add. "I don't even know if I'm going to keep it once it's fixed up. I just need a change, a new vision, to get away, and — I don't know that I want to live in Oakwood. Permanently."

"But it's a *historic* landmark, Kaine. And according to Grandpa Prescott's old family Bible with the family tree, our great-great-grandmother lived in the same town. That alone should excite you. Not to mention it must be beautiful there. The realtor said it was purchased after the turn of the century and restored. But now it needs some TLC. And you know Danny would've been behind this one hundred percent."

Poor Leah. She was grasping at straws trying to give Kaine encouragement. Kaine's eyes filled with tears, but she blinked them back.

"We don't know much about Grandma Ivy, but I'm not here to play Ancestry-dot-com. Besides, the house might be historic for Oakwood, Wisconsin, but the fact I got it for a steal is what still makes me leery. No one sells historic landmarks for less than a quarter of an average mortgage in California."

"Yeah, well, our realtor wouldn't steer you wrong. He found our house here, and with his cousin in the same field in Wisconsin, it was a perfect connection since you couldn't exactly fly cross-country to inspect it."

Kaine sincerely hoped the cousin of Leah's real estate agent had the integrity Leah was so certain of. Most people had an inspection done on a house, but it had been a short sale. Offers were contingent on skipping the inspection, with an "as is" clause. Call it stupid and impulsive, but Kaine wanted out of San Diego. The pictures on the listing had been blurry and very unprofessional, yet what she'd seen looked mostly cosmetic. A gabled house, Gothic and East Coast in style, unique to the area, with three bedrooms, a parlor, updated plumbing, and a broad assortment of other rooms labeled with Victorian-era terms. While Kaine wasn't very interested in old architecture, Danny had been. Still, she was taking a financial risk to come here, and she wasn't convinced she hadn't completely lost her mind. Especially with a few days alone in a

26

car to think, calm down, and have a sense of reason invade her emotional angst.

Kaine had already sunk the remainder of Danny's life insurance policy into buying the old place on pretense of a new beginning but charged with the reality of a hopeful escape. Just because she had some savings to fall back on for repairs and living expenses didn't mean she could afford an entire renovation. Maybe if she did this, she could keep Danny close. Perhaps he would be able to look down from heaven and be reassured that, in the end, she really did love him.

"Are you okay?"

The question was simple, but the answer was so complicated all Kaine could muster was "Yeah."

"I don't believe you." Leah. She was a mother. Protective, nurturing, and full of emotional comfort.

"I'll be fine, Leah."

Kaine started reading the fire numbers. That's what they called them here in Wisconsin. Fire numbers were addresses on blue, narrow, rectangular signs attached to metal posts, located at the ends of driveways.

"Video-call me when you get there." Leah's voice became a distant echo in

Kaine's ear.

W12943 Foster Hill Road

Kaine turned onto the gravel drive, and the woods opened to a clearing. A hill sloped with rocky boulders, enormous oak trees, and pasture grasses waving in the spring breeze.

"Oh, my landy-love." Kaine used her grandfather's substitute cussword.

"What? What!" Leah's eagerness clashed with the disappointment that slammed into Kaine's body.

"I gotta go." Kaine hit the End button on her phone and tossed it on the passenger seat. Video-chatting with Leah, in this moment, would not end well. So much for God's intervention and leading. Kaine had officially taken a dive off the deep end of sanity. No wonder the San Diego police didn't believe her when she claimed her husband had been murdered and the killer was stalking her. It was too . . . nuts. *She* was nuts.

Cavernous windows opened in a silent scream on the face of the Gothic house that tilted on the crest of Foster Hill. Its gables towered as if to mock her, and balconies curved in permanent, evil grins. The front door gaped open with a black shadow, evidence that somewhere, at some time, it had been opened and never closed. Abandoned.

The tires crunched on the gravel as her car rolled up the hill, slowly, as if it didn't want to get any closer. Her reticence was reflected in the speed. This was more than a little fixer-upper. This was a demolish-and-start-over! The pictures she'd seen on the realty site had been taken from creative angles to downplay the state of the house.

The clapboard siding was hanging lopsidedly on the east gable, but seemed somewhat intact on the other gable. She could hear the real estate agent in her mind: Snap a pic of that nicer gable! The brick foundation looked as though an earthquake had rendered its mortar ineffective. The house summoned old imaginings of Nathaniel Hawthorne's *The House of the Seven Gables*. Kaine had read the book in high school and never forgotten it. *Haunted* was too cliché a word for this house, its deed now branded with her signature. Even ghosts would have abandoned the home years ago.

Could she truly credit God with leading her here? He knew she hadn't credited Him with much lately, and it was for reasons like this. Not to mention, you didn't thank the Lord for the murder of your husband and the fact that not even the police believed you. That they thought you were crazy to think he'd never have been a bad enough driver to face off with a concrete pillar of an underpass. That someone kept intruding into your house while you were away, moving things and leaving daffodils to taunt you. Nor could she thank the Lord for the displacement of her life and a career so depressing it hurt to even remember it.

"Okay. I can do this." Kaine's car rolled to a stop. She craned her neck to stare up through the windshield. "I can't do this. No. I can't."

It was too creepy. Too dark. Now she was talking to herself. And that was getting old. She needed a dog. For protection. A guard dog. Yes. She would adopt a dog.

She shook her head to collect her thoughts from random escapades. Exiting her car, Kaine made her way past the crooked fence to the front stairs that led up to a porch void of paint and weathered from the sun.

Her throat closed, and she clapped her hand over her mouth.

It couldn't be. *No, no, no!*

She backed away a step. Her eyes were fixed on the flower propped against the doorframe of the entrance like a wax garden ornament. A daffodil. Its sunny color mocked the taunting nature of its existence. *He* had left it. Just as he had left them in her house in San Diego. He had met her here.

Kaine spun on her heel and raced across the barren yard, her hip smashing against the edge of the fence and sending a rotted slat flying. She scrambled into her car and slammed the door shut, hitting the lock button.

Turning the key, Kaine cast one more glance at Foster Hill House and the daffodil that had been left to greet her. This house was a reflection of what was in Kaine's soul. This house was terrifying. This house was dead.

Kaine's foot was solid on the gas pedal as she sped toward town. *Population 2,000* was posted just below the *Welcome to Oakwood* sign. Numbers offered security, didn't they? But two thousand seemed paltry compared with San Diego's one million plus. This was a dark little village with a creepy old house, not the country home with wildflowers Kaine had imagined in her mind. A relaxing bed-and-breakfast type of a house. An oasis in the countryside.

Kaine massaged the steering wheel with cold, clammy hands. Crowds. No matter the size, she'd be safe there. There was something reassuring about the stimulation of a crowd, the sound of hundreds of voices murmuring around her. She was safe, and she wasn't alone. Kaine counted at least two, three, okay, five taverns down the main street. Welcome to Wisconsin, she supposed, one of the leading states for drinking and alcoholism. A woman jogged along the sidewalk, her Nike shirt a fluorescent yellow. Kaine glanced at her as she passed. The woman lifted her hand in a wave. At least someone seemed friendly.

The vision of that glorious daffodil stabbed deeper than any knife. Her tentative thread of security was lost. Broken. Where was the witness protection program for the abused and hunted? Kaine had long wondered that. In her line of work, she had seen it over and over again. The prey, the hunter, the victimization. Now it was her turn.

Harvey's Auto & Gas. Well, that was a welcome reprieve. Any living body at this point might be at risk of being hugged, and Kaine wasn't a hugger. She leaned her head back against the seat. The corner station boasted a green metal roof, three gas pumps that didn't accept credit cards, and a small store. Maybe she'd grab a candy bar. A

Snickers. She deserved chocolate, even though it wouldn't fix this problem.

Kaine crawled from the car, her legs still stiff from her four-day cross-country drive. Her hand brushed the small wooden cross that dangled on a pink ribbon from the rearview mirror. It was a remnant of her faith. A bruised faith.

A robin hopped across her path, then fluttered away as Kaine walked to the building. The tinny clang of an old bell greeted her ears as the gas station door pulled inward just as she reached for it. Off-balance by the unexpected swing of the door, Kaine stumbled. A firm grip on her upper arm steadied her.

"So sorry."

Kaine met an apologetic pair of hazel eyes. She didn't typically find scruffy men striking, but this one was — in an artsy, earthy sort of way. His black plastic-framed glasses were trendy, and his sandy-blond hair was in enough disarray to make her question whether it was purposefully styled to look like he'd just crawled out of bed.

Kaine pulled her arm away. She was betraying her dead husband with her appreciative flutter toward the good-looking stranger.

"It's all right." She rubbed her hand over

the sleeve of her jacket.

"Are you okay?"

Oh for heaven's sake, she'd tripped, not flown over the edge of the Grand Canyon. Kaine sucked back her defensive retort. He didn't deserve it. He gave her such a remorseful look, she got the distinct impression he was a mama's boy.

"Fine. I'm fine." She really wasn't, but that was on so many levels deeper than tripping over a man in the doorway of a gas station.

" 'Kay."

They danced in the doorway. He moved one direction as she did, then the other, and then he chuckled and stepped aside. "Go ahead." His arm extended toward the inside of the station.

Chivalry wasn't dead.

Kaine avoided his gaze. It was — unnerving.

The smell of coffee slammed into her senses as she entered the store, accompanied by the reedy sound of a polka playing through an archaic radio perched behind the counter. A display of brilliant yellow foam cheese triangles greeted her. Ahh, yes. The famed Wisconsin "cheeseheads." Mama's boys and cheeseheads. This town was . . . promising?

34

Kaine couldn't fathom putting that yellow foam on her head and sporting it as a hat. Who would be silly enough to wear such a thing?

Apparently, the older woman behind the counter.

Sparkling brown eyes greeted Kaine as she paused to control her reaction.

"What can I help you with?" The attendant had to be nearing sixty. Her short brown hair was permed and squashed beneath the foam hat. An oval nametag informed Kaine of her name. *Joy.*

Kaine snatched a Snickers bar from the display in front of the counter. Her hand shook with nervous energy as she set it on the Formica countertop. "Only the candy, please."

She glanced out the gas station window. No daffodils. No faceless stalker. Just her car, and the handsome stranger jogging across the street toward a brick office building.

Joy waved the candy bar under the infrared scanner. "Are you passing through?"

No. She wished she was. To Canada, maybe. But she'd signed for that rotted house. How could she walk away? She'd be throwing away everything Danny had left her. But then how could she stay?

35

"I'll be here for a bit." It was all she wanted to offer.

Joy smiled and slid the candy bar back to Kaine. "Where ya staying?"

Were all Midwesterners this nosy? Kaine handed two one-dollar bills to Joy. "I'm — not sure." Some place with about thirty dead bolts, grilles over the windows, an alarm system, and a closet full of high-powered automatic rifles would be nice. And, she was from California where gun control was popular. Kaine bit back an ironic smile. Circumstances certainly changed a person's ideals.

"There's a motel not far from here. Just head down the road about a mile. It's small, but it's clean."

That sounded comforting. Four walls would be better than four car windows exposing her to the dangerous world outside.

Kaine took the quarters Joy offered. "Thanks." She had planned on camping out in her new house, but now it was an utterly horrific idea.

"Where are you from?"

Good grief. Kaine pocketed the change. "San Diego."

"San Diego?" Joy parroted.

Was there more than one? Kaine nodded.

"You don't say!" Joy's brows raised, the lines darkened from the overuse of an eyebrow pencil. "I have a brother in California. But not in San Diego. He lives closer to Oregon."

"Mm." Kaine nodded. As if she cared. She should care. She had always cared about people before.

"What brings you to Oakwood?" Joy leaned against the counter. "I'm sorry, we don't get many tourists here. Just a tad too out of the way. Wisconsin Dells is the place where they like to congregate, what with all the water parks and the circus nearby. But we're too far north for them to care."

"I'm . . ." What could she say — that she thought God wanted her to buy a dilapidated house in the hometown of her ancestors just so she could fulfill a dream of her dead husband? Her stomach rolled. If only she had listened to Danny three years ago, when her job started eating her contentment.

"You all right, buttercup?"

Drat. Kaine swiped at her eyes. The wetness on the back of her hand betrayed her.

"Aww, sweetie." Joy snatched some Kleenexes from a box behind her and shoved them toward Kaine. "Don't mind me and my questions. I can be a motormouth."

Kaine took the tissues. She wasn't accustomed to being on the receiving end of care. She was the one who cared. The social worker who could read a broken woman simply by the way her shoulders bent and her head hung.

Joy rounded the counter. "Do you drink coffee? You do, don't you? Who doesn't?" She filled a styrofoam cup with coffee from a utility-sized carafe. These Midwesterners and their styrofoam. Whatever happened to going green?

But Kaine didn't argue when her hands wrapped around the cup. She didn't even argue when she tasted the burnt gas-station coffee. The warmth in Joy's eyes comforted her raw nerves. Joy's smile, even though it was bordered by red lipstick that bled into the wrinkles around her lips, reminded her of a mother's. Kaine's mom had died when she and Leah were preteens, and their dad had disappeared years before that. They'd been raised by Grandpa Prescott. There'd been little feminine influence in their lives after Mom. Joy appeared to be what every little girl imagined in a mother — at least at first impression.

"I bought the house on Foster Hill Road." Kaine offered it up in exchange for the complimentary coffee.

38

Joy's caterpillar brows hunched upward again. "Foster Hill House?"

Kaine sipped the coffee and nodded.

"Well, I'll be." Joy filled her own cup with brew. "That place is — well, I — hmm."

Even Joy didn't have words.

Kaine nodded.

Joy grimaced.

They laughed.

Kaine heaved a shaking sigh. "I have no idea why the realtor sold it to me." Sure she did. Unsuspecting out-of-state sale, easy money, effortless off-load of a property that had probably been tacked to his bulletin board for years. She, the out-of-her-mind, still-grieving widow, jumping at a chance to escape. Smart.

"It's a mess." Joy nodded. She slurped her coffee as if cooling it between her teeth. A flicker of concern flashed across her face. "I keep telling my daughter to stay away."

"Your daughter?" Kaine knew the house had been deserted when she arrived. But maybe that explained the open door.

Joy blinked rapidly.

Oh no, now the gas-station lady was going to cry.

"Please, don't be upset." Joy sniffed. "I know it's your property now. But, Megan is — well, she likes to wander, and that old

place . . . she pretends it's her playhouse."
She waved her hand in her face as if to dry
the tears.

A playhouse?

"Megan is twenty-two, but she has Down
syndrome. Sometimes my friend Grant
watches her when I'm at work, but God love
him, he gets sidetracked and . . . well,
Megan loves to wander for flowers and hiding places. Foster Hill House is that to her.
Yesterday Grant found her there and she'd
picked all the daffodils in a patch at the
corner of the house. I'm so sorry."

Daffodils?

Daffodils! Thank God Almighty! And then
her inward praise turned outward, and
Kaine's breath released in a whoosh of
anxious relief.

"Oh, thank God!" Kaine's exclamation
turned Joy's expression quizzical.

It wasn't him. He *hadn't* followed her
here. It was a horrible, awful mistake caused
by an innocent special-needs young woman
who lived in a fantasy world of flowers.

"You're not upset?" Joy charged on. "The
flowers are the only nice thing about that
place. I wasn't concerned when Megan
picked them, but I hadn't a clue the house
had been bought. I mean, that place
should've been bulldozed years ago. No one

wants to touch it."

"I'm not upset. I'm just surprised your daughter even wants to go there." Kaine set the coffee on the counter and ripped open her candy bar. Her first bite was celebratory.

"Megan has an imagination, and Foster Hill House inspires that." Joy shrugged, her beaded earrings hanging low enough to brush her shoulders. "But it creeps everyone else out. Superstition, y'know?"

"I suppose they say it's haunted." Kaine spoke around a heavenly mouthful of peanuts, caramel, and chocolate. Blessed relief.

"Some do." Joy squeezed a plastic lid onto her coffee cup, her eyes widening as if she knew far more than she was willing to spill over gas-station brew. "But, it's more what happened there."

"What happened there?" What could be worse than a haunted house?

"Of course, the realtor didn't tell you." Joy sniffed. "Foster Hill House has a litany of oddities. All the way back to the 1860s. Legend says people saw strange lights there in the middle of the night, lanterns glowing, and they heard piano music. Little things would be moved in the house. A candlestick or an old umbrella stand. Rumors that people were coming and going, but in the

41

daytime no one could ever find anything to explain it."

Kaine swallowed the candy, the mouthful suddenly as big as a softball in her throat. The relief from knowing Megan had left the daffodil oozed away, forced out by the house's legend. It was eerily familiar. The coffee cup she'd left at her bedside table moved to her dresser with a daffodil propped in it. Her red cardigan flung over the back of the chair when she was sure she'd hung it in her closet. Her kitchen light on when she was positive she'd turned it off before leaving for work in the morning.

The police blamed it on post-traumatic stress disorder. Any wife whose husband was killed in an accident, but insisted it was murder, could be shaken enough to see things, even hear things. It didn't mean it was real. But she'd never prop a daffodil in a coffee mug. It deserved a vase. Her favorite flower.

"And then the murder."

"The murder?" Kaine choked, and it wasn't because the coffee was awful. The knot in her stomach grew larger than when she'd first laid eyes on Foster Hill House.

Joy nodded, her yellow cheesehead not shifting at the movement. "She's become something of a renowned mystery."

"Who? What happened to her?" Kaine didn't want to know, but reflex forced her to ask. It was dumb luck she'd flee the memories of death only to buy a house shrouded in shadows of the grave.

Joy sucked in a breath. "That's the mystery of it. It's been over a century and now it's more folklore than fact. No one really knows any more. I'm not certain if anyone back in 1906 really understood it all. Just a young woman. Her body was stuffed into a massive, hollowed oak tree at the bottom of the hill. Some like to say she's the one who lit the lanterns at night. They stopped shining after she died. At least" — Joy flicked the air with a green fingernail — "that's what legend says."

CHAPTER 3

IVY

Stillness shrouded the examination room, but *peaceful* was not a word Ivy would use to describe its crypt-like atmosphere. The body on the table revealed all of the young woman's secret wounds with stabbing reality. There would be justice for her, if Ivy could commandeer the future. But paramount to justice was a mission to search and save, and one that Ivy would not be left out of. She'd had that same desperation when Andrew died, watching him as he disappeared beneath the ice on the lake. But this time, death would not — could not — become the final signature penned to the end of this woman's tale.

Gabriella had borne an infant. Within the last two or three weeks. Alone with the body, Ivy held the dead girl's hand in the bowl of warm water and ran the washcloth over her pale skin. The mud caked under

Gabriella's fingernails dirtied the water.

"Where is your baby?" Ivy whispered. But, did it matter? Yes, Gabriella had been murdered, but perhaps her child was safe. Or was the babe out there, alone for the last thirty-six-odd hours? Would it even be able to survive such a stretch on its own?

Ivy scowled in concentration as she passed the wet cloth over Gabriella's bruised wrist. Her father had exited the room to soothe his own unsettled nerves in a cup of coffee. She heard the front door shut with a *thud.* As promised, Joel had returned from the sheriff's office to hear the analysis of the cause of death.

She wrung water from the cloth and laid Gabriella's hand over her sheet-covered chest. Drying her own hands on a towel, Ivy tucked a loose strand of her hair into the pinned mass on the top of her head. Her own dark hair and olive skin were a severe contrast to the ethereal paleness of Gabriella. Eyes that were as blue as the sky were now covered with closed eyelids. Ivy knew her own eyes, hazel and catlike, sparked with spirit that Gabriella could no longer claim. Life.

The door pushed open, and Joel entered, Dr. Thorpe on his heels with a pointed look at Ivy. Her father was beseeching her to cooperate. Now would not be the appropriate time to challenge Joel Cunningham's reappearance in Oakwood, in their lives. Not with a murdered woman and the reality of a missing child.

"Thank you," Joel's cool politeness rankled Ivy's nerves, and he was clearly already well engaged in conversation with her father. "I do take my role here very seriously. I have an obligation to find the truth."

"I believe the truth may be hard to reconcile," Ivy inserted before she could bite her tongue.

Their eyes locked. His narrowed, but Ivy preferred to foster an unaffected expression, even though her stomach churned with the intensity of his stare. Their foundation was already well on its way to being irreparable, yet in this moment they were forced to get along.

Under duress. She laid a possessive hand on Gabriella's shoulder.

"I am not intimidated by difficult truth." Joel raised an eyebrow, his gaze burrowing deeper into hers, blazing with conviction that implied he had the right to defend not only his position in the room but also his past actions.

Dr. Thorpe cleared his throat. The connection between Ivy and Joel evaporated as

Ivy shifted her attention to her father, whose sharp expression communicated he'd missed none of the underlying messages tossed between the two of them.

"It is very clear the woman died from asphyxiation." Ivy's father's white walrus mustache wobbled as he sniffed. His spectacles slid down his nose when he looked down at Gabriella and pointed toward her eyes. "The burst blood vessels in the eyes, the bruising around the neck — both imply strangulation." He traced the bruising while Joel leaned over the body to examine it. Ivy edged aside as her father pushed his way in. Frowning, she repositioned herself at the head of the table and allowed the two men to go about their discussion, effectively excusing her from it.

"The killer's fingers left their mark, to be sure." Dr. Thorpe ran his finger along the distinct edge of a bruise. "And it is evident she fought back," he concluded.

"How so?" Joel was so focused, so intent on the body before them, that it allowed Ivy a moment to study his face. His jawline was clean-shaven, his dark hair trimmed with a slight wave around the ears, his starched collar touched his Adam's apple, and his blue eyes were bordered by thick lashes. Everything about Joel Cunningham was

47

straightforward. Except where he had been for the last twelve years.

Her father's voice brought Ivy back to the explanation of his postmortem examination results. "We found skin particles underneath her fingernails, mixed with some mud that would be consistent with the earth near where she was found."

"Was there a scent?" Joel inquired.

"A what?" Dr. Thorpe drew back with a perplexed frown.

"A scent on the skin or even to the mud," Joel clarified, and

Ivy had to begrudgingly admit Joel was sharp. "Of soap, or perhaps a cleaning solution? Manure or pond algae? I'm looking for something that may help us identify the killer and perhaps the exact location of death."

Ivy shook her head and answered before her father could. "The skin beneath her nails was too tiny to tell a scent. The mud smelled like earth after the snow melts. Her body has no distinctive smell." *Other than death itself.*

Her father gave her a quick glance. *Yes, Daddy, I smelled it.* She loved her father, but he often questioned her sensibilities, if not her own sanity.

"What else?" Joel brushed past her explanation.

Dr. Thorpe lifted Gabriella's hand and turned it so Joel could see. "This strikes me as odd. The bruising around her wrists is older but not consistent with a struggle. It's almost as if she had been bound once, not terribly long ago, but also not within the past few weeks. She has some scrapes and cuts that are scabbed."

"She was held against her will, then. Are there other wounds?"

Dr. Thorpe scratched a spot above his ear and cleared his throat, looking at Ivy. She raised an eyebrow. She had already been through the examination, but she assumed her father thought it terribly improper to discuss it with another man present. Considering they'd already far breached the boundaries of propriety, Ivy tried to muster an encouraging smile for her father and realized it probably came out more like a grimace. He coughed again, then proceeded with a final nervous glance in her direction.

"There was a child."

Joel raised his head from his inspection of Gabriella's wrists. "Excuse me?"

"A baby," Ivy said, drawing Joel's icy-blue attention to herself. "She gave birth no more than two or three weeks ago." Urgency

49

filtered into her voice and Ivy didn't try to disguise it. "Somewhere out there" — she waved toward the window — "is Gabriella's baby."

Joel followed the wave of her hand to the black-and-white, snow-melting landscape outside. Ivy could read his thoughts. Cold. Ice. Dark nights. Little warmth.

"How long has she been dead?"

Ivy hoped Joel was doing the math in his mind. A baby left alone for more than eighteen to twenty-four hours would have little chance of survival.

Her father did not waltz around the horrid truth. "She has been gone at least thirty to thirty-six hours. Doubtful any longer."

"There isn't any way, if the infant was left to fend for itself, that it would survive that."

Joel's conclusion, coupled with the cold tone of his voice and the unapologetic delivery of fact, incensed Ivy. She stared at him, curling her fingers into the sheet that covered the examination table. She tipped her head.

"You cannot draw such a blatant conclusion." Ivy drew in a shaky breath, not from tears but from a frustration enhanced by their past, by Andrew's death, and by the lack of empathy Joel had a history of displaying.

He matched her sigh, only his was stable and unemotional. "If the infant was abandoned, then I can conclude little else, outside of a miracle by the hand of God."

Ivy opened her mouth to protest, then snapped it shut. He was right, of course, but he didn't seem convinced that God would choose to work miraculously. She had seen enough in her life to know He usually erred on the side of tragedy. But until she knew God's decision, there was a little life that needed to be accounted for — and she was determined to see it was done.

CHAPTER 4

Nighttime crept upon them with its frigid clutches, sending Gabriella's body on its way to the mortician's table and leaving Sheriff Dunst and Joel behind in the examination room to deliberate their next move. Ivy shouldn't have eavesdropped, but when the words "wait until morning" passed across Sheriff Dunst's lips and Joel did nothing to protest, she knew she had to listen on behalf of Gabriella and her child. She pressed her ear to the door, her hand gripping the knob under debate of whether to barge in or remain silent.

"There's nothing we can do tonight. We don't even have a solid point of reference as to where the murder took place. Foggerty has trapped all over that land and he said he's seen nothing." Sheriff Dunst's words brought no comfort to Ivy as she rested her ear against the door. "We won't be able to find any evidence in the dark."

"She was by Foster Hill House — start there maybe — baby out there alone." Joel's words were broken, his voice less booming than the lawman's.

"I walked through the house after we transported the body here. I didn't see anything. No child. It is likely that it's safe and tucked away with the girl's family and her death is random and unrelated. She may not even be from these parts. To go out now would be like searching for a ghost we aren't even sure exists."

At those words, Ivy's actions were swift. Swiping her wool coat from the hall tree and shrugging it on, she snatched a lantern off its cast-iron arm where it hung on the wall. The cold air that hit her face when she opened the door was the exclamation mark on the reality that a baby left abandoned could not survive another night.

Ivy's shoes crunched in the snow as she hiked down the road toward Foster Hill. An owl swooped overhead, the girth of its wingspan draping over the path ahead of her. She squinted her eyes as she lifted the lantern so the light spread into the woods on either side of the road. The uneasy gnaw of reality ate at her calm. A young woman had just been found murdered, and Ivy was very much alone in the dead of night.

Unreasonable? Completely. But Gabriella had been dead well over a full day and night. The likelihood was the killer had already fled. If not . . . Ivy stifled her fear as the image of a baby shivering and crying in the cold urged her forward. Someone had to be proactive and assume the worst, and evidently that responsibility fell to her. It didn't appear the men of the law shared her sense of urgency or the sacredness of fighting for the baby's life.

She prayed the sheriff was right, that the baby was secured with its extended family somewhere. But she wasn't going to bed that night beneath covers and quilts if there was any possibility Gabriella's infant was in such desperate need. Maybe the sheriff didn't understand what it was like to have that desperation tighten every muscle in your body, shorten your breath, and incite your cries for hope. But Joel did. Ivy blinked and cleared her vision that suddenly teared. He knew it, and was ignoring it. Again.

She paused at the base of Foster Hill, by the skeletal tree that had been Gabriella's momentary burial place. In the moonlight that reflected off patches of snow and dark shadows of earth, Foster Hill House gave the appearance of evil. Even the lantern light was a dim glow. The rickety fence that bordered the abandoned house tilted, its rotting slats wobbling in the wind. Windows reflected black, like eyes staring down upon her.

Prayer wasn't something that came naturally to her anymore, but Ivy breathed one anyway. For the baby, for herself. *If it's here, help me find it.* Then let her flee home to the safety of a locked door where she would triumphantly embrace the rescued child and glare at the stunned faces of the sheriff and Joel.

Ivy passed by the fence and an iron lamppost. Her shoes were quiet against the wooden steps that rose by four to the porch bordering the front of the house. The front door loomed in front of her, with stained glass intact and brass knob tarnished to a dull black.

She turned it and met little resistance. That must be what happens when houses stand empty for years. Locks erode and barriers vanish as it becomes an empty tomb. Ivy perched in the doorway, ears straining to hear the tiny whimper of an infant, a sniffle, a cough. Sheriff Dunst may have been here earlier, but he hadn't been focused on finding a baby. She braced her hand on the splintered doorframe as she let the lantern light wash across the vast entryway. A staircase climbed to the second level, doors gaped on both the east and west walls, beckoning her to search the rooms beyond. An old chandelier hung precariously from the ceiling, which she hoped didn't come crashing down on her.

Rumors long abounded surrounding this place. Lights seen flickering in its rooms in the dead of night, piano music filtering through the air only to cease abruptly. Ivy tiptoed to the first room on the right. There was no solace that the lantern light revealed the very piano she'd just been considering. With a sweep of her gaze around the room, Ivy approached the piano, its warped keys a pathetic reminder of the damage of the passage of time. A piano cover draped over the top in a shroud of white lace grayed by spider webs and dust. Sheet music was propped up.

"Beethoven." Ivy breathed the name as her fingers traced Opus 27, the *Moonlight Sonata*. A vague memory returned to her. Andrew, years before, whispering in strict confidence to her and to Joel that on one of his nighttime escapades, he heard Beethoven's haunting melody floating across the wind from Foster Hill House. They'd teased him mercilessly for his superstition, while being equally as intrigued. But after three nights of repeated sneaking off to the tree line to listen, the music wasn't heard again.

Ivy drew her hand back as she stared down at the keys. Odd. There was no dust on them. Their ivory, though chipped, was clean. As if played recently.

She shivered. Now she was imagining things. Memories of Andrew were never a good thing. She lost herself in them, in the days before he'd drowned beneath the pond's crust of ice, and with them lost her sense of reality.

Ivy retreated to the foyer and paused. If only there were a sound. She'd give anything to hear the baby's wail. But Foster Hill House was still in the horrible darkness. She drew a deep breath and adjusted her grip on the lantern. Bedrooms would be up the stairs. If Gabriella had abandoned her baby, Foster Hill House would provide shelter and a bedroom might provide blankets — if there were any left over from the Fosters, whose abrupt move decades before left the house half-furnished but never lived in again.

The steep staircase to the second floor drew Ivy up its steps. Ribbons of spider webs and dust hung between the rails of the banister. Her hand pushed away a thick layer of time's collection as she ran her fingers along the old walnut wood.

A bat swooped from the mouth of the unknown second floor, its wings millimeters from Ivy's head. She ducked with a stifled shriek. Her lantern hit the wall, and the glass chimney protecting the flame shattered. The scent of kerosene filled Ivy's nostrils, and she squinted into the darkness that wrapped its chilling arms around her body. The lantern flame had surrendered, plunging her into faint, pale light. Only moonlight from the foyer windows below lit her steps now.

Turn back. Go home.

Ivy could hear the voice of warning in her mind. Maybe Sheriff Dunst was correct. What could be found in the dark? And there wasn't evidence to tie Foster Hill House to Gabriella anyway. She hesitated. No. She was here now. The danger was more than likely passed, and if there was even a slim chance a baby was here . . .

Ivy took another step, her foot sending an echo through the house.

When she reached the top of the stairway, a long hall stretched ahead of her. Dim shafts of light cast their shadows from doorways to rooms that held more mystery. Ivy passed two of them, both opening into empty voids. A quick perusal showed bare wood floors and nothing else.

Ivy approached the third door. Its knob was clean, almost shiny in the night's faint light. She reached out to grasp it, but her hand hovered. Clean. Shiny. A doorknob in an abandoned house should be grimy and dull. Here was another sign of life. Someone had been here before her. Her heart lurched with sudden hope. The clean piano keys, a smooth doorknob . . . if Gabriella was the one to have cleaned them, that meant her baby might lie beyond this door. Ivy closed her eyes. *Please, God.* She wasn't afraid of death. Her journal was page after page about those who had passed on. Yet, there was something horribly different considering it might be an infant.

Not willing to let her fear become bigger than the moment, Ivy pushed the door open. The hinges offered a momentary creak before losing their voice. A lone bed was pushed against the far wall. Its curved wooden headboard held more evidence of spiders. But it was the scarlet velvet blanket draping off the side that gripped Ivy's attention. Plaster from the ceiling had fallen to the floor, onto the mattress and blanket. She hurried to the bed, hope colliding with disappointment. Empty. She splayed her fingers over the soft velvet. Yes, it was empty, but it was further evidence to support that someone had inhabited Foster Hill House in secret.

On the other side of the bed was a closet. Ivy hurried to it and flung the door open. Her sigh of relief broke the stillness. No one was hiding inside to leap out at her. Just an empty, boxlike room.

Ivy cast a glance over her shoulder at the open doorway. The room, the bed . . . everything about it made her skin crawl. She didn't know if the absence of Gabriella's baby relieved her, or frightened her.

A book lay overturned on the floor beside the bed, its hard cover collecting dust. *Great Expectations.* Her fingers traced the inset black letters on the cover as she squatted beside it, her eyes now adjusted to the light that glowed through the bedroom's lone window. She knelt and picked up the book, turning it over. Some of the pages were intact, others ripped from the binding and missing.

Ivy thumbed the pages still there. A musty smell tickled her nose, but the pages were clean. Old but clean. A tiny ink scribble laced the margins. She squinted to try to read it, but she couldn't make out the words. The light wasn't enough, and Ivy wished she hadn't broken her lantern.

Still kneeling on the floor, she held the book up and turned it toward the window. She sucked in a breath, finally able to make out a few words in feminine script.

All houses hold secrets, and I am one of them.

Rough hands yanked Ivy backward and upright, and the book fell from her grasp. Her scream bounced against the window-pane and echoed in the room. Her shoulders slammed against a burly chest. Wool sleeves scraped her face as her assailant smothered her mouth with his arm.

"Scream all you want." The words were a hiss, the voice unrecognizable but hot in her ear. "None to hear you. None to care."

She wasn't about to give in. Terror provoked her instinct to survive. The image of Gabriella's bruised neck and face flashed before her eyes, and Ivy buckled her knees, slumping toward the floor. The movement caught her attacker by surprise and he tripped, crashing down beside her.

"Where's the baby?" she demanded as she scrambled for her feet. But he was quick and grabbed at her ankles.

"What baby?" he growled.

Ivy sidestepped his grip, yet his hand caught the hem of her dress. It ripped as she struggled to get away. She managed to stumble to her feet, clutching at the door-frame for balance. His fingers clawed at her hair, dragging her back into the bedroom.

"No!" She would *not* die.

Ivy's scalp stung as she jerked away. The man's grip took hair with it as he lost his hold on her. She ran from the room to the stairway, and her foot caught on a warped floorboard. Her shoulder slammed into a framed portrait that tilted on impact.

For an instant her eyes met the black, empty gaze of a woman. She spun away from the portrait and sprinted for the stairs. Her hand gripped the banister just as her assailant grabbed her shoulders. He jerked her back against him, his arm around her throat, squeezing. Ivy clawed at his hold as spots floated in front of her eyes.

"You shouldn't have come here." His words chilled her. Then there was nothing solid beneath her feet. He shoved her off the top stair, and she twisted as she fell. The blackness of Foster Hill House engulfed her.

CHAPTER 5

KAINE

Kaine stood in the parlor of the dilapidated house, staring up the staircase that disappeared into the second floor. She frowned and spun on her heel to face the front entrance and reassess the doorless frame. It was a sorry sight. Not to mention the walls. Ugh. Wallpaper that screamed 1960s peeled from the walls, its garish pattern providing splashes of mustard-yellow nosegays. Oh yes, and the cobwebs. Horrible, fluffy traps of eight-legged fiends. She blew a huge breath through her nose and looked up at the ceiling. It had been patched, the original plaster repaired with more plaster a few decades old now. It appeared there was an old fixture where a chandelier may have once hung.

"Probably full of asbestos." Kaine stuck her tongue out at the ceiling, because sometimes she felt better when she acted juvenile. Who knew what other problems she would find?

Oh, Danny.

When they first married, she'd been fresh out of college and he was a dreamer. It was an attractive quality. He wanted to flip houses someday, old houses. With character, he'd said. Kaine hadn't wanted to leave California, her job, the people she was ministering to, and of course Danny supported her. Like he always had.

I'm so sorry.

Kaine had cheated him out of his dream. Maybe not intentionally, but now that he was gone, it felt that way. As silly as it seemed, if she could make amends here, and start a new life, it would all be worth it. She needed to fix her eyes ahead, or on Jesus, as the Scripture stated. But it was so difficult when memories surfaced of Danny, of his suspicious death, and even of the events that shaped her into who she was by the time she married Danny. Events she had spent years learning to forget. All of it God could heal. Kaine tugged at the hem of her sweater. If she knew how to let Him.

Kaine moved into one of the side rooms. A bathroom. She stared into a cracked mirror hanging crooked over the sink. Her brown eyes stared back at her, doubtful and questioning. What was she going to do with this place? The gas-station lady, Joy, may have relieved Kaine of her initial panic over the daffodil, but the history around this house was far too parallel to her own story.

"God, maybe you could say something right about now?" Kaine's whisper shattered the silence in the ancient house. She gripped the sides of the porcelain pedestal sink and eyed the oxidized copper pipes that rose from the back of the old toilet and into the wall. The plumber had just left. It would do for now, he'd said, but eventually the pipes would need replacing.

"The plumbing was supposed to be updated," she whispered, still praying out loud as if God would respond. Apparently "updated" meant when it was last installed in 1983. "At least the toilet flushes." She pulled the toilet handle, and water rushed into the bowl. High in iron, the orange water stained the bowl. Gross. If the toilet water was that orange, she would most definitely need to buy bottled water to drink until the well was tested and a filtering system put in. Which required money. Her savings was going to dwindle faster than she'd planned.

She needed to get Wi-Fi asap so she could log on and complete some of her deadlines for her new position as a virtual assistant for Leah's husband. It helped that she could do his law firm's blog from states away. It didn't help that she was going to need to market herself and get at least four more significant paying clients to make ends meet. Trying to pass herself off as a capable blogger, someone with skills in writing employee manuals and social documents for private companies, was going to be tricky. She'd minored in business, but social work had taken precedence for the last eight years.

There were times she missed the job she'd fled. But now it was mostly because of the money and not the people. In fact, she'd cut herself off from everyone back home, with the exception of Leah. Her passion in life had taken a horrible swing toward surviving, and the pendulum didn't look as if it'd find its way back in the other direction where Kaine had once served broken hearts. It was hers that was shattered now. Shattered and very alone.

Kaine exited the downstairs bathroom and made her way to a room that was far more intriguing than a bathroom with nasty pipes. It had been a study at one time, or a library. The built-in shelves held only blankets of cobwebs and dust that had collected in the corners and reached down to touch the shelves below.

A mouse nest of bundled straw, droppings, and dust bunnies piled in the corner of the bottom shelf. Mice. Spiders. Murder and mayhem in its history. Her own stalker. The only thing missing was that dog she'd promised herself.

Kaine pulled a dustcloth that hung from her back pocket. Well, this room was as good as any to tackle. It might be one of the only rooms that didn't need major renovation. Besides, cleaning off the bookshelves would just feel good. There would at least be a sense of accomplishment on her first day here. She'd finish this and then go back into town, grab some dinner, and afterward head to the motel to get some paying work done.

Kaine spent the next hour wiping and sneezing. With a few more swipes of the now-black dustrag, she knelt on the floor by the shelves closest to the bay window. The bottom molding of the shelf jutted out, warped by time and wear. She pressed on the wood and, as she expected, there was no give. The walnut molding was tough and aged into a permanent warp. She wouldn't be able to just pound a nail in and tighten it that way. Pound a nail? She didn't even own a hammer.

She ran her hand along the molding one more time, trying to draw hope from its aged beauty. She wanted to imagine the house as it could be instead of as it was. Her future needed to take on some sort of hope or Kaine might well lose her mind.

Her fingers played with the end of the trim piece and edged into a gap behind it. She frowned as her index finger slipped up to her knuckle into the cavity.

"If I scream," Kaine spoke aloud to only the mice, "it's probably a gargantuan spider eating my finger, so go get help." Kaine's admonition to the hiding rodent and its eight-legged friends didn't leave her feeling hopeful.

She bent and inspected the gap. Huh. The shelves had a hollow behind the trim work and beneath the bottom shelf.

"Umm." Kaine's perplexed pause earned her an echo off the ceiling. Her finger felt the edge of something. A leaf? Paper? Curious, she wedged her thumb into the gap and struggled to reach it. Finally, she grasped it and tugged, maneuvering the paper through the inch-wide gap. It was larger than she'd expected and folded into a long strip.

Kaine pulled it toward her. It was a page from a very old book. She carefully unfolded the page and pressed it against her jeans-clad leg.

Great Expectations.

A page from the old classic by Dickens. Kaine curled her lip. She'd never liked Dickens. He took four pages to explain one setting when he only needed a paragraph. She noticed faded ink in the page's margins, scrawling, as if someone had taken notes on the story.

Kaine held the page toward the light coming from the bay window.

I am not meant for this life.

Weird.

He will come and take me, and I'll never find my way home again.

Kaine swallowed. The same anxious feeling she was running from washed over her with renewed vigor. It was as if the words on the page reflected her own soul.

He's always watching. My life is no longer my own. Hope is difficult to find in the darkness.

Kaine turned the page over and focused on the handwriting in the margin.

69

But there is hope. I will remember that tonight when he comes for me.

Kaine stared at the page of *Great Expectations* scarred with the feminine handwriting. When? Who? Someone had hidden this message behind the warped bookshelf. Someone had chronicled a brief moment in her life. One of quiet desperation, and a mirror of Kaine herself.

She folded the paper along its original seams and slipped it into the back pocket of her jeans. With a quick sweep of her gaze around the musty library, Kaine lurched to her feet. She needed to shake this — the feeling of being watched. It was all supposed to be left behind in California. The suspicions, the memories, the unproven break-ins. But the note from decades before fed the emotion that Kaine once again jammed under the surface calm she tried to etch on her face. Even though no one could see it, she needed to sense that power, that control. *She* was in control of her life. Not *him* or whoever it was who had made her existence post-Danny a nightmare that no one could share with her.

Kaine speed-walked from the library as if at any moment the apparition of the one who had written the message would appear.

She narrowed her eyes at the broad, winding staircase in the entry. She could almost envision the pre-Civil War-era owners in their silks and cravats, but her vision disintegrated as she noticed half the banister was tilting to the left, as if it were about ready to give up its ghost and die. She was going to have to start a to-do list.

Thumbing to contacts on her iPhone, Kaine selected to Face-Time Leah. Her sister was the queen of organization with her colored pens, notecards, planners, and neon Post-it notes. Unlike her own bad habit of jumbling must-haves, to-dos, and should-haves in her mind. Maybe Leah could help Kaine find a reference point at which to begin — or at least pick a color scheme for her list.

The data connection was sketchy. Leah's face appeared on screen, albeit pixelated and delayed.

"Wha-for the-wallpaper-pretty." Leah's sentence was so broken, Kaine tapped the End button on the video-chat. So the house sat in the black hole of LTE wireless activity as well, huh?

Figures.

Kaine sagged against the wall. Her lack of confidence was synonymous with being alone. She was never good at silence.

71

Her phone pinged.

Text message from Leah. *No data?*

Nope, Kaine texted back.

Phooey. Call. Or get Wi-Fi stat. I need to see this place.

Wi-Fi was probably not going to happen here in the boonies. And yes, Leah *did* need to see this place so she could help Kaine file a complaint on this revered agent who was so honest he would never sell a ramshackle house to a grief-stricken widow.

The sarcasm oozed into Kaine's thoughts like a poison. She would call Leah. But not now. She would say something she'd regret, and in the end it wasn't Leah's fault that Kaine had been this stupid. The house closed in around her like a coffin. Danny would have been on his tablet right now, tapping out a to-do list for renovations in Evernote. Kaine was out of her depth . . . and out of her mind.

Footsteps on the front porch jerked her attention from her melancholy. She was startled at the outline of a man in the doorway. For the split second between the confirmation that her stalker from San Diego really *had* followed her here and the moment she recognized Artsy-Probably-Lives-With-Mom man from the gas station, Kaine realized how truly susceptible to danger she was.

This was not what she'd wanted from Foster Hill House. She had wanted to regain a desire to live. Instead, death continued to chase her.

CHAPTER 6

"Why are *you* here?" Kaine hoped the apology showed as much on her face as she felt it in her heart. Her fear added an element of defensiveness the man from the gas station didn't deserve. Or did he? Kaine wished for a front door. But then, if this guy was a threat, he'd probably just kick it in and have his way with her. Yes. She needed that dog. A vicious guard dog. As well as a case to clip her can of pepper spray to her jeans and Captain America for a bodyguard. Or maybe the Green Arrow. Yes, definitely Oliver Queen.

"I wanted to make sure you were okay." Good-looking artsy boy shrugged and extended his hand slowly in greeting. "After almost running you over at the station."

He cast a cursory glance into the house over her shoulder. Kaine reached out and took his hand. *Firm handshake. Show you're confident, even when you're not. Eye contact.*

All the years of coaching and counseling battered women entered her mind. Now she was coaching herself.

"It's not like I was critically injured." She couldn't refrain from sarcasm. It was still running rampant through her.

"I know," the man admitted with a sheepish shrug. His blue flannel shirt gave him a casual air. Instinct told Kaine he posed no threat. Logic told Kaine she'd be dumb if she trusted her instinct — look where it'd gotten her so far.

"Joy sent me," he continued. "She was worried about the new owner of Foster Hill House."

"Ahh." Kaine offered up a hesitant smile.

"Grant Jesse." He still held her hand. So this was the man who sometimes watched Joy's daughter.

"Kaine. Prescott." She yanked her hand back when she realized she had been squeezing his far longer than a casual greeting. "Kaine Prescott," she repeated.

"Yep. Got that."

"Joy sent you?" Kaine tried to wrap her mind around the fact the station attendant was concerned about her. But, maybe the older woman felt she owed Kaine in exchange for the daffodils?

"When Joy calls, I answer." Lopsided grin

warmed hazel eyes. Gracious. He reminded Kaine of some actor she'd seen in a TV show. One who married the heroine, and then turned into an ogre, and then morphed back into a hero. Unpredictable at best.

"Some place you got here."

Well, he's a good fibber. The house was a wreck, and Grant Jesse knew it.

Kaine offered a plastic laugh. "Yeahhhhh. It's a castle."

"You're not really going to stay here?"

Kaine eyed him. Why did he want to know? "I — sure. Yes." She wasn't really, but he didn't need to know that. Kaine tugged at the bottom of her sweater and crossed her arms in front of her. It was the third time she had done that.

"There's a nice mo—"

"Motel," Kaine interrupted with an edgy laugh. "Yeah. I know. Joy told me."

"Ahh." Grant moved back a few steps as if he read her nerves. He searched her face, and a small, knowing tilt to his mouth told her he had drawn some sort of conclusion. Obviously the correct one, she determined, when he backed away from the doorway to stand farther out on the porch. Giving her space. Smart man. But he was lucky his foot didn't go through the floorboards.

"You might want to take Joy up on the offer of that motel." Grant tipped his head back to look up at the dilapidated house. Kaine caught a whiff of deodorant or cologne, she wasn't sure which. It was crisp, masculine, and reminded her of the marina in San Diego.

She followed him onto the porch. "I'm fine, thank you. And thank Joy as well, please. I've camped before, and this place isn't so bad." Let him believe she was fearless instead of planning on cowering under the covers at the motel — with her can of pepper spray. Where had she set it, anyway? This was why she needed organizer Leah around.

Grant's smile broadened and created crinkles in the corners of his eyes. Kaine could tell he knew she wasn't being honest. He shifted, and his heel caught a nail sticking up from the porch floorboard.

"You have supplies, then? Sleeping bag, food, camp stove?"

Darn. He was calling her bluff. Kaine pursed her lips and matched his cross-armed stance.

"Porta Potty?" Grant tested her sense of humor.

Very funny. "Actually, the plumbing here works okay. I'll be fine. Thanks." Kaine bit the inside of her lip. The guy made her want to smile at the same time she narrowed her eyes, trying to read him.

Grant bent and yanked on the offending nail. It came out with a minor tug. Old, rusted, worthless. He handed it to Kaine. She reached for it, and as her fingers closed around it, Grant kept hold of his end, forcing her to look at him.

"Going to be one heck of a house to restore yourself."

Kaine raised an eyebrow. "I like a challenge."

Grant released the nail. "So do I."

It was a new day. Sleep helped, Kaine had to admit. The Oakwood Motel was a strip of five small rooms available for overnight or long-term rent. A double bed with white sheets and a bedspread made of shiny polyester from 1994. The walls had wooden-framed pictures of the ocean, something Kaine found to be quite ironic since she had fled that very scene. A sink, a toilet, a digital alarm clock on a nightstand, and about the only up-to-date thing in the room: a flat-screen TV with cable. And Wi-Fi. She'd gotten in some blogging for Leah's husband and answered a few emails. A client referral proved to be good, so she sent a contract of agreement to consult for them.

More money would be essential.

Not far from her thoughts for the evening was Grant Jesse. Joy too. The only people she'd met in Oakwood, outside of the red-lipped teenager who'd registered her at the motel. They'd been kind, really. She needed to work on relaxing now and allowing herself time to process Danny's death from two years before while not constantly looking over her shoulder. It was hard to swallow that justice wouldn't be meted out on Danny's behalf, but maybe it was time to put it aside. Since she was the only one who kept alive the idea that he'd been murdered, not just killed in a random car accident.

Foster Hill House greeted her in the morning, not looking any friendlier than the day before. But, Kaine mustered her will to continue and focused on the good memories of Danny. His satisfied grin when he finished a project. He would be proud of her when she completed restoring this place.

Kaine tried to remind herself of that as she looked up the stairwell to the second floor. She felt for her back jean pocket. Pepper spray. Check. God help her. She was a paranoid mess. In another life she could see Danny right now, as if he were beside her. His brown eyes would be sparkling with anticipation for the latest hands-on project.

His brown hair would be ruffled and his tailored shirt untucked over blue jeans. But it was more than the attractive life that radiated from him that first caught her eye at the church she'd visited at the behest of a fellow social worker. It was his love of everything. Unabashed. Uncorked. Even for her. She held her secrets to herself, yet he gave her the room to do so. Even when her career began to drain every last ounce from her, he watched her go each morning, waiting . . .

She swallowed the lump that crowded her throat. She owed him this. For the morning that she didn't come back when he stood there at the door and asked her to stay. For the kisses she shrank away from. For the day that he died.

The stairs creaked beneath Kaine's feet, but they held. That was a plus. One check mark in the pro column of Foster Hill House. She let out a breath as she reached the top of the stairs, where a long, dank hallway, as creepy as a horror movie, met her. It was barren, with the exception of more spider webs, another large mouse nest, and a disintegrating painting that hung askew midway. She tiptoed over to it, the walls closing in and suffocating her with the presence of imaginary ghosts. What footsteps had walked these hallways? Young, old, child, elderly? The note-riddled page from *Great Expectations* was still in her pocket. She felt for it. Had the person who left it walked this hall?

Kaine's skin crawled and goose bumps rose on her flesh as if she were being watched. She rammed her hands into her yellow hoodie's front pocket as though that would somehow make her invisible.

The painting was so covered in dust, Kaine couldn't make out much color, let alone figures. Running her hand across it, she regretted that choice immediately and swiped it against her jeans, attempting to wipe the grime off her palm. It was weird there was still a painting in this house, as if all previous owners had been afraid to take it down.

A face stared back at her from the cracked, peeling canvas. An ancient woman in a black dress that appeared to be from the Civil War era. Kaine tipped her head, locking eyes with the vacant dark browns of the woman long dead. She couldn't be more than forty. Her face was average, her lips pulled tight. Maybe from sitting so long while the painter painted her? Kaine wondered what she had been thinking or what her eyes had seen. The war, newspapers with Abraham Lincoln in bold letters and quotes, maybe death? Kaine swallowed. She could connect with this woman, if only by that one thought alone.

Her cellphone shattered the chilling stillness. It flipped from Kaine's hand as she jumped at the sound. Catching it in midair, she rammed her finger down on the screen's green answer button.

"Leah. Sheesh!"

"Are you all right?" Leah's voice, so familiar, brought reality rushing back to the historic tomb into which Kaine had wandered.

She wrinkled her face in disgust as if Leah stood in front of her. "I'm creeped out, that's what. This house — it's sketchy."

"That bad?"

"Well, it's not good," Kaine countered, biting back the added accusation that the realtor Leah had sworn by had, indeed, scammed Kaine.

She gave the woman in the painting one last study. Kaine could almost feel her gaze searing into her back, begging her to step back into time and rescue her. That was it — the woman looked afraid.

"Are you going to stay?" Leah's question followed Kaine into the first room. A bedroom, empty and cold.

"I have to. I'm saddled with the place now."

"No, you don't. Come home to San Diego if it's so horrid. We can put it back up for sale and you can live with us until you get back on your feet."

"No one but me would be stupid enough to buy this place. Besides, you know why I left San Diego. I can't come back. I can't —"

"Are you sure there isn't an element of truth to what the police said? Maybe you really do need to take some time and just rest. Get more counseling. It was helping you. I could tell it was and —"

Kaine froze in the doorway of bedroom number two. "Don't, Leah."

Silence.

"I just —" Leah paused — "I just want you to be sure."

Kaine sagged against the doorframe and stared into the empty room. Be sure? Of what? That her life as she'd known it was over the day the police showed up on her doorstep and said Danny had been in a wreck? Or how about when the police told her the witnesses said his driving had been erratic? Like he was drunk or falling asleep at the wheel. Danny's autopsy ruled out alcohol, but Kaine knew that the drugs they found in Danny couldn't be the full explanation. He'd never used. He wasn't *that* type of man. They closed the case as accidental, and they labeled her the crazy wife who insisted her husband wasn't an addict and that someone had drugged him. Why did she think that? They had asked. But she didn't have an answer. So it was posttraumatic stress disorder, they assumed. Because of the accident. Because of the violence she'd witnessed in her career, maybe even in her own past. A past Kaine had no desire to remember, let alone admit to. So no, Kaine wasn't sure. Of anything anymore. It had been years since she had been sure.

"Don't question me now, Leah, please," Kaine whispered to her sister. She could picture Leah's eyes, large and earnest, filled with concern. She probably thought she was coming alongside her, urging her forward with baby steps. Instead she was whacking Kaine across the face with every doubt, angst, and wound Kaine carried inside.

"Kaine, you ran out of San Diego like a cat out of a dog kennel."

"I was scared. I still am."

More silence. As if Leah was choosing her words carefully. "You need to talk about it, Kaine. About Danny, about the break-ins . . . about your job."

"I left my job behind." Kaine held the phone away from her face and glared at it, pacing out of the empty second bedroom toward the third and final room. Leah had to bring up her job? It had sapped every ounce of life from her *before* Danny died. It was her passion, her mission, even her ministry, if she spiritualized it. The women she had helped, the stories . . . the violence.

Kaine put the phone back to her ear. "Listen, Leah. Please — give me some time, all right? I need to find my life again. I need to stabilize. Explore our roots and do something for Danny." Because she hadn't done enough when he'd been alive. The hours away, the lack of romance, the slow drift apart. Six years of marriage, and now here she was.

"You know I love you, and I'm proud of you." Leah always needed affirmation, so that's what she usually offered too. Kaine could use something more tangible.

"I love you too."

"Kaine?"

"Yeah?"

"I put a box in your trunk before you left. I wanted to be sure you had it when you returned to Great-Great-Grandmother Ivy's old stomping grounds."

Maybe Leah had learned something about Kaine. The first seedling of hope grew in her chest. Something tangible was in her car, right now, a gift from Leah.

"What is it?"

"It's our great-great-grandmother's quilt." A smile touched Leah's voice.

"Where did you get that?" Kaine recalled it from years before, folded at the foot of their grandfather's bed.

"After Grandpa died, you were away at college all preoccupied with your pre-Danny boyfriend when I went through Grandpa's stuff. I had it stored in my closet. But I thought now that you are in Oakwood, where Ivy grew up, you might want it." Leah's voice waned, as if she didn't know what to say anymore.

But it meant everything to Kaine. Maybe, since she was in Oakwood, it was time to find her foundation in family roots. What part did the family legacy play in shaping her into the driven, assertive, and now very lost person that she was?

Kaine stepped across the threshold into bedroom number three.

"I'll cherish it, Leah, I'll —"

"Kaine?" Leah pressed into Kaine's choked silence.

Kaine couldn't respond, couldn't answer.

Her hand lowered, the phone clutched in her hand. The walls of the room closed in, then expanded, and she blinked several times to bring it back to proper proportions. The shaft of light from the four-paned window on the opposite side of the room stretched across the weathered wood floor. The object propped in its path stole her breath, and the last vestige of tentative peace Kaine had found exploded into a thousand invisible pieces.

CHAPTER 7

IVY

Her favorite scent of lavender wrapped around Ivy as she opened her eyes a small crack. Her vision was blurry, but she made out the deep green-striped wallpaper that met the white wainscoting in the middle of her bedroom wall. Oh, the ache, the deep ache. Ivy closed her eyes again. Darkness. Stairs. She remembered the hazy sensation of falling.

"What's her condition?" The voice by her bedside startled her, but Ivy didn't open her eyes. It was Joel Cunningham. In her bedroom. She wanted to argue him away, but the words wouldn't formulate in her foggy brain, let alone escape her tongue.

Her father's voice shattered the remaining blur. "Who did this to her, Joel? I want this fiend caught!"

"Was she — ?" Joel let his question hang.

No. I wasn't. Ivy responded in her mind.

Neither of the men were answering each other's questions, and Ivy had yet to summon the stamina to open her eyes again.

"No. No. She wasn't." Finally. Her father answered for her. "She's badly bruised, as you can see, not unlike the girl we found. I swear someone tried to strangle her, but I don't think anything's broken. It appears she was pushed down the stairs in Foster Hill House."

She wasn't half dead after all, thank God! But she felt like she was. Ivy tried to move, but her body throbbed in protest.

"How do we know what happened?" Joel was fact-finding already. He was on a case, and now, Ivy realized, she was part of the case. She could have easily been lying on the same table Gabriella had lain on, and in the same condition. The realization was frightening enough and it bought Ivy's continued silence.

"She was coherent enough when Foggerty found her to tell him she'd been attacked." There was a tremor in her father's voice.

"How is it Foggerty found Gabriella and now Ivy?"

"He traps the property, and he wanders. He said he heard moaning in the house and that's when he came across Ivy." There was a break now in her father's voice. *Dear Papa.*

"Whoever did this to Ivy must have thought she was dead." Joel seemed to hesitate. "She's blessed, or else they may have tried to make sure that was the case and hid her like they did the girl. We may never have found Ivy."

"Dear God." Her father's quivering plea sliced through Ivy's consciousness. She should open her eyes, assure him she was going to be all right, but Joel continued.

"She'll recover?"

"Physically, yes." Ivy could feel her father's fingers pushing back the hair from her forehead. "Emotionally? After all she's been through . . . with Andrew? She's never been the same since. I lost them both the day he drowned. In different ways. So, I don't know, Joel. I don't know if she'll ever recover," Dr. Thorpe said.

Darkness crowded in on Ivy once more, except this time it was different. It summoned the pain she'd never buried. The pain of Andrew, the pain of Joel's abandonment, and the aching question: Why had he come home?

The second time she awoke, the memories came with force. Foster Hill House, the scarlet bed, a volume of *Great Expectations,* and the attack.

Ivy's eyes flew open and she sat up in a swift motion. The room spun, and she blinked rapidly as shutters of black closed across her vision.

"Slow down," the voice beside her murmured. She had no choice but to yield to the pressure of a hand on her shoulder, urging her back onto the pillows.

Ivy turned her head, her gaze landing on a muscled forearm, rolled-up sleeves of a blue cotton shirt, and the clean-cut jaw of Joel. She closed her eyes. More to avoid seeing his disapproval than from the spots still swirling in her vision.

Yet he didn't say anything, so after a few moments Ivy attempted to open her eyes again. Her body awakened to the sore muscles from her tumble down the stairs. Her jaw hurt from where she had struck it on a step as she'd twisted from beneath the man's wicked grip.

Her eyes met Joel's. There was no criticism in his expression. She was taken aback by the tenderness she saw there, until it disappeared and his face transformed into the detective he was instead of the friend he'd once been.

"Did you see the man who did this to you?"

Yes. This was the Joel she was fast becoming accustomed to. Ivy looked away, toward the window and the trees that waved black, bare branches against a blue sky.

"No." There wasn't any need to expound further.

"Any physical features at all?"

"Outside of the fact that his arm around my throat was like a steel bar? No."

Silence. Ivy should feel bad for snapping at Joel. But with awareness seeping into every cell of her throbbing body, the need to distance herself from this man at her bedside grew.

"Did he speak to you? Did you recognize his voice?"

Ivy bit her lip, then reconsidered when she bit down on a bruise. Tears burned her eyes but didn't fall. She wanted to sleep, to curl deep into the covers and not see the light of day for hours, days even.

"Ivy?" Joel pressed.

She turned her head on the soft pillow but kept her eyes closed. "He spoke, but I didn't recognize his voice."

"What did he say?"

"Stop, Joel." Ivy lifted her eyelids. "Please."

His blue stare drilled into her. In another time and place, she might have been able to interpret the look in his eye. Now he was a stranger. A stranger who still stirred some-thing deep inside of her. She resisted that. "Please, stop fact-gathering."

"I need to know, Ivy. This man — he could have hurt you worse. We need to find him to determine why he's targeting beauti-ful women."

Beautiful. Ivy picked at a loose thread on the blanket that covered her. She'd never known he considered her beautiful. She stole a glance at Joel. In all her resentment toward him, she'd neglected to notice his demeanor had shifted over the years. Gone was the boy who smiled, who laughed, and who put her in her place as he toyed with the ends of her braid. The pragmatic and calculating personality hints she'd witnessed in the orphan boy had swallowed the mis-chievous boy whole.

Andrew's death had darkened them both.

Yet, in spite of what happened, in spite of what Joel had done, she still missed him.

"Why did you come home?"

Joel blinked, his expression remaining impassive. "I was hired by Sheriff Dunst."

It was a bland answer. Unsatisfactory, and the vagueness of it hurtful.

"Because of all the crime in Oakwood?" Ivy regretted speaking, the irony in her tone not only sounded wicked, but the quick

93

flash of hurt in Joel's eyes made guilt clutch her heart. But she shouldn't feel guilty. He owed her an explanation she could accept.

"Because I inquired, and because it was offered."

Fine then.

"Ivy, not now." Joel's eyes connected with hers, searching, pleading.

He was right. Now wasn't the time. Not when her brain was fuzzy, muddled from her fall, when Gabriella's baby was unaccounted for, and when a potential killer was still haunting Foster Hill.

Joel's hand rested on the edge of her bed, its weight tugging the blanket tight at her side. The scent of his spicy cologne tempted her with its warmth, as if he himself were a safe refuge. So contradictory to her memories. It was an invisible pull, and one Ivy didn't have the strength to resist. She moved her hand down her side until her smallest finger touched his skin. His hand didn't stir, didn't even twitch. She considered pulling away — she *should* pull away — but just as Ivy determined to, Joel's finger curled around hers. There was no forgiveness in their connection, only longing for what should have been, instead of what was.

CHAPTER 8

The third bedroom was far less daunting in daylight. Even the bed, with its scarlet blanket askew and the mattress covered in debris and mice droppings, was sad. It was Joel who was intimidating. He glowered at Ivy from the doorway, his arms crossed, the scowl on his face harsh. Their carriage ride to the house on Foster Hill had been one of silence. He preferred she stay in bed, but Ivy had had enough. Twenty-four hours in bed had only sealed fate if Gabriella's baby had been left behind in the cold. The very idea ate at her insides and made Ivy's own pain unimportant.

"Stop looking at me as if I'm a pariah." She twisted one of her dark strands of hair around her finger. It was hanging loose. It hurt too badly to put it up proper.

"I've not disowned you, but I'm coming awful close."

She gave Joel a sharp glance. He *hadn't*

disowned her? Then what did the last twelve years without even a letter mean?

"I need to tell you what happened to me here, before I forget the details." Ivy chose to ignore the more personal train of thought and focus on Gabriella and her baby instead. "The baby —"

"Ivy." Joel's hand on her arm caused her to pull back. He hesitated before he returned it to his side. "You need to trust that Sheriff Dunst and I are putting forth every effort to find out who Gabriella was and where her baby is."

"I do." She didn't, but for now she preferred to lie.

The look he gave her was dubious at best. He ignored exploring further the truth behind her assertion. "What do you remember?"

Yes. Anything. She would do anything to help find Gabriella's killer and now her own attacker. Ivy pushed a curl behind her ear and the movement made her grimace. Her shoulder was sore and bruised from hitting the stairs when she'd been pushed. It even hurt to talk.

"I was standing here. No. No, I was kneeling. By the bed." Ivy remembered now. A beam of light through the lone window had illuminated the floor at the end of the bed.

96

"I noticed the blanket. It was very red in the moonlight. I thought maybe Gabriella had slept on the bed before."

"That's conjecture, Ivy."

"I am fully aware of that." She shot a stern look at Joel. "But it may have happened."

"True, but it changes nothing."

"You said you needed all the details. That's what I was *thinking* at the time." Ivy pursed her lips. Dust particles danced between them in the sun's ray.

Joel cleared his throat. "I would prefer the details of what you *saw.*"

"Of course." She knew what he wanted. Straightforward facts. But one must theorize to shape the facts into any kind of potential. She mustered a small smile, a truce of sorts.

Joel blinked and his features relaxed. "All right then. Continue. What did your assailant look like?"

Ivy cleared her throat. It hurt to swallow. The sensation of her attacker's arm around her throat returned, along with the memory of the scratchy wool of his sleeve chafing her skin. Her breaths shallowed. She needed to breathe, yet a suffocating fear gripped her as the memories overwhelmed her.

"I-I don't know. He came up behind me." The memory assailed her. Fear crawled into her stomach and up to her throat, squeez-

97

ing at Ivy's breath like it was happening again. "I never saw his face. His voice — I didn't recognize it. It was —" She needed to breathe.

Ivy grabbed the bed frame. Joel was beside her in a moment, his hands on her shoulders. He lowered his face to match hers, eye to eye.

"Take a deep breath, Ivy."

She was. Or she was trying to. Fear was a vicious enemy. She couldn't let it best her. Ivy closed her eyes, wishing she had reconciled enough with God to pray, to feel the old assurance of His presence beside her. But her mind was empty of prayer. Instead she heard Joel's quiet breathing, and she matched hers to his.

When her panic lessened, Ivy shrank from Joel's touch. She didn't want to be mollycoddled. She didn't want to be ministered to or treated like a swooning female.

"There was a book." Ivy reinserted herself into her memories and avoided Joel's searching eyes.

"Where?"

"It was . . ." Ivy tried to remember. It had been dark. So dark and then — "There." Ivy remembered. She turned to Joel as she pointed at the floor next to the bed. "It was a copy of Dickens's *Great Expectations.*

Someone had written in it. Scrawled with a pencil, 'This house holds secrets. I am one of them.' "

Joel did not seem triumphant at their first real, tangible clue.

"Well?" Ivy rested her hand on the dusty footboard of the bed. She was still dizzy, but loath to admit it to Joel.

"Anyone could have written it."

"What if Gabriella wrote it?"

"Was her name in it?"

Ivy leveled a look of derision on him. "We don't know her name."

"Exactly." Joel nodded. "There's nothing to indicate that it was Gabriella's, or who-ever she is. The book isn't even here any-more."

"I realize that." Heaven help her, she might align herself with her attacker and strangle Joel. She frowned and tightened her grasp on the bed. "But, if it was Ga-briella, then she's trying to tell us some-thing. Something about Foster Hill House. Something about how she died."

Joel drew in a deep breath and looked beyond Ivy to the floor where the book had been the night of her attack. He braced himself with his hand on the mattress and gave a cursory glance beneath the bed. It was apparent the book hadn't been kicked

99

beneath it during the struggle when Joel stood up empty-handed. "While I see the importance of theorizing, we must be careful it lines up with evidence. Otherwise we're chasing ideas."

"Desperate situations sometimes call for it. I think the existence of a baby warrants even extreme speculation, don't you? I don't believe it's farfetched to consider the fact that Gabriella *was* here in this house and *did* write that note. She was, after all, found just down the hill from here."

Doubt flickered in his eyes. "And now the book has disappeared."

Ivy tapped her toe on the wood floor, impatient and disconcerted all at the same time. It didn't seem that Joel was implying someone had swiped the book after attacking her, so much as suggesting she might have never seen the book to begin with.

"The book *was* here." Ivy stopped her toe from its agitated dance.

Joel nodded. His silence was a stronger answer. He turned his attention from her and began to poke about the room. He opened the closet door and peeked in. Empty. He moved to look behind a dusty bureau and the miniscule gap between it and the wall.

So be it. Ivy let the conversation rest

alongside its bedmates of doubt and mistrust. Her breath caught, partly because of her bruised ribs and partly due to the ache in her spirit. She wanted to contemplate the what-ifs, but Joel was only focused on the what-is.

Joel pulled out a drawer from the bureau and a poof of musty, dank smell invaded the room. Ivy wrinkled her nose as she came up behind him. There was nothing inside. Nothing to indicate anyone had lived here since the Fosters abandoned the house forty years ago.

"The mice are loving this place." Joel pointed to a pile of droppings.

Ivy backed away. She reached the window and pressed her hand against the glass as she stared out over the hillside, its grasses heavy with spring's thaw. She knew, deep inside, that Gabriella had been here, had been in this room, and had looked out this very window. But Joel was right. There had been no name in the book along with the cryptic message. Even if there were a name, they couldn't attach it to the nameless woman found dead in the hollow tree. And now the book had disappeared. Had her attacker swiped it? That was the most logical conclusion, but again, it was speculation.

Ivy slid her hand down the window and

rested her fingertips on the wooden strip that crisscrossed it. She needed to show Joel the piano downstairs, its clean keys and the sheet music. Maybe that would be the evidence to convince him someone had been in Foster Hill House recently.

"Joel, I —"

He interrupted. "I'm sorry, Ivy, but there's nothing here. If I'm going to pursue the possibility that the book you saw was truly scribbled in by Gabriella, I need proof she was here. I can't go back to Sheriff Dunst with pure assumption."

"I realize that." Ivy turned. It was a mistake. Her eyes dropped to his mouth, then rose to meet his narrowed gaze. There was savvy there, but a touch of tenderness at the edges. She tried to soften her voice, but wasn't sure she was successful. "There's more you need to consider."

"*I* am already considering some leads."

She didn't miss the inflection in Joel's words, an inflection that excluded her. Ivy turned back to the window and rested her hands on the sill. She made pretense of watching a robin flutter by to its perch on the hollow oak tree that had been Gabriella's initial grave.

Ivy knew Sheriff Dunst was visiting some of the outlying area, inquiring as to whether anyone knew Gabriella or could identify her. What leads could Joel possibly have?

"The piano, downstairs." Ivy spun around to explain to Joel, but her sleeve caught on the windowsill. The rip of her cuff stilted her turn. "For heaven's sake," she muttered, and inspected her dress.

Joel pushed up against her, and she jerked her head up in surprise at his close proximity. But his attention wasn't on her. He reached for the jagged edge on the windowsill, the wood beginning to rot from moisture and age. When he pulled his hand back, there was a small piece of material in his fingertips, no larger than a penny.

"Here." Joel handed it to her as if she would be able to piece it back onto her dress.

Ivy frowned and reached for it, but her fingers stilled as they reached his. "That's not mine."

Joel looked closely at the scrap of material in his hand, then gave her dress a cursory glance. The faded gray calico was nowhere near the same shade as her serviceable blue.

A thousand prickles met her skin again, but this time they had nothing to do with Joel. Ivy carefully took the calico from him and pressed it into her palm, lifting it so they could both see. There it was. The tiny piece of material. Proof that Gabriella had been in Foster Hill House.

"It's Gabriella's. This is from the dress she was wearing when she was found."

Joel's voice dropped a few bars. "You're certain? No doubts?"

"None." Ivy couldn't help the slight upturn of her mouth as she locked eyes with Joel. Gabriella *had* been one of the secrets the house on Foster Hill concealed. A definitive starting point was identified. It was one painfully small step toward finding out who Gabriella was and, most important of all, what had happened to the little baby she had birthed only weeks before her death.

CHAPTER 9

KAINE

He was here. He had followed her. Kaine's knuckles whitened on the steering wheel. She should have told her sister, but Leah would have insisted Kaine come home. And why couldn't she? Because she didn't want to. The memories, the grief, not to mention the most blaring reason: Her leaving San Diego was to get away from this terror.

She braked as she rounded a corner in her Jetta, casting a glance at the picture of Danny that lay on the passenger seat where she'd tossed it. The picture that had been sitting in the middle of the barren floor was an 8-by-10 print from a color ink-jet printer, stolen from one of her online photo galleries. She'd thought she deleted them all, but apparently not. Danny's smile ripped into Kaine's heart. She stifled a sob and adjusted her grip on the steering wheel, staring at the road ahead.

Who was this dedicated to playing such horrific psychological games? Why had they taken Danny's life? Now they were pilfering pictures of him off the internet? Kaine needed to find a coffee shop with Wi-Fi and do a Google search of her name again to find which online photos still existed in cyberspace. She'd already changed her email, ditched her original cellphone for a new one, and erased her Instagram, Facebook, and Twitter accounts.

Oak trees whisked by her car in straight lines, like soldiers. Had her stalker driven past them? Kaine was no stranger to stalkers. Her entire career as a social worker for abused women had her shielding, defending, and helping women escape the beasts in their lives. Some of the women were victims of sex trafficking, bound to a pimp who valued their worth only in a monetary sense. Escape was never easy and too often ended badly. Kaine's fervor to save had ended abruptly with Danny's death. Her life was surrounded by violence, and she'd reached the end of her tolerance for it.

"God, please." She begged the Lord through clenched teeth as she rounded a corner. Why would this elusive unknown follow her across country? She'd been more than happy to dismiss the daffodil on day one as Joy's daughter's accidental token of greeting. But now? Kaine blew out a puff of air. She hadn't been paranoid after all. Once again, circumstances proved to her she wasn't suffering from PTSD any more than Elvis was actually alive.

Her car brought her into view of downtown Oakwood. Her phone GPS called out her next turn, and she rounded the corner to pull into her destination. Tilting her head, Kaine peered through the windshield at the Oakwood Police Department building — a tan brick structure with a glass door and two windows on either side. Not at all like the San Diego precinct.

She closed her eyes. The memories of past police interviews filtered through her mind. The doubt written across the detective's face, his reminder that she had just lost her husband in an *accident,* and the implication that her stress caused her to forget *she* had moved the items, not some stalker. Kaine squeezed the steering wheel. If the San Diego Police Department didn't believe her and couldn't find substantial evidence to support her claims of break-ins, then what would the Oakwood Police do? In a rinky-dink town whose worst crime in the last fifty years was probably an elementary student stealing bubblegum from the local grocery store.

Still. Why take chances?

Within minutes, Kaine pulled open the station door, Danny's copy-paper picture clutched in her hand.

A window of plexiglass separated Kaine from the officer at the desk.

"Can I help you?"

"I need to file a report." Kaine prepared herself for the all-too familiar barrage of questions. Soon she was seated across from a robust detective holding a spiral-bound notebook and clicking a pen against his teeth.

"Detective Carter."

"Kaine Prescott." She wanted to scream. Her foot tapped a nervous cadence against the leg of the wooden chair. Detective Carter glanced at it. Kaine stopped.

"So, you experienced a break-in?" he inquired.

"Yes." Kaine explained the location, the circumstances, and ended by placing Danny's picture on the desktop. She had to avoid looking at it. His grin lit up the room from the paper and drove the knife of guilt deeper into her soul. He'd died not knowing how much she really did love him. "This picture was left in an upstairs bedroom. It's of my husband, who died two years ago."

"And there was no vandalism?"

"Not that I could tell." But really, it was Foster Hill House. Someone could bust down a door, and unless Kaine had made mental note of it standing, she'd venture it matched the rest of the dilapidated structure.

"Huh," the detective said. "Do you know anyone in the area? Anyone who would think leaving a picture of your husband would be . . . a bad joke?"

A bad joke? "No."

"And your husband, how did he pass away?"

What did she say? Her husband was murdered two years ago? The nice detective would contact the San Diego Police and find out it'd been an "accident." She was being stalked? Oh, yes, the police would identify her as exhibiting symptoms of an anxiety disorder and tell him she'd been warned she could be charged with making false claims.

"He was in a car accident. In San Diego. The case was closed as an accident, but —" Kaine stopped and picked at a fingernail.

"But what?"

She lifted her eyes and met the detective's. What could it hurt? "I never thought it was an accident."

He frowned and tapped the photo. "Why's that?"

Kaine noticed he had a line of dirt under his fingernail that kept poking at Danny's face. "They said it was drug-induced, only Danny was never a user. And afterward, things like this — the picture — kept happening. But, no one could explain it to me."

A long moment passed while the officer contemplated her words. "Here's what I'll do. I'll send a dispatch out to check over the place," Detective Carter assured her. He lifted Danny's picture. "May I keep this?"

"Absolutely." He was taking her seriously. Kaine would do anything for the man.

"I'll touch base with the precinct you worked with. Familiarize myself with your case. But, frankly, outside of this, there's not much to go on. We can run the paper for fingerprints and see if anything comes back. While I'm sorry about your husband, you have to know if there was no credible evidence for your husband's death being a murder, there's nothing I can do here."

His eyebrow rose. There it was. The familiar, unspoken warning that she would end up walking the line of being accused of making false claims. She was starting all over again. Square one.

Kaine stood and reached back to tighten her ponytail. "Thank you." She didn't know what else to say.

Detective Carter filled in the awkward silence. "Ma'am, Foster Hill House always has strange things happening. Kids break in all the time and have parties and whatnot. It may be some kid got on the internet and read your story and is playing a prank."

Kaine nodded. Certainly. That was it. A prank.

She politely shook hands with the detective and left the station. Now she had two police files in two states with records of the strange occurrences. At least this time she had something tangible, Danny's picture, to leave with them.

Defeated, Kaine drove around the city square. Not even the quaint village shops inspired her, yet she had no desire to return to Foster Hill House. Not alone.

To the right of the road sat a medium-sized building with vinyl siding inside dark brown metal fencing, and a sign boasting a picture of a dog and a cat. Remembering her impulsive promise to herself, Kaine followed the whim and swung into the parking lot. If she was going to be alone, she was definitely getting a dog.

Crawling out of the car, she tugged her shirt over her hips and strolled to the front door. The idea of a cuddly dog warmed her, but she hoped it would also boast fangs. When she pushed open the door, a cat scampered past her feet and across the linoleum floor. The distinct smell of fur and animal shampoo tickled her nose. The entryway was empty. A lone counter that apparently served as a receptionist desk stretched in front of her, a vacant chair behind it. A small empty kennel was in the corner, its door open. A beat-up leather chair sat in the middle of the room, like it was awaiting an occupant in an interrogation room.

"Hello?" Kaine ventured down the hallway in the direction the cat had fled. The sound of barking dogs greeted her as she pushed open a door. The kennels. Two employees wearing jeans and blue polos stood in the room, and one of them raised his head.

Well then.

Grant Jesse's welcoming expression froze on his face for a second before it transformed into a grin that reached the corners of his eyes. So he worked in an animal shelter?

"Kaine, what brings you here?"

"I need a dog." Kaine heard the fear in

her own voice, and for a moment she got the feeling Grant recognized it too. No one who met her now would ever guess that only five years ago she'd been a caring, effervescent person.

"A dog?" He jammed his hands in his pockets. He tended to do that, Kaine noted.

"Yeah. I . . ." She was tired of trying to explain herself. Detective Carter had sucked out her will to explain herself ever again.

"Foster Hill House is pretty creepy." Grant offered up his own suggestion, and Kaine latched on to it.

Thank God. Yes, blame it on the stupid house. She mustered a smile to try to look friendlier than she felt. "It gets lonely there. I'd like some company and I've had dogs in the past. I had a golden retriever when I was a teenager."

The light of interest that flickered in Grant's eye wasn't what she'd intended. She just wanted to convince him she was capable of being a responsible dog owner. He ran a hand over his day-old scruff, then shoved his fingers through his light brown hair.

"Sure. I get that. What kind are you looking for?"

"A pit bull," Kaine offered without hesitation. They were the brutes, right? The ones who attacked to kill and never let go?

113

Grant choked, laughed, and cocked his head to the left. "Well, that's a great breed of dog. They're very loyal, faithful, gentle. . . ." He went on to extol the virtues of the pit bull. By the time he was finished, Kaine was convinced it was the cuddly animal she'd been hoping for. But what about lion-toothed defenders?

"Aren't they fighters? Killers?" she interrupted, adjusting her purse on her shoulder.

Grant's eyebrows went up. "You need a killer dog?"

Kaine averted her eyes, fighting an instinctual attraction that just felt wrong. She was married — or she had been. And for all she knew, he was married with four kids. "Well, a guard dog would be nice," she finally said.

"They are very loyal dogs, and protective. But contrary to popular belief, pit bulls are killers only when trained, and usually they're abused in the process."

There it was again. Abuse.

Kaine was so tired of how that word followed her.

"Maybe I don't want a pit bull." At this point, Kaine wondered if an ankle-biter dog would be more effective. One of those little rats that ran around and yipped at a frequency so high it could shatter crystal.

Grant waved his hand toward the kennels.

"We actually don't have many dogs here right now. We just had a free giveaway in order to place most of them in homes. We do a lot of rescues from the big-city shelters that put an expiration date on their lives. You see, we don't euthanize here."

"That's nice." And it was. But Kaine didn't even know where to go with this education. She just wanted a dog. Company. An animal smart enough to alert her if there was a stranger on the premises. If she ever went back to Foster Hill House, that is.

"Here." Grant grabbed her hand as if they were old friends.

Goodness, he was touchy-feely, but Kaine didn't pull away. His hand was strong and comforting — and not wearing a wedding ring.

Grant steered Kaine down a row of empty kennels to the one at the very end. The soulful brown eyes of a black lab stared back at her. The muzzle was peppered with gray, the dog's hips lumpy with aged muscles, and the ears drooped around the furry face. It blinked at Kaine, then lowered its muzzle between its paws. Resigned. Knowing that Kaine wouldn't adopt, wouldn't save, wouldn't rescue.

But the dog needed her.

Kaine was surprised by the return of her

innate urge to rescue. She saw something in the dog's eyes she connected with. The dog was alone. Like her.

Grant was speaking. "She's the only dog we couldn't place. Olive is eight years old and a lot of folks don't want an older dog. Not to mention, she was abused, so she's shy of male strangers."

Not exactly a killer, but if she didn't like strange men, maybe she would at least bark.

"Olive. That's a cute name."

"Sure. Black olives. Black lab." Grant gazed down at Kaine as if waiting for her response. When she didn't give one, he opened the kennel door. "You'll want to go slow. Olive doesn't respond well to fast motions."

Kaine knew all about that. The same thing could be said of abused women, or women with stalkers. She crouched by Olive and extended her hand, palm down. The dog sniffed it, withdrew, then returned to nudge her.

"She likes you." Grant's affirmation brought a tiny flicker of hope to Kaine's raw emotions.

"I'll take her." The words escaped Kaine's mouth before she had time to consider any further.

Grant snapped the leash onto Olive and scratched the dog behind her ears. "Well, girl, you've got a new home." He gave Kaine a sideways glance, accompanied by a lopsided grin. "Not every dog's dream to live at Foster Hill House, though."

Kaine offered a tiny smile back as she passed him, using her key remote to unlock her blue Jetta. She pulled the door open, and Grant knelt beside Olive, her haunches quivering.

"She's a bit afraid of vehicles," he explained to Kaine.

"I see that." Poor thing. Kaine's hands had only just stopped shaking from the morning's discovery. She could relate.

Grant lifted Olive and carefully placed her in the back seat of the car. Kaine tried not to notice the way his biceps strained against his shirt. The dog scrambled to get out, so Grant slid in next to her. With a calming hand, he stroked Olive's black fur.

Kaine leaned against the car and peeked in. "Is she going to be all right?"

"She might get some comfort if you have a blanket or something she can make her own." Grant scratched behind Olive's ear.

"I'll just sit here for a minute."

"I might have one in the trunk." Kaine spun on her heel and popped the trunk with her key fob. What was she doing? A dog? She wasn't prepared for this, but her impulsive need for companionship and security wasn't something she could go back on now. Nor was she certain she wanted to. She pulled out a few boxes of belongings from California and stacked them. A flash of fuzzy navy blue caught her eye. Reaching for the familiar blanket she'd always curled up with in front of the TV back in San Diego, Kaine paused at the quilt beneath it. Leah's gift. Great-Great-Grandmother Ivy's quilt. Kaine had forgotten about it in the terror of the day.

She pulled the fuzzy blanket from the trunk and shut the lid.

"Will this work?" Kaine handed the blue blanket to Grant as she hung Ivy's quilt over her left forearm.

Grant reached out and took the blanket. "Perfect." His smile revealed a small crease in his left cheek. Kaine looked away from him. She listened to him crooning to Olive as she unfolded the quilt from Leah. It was pieced together with varying squares of material and, while quaint, not particularly beautiful.

"Hey." The surprise in Grant's voice drew Kaine's eyes back to his. Olive nuzzled the blanket on the car seat and then plopped onto it with an *oomph*. Grant slid from the car, an unspoken question bending his brows. He pushed his glasses up his nose with an index finger as he tipped his head toward the quilt in Kaine's hands. "That's, um, some quilt you got there."

"Oh." Kaine glanced down at it. "Yeah, it was my great-great-grandmother's quilt. My sister gave it to me when I left San Diego."

Grant narrowed his eyes. "Was your great-great-grandmother from around here?"

"I guess. I don't know much about her really. For that matter, I don't know much about my ancestry at all, pre-my-grandpa." Kaine stuck her hand inside the car. Olive sniffed it, then laid her muzzle back on the blanket she'd clearly claimed as hers now.

"What was her name?"

"Ivy Thorpe. She's in our family Bible, and the family tree ends there. It doesn't list her married name, even though she obviously did marry. My grandpa's name, Prescott, is the only family surname I know after that." Well, that was info dump. But it was obvious there was something about the quilt that captivated him. His eyes kept dropping to it.

119

Grant cleared his throat. "I see."

Kaine edged around him and opened the driver's side door. She tossed the quilt onto the passenger seat out of sight. "You see what?"

Even Kaine could hear the sharpness in her voice. Grant Jesse's cryptic behavior wasn't complimentary to the anxiousness still riddling through her.

"It's nothing," he said with a shrug, making a pretense of waggling his fingers at Olive. "My mom likes old quilts, and my brother owns an antique shop south of here."

"Try again." Kaine crossed her arms. "Why the fascination with my family quilt?"

"It's true," Grant went on. "My brother does own an antique shop. My family took vacations to museums growing up, and my dad was a history professor at the university before he and Mom retired in Arizona. We're all history buffs."

Kaine raised an eyebrow.

Grant's jaw muscle twitched and he released a sigh. "Look. Ivy Thorpe is sort of a household name in Oakwood's history books. And that quilt? It went missing from the museum here in Oakwood back in the sixties. There are pictures of it at the museum."

120

Kaine squeezed her eyes shut, then opened them again. Nope. He was still there with his silly story of a stolen quilt. She didn't need this right now. Not after this morning. "My sister gave me this quilt. It's been in my family for years."

Grant pulled his hands from his jean pockets. "I didn't mean to accuse you of anything, really. It just took me by surprise — seeing it."

Kaine whispered around the lump in her throat, "You've no right to question my family, or me."

Regret filtered across his face. His poignant stare rocked her, as if he was studying her, reading her, seeing inside of her.

"I need to go." Kaine turned sideways to get into her car, but Grant's firm grip on her arm stopped her. She looked down at his corded hand, then at him.

"I'm sorry, Kaine. I didn't mean to offend you. There's just a lot of history in Oakwood, and your being here sort of stirs it up."

Kaine shrugged off his hand, his touch burning through her sleeve. "How so?" Did she really want to know?

Grant hesitated, seeming to weigh his words before continuing. "You know the story about the dead woman found at

Foster Hill House way back at the turn of the century?"

Kaine nodded, not keen on remembering it. "Joy told me."

"Well, Ivy . . ." Grant paused.

Kaine waited expectantly. Grant cocked his head to the right. He was doing that studying thing again.

"Yes?" she pressed.

Grant shook his head slowly. "You really don't know, do you?"

"Know what?"

"Ivy was the second woman found at Foster Hill House. She was attacked and left for dead. That was what made her a legend here in Oakwood."

CHAPTER 10

Joy was perched on a stool behind the counter at the station when Kaine entered. The cheesehead from their previous encounter had been replaced with a faux ruby-studded tiara. With her navy blue blouse and gaudy pearl necklace, Joy gave the appearance of someone past her prime playing dress-up with toddler princesses. Kaine envied the older woman and her unabashed identity.

"Kaine!" She slid off the stool and surged around the counter.

Before Kaine could react, her face was pulled into Joy's shoulder, and she was embraced in a motherly hug of concern.

"You're all right!"

"Mppfff . . ." Kaine tried to answer, but could only breathe in the flowery scent of Joy's laundry detergent.

"Oh dear." Joy pulled away. "I'm suffocating you." She released Kaine and stepped back a few feet. "But, oh my, you had me worried. That creepy old house, and you in it, alone."

Worried? Kaine hadn't expected Joy to waste her time fretting over a perfect stranger. She couldn't deny it felt nice, though, to know someone here in Oakwood cared.

"I'm fine." Kaine didn't want to burden Joy. "I'm staying at the motel."

"Oh, good." Joy smiled and waved a hand adorned with a fake ruby ring. "That motel is so old-fashioned. They don't even have keycards! But it's clean and welcoming."

Kaine laughed in spite of her day. The massive blue plastic keychain emblazed with the number four for her room took up way too much space in her purse

"It is clean." And it felt safe. For now.

"That it is. I'll sleep better knowing you're not fighting off evil spirits in that old place." Joy's concern soothed Kaine's frayed nerves. Grant's revelation about her great-great-grandmother Ivy Thorpe sent Kaine's mind wandering in a direction she didn't like. Ivy was linked directly to the house she'd purchased — she had almost been murdered there, shortly after the mysterious young woman. Grant had told her that history recorded the dead woman as Gabriella.

124

Kaine hadn't wanted a name, even a nick-name, associated with the story of a murder victim. But, unfortunately, now there was one, and *Gabriella* rang through her mind repeatedly, alongside Danny's name.

"No. No evil spirits." Kaine swallowed the familiar rise of panic in her throat. Just evil people. A person, actually.

"Well," Joy said, toying with her pearls, "anyone who spends more than a night in that haunted house would need to be exam-ined for sanity."

"It's not haunted." Kaine's thoughts swooped to Danny's picture propped in the middle of the abandoned bedroom. No, not haunted. Worse. "Has — has Megan maybe been wandering over to the house again?" It had been the second crazy impulse of the day. First, adopting Olive, and now swing-ing into the gas station with the vague hope that somehow she could find a reason to explain away the intrusion of her nightmare into her fledgling peace. But she knew, even as she asked, that Megan wouldn't have the slightest clue where to find a picture of Danny, and zero motivation to place it in the bedroom.

"Oh no. Has something happened?"

"Um, just a picture from the internet of a family member of mine. It was in the house,

and if it was from Megan, that's okay, I just
—"

"Got a little jumpy?" Joy supplied.

That was an understatement. "Yeah." Certainly. Jumpy.

Joy's drawn-on eyebrows dipped into a befuddled V between her eyes. "I don't see how Megan would know to do that, or why she would. But I can ask." She turned toward a back room, speaking over her shoulder as she walked. "I had to bring Megan to work today. Grant had things to do, and my other options aren't that great."

Calling for Megan, Joy waited. Kaine regretted stopping by the gas station. There was no explaining the picture away, and she hated pinning even a suggestion of blame on Megan. A few seconds later, a young woman with Down syndrome shuffled out from the back room. She was adorable for twenty-two. Her hair was pulled into a ponytail, a large silk sunflower sticking out at the top of it. Megan was dressed in inexpensive but stylish jeans and a cute plaid shirt.

Joy reached for Megan, and Megan took her mother's hand, a friendly smile stretching her rounded cheeks, reaching eyes that shone with spirit.

"Megan, honey." Joy tucked a loose tendril

of dark blond hair behind Megan's ear. "This is Kaine."

"Hi, Megan." Kaine reached out her hand, and Megan took it as she offered a toothy grin. Kaine instantly wanted to be Megan's best friend. She embodied life.

"Hi, Kaine!" She shook Kaine's hand with exuberance.

"Honey, have you been back to Foster Hill House?" Joy straightened her daughter's collar. Megan stared at her mother, as if attempting to judge whether she was in trouble.

"Since the daffodils, sweetie," Joy added.

Megan glanced at Kaine, and honesty oozed from the girl's sweet blue eyes. "No. Mama, you told me no and I obeyed."

"Thank you, sweetie." Joy rested her hand on Megan's shoulder, and they both turned to Kaine expectantly.

She had known the answer before Joy ever asked Megan. But this confirmation robbed Kaine of her last sliver of irrational hope. The truth slammed into her with force equal to when she'd first found the picture.

He had followed her here and found out she'd bought Foster Hill House. A house that hid mysteries about Gabriella and Great-Great-Grandmother Ivy that were still unsolved. A house with a history of violence. A house that seemed to promise more to come.

Chapter 11

Ivy

Joel's incessant pacing made Ivy nervous. He marched from one end of the room to the other in the front parlor of Foster Hill House. The piano mocked them from the corner, its cleanliness once again emphasizing that the house was not as abandoned as most believed. Ivy could see Joel's mind churning with possible explanations and many unanswered questions.

She still held the scrap of material from Gabriella's dress, rubbing it back and forth between her index, middle finger, and thumb. But her focus was on the piano music. While a conversation from long ago flooded her memory, she was reluctant to bring it up. Especially with Joel, who would share the memory. It would only bring life to the past neither of them had mentioned.

Joel stopped before the piano, his hands at his waist and his coat shoved back. He stared down at the keys, then his hand reached out and a finger followed the notes on the yellowed sheet music. His shoulders raised in a deep sigh, and when he spoke, he didn't turn around.

"Do you remember?"

Ivy almost didn't hear him, his voice was so low. It took a different tone altogether than the one he'd used up until now. This time it was personal. Intimate. She couldn't answer. Instead, Ivy crossed her arms, her wool coat stretching over her back with the movement. The window was a very good place to focus her attention, along with the gray and damp woods beyond.

"Andrew and his Beethoven?" Joel's question raised bumps along Ivy's skin. He had neared her and reached out to touch one of her curls. "Dark like coffee," he'd always said. Only he didn't say it now. He was quiet, as if waiting for her to answer. How could she? This was what she'd avoided for years. The memories, the feelings, the pain.

Ivy hugged her arms around herself tighter and pulled away so that the curl slipped from Joel's hand.

"He loved his music." Joel wouldn't stop.

Ivy walked away from him and pressed her forehead against the cloudy, dirty windowpane. It was cool against her skin.

"Yes," she whispered. Grief was fast to sweep over her. The same grief she witnessed with almost every death since Andrew's. With every stroke of her pen as she wrote the stories of the ones who'd passed away in Oakwood. Remembering anyone and everyone but Andrew. Their stories must be kept alive, remembered, because she understood what it was like to see a loved one forgotten. No one seemed to remember Andrew. Even her father avoided all reminiscing of him. He had faded into the annals of time, until now. But Ivy didn't want to remember Andrew with Joel. Never with Joel.

Joel cleared his throat. "Do you remember the time Andrew said he heard Beethoven coming from this house?"

Of course. She'd recalled that memory the night of her attack, though now she couldn't avoid it. Ivy turned, and Joel's gaze slammed into her. "We told him he was crazy."

Joel nodded. "That we did."

They shared a long look, laden with sorrow and the unspoken words that hung between them since the day Joel abandoned her in her grief.

Joel grimaced. "It wasn't fair. Andrew heard music in everything, but we should have believed him."

Ivy brushed past Joel to the piano. She lifted the sheet music from its stand. "It wouldn't have changed anything. He still would have died." Ivy leveled a glare on Joel. "You still would have left."

"Ivy —" Joel's jaw clenched. He stepped toward her, but she whirled away from him and slapped the music back into place.

"All Andrew's observation tells us now is that someone has been using this house for well over a decade. Maybe random vagabonds."

"Random doesn't fit the fact it's Beethoven, and the same melody Andrew told us about twelve years ago." Joel's voice switched back to a distant professionalism.

Ivy hid a shuddered sigh. Good. They were always a fair team at concocting a balance between her creative thinking and Joel's logical frame of mind. This was much safer.

"The facts. We need to list them." Joel traced a path across the floor to stand beside her. Ivy moved to her left to avoid even the feeling of warmth from his body.

"We know Gabriella was here, in Foster Hill House, for some reason. We know she recently had a baby. We know she was strangled," Ivy began. She brushed a cobweb from the candelabra that sat atop the piano.

Joel nodded. "*You* were almost strangled."

Ivy swallowed. The memory was raw. "I was. But he pushed me down the stairs as opposed to stuffing me in a tree."

"Why didn't he bury Gabriella? Why try to fit her into the trunk of a dead oak? He had to know someone would find her."

Ivy nodded and turned toward Joel, capable of controlling her emotions once again. "Maybe he was in a hurry. It was unexpected. He hadn't planned on killing her?"

Joel curled his lip and shook his head. "We're assuming it was a *he* who murdered Gabriella."

Ivy fiddled with the button at the cuff of her dress sleeve. "Well, it was a *he* who tried to kill me. I would say the odds are high there's one person we're facing rather than two potential killers. In that case, then, he's male."

"That's a safe assumption. What further evidence do we have?"

Ivy knew Joel's question was rhetorical, that he was thinking out loud. She could see the gears of his mind turning, calculating and compartmentalizing. She was eager to assist.

"The piano." Ivy glanced toward it. "It's

obvious it has been somewhat cared for —
at least the keys kept clean. And the sheet
music is the same as what Andrew heard
years ago."

"Someone has a penchant for Beethoven.
And Dickens, assuming you're correct
about the book you saw."

Ivy started for the doorway of the parlor.

"Where are you going?"

She called over her shoulder, "I'm going
back upstairs. I *did* see the book. If whoever
attacked me moved it, but didn't take it
from the house, then it's still here. And if it
is, we need to find it. Gabriella may have
written about her baby in it, and that is the
most critical *fact* right now. We haven't
explored the attic yet, and we should." Ivy
pulled her skirts up with her hand and
began to ascend the stairs.

Joel followed her. "I'm coming with you."

"I wasn't holding out hope that you'd let
me go alone." Ivy rolled her eyes at the
empty hallway that greeted her at the top of
the stairway.

"Why does that offend you?" Joel's voice
was incredulous, but Ivy didn't look behind
her to read his expression.

"Because you're implying I am helpless,"
Ivy mumbled, hiking down the hallway. She
reached the door at the end of the hallway

and stared up into the dark void of the attic.

"You did almost die here."

Ivy bit back a yelp but couldn't hold back a flinch as Joel's words whispered eerily into her ear, awakening the fear she'd been attempting to suppress.

"Stop it!" Spinning around, she made a move to push him away with her hands.

Joel took hold of her raised forearms and drew them against his chest. His blue eyes speared hers.

"I am not a monster, Ivy Thorpe."

She stiffened, tugging on her arms. "I never said you were."

"Can we set the past aside?"

Was he sincere? Frustration boiled inside her, making her bite her lip until she tasted blood. "Set it aside?" Ivy regretted the tremor in her voice. Like an old pair of shoes? That cavalier? Joel's thumbs stroked her hands as he gripped her wrists. She tugged against his hold again.

"I know we have history, Ivy, but can we move forward instead of holding past regrets so close?"

Ivy tipped her head in disbelief. "Yes. Certainly. We shall toss away the years of silence, the fact you left me alone to tell Andrew goodbye. That you, the poor orphan boy with no family, pretended to be part of us and then left without a backward glance, as if the Thorpes meant nothing to you. That you didn't save Andrew!"

The last words hissed through clenched teeth. She didn't have tears; she didn't even have grief now. It was anger, pure and just. Ivy wrestled her wrists free and stumbled backward.

Joel worked his jaw back and forth. His eyes narrowed, his expression hardened. "You have always been so sure of yourself. That you were always right and that you had a complete grasp of the circumstances."

The icy words were not what Ivy expected, and they did not cool her fury.

"Shall we go up?" She waved at the stairs. They were at an impasse. She needed space from the conversation. He riled her emotions, and she had precious little patience for emotions.

He extended his arm as if to say *carry on.* His movement made the unseen wall between them even higher. Their footsteps matched as they climbed the stairs to the attic. Ivy could hear Joel's breathing was controlled, but not at all rhythmic. He was angry too. He always breathed that way when angry. She tightened her hold on her dress, lifting the hemline so she didn't step on it.

The attic was stale, and dust particles danced in the air as their feet disturbed the dirty wood floor. It took a moment for Ivy's eyes to adjust to the darkness.

"There's a lot of old furniture up here."

Ivy waited for his reply, but Joel didn't respond. He moved past her and inspected a chair. His hand moved over the upholstered seat and back, eaten away by mice and moths.

"Worthless," he muttered.

The tension was thick. Ivy ignored it, instead pulling open the drawer on a small end table. Empty, with the exception of a dead cockroach. She slammed the drawer shut.

"There's nothing here." Joel was leaping to a conclusion. Another sign he was upset. His logical approach was influenced by his emotions during times of stress.

"We've hardly looked." Ivy was the opposite. Emotion in herself irritated her as weakness.

Joel yanked open a door on an old wardrobe. His eyes widened, and he quickly shut it in a plume of dust. Coughing, he waved his hand in the air to clear it. Ivy stared at him until he offered her a sheepish look.

"There was a bat in there."

Ivy shivered. The expression on Joel's face altered as he looked beyond her. Ivy followed his line of vision, and her breath hitched in surprise.

"Is that . . . ?" Her hand flew to cover her mouth.

"A baby cradle," Joel said, his mouth tightening into a firm line. He stalked across the floor and ran his hand over it.

"And it's not dusty, is it? Not one cobweb?" Ivy questioned while already knowing the answer.

"No. It's clean." The grave tone in Joel's voice matched the horrible sensation in Ivy's stomach.

Straight lines, applied carving on the headboard, nine pierced slats, and outswept legs formed a beautiful specimen of craftsmanship. But it was the baby blanket inside, piled at the end of the cradle, clean and fresh, that sent spears of horror through Ivy.

"A *baby* was here." She reached for the blanket, imagining an infant swaddled in cotton and lace kneading the air. Its innocence in a house that sheltered mysteries.

"I *told* you." Ivy couldn't help it. She couldn't resist the need to make sure Joel saw her urgency as validated. That she hadn't been foolhardy or emotional when she came to Foster Hill House the other night.

Joel cleared his throat. "So you did."

Their eyes met, and this time all animosity dissolved between them.

"But where's the baby?" Ivy's whisper echoed through the attic like the quiet breath of a ghost.

CHAPTER 12

KAINE

A sharp rap on her motel room door jolted Kaine awake. She scrambled across the bed, taking the blankets with her on her fall to the floor. Olive scampered to her feet, three deep *woof*s emanating from her throat.

"Kaine? Love?"

It was Joy.

Kaine ran her fingers through her dark straight hair that was snarled from sleep. Olive's tail thumped the floor as she sensed her mistress relax.

"Hold on!" Kaine called, untwisting herself from the covers. She tugged her tank top over her red pajama bottoms and scratched the middle of Olive's head as she passed by the dog. Not willing to leave Kaine alone, Olive followed close at her heels.

Kaine peeked through the door's peephole. Joy's red-lipped smile greeted her with magnification. Sliding the dead bolt back and twisting the lock on the knob, Kaine opened the door. A blast of fresh spring air hit her in the face.

"Oh my. I woke you, didn't I?" Joy hoisted her flamingo-pink purse on her shoulder. Her T-shirt was emblazoned with a Green Bay Packers helmet, and her yellow cardigan begged to be worn by someone twenty years her junior. Kaine originally thought she was in her sixties, but her flamboyancy could have landed her easily in her fifties, if not forties.

Kaine smiled. Maybe her first genuine smile in two days. After Danny's picture showed up at Foster Hill House and Detective Carter called to let her know they weren't able to pull any prints from the photo, Kaine holed up in her room with Olive. She had to think, to pray, to figure out what she was going to do next. Witness Protection Program? Not an option. Return to San Diego? That wouldn't help anything. Sell Foster Hill House? There wouldn't be another human alive who would be as gullible as she had been, and she wouldn't be able to ethically hide the truth to some out-of-state buyer as the real estate agent had done with her.

"C-can I help you?" Kaine wasn't sure

why her voice broke. Maybe she was lonely. A dog could only offer so much companionship, especially when you jumped at every noise.

Joy reached out and squeezed Kaine's upper arm, then pushed a lidded Styrofoam cup into her hand. "I'm not working for the next few days — goodness, I wish that were all the time. I'm sixty-two, but when Megan's daddy passed a few years ago, his social security just wasn't quite enough. Anyway, Megan is waiting in the car."

So she *was* in her sixties. Kaine glanced over Joy's shoulder to see Megan focused with intent on a tablet. She turned her attention back to Joy in time to catch her words. "So I'm taking charge." Joy smiled and pushed past Kaine. Marching across the small motel room, she pulled out a dresser drawer, then gave Kaine a quizzical look.

"You haven't unpacked?"

Kaine smiled and took a sip of the awful gas-station coffee. "I'm not big on settling in." A lame excuse, but if she needed to flee, having her clothes lined up in the drawers and closet wasn't conducive to a quick getaway.

Joy tapped the duffel bag on the luggage rack at the end of the bed. "God told me

142

this morning that you aren't to be alone at Foster Hill House. So, Megan and I are coming with you today."

God told her? A bit charismatic for Kaine's taste, but she *had* been praying for an answer. Not like Joy would pose much threat in the face of violence, but typically offenders preferred to get their victims alone. Kaine blinked a few times to clear her mind. So far, her stalker hadn't threatened her bodily harm. Yet.

Olive's cold nose touched the back of Kaine's hand. She buried her fingers in the fur on the back of the old black lab's neck. Going back to Foster Hill House? The image of Danny's picture in the middle of that haunting, empty bedroom chilled Kaine.

"I wasn't sure if I was going there today."

Joy shrugged, her shoulders brushing the long earrings that hung from her lobes. "Honey, I can *feel* the ache inside you." She reached out and wrapped Kaine in a motherly embrace. Kaine stood there, stiff and uncomfortable, enveloped in the older woman's arms. "But I listen to the One who sent you here to me. We have things to do at that crazy old house. Floors to wash, dust to banish, and maybe some stories to uncover. Yes?"

Stories to uncover? For Joy, the old house

was an adventure. Kaine's gaze drifted to the top of the dresser where a page from *Great Expectations* lay beside Ivy's ancient quilt. She had enough stories of her own to find the ending to, why would she want to uncover more?

Joy tossed a pair of blue jeans on the bed, pulled from her rather presumptuous but forgivable dive into Kaine's duffel. As if she had no choice, Kaine went to retrieve the jeans. A quick change in the bathroom, zip of her jeans, and throwing on of a flannel shirt over a T-shirt made her feel more human. She ran a comb through her hair and tied it back in a low ponytail. Forget makeup. There was something to be said about this Midwestern organic honesty when it came to appearance. Finished, Kaine emerged, and Joy's smile confirmed she was making the right decision. Following Joy, Kaine snapped her fingers at Olive. She paused on her way to the door to snatch up the page from *Great Expectations* and stuff it in the breast pocket of her shirt. For some reason, she needed it close to her heart.

"Hey."

Kaine jumped in unison with her squeal. Spinning from the window in the third bedroom, her ponderings were shattered by the sight of Grant in the doorway. Kaine shot a look at Olive, who lounged in the corner of the room. Some guard dog. Olive's tail thumped the wood floor, and her soulful eyes cast apologies in Kaine's direction. Kaine made a pretense of acting casual and re-twisting the rubber band around her ponytail. Joy and Megan were downstairs wiping down the parlor walls. Light from the sun shown in every room with warmth and even welcome. Though Grant was no threat, still, she was edgy.

"You don't believe in ringing a doorbell?" Ouch. She tried to infuse her voice with humor, but it didn't work.

Grant was undeterred. "Foster Hill House has a front door?" He chuckled.

Funny, and good point. The missing front door had given Joy reason to lecture Kaine to hire a contractor as soon as funds allowed.

"How's Olive?"

Of course, that was why Grant had come. Kaine avoided his searching stare. Why did he have to be so perceptive? Like he was searching her soul instead of inquiring about a dog. She reached for Olive, who rose to her feet and padded over, pushing her nose into Kaine's hand.

"We're building a solid relationship," Kaine offered with a half smile.

"That's good. We like to encourage long-term commitment at the shelter." Grant's lopsided grin widened Kaine's. He was either super intelligent behind those black glasses or endearingly artsy. She wasn't sure which.

The moment grew awkward. Silence. Yes, silence was awkward, but Kaine couldn't think of anything to say. She looked away. The man hardly blinked. He was like some Jedi from *Star Wars.* No mind tricks on her today, no thank you.

"So I was thinking — maybe I could help you out here? With whatever demo you're going to do. You've already engaged Joy and Megan, but there's only so much dusting they can do." His nose wrinkled when he grinned, but the scruff on his squared jaw gave him a charming appearance rather than boyish.

Grant's offer was either creepy or downright heroic, Kaine wasn't sure. If her life were a novel, Grant could end up being the villain who edged his way behind her defenses and then finished the job some day in one fell swoop. But she was letting her imagination run wild.

"I don't know. . . ." Kaine hesitated.

"I'm not a creep, you know." Grant called out her worst fear.

Kaine mustered a laugh. "Said the creep."

Grant held his hands out, palms forward. "Really. I'll give you the résumé of my life and you can check my references with Joy."

Kaine waited and curled her fingers into Olive's fur.

"I volunteer at the animal shelter about ten hours a week," he offered.

Of course he did — he had nothing else to do?

"Contrary to common assumptions, I do not live with my mom."

Crud. He'd read her mind. He *was* a Jedi!

"I'm a bachelor. I was engaged once about six years ago, but we called it off. It wasn't dramatic. Mutual decision. She liked the sun and surf of Florida and I'm a native Wisconsinite. So, after I finished my master's at UW-Madison, I moved back to Oakwood because it's home. What can I say? I'm a homeboy."

Kaine couldn't help but laugh. He was reciting his past as if it were a job interview.

"I have a house just outside of town, about half a mile from here. That farmhouse down the road?"

Kaine nodded. So he was her neighbor? That explained how Megan could walk here

147

from his house.

"For my day job, I'm a counselor. A grief counselor, actually. I do most of it out of my home office, and my assistant and I also hang with Megan on occasion."

Whoa. She hadn't seen that one coming. Kaine's image of the artsy mama's boy began to fade into a different picture. No wonder he always seemed like he was reading her.

Grant's face softened as he saw the question on hers. "I sort of have a thing for tough cases."

Tough cases. So did she. Or she had. Before she'd become one herself.

"I have a pit bull, Sophie. I play guitar for worship at a church just outside of town, and I like to read. Louis L'Amour westerns, preferably."

Yep. That solidified it. The man was good-looking, creative, smart, *and* nice. God help her. She hadn't paid attention to another man since Danny's death, and now probably wasn't the best time to start considering the opposite sex again.

Kaine crossed her arms over her chest, pulling her thumbs inside the fingerless gloves she'd donned for comforting warmth. The mustard-yellow yarn was a tiny bright spot in the gray of the house.

"Do you go to church?"

Now wait. Wasn't this his life résumé? Not hers. She answered anyway. "I used to." Kaine pushed her thumbs back through the thumb holes and picked at a loose thread. "It's a long story."

"Gave up on God?"

Wow. He didn't pull any punches. She gave him a direct look. It wasn't any of his business, and she wasn't his client. Grief counseling had been on her agenda for the last two years, and she wasn't a stranger to counseling in general, but life circumstances made reconciling with the past a living nightmare.

Fine, she'd be honest. "No. Just . . ." Kaine searched her mind for the right answer but couldn't find it. "Just trying to find my life again."

Silence invaded the room as Grant's eyes deepened with concern. But he didn't push any further, and Kaine was grateful.

"Well." Grant crossed his arms, his blue long-sleeved T-shirt stretching over his muscles. "How about we work on getting this place into shape so you can start your new life?"

Kaine couldn't refuse him. Starting a new life had been her original objective in coming here, and if Grant's presence, along with

Joy's and Megan's and Olive's, wasn't enough company to keep danger at bay, then she might as well give up altogether.

Kaine handed Grant her list of to-dos as they perched on the front porch and ate sandwiches made from ingredients she stored in a cooler. Joy and Megan could be heard singing songs in the parlor from the Top 40 music charts from the 1970s. Kaine took a bite of her sandwich and watched expressions filter across Grant's face.

"You think I'm out of my league, don't you?" She spoke around a mouthful. Might as well be candid.

Grant pursed his lips and shrugged. "Well . . . these are all only surface repairs. Have you met with a contractor, a plumber, anyone?"

Kaine nodded and sipped her Pepsi. "Both. The day after I arrived here."

"Huh." Grant ran his finger down the list. "So they recommended mold remediation, window replacements, and porch repairs. What about the foundation? The roof? That's a whole lot of expense if you throw it all together on an invoice."

Kaine eyed him over her sandwich. He hadn't earned the right to question her judgment or even her available finances.

"The foundation was sound. The roof . . . I'll get to that."

Grant simply nodded. He was wise enough not to question her further. He was going to have to move slowly if he wanted to gain her trust. Kaine brushed crumbs off her gray T-shirt. It was oversized and emblazoned with *Yosemite National Park.* It had been Danny's. She needed to remind herself of him and focus less on Grant.

"Do you have any family?"

Kaine blinked. "Is this a question stemmed from friendship or are you analyzing me?"

Grant chuckled as he picked up his sandwich. "My dad says I'm always trying to understand everyone." His eyes took on a studious glint and he tipped his chin out. "You're most definitely not an open book, but I can tell you want to be."

Bam. Nailed it. Kaine looked away and brushed more imaginary crumbs from her shirt. Of course she wanted to be. Leah called her Tsunami Kaine. She normally word-vomited all her thoughts on any unsuspecting soul as a means to process them. But this time? This was different. She'd never been accused of being unstable, or making false claims, or putting herself on the brink of trouble.

"No? Don't want me to go there either?" Grant nodded again. "That's fine."

He popped open a can of Mountain Dew. *"Syrup in a can,"* Danny used to call it. Kaine was prone to agree.

She supposed honesty wouldn't hurt her in this scenario. "Um, I have a sister."

"She's in California?"

Joy must have told Grant where Kaine heralded from. "Mm-hmm. She's married. I have a little niece."

"Do you have a boyfriend?"

Wow. For a counselor, he didn't tiptoe around.

"Husband." Kaine's sandwich bite went down much harder this time.

"Ahh." Grant's expression was unreadable. She wasn't sure if what she said bothered him or if he'd expected it.

"He's dead," Kaine added, unable to stop herself.

A robin chortled from the soggy yard in front of them. Spring's crisp freshness was in the breeze, which lifted Kaine's hair in her ponytail.

"I'm sorry." Grant's tone was even. That made sense. He was accustomed to working with people in the throes of grief.

Kaine's lips worked back and forth trying to determine whether she wanted to cry, share her story, or just stay quiet. "He was killed in a car accident two years ago. We were married not long after I graduated from college."

Grant gave a nod and took a bite of his sandwich, chewing slowly. He didn't say anything. His lack of response encouraged her, like an open invitation to continue.

"Danny always wanted to do a home restoration and he was raised in the Midwest. So I wanted to do this for him."

She looked to Grant as if he were a temporary stand-in for Danny. But that was silly. He wasn't.

"Cool."

The word brought some assurance to Kaine and she smiled. "I found Foster Hill House online, and my brother-in-law lawyer is checking into the realtor. The pictures of the house were a misrepresentation. Even though the realtor came with references, he wasn't as honest as we thought. Or else there's some other weird explanation."

Grant smiled but let her continue.

"Oakwood was where my grandpa was born. He left for California when he was eighteen. So when I saw Foster Hill House was for sale in the town where my family tree seemed to start, it made sense."

"So is your surname of Prescott your husband's?"

Kaine shook her head. "No. It's my grandpa's. Danny supported me in honoring Grandpa by keeping it. I wanted Grandpa alive in a small way. Is that strange?" Her question was honest.

"Not at all. It's interesting." Grant took another swig of his soda, his brows drawn together in thought. "My mother can trace our history back to the Vikings. But I know a lot of families, especially broken ones, who find those genealogies get lost."

"I never paid much attention to my genealogy, and my grandpa lived during the sixties when everyone wanted free love and separation from tradition. So he wasn't exactly one to foster the preservation of our lineage."

"And your parents?"

"My father ran off when I was three," Kaine said matter-of-factly. "That's why my mom kept Grandpa's name. She didn't want us known by my deadbeat dad." Kaine was indifferent to him really. Grandpa had always been her strong male influence. "My mom died when I was eight, so Grandpa raised my sister and me. She had breast cancer and, well, you know how that journey goes for some." She paused, reflecting. Her memories of Mom were dim now. "You'd think I'd be used to losing people."

"You never get used to that," said Grant.

"I guess." Kaine let out a sigh. "Anyway, it was me, Leah, and my grandpa until Danny came around. I had a ton of friends, co-workers, but Danny was — he was my foundation." She chuckled at a memory. Grant had a way of drawing a person out. "Danny and I took a trip to Montana once. We were camping and there was this huge thunderstorm. I was sure we were going to have trees come down on us. Danny sat on top of me, put his hands up in the air, and said, *'I'll just sit here and catch them for you.'* He was mocking me, in a loving way, but that was Danny. Always trying to take care of me in his zany way."

A companionable silence followed. Kaine drew in a deep breath, closing her eyes for a moment. It was comforting to remember Danny as he was, not how he died. Nor how she'd distanced herself from him as her job resurrected old memories, and the weight of the abuse she daily saved women from overwhelmed her.

"Sounds like he was a stand-up guy."

Kaine gave Grant a thankful smile. "He was."

Grant returned her smile, understanding and compassion on his face. "So . . ." Kaine saw something flicker in Grant's eyes. Curiosity, intrigue? She wasn't sure until he voiced his question. "Do you know how your grandfather got Ivy's quilt?"

Kaine cast Grant a perplexed look. "I have no idea, but I know Grandpa wouldn't have stolen it. I mean, Grandpa was a good man."

Grant was immediately apologetic at her fervent defense of her grandfather. "I didn't mean to imply that he wasn't. It's just odd. Like one of those unsolved mysteries on the History Channel."

"I agree." Kaine twisted on the stairs to better face Grant. The more she thought about it, the more curious she became. Ivy's quilt, the note from Foster Hill House, and Grant's previous claim that Ivy had been attacked right here, on this property. "Do you know what happened to Ivy? After her attack?"

Grant set his sandwich down on the ziplock plastic bag on his lap. There were only a few bites from it. He must not like alfalfa sprouts and turkey. "This is why this stuff intrigues me. My dad and I used to study Oakwood history for fun. Weird, I know. Anyway, Oakwood Museum has a few things about Ivy Thorpe and Foster Hill. A display about the dead woman found in the old oak tree, Gabriella, and Ivy's subsequent attack.

The lack of detail keeps the legend alive because it's like that forever story that has no end or resolution. The story says that Ivy was engaged in trying to uncover Gabriella's murder and got too involved. As for the quilt, it was one of the main pieces of Ivy's memorabilia, and when it was stolen, well, outside of history junkies like me, and superstitious folk like Joy, it's all but forgotten. I don't know that most people really cared in the long run."

Kaine reached for the flannel shirt she'd discarded next to her on the porch so she could sit in her T-shirt and soak in the warmth of the sun. She grasped the old page from *Great Expectations* and pulled it out of the shirt pocket. Maybe Grant could shed some light on it. She handed it to him.

"I found this. In the house."

Grant took the page from her and eyed the handwriting in the margins. "Where was it?"

"Behind a baseboard in the library. Read it. It's creepy."

Grant skimmed the words. "That is creepy." He eyed the text of the novel. "This looks like late nineteenth century, maybe turn-of-the-century type print."

"How do you know that?"

"My brother. Antique-store owner, remember? He collects and sells old books. I told you my family is full of history buffs. Except for Mom. She just likes to garden. Do you think this belonged to one of the occupants of Foster Hill House?"

"I've no clue." Kaine watched him turn the page over to the printed text on the other side, then return to examine the handwriting.

"You know . . . it'd be freaky if the dead girl wrote it."

"You mean the one my great-great-grandmother found? Gabriella?"

"Yeah."

Kaine had considered that, but thought it a stretch. Now that Grant voiced it aloud, she wondered if maybe it wasn't so far-fetched after all. Kaine remembered the words, the aching plea behind them. If this Gabriella had written it, then more than one horror had occurred in this house. Now, it seemed, the horrors were following the next female over a hundred years later. Her. Kaine reached for Grant's knee before she could stop herself.

"I want to find out. I've bought the house my great-great-grandmother almost lost her life in. A house that a young woman was either murdered in or nearby. And with what happened to me the other day, I —"

158

She caught herself and snapped her mouth shut.

Grant frowned. "What happened the other day?"

"Nothing." Kaine jumped to her feet and wiped her hands down her jeans. Subject change needed — stat! "So, how about heading into town for some garbage pails? I'm going to need them if I'm going to start ripping out stuff. And some masks so we don't breathe in the mold." The forced cheer in her voice erased her initial excitement. "I want to do as much as I can myself. It'll be cheaper that way."

"Of course." Grant tossed the sandwich of sprouts and turkey into the bushes. A sideways grin tipped his mouth. "And get some real food."

She managed a smile. A hamburger did sound good, and chocolate, and carbs, and lots of sugar. Anything to mask her grief, the fear, and the door that made her slam it all into a secret place inside of her. A place that held Kaine captive.

CHAPTER 13

Kaine's hips ached as she adjusted her position on the motel bed. Her laptop was heavy on her lap, and she moved the blankets away so it didn't overheat. The TV played an old episode of *Friends,* and while Kaine usually related to Chandler, tonight she understood the melancholy nature of Ross. Olive moaned from her spot on the floor, stretching her hind legs out and then pulling them in closer to her body.

Kaine's phone vibrated against her hip, and she yanked it from underneath her. It was midnight here in Wisconsin, but Leah was wide awake back home.

"Kaine, we need to talk." The absence of warmth in Leah's greeting heightened Kaine's senses. She closed the lid on her laptop.

"What's wrong?"

"Did the police call you?" Leah's voice trembled.

Coffee. She was going to need coffee. Kaine reached for her thermal mug on the nightstand and popped open the lid. She took a long sip and shook her head even though Leah couldn't see her. "No. They didn't."

"There's been a change in Danny's case."

"A change?"

"Apparently they reopened it. Something about the detective who was on the case losing his job for covering up stuff and being sloppy. He's not on the force anymore, and they're looking into some of his past cases for accuracy."

Leah's words didn't inspire celebration or relief. Kaine wasn't sure what she felt. She bit at a chip in her fingernail.

"That's wonderful." Kaine couldn't hide the sarcasm. "Because obviously Danny's wife was insane, so it took some cop to get fired to get them to look into it more seriously?"

"Don't be bitter, Kaine. Be thankful." Leah's plea reached through Kaine's jaded thoughts. Thankful? It was hard to find reasons to thank the Lord for the past few years of her life.

"I'm sorry." Kaine fought back a sudden rise of frustrated tears. "It's just, after being told I was wrong so many times over . . ."

161

Her voice trailed off.

"But look at it from a different perspective. It's not in your timing, but the Lord has someone in your court, Kaine. This cop, Detective Tamara Hanson, called me the other day when she couldn't reach you. She questioned me, since you named me as a witness, about the police reports filed after those first times things were moved in your house."

"You mean when they said I had PTSD?"

"Kaine," Leah scolded.

Kaine swallowed her anger. She should be thrilled. Finally someone was willing to risk believing her. Finally someone in law enforcement would listen when daffodils were left on counters or in the middle of an entryway floor. When her husband's picture was left in an upstairs abandoned bedroom. Except she was in Wisconsin now.

She squeezed her eyes shut as she battled her cynicism. Detective Hanson may not be able to protect her here, but if she could uncover who had killed Danny, then they'd also know who was after Kaine. Local authorities could be alerted.

"Detective Hanson said she'd be calling you. She wants to dig into Danny's history, and yours too. Even your career here helping abused women. She said that wasn't exactly a low-risk career. How many women did you help escape their husbands or pimps, Kaine?"

Leah spoke with a thread of excitement in her voice. She had no idea what her announcement was doing to Kaine's stomach. Even the possibility that something in her career, which had consumed so much of her life and alienated Danny, had anything to do with his death raked her insides into a sickening pile of guilt.

"Is she saying Danny was killed because of me?"

The silence on the other end of the line communicated Leah's comprehension. "Kaine. Oh, I'm sorry. I didn't mean — I mean, I didn't want to imply that — you're not responsible for Danny's death."

Kaine couldn't answer. A lump lodged in her throat.

"Besides," Leah continued, "the detective is just fishing. Speculating and digging for possibilities."

Her head down, again Kaine squeezed her eyes shut. Danny had been an engineer. He didn't make enemies. He'd get excited over building model airplanes in his spare time. He preferred solitude to social activities. He'd been devoted to Kaine, but she was devoted to life. To people. To saving them and fulfilling a mission and pursuing a passion. Danny's worst enemy had been dried-up model glue.

"Well, hopefully Detective Hanson will find something." Kaine's response was lame, but her hands were shaking now. "Prove that Danny wasn't on drugs and didn't kill himself."

"I told her you'd moved to get away. That nothing else had happened since you left."

Kaine ran her palm over her eyes.

"Please tell me nothing's happened." Leah's plea reawakened Kaine's fear. Danny's car wreck had been intentional. Danny had been murdered, and someone was really out there, following her.

"He's here, Leah."

The instant her finger pressed the doorbell Kaine regretted her impulsiveness. A dog barking wildly from inside the house was like a slap of reason against her irrational fear. The phone call from Leah encouraged a panic attack like none she'd had since the day she found out Danny was killed. Her hands were shaking, her heart palpitating. It was like an out-of-body experience. She could *see* herself reacting with no logic whatsoever but didn't have control over it.

She swiped at the tears that slipped down

her cheeks. Stupid. What inspired her to leave the security of her flimsy motel room and leap into her Jetta with Olive to drive four miles out of town and pull into Grant Jesse's driveway? Why hadn't she gone to Joy's house — other than the fact she didn't know where Joy lived? Safety. That's what. Kaine could still sense the strength that emanated from Grant in the limited time they'd spent together. She was alone in Oakwood, with no source of comfort, save God who was pretty silent at the moment. While she was a strong woman, even the strongest sometimes needed someone to calm them. Joy was too spasmodic and excitable. Kaine needed calm right now.

Moonlight shone down onto the welcoming front porch of a white farmhouse while Kaine's senses argued with her emotions. *Go back to the motel. You're exposing yourself as emotionally unstable. No one needs to see this side of you. Suck it up, Kaine Prescott.*

So she did. Just as Grant opened the door, the light from the entryway silhouetting his body. Grant held his tan-colored pit bull back by its collar as it roared to life with a series of deep-throated barks and growls.

"Shush, Sophie!" Grant opened the door wider. "Kaine? What's wrong? What happened?" He stepped aside, pulling his

165

energetic dog with him.

Olive moved before Kaine did, sticking out her nose to sniff at Sophie. The two dogs danced around each other, then quickly made friends, their hindquarters wagging along with their tails. Kaine remained frozen in place.

"Kaine, are you okay?"

"Umm . . ." She paused and glanced at her car. She took a step back. "I'm s-sorry. I was stupid. Come, Olive." Turning, she hurried down the porch steps, Olive on her heels. Seeing Grant face-to-face was a cold, hard slap of reality.

"Stay," Grant commanded Sophie, and shut the door in his dog's face. He leaped down the two porch steps and chased after Kaine, who couldn't run fast enough back to her car.

The song of crickets surrounded them as the crisp air chilled Kaine's coatless body.

Grant's hand closed around hers and tugged. "Hey."

Kaine stopped, and apologies poured from her without pause. "I'm really sorry. Waking you up. I shouldn't have come. I-I'm going to head back. Please. Just — go back to bed. I'm fine."

"You're not fine." Grant placed his hands on her shoulders and urged her to turn and face him. "Did something happen?"

Kaine lifted her chin, her gaze directed at the sky. She bit her bottom lip. "I feel like an idiot."

"Don't." Grant squeezed her shoulders. "What's wrong, Kaine? Talk to me."

Kaine pressed her lips together, opened her mouth, and then snapped it shut again. Her eyes glistened with tears and she blinked several times. A gust of wind brushed over them, and Kaine shivered.

Finally she whispered, wincing as she did so, "My husband . . . he was murdered."

CHAPTER 14

IVY

"It was nice of you to invite me for a walk."

Ivy gave the girl strolling beside her an encouraging smile. She'd met Maggie just this morning on a stop for Ivy's father to drop off medicine for Widow Bairns. She knew her father was trying to keep her occupied and busy. Since she and Joel uncovered the cradle at Foster Hill House yesterday, Joel had made no secret that she was not to become further involved or put herself in danger on her own crusade to find the missing child. So her father saw fit to create a list of to-dos that was busy work at best. But, perhaps meeting Widow Bairns's new live-in caregiver was a blessing of sorts. She reminded Ivy a little of what Gabriella may have been like. Of course, she'd never tell the mousy, timid girl that. No one wished to be compared to a dead woman. Nor would she tell the girl that she'd requested her accompaniment not so much to be charitable and get to know her, since she was the widow's great-niece from out of town, but because she knew it probably wasn't wise to go on her secret jaunt alone.

She glanced at Maggie from the corner of her eye. The girl picked at her fingernails as they walked, her gesture nervous, and her shoulders stiff as though she was horribly shy. Ivy felt a moment of conscience prick her. She'd hate to be the cause of trouble for Maggie. But Ivy also didn't particularly trust Joel with the responsibility of finding Gabriella's baby. Sheriff Dunst was organizing a search party, and Joel was drumming up men to assist. In the meantime, no one was canvassing the town to investigate. No one except Ivy.

"Are you finding Oakwood pleasant?" Ivy owed some extension of genuine friendship to the girl.

Maggie nodded short, shy nods. She gave Ivy a quick wide-eyed look. "It's very nice."

"You must be delighted to foster a relationship with your great-aunt." Ivy sidestepped a rock in the road, her eyes scanning the tree line on either side. Dark shadows played against bare trees and patches of snow. A squirrel hopped over a dead tree and chattered at them as they passed.

"Have you been here long?" Ivy adjusted her grip on her purse, her mind traveling a thousand steps ahead to the orphanage and to the moment she would inquire about a baby. What if there was an infant there? Could it be that simple?

"Only a week." Maggie's answer brought Ivy back to the conversation. She tightened her coat around herself, fiddling with the buttons, and smiled a timid, fast smile. "I like Aunt Edith."

"Everyone adores your aunt," Ivy reaffirmed.

Maggie stared down the road with squinted eyes. "How far are we going to walk?"

Yes. Walk. Ivy realized she'd invited Maggie for a friendly stroll, which Widow Bairns had encouraged, but Ivy hadn't explained they had a destination.

"I need to make a stop at the orphanage, if you don't mind."

Maggie tugged at the warm gloves on her hands. "Oh. Yes. Yes, that's fine."

Ivy nodded. Good. They walked a bit more in silence, and then Maggie stopped, her eyebrows drawing together. "Oh dear," she sighed with a quiver to her chin. "I completely forgot. I didn't set out anything for my aunt for lunchtime. She isn't able to prepare her own food."

Drat. Ivy glanced up the road toward the orphanage roof that peeked above the treetops, then back toward town and Widow Bairns. So close.

"I'm so sorry." Maggie read Ivy's indecision as offense.

She couldn't miss this opportunity to find Gabriella's baby. Ivy reached out and patted Maggie's shoulder. "You go on back." Maggie would be safe, wouldn't she? Ivy grimaced. The only danger would be to herself. She'd seen the book with writing in it, and for all her attacker knew, she'd seen him. Maggie was an innocent, but Ivy would need to retrace her steps home. Alone. Maybe she should return with Maggie. Before Ivy could reach a conclusion, Maggie smiled shyly.

"Thank you for understanding." She whirled and hoisted her skirts, hurrying down the road without so much as a backward glance.

A stick snapped behind Ivy, and she spun back toward the orphanage, scanning the path and the dark edges of the woods behind her. She was committed now. Ivy hurried the final quarter mile to the orphan-

171

age and up the home's stairs, stopping only long enough to brace her hand against the porch rail and survey the road one last time. A murder of crows fluttered from the trees nearby. Something had disturbed them. Most likely her own frantic pace and Maggie's retreating form.

Ivy rapped on the orphanage door, her furtive glances over her shoulder revealing nothing but the birds. *Murder of crows.* Horrible term, considering the circumstances. Why couldn't they be flocks like other birds?

The orphanage door opened, and Ivy saw the familiar inside of the home. Its interior was plain, just as she remembered. Mr. Casey, the orphanage director, peered at her, his expression a scowl. He'd never been pleased with her visits, and apparently nothing had changed. She and Andrew had met Joel when their small Sunday school group had come for an afternoon to recite Bible verses for the orphans and share homemade cakes. Something had been markedly unique about Joel. The mischief in his eyes perhaps? The way he could stare right into her eyes and read her mind? Whatever the case, she and Andrew hadn't wanted to leave with their group because they'd found unusual comradery in the orphan. So they'd returned the following day with the excuse of bringing Joel a storybook. The day after that, it was a wooden whistle in hand as a gift, after which Mr. Casey put a stop to their almost daily visits to see Joel. Yet the refusal to allow them friendship was not to be entertained by the trio. Because of that, their childish selves snuck out at nighttime to seek adventure in the woods and to be together. It continued into their teenage years, Joel savvy enough to avoid his absence at night from being detected, but then their escapades halted abruptly when Andrew —

"Well, well, Miss Thorpe." Mr. Casey's deep voice broke into Ivy's chaotic nostalgia. "It's been quite some time." His hooked nose reminded her of a pirate, or a villain, or — Ivy blinked to clear her thoughts. Her mind was running wild, something she rarely allowed it to do. She was just unnerved. *Joel* had unnerved her — on many levels.

"What can I do for you?" Mr. Casey opened the door with a grimace that indicated he did so more out of etiquette and obligation than hospitality. For twelve years she had avoided this home and its memories of Joel. Twelve years she'd denied the orphanage even a charitable service. Mr. Casey had the right to hold some sort of grudge.

173

Ivy stepped inside, thankful when the orphanage door closed with a solid thud behind her. She never conceived of taking refuge in the orphanage, but for now it served its purpose and hid her from the shadowed woods.

"I need to make an inquiry about the children here." Best to remain polite and pleasant. Ivy smiled with as much charm as she could manage.

"Ah, I see. Looking to adopt an orphan, are we?" Ivy didn't miss his sarcasm as he smoothed back his thinning gray hair. Mr. Casey made no effort to hide his sigh as he led her into his office. He moved behind his desk as if he was most comfortable there in his place of authority.

Ivy shifted her weight onto her other foot. "It will only take a moment."

"Very well." Mr. Casey motioned for Ivy to sit, so she eased onto a green leather chair with wooden arms. "But, I should tell you, unmarried women are not allowed to adopt."

Ivy nodded. "I know." For goodness' sake, he was going to make this difficult.

"Least of which, being yourself," he muttered under his breath.

Ivy stiffened, her ire raised. "Pardon me?"

Mr. Casey eyed her as he made a tent with

his fingertips and tapped them together. His eyebrow raised. "You're the memory keeper. Your death journal? There is much about you, Miss Thorpe, that has become . . . shall we say, a bit concerning, especially since everything that happened some time ago."

"I merely write the stories of those who have gone before. Nothing more." Ivy resisted having to defend herself. Why couldn't others understand that keeping memories alive wasn't a fascination with death? Life was so important. The image of Andrew fluttered through her mind, and Ivy blinked it away. She loosened her grip on her purse before she strangled it. "I'm not looking to adopt, Mr. Casey, although I did want to inquire if you've received any babies recently."

Mr. Casey choked and eased onto his chair. "Babies do not fall from the sky, Miss Thorpe."

Ivy bit back a retort. "Mr. Casey," she began, choosing her words carefully, "I only meant to inquire as to whether you have taken in a baby that might be traced back to Gabriella." She winced. Applying a name to an unidentified body would only build his case that she did in fact have an unhealthy friendship with the dead.

"The murdered girl?" Mr. Casey pursed his lips.

"Yes." Ivy had a fleeting moment of sympathy for Joel, growing up under this man's care.

"How recent would you like me to report to you?" There was no missing the scorn in Mr. Casey's question. "A year? A month? A week?"

No one knew how long Gabriella had been living in Foster Hill House, but the physical evidence pointed toward childbirth no further back than a couple of weeks.

"Any time in the last month?" She hoped the time frame would give some range for the director to work within.

Mr. Casey clasped his hands over a ledger on his desk. "We did. A girl."

She'd been right! Ivy's excitement pushed her to the edge of her seat. But Mr. Casey's smug expression sent her hope crashing as fast as it had risen.

"The girl was left here several days ago. But she was brought by her mother herself. She was simply a young lady in a position of serious indiscretion."

"What did she look like?" Ivy wasn't willing to accept his dismissal. The timeline was perfect.

Mr. Casey frowned even deeper as he

reached for a quill pen and tapped its tip with his index finger, fixing his stare on her. "Brown eyes, dark hair, and she wore a blue dress."

Ivy's shoulders sagged. That was nowhere near the angelic Gabriella with her nearly white hair and pale blue eyes. "You're certain the woman was actually her mother? Perhaps there was another baby that you received."

Mr. Casey lifted his spectacles from the desk and slipped them on his face. "Miss Thorpe, contrary to rumor and common perception, orphans are not delivered to us like used inventory to be logged and shelved."

"I didn't mean to imply —"

"And" — Mr. Casey lifted his hand to stop her — "the ones that do arrive here I most certainly remember. So to imply I have a baby brought by the dead waif who was murdered on Foster Hill and I merely misplaced it is heinous."

Ivy had no words. There was truth in what he said.

"Now, if you'll excuse me." Mr. Casey rose to his feet, a sure sign any further inquiry was not welcome.

Ivy stood reluctantly. "Thank you for your time."

She followed him out of the office, noting the way his polished black shoes took firm steps toward the door with no hesitation. He certainly didn't seem like he was lying or hiding anything, and he had no reason to. Once he pulled the front door open, Mr. Casey looked at her and said, "Best of luck in whatever it is you believe you're trying to do."

She paused at the base of the porch stairs and glanced back at the house where Joel had spent the majority of his childhood. It was certainly more welcoming than Foster Hill House, but there was a chilly air surrounding its asylum appearance. Ivy sighed. When Andrew died, it was clear she needed Joel more than she ever had before, and when he didn't show at the grave that night, she was more than crushed. She was betrayed. But now, as she pondered the civil but stern interaction she'd just had with Mr. Casey, a twinge of conscience made her wonder whether she'd misjudged Joel.

Ivy walked across the barren yard and past the picket fence that bordered the orphanage acre. She reached the road, then hesitated. Its gravel was packed but moist, and stretched longer and emptier than she wished.

She startled as a bulky form rounded the

corner of the fence. Her body tensed, poised to run back into the orphanage, but then her shoulders sagged in relief. "Hello, Mr. Foggerty."

The trapper's bushy eyebrows raised in recognition. His hat was squashed onto his head, making his wiry gray hair stick out like horns over his ears. "Ivy, hello. Any word on that poor girl yet?"

Ivy eyed him for a moment. He was the first to discover Gabriella. She either owed him a great debt or . . . a great amount of suspicion. She shook her head. That was unfair. Mr. Foggerty had been trapping in these woods since she was a child. "Nothing yet," she finally answered.

Mr. Foggerty clucked his tongue. "Such a shame. Pretty little child."

Child. Yes. Gabriella had been quite young, it appeared. Ivy nodded. "We *will* find her killer."

Mr. Foggerty adjusted the burlap sack over his shoulder. Ivy stared at the bottom of it, soaked in dark red, the blood of his trapped animals that must be piled inside. Her stomach turned. There was something violent about the sack, intimidating and threatening.

"I'd best be on my way." He pointed to the woods beyond the orphanage. "Mr. Casey let me set traps over yonder at the creek. I'm hopin' for some otter today."

Otters. Dead, trapped otters. Ivy swallowed at the idea of the trap's vengeance on the little animals. "Goodbye then." She waved at the older man. He returned the wave and set off in the opposite direction. Thankful he wasn't going her way, Ivy regretted not returning with Maggie, especially now that she'd uncovered nothing at the orphanage.

Hurrying forward, Ivy followed the footprints in the patchy snow she had left on her walk there. They overlaid some carriage tracks and one of an automobile, until she joined with Maggie's footprints coming toward the orphanage and then returning to town.

Ivy increased her speed. An unnerving sensation of being watched had raised bumps on her arms. Had Mr. Foggerty opted to follow her instead? He and his sack of dead animals?

A raindrop hit her cheek, and she swiped it away with her hand. The clouds were dark and churning. A spring storm with its icy drops and thunder was exactly the ambience she didn't need on her lonesome return to town. Ivy rushed down the aisle of trees, their scraggly arms reaching for her.

Her toe caught on a stone in the road and she stumbled, righting herself as her left foot planted alongside her footprint from earlier.

Ivy froze.

Beside it was the impression of a larger set of footprints. Most assuredly not hers or Maggie's. They were booted and deep. The weight of a man that overlapped her original steps.

A frigid gust of wind surged through the woods and plastered loose tendrils of hair to Ivy's cheek. Shivering, she fastened the top button on her coat. She searched the woods for a face, a form, a pair of eyes, anything.

"Mr. Foggerty?" Her voice quivered as she called. Perhaps he'd followed her and Maggie, innocently checking traps. But traps were set in the woods, not on the road.

Movement by the trunk of a maple tree made Ivy squint. Rain began to fall in earnest, the drops like tiny knives assaulting her face. The figure of a man came into view, and her eyes widened. He stepped from behind the tree, his features hidden by the downpour and shadows.

"Mr. Foggerty?" she called again, unable to make out details in the heavy rainfall. Thunder rumbled and rolled its warning through the thick clouds.

"None to hear you. None to care." The figure's voice mocked her, mingling with the pounding of rain against the canopy of trees. She didn't recognize the voice but could distinguish its tone as thunder swallowed the words.

Terror catapulted Ivy into a sprint. Her feet slipped in the mud as she ran. He was right, whoever he was — there was none around to hear or see. She was alone. Foolishly alone.

CHAPTER 15

KAINE

She'd been selfish to pester Grant Jesse at one in the morning. But it was too late now, so Kaine took a deep breath, and the truth fell from her mouth, escaping like it didn't want to be held captive a moment longer. Grant let her spill without interruption, but his face tightened as she told him an abbreviated version of what brought her from San Diego, of her stalker, and now the refocus on Danny's death.

"Man, Kaine. Come here." Grant didn't address the word vomit she'd just expelled. He reached for her hand and led her back to the house. His grip was comforting and confident. Right now, Kaine needed someone who could inspire her own sense of self-confidence that warred against the feeling of being hunted. She and Olive followed him up the porch steps. As the red farmhouse door pushed open beneath his hand, the sandy-colored pit bull lunged toward her. Kaine squealed, but Grant put out his free arm.

"Down, Sophie." He gave Kaine a crooked smile. "She's friendly, just super exuberant."

Kaine scratched the dog's head, and Sophie licked her hand. Olive hurried in after her, the dogs sniffing noses again.

Grant closed the door and locked it. The sound of the dead bolt sliding into place eased the last of Kaine's panic.

"In here." Grant showed her into the living room. An oversized black leather sofa tempted Kaine's overtired body. A love seat angled to the right of it and formed a half square in the middle of the room, with a massive stone fireplace in the corner. There were coals in the firebox, and Kaine wondered if it would be rude to pull the couch right up to it and stick her feet on the hearth.

The lights were dim and emanated from iron floor lamps with shades in two different hues of burnt orange. The plaster walls were painted in a subtle khaki, and a large rug in the center of the floor was vibrant with more oranges and reds, browns and blacks. Kaine was ready to peel off her shoes and dig her toes into the rug. Everything about this space contradicted the dark, gray hollowness of Foster Hill House.

Kaine sunk into the welcoming couch cushion, and Olive settled over her feet, her body warmth a special kind of comfort. Grant grabbed a blanket from the back of the couch and handed it to her. Sophie eyed them from across the room, then dropped to the floor by the fireplace.

"Coffee?" Grant's complete lack of response to her unannounced visit and shocking pronouncement was soothing. It must be his career that enabled him to hide any reactions to emotionally charged situations.

Kaine nodded, then shook her head. No. She really shouldn't. "No, no. That's okay. I really need to go and let you get some sleep now that I've dumped my drama all over your home."

"You're not going anywhere." Grant's smile was gentle but protective. The kind that told her she'd be safe with him even in a zombie apocalypse. He pushed his blond hair back from his forehead. His chunky black glasses framed eyes that pierced her with their sea-green intensity. "I have a Keurig. Colombian or Guatemalan?"

She would have preferred hazelnut, but Kaine was in no position to be picky.

"Guatemalan."

"Perfect. Sorry, it's not decaf."

"That's fine." She wasn't going to sleep anyway. Kaine picked at a loose thread on her yoga pants as she waited. A clock ticked on the wall. A worn Bible sat on the coffee table, along with a highlighter and a Louis L'Amour western. Finally, Kaine could breathe without fear lacing each intake of air.

Grant returned with two mugs of coffee. He handed her one, teal-and-brown pottery. His orange mug had a silhouette of buck antlers on the side. He settled on the couch next to her, close enough that Kaine could feel the warmth of his body. Grant took a sip of his brew, then lowered it from his mouth. His upper lip had an indentation in the middle. Kaine used to kiss Danny on his. She looked away.

"So . . ." He took another sip of coffee. "Danny."

Kaine stared into her mug. The dark liquid was hypnotizing as it swirled with creamer he'd failed to mix in with a spoon. She couldn't meet Grant's eyes. He was too tender. She was vulnerable tonight. The broken part of Kaine longed to cover the few feet between them and curl into his broad chest, feel his strong arms around her, and the assurance she was safe. This was what it was like to be on the side of the abused. To run until exhaustion and fear either drove you mad or pushed you into the grip of someone who would pull you to safety.

"Danny," Kaine whispered, reminding herself that Grant wasn't him. She sipped the coffee, her eyes following a particle floating on its surface.

Grant shifted in his seat but didn't say anything.

"I saw Danny in the morning before I left for work. He . . . was drinking from a water bottle and had just been for a run." Her voice cracked. "I blew him a kiss. He was sweaty and I didn't want to . . . I didn't want him to hold me."

Lying at her feet, Olive sighed and stretched her four legs out.

"And that was the last time you saw him?" Grant said.

Kaine lifted her eyes. Grant's were serious and searching. Somehow she could tell he understood not just her pain but her guilt. She should have held Danny. She should have let him love her that morning. But, like every other morning, a list of names riddled her mind. Names of women she needed to check on, to help, to shelter, to save. Her kiss had been blown with familiar complacency. How Danny's hand had swiped the air as he caught the imaginary kiss would forever be tattooed in her memory. He'd held his hand to his lips, his eyes pleading with her to stay, deep with desire to love her. Then they had dimmed as she reached for her car keys. He never understood the compelling drive she had for her work. He never understood what she'd always hidden from him. But he had supported her, in spite of it.

"Kaine?" Grant's soft voice broke into her reminiscing.

She bit her lip. Hard. "He's dead."

"Yes," Grant acknowledged, and his head tipped to the side.

"Someone killed him and now . . ."

"Now?" Grant leaned over and set his mug on an end table.

"Now his killer is after me." Kaine watched concern return to Grant's face. "He followed me from San Diego. He's playing with my mind, Grant. He leaves daffodils for me, my favorite flower. He used to break into my apartment and move things around. It was subtle. But I knew he was there. I knew he killed Danny. It's as if he's trying to tell me something and I don't know what it is. I don't understand why he took Danny's life. I don't know what he wants —" Rising fear choked Kaine's words.

Grant reached out, taking the mug from her hands.

"Maybe I know how my great-great-grandmother felt," she whispered. "That house — it draws wickedness. I thought I could come here to escape, but I've come full circle to the place where someone tried to murder her. Where they murdered the girl called Gabriella." Kaine clutched the blanket, pulling it higher. "I'm afraid it'll happen to me."

"Kaine." Grant's deep voice barely broke through her growing panic. "They're not connected. Ivy's story is different from yours, and so is Gabriella's. Don't associate Foster Hill House with your husband's death and this stalker." Grant shook his head.

The blanket wasn't enough anymore. She pulled her knees to her chin and rested her feet on the couch. "Maybe the circumstances aren't connected, but we are." Kaine wiped a tear from the corner of her eye. "I am not giving up. I'll find out who he is and I'll stop him. I'll —" Kaine stopped and drew a deep breath, gathering her courage — "I'll survive this, Grant. I'll fight."

CHAPTER 16

They said Hell was a place of darkness. Kaine flicked on her flashlight, and it lifted the shadows. Nothing good ever came from wandering in the dark. The attic of Foster Hill House was barren, the rafters low, and Grant was forced to duck in some areas. His six-foot-one frame wasn't going to be friends with the low ceiling. Kaine shifted her attention from him. She battled guilt over his decision to take a weeklong vacation from work. She was practically a stranger to him, and being on the receiving end of sacrifice was far more difficult than giving of herself. At least he wasn't treating her with pity or patronizing her with random, sad smiles.

Grant bent to peer out one of the small attic windows. "You can see a long way from up here."

"I know." Kaine never wanted him to leave now. She'd had the most peaceful night's sleep on his couch. He left Sophie with her and Olive, along with the comforting statement, "She was an abused dog the shelter rescued, so she hates men and will alert us if your stalker tries to get in." His wink was meant to ease her anxiety, and it worked.

In the morning, she awoke to the smell of fresh Guatemalan coffee. Grant had showered — his hair was damp and he smelled like minty soap. Kaine watched the morning news with him and avoided the idea of returning to her motel or Foster Hill House. Avoided it until Grant announced his impromptu vacation from work and his intention to continue to help her with the repairs and renovation.

She stole a glance at him now. He still stared out the window like he was studying the landscape. His worn sweatshirt wasn't exactly sexy, but it was passable considering Grant wore it.

"So, where do we start?" Grant turned and brushed his hands down his jeans.

Kaine turned away quickly so he didn't catch that she'd been watching him. "The moldy wall, downstairs in the bedroom. It's not the dangerous mold that has to be removed professionally — at least that's what the contractor thought. Also, the floorboards are very warped. I need to pull them up and have them replaced. I guess I'd rather start there and make an appointment for someone to come out to do a mold test, just to be on the safe side."

Grant grimaced.

"What?" Kaine pressed.

He shrugged. "You're right about the mold test, but floorboards? Seems to me there's more concerning things. Like the roof, for one."

Kaine knew he was right, but she would need to hire a roofer to do that. Besides, cosmetic repairs were less daunting than the list of other, more involved repairs. The surface fixing only required a few crowbars, hammers, face masks, and aggression. And she had enough aggression inside her to tear down the entire house.

"I'd prefer to tackle the easy stuff first," she said. It was her house after all, and she really didn't have any obligation to Grant Jesse. He might make her feel safe, but outside of that . . . yep, no obligation whatsoever.

"The easy stuff doesn't take care of the root issue."

Part of Kaine bristled against his stating the obvious. He was making a barely veiled point.

"If the roof collapses, new floorboards

won't matter." Grant stomped on the attic floor. It was sound, unlike the floor in the third bedroom.

"Fixing the big stuff is painful," Kaine admitted. She swiped at a tiny spider that swung from the ceiling.

Comprehension filled Grant's eyes, empathy that made her own eyes sting with tears. He didn't pity her, he understood her. There was a big difference.

"I know."

Two words. But they were poignant.

Kaine wrestled with her swirling emotions as she moved toward the stairs leading out of the attic. It was one thing to face the loss of a spouse, but it was entirely different when he'd been murdered and her own life was —

Kaine halted, and Grant caught himself on the wall before he stumbled into her.

"What's the matter?" he asked in her ear.

Kaine squinted. She had caught a glimmer of a shining reflection in the far corner. But she didn't see it now. She backed up a step, and Grant moved with her.

"I thought I saw something." Kaine edged past him. She rocked from her left to her right foot, hoping to catch a glimpse of the reflection. Nothing. She took another step. The sunlight through the attic window bounced off something tiny in the corner of the bare space. "Over there." Kaine pointed.

Grant looked in the direction she pointed. "I don't see anything."

"It's shiny. Or it was." Kaine reached the corner of the room and knelt on the floor. She couldn't see it anymore. Palming the floor, the filth collected on her hands as she ran them across it hoping to feel whatever it was she'd seen.

Grant knelt beside her. "Like glass? Be careful you don't slice your hand."

"I will." Reaching the corner, Kaine ran her fingers by the floorboard where the sun shaft was brightest. The tips of her fingers met something smooth, wedged in a small gap between the floor and the wall. "I've got something." She tugged at it.

"Careful." Grant's breath was warm on her neck as he leaned over to watch.

Kaine worked her fingers beneath it and pulled. It released. A gold locket. Its tarnish layer was thin and barely darkened the reflective surface.

"Whoa. That looks old." Grant's statement echoed Kaine's thoughts.

They both straightened and looked closer at the locket resting in her palm. Its chain dangled off and swayed below her wrist. She touched the engraved foliage on the front.

"I'm surprised it could even be wedged in there without someone seeing it," Kaine said.

Grant tapped it lightly with his index finger. "You never would have seen it if it hadn't caught the sun."

She pried at its tiny clasp with her fingernail, slowly opening the locket. She blinked in surprise. The inside of the locket was lined with an aged ivory material. What caught her attention, though, was a navy blue ribbon, embroidered, which held strands of baby-fine blond hair.

"Hair?" Grant appeared fascinated by it.

Kaine shook her head. "Weird. Why would someone put hair in a locket?"

"Well, in centuries past, hair was kept in memory of a loved one, or as a token of love."

"You mean they cut hair off a corpse?" Kaine handed the locket to Grant so he could get a better look.

"Or a lover." He studied the hair and ribbon.

Why did that make her blush?

There wasn't a chance Kaine would want a lock of hair in a necklace around her neck whether the donor was alive or dead. She preferred the more contemporary token of a gemstone.

"It was to remember them by," Grant explained. "Like if I gave you a lock of my hair to keep near your heart."

Kaine raised her brows. "Did guys really do that sort of thing back then?"

He nodded. "Exchanging hair wasn't uncommon."

"A love note wasn't enough, huh?" Kaine received the locket back from him and carefully snapped it shut, hiding the token of memory or love. An etching on the back caught her eye. Holding it closer, she read the inscription and reached out to grip Grant's wrist.

"Grant, look." As she bent over the locket, her heart pounded. Grant's whispered "What — ?" only enhanced her surge of adrenaline. They turned toward each other, and Kaine knew the astonishment in Grant's eyes mirrored her own.

"Ivy." Kaine traced the engraving with her finger. "My great-great-grandmother's name. Is this her locket?"

Grant leaned back against the attic wall. "Unless there was another Ivy we don't know about."

Kaine closed her hand around the locket. "Why is it here in Foster Hill House?"

Jamming his hands into his pockets, Grant

looked her in the eye. "The bigger question is, whose hair is that?"

CHAPTER 17

IVY

She would not survive. Ivy's feet slipped and slid in the mud as the rain continued to beat down on her. She threw a glance over her shoulder. No one. Had she outrun him or had he given up the chase as she approached town? Joel's boardinghouse came into view as she ran into the village, glad she'd overheard him telling her father where he was living and his room number in case he was needed. Her home was at the opposite end of Oakwood, and she told herself the distance, rain, and fear was what sent her in a fast run toward Joel and not her home. She was running from the same shadow of a man who had killed Gabriella. It had to be. If he caught her, this time he wouldn't fail in killing her too. Safety was her first concern, propriety a distant second. That reasoning catapulted her into the boardinghouse and up the stairs to Joel's room.

Her fist connected with his door in a frantic knock. Nothing. Ivy knocked again, a three-time rap. Her wet hair clung to her face, and she raked it away with her fingers. Her dress clung to her in damp folds. She looked over her shoulder again as if convinced the man from Foster Hill House had followed her into the house and would charge up the stairs any minute.

She was about to knock again when the door swung inward. Joel stood framed in the doorway, his pinstriped shirt untucked and hanging over his trousers. His rumpled hair sprang up from his head. Ivy ignored his impressive physique and pushed her way inside, ducking under his arm that held the door open.

"Close it. Please!" Ivy's command was met with compliance.

"Ivy Thorpe, have you taken leave of your senses?" His raspy voice sent shivers through her. He shut the door firmly with a glance into the hallway. "You shouldn't be in my room."

"He followed me." She ignored his scolding and sank onto a ladder-back chair by the lone desk and a bed with a white iron frame opposite her.

"Who followed you?" Joel hadn't left the door. His hand still gripped the knob as if ready to toss her out.

"I don't know!" Ivy peeled off her wet gloves. "*Him!* The man who attacked me. The man who killed Gabriella!"

"Slow down." Joel pushed up his sleeves and leaned against the door. "You *saw* him?"

"Just a glimpse. A man. I didn't recognize him." Ivy drew a deep, shuddering breath. "And I'd just seen Mr. Foggerty. What if it's him? What if Mr. Foggerty is trapping more than otters?"

Joel pushed off the door. "Stop, Ivy. I need you to collect yourself."

"I am collected." She skewered him with a glare. "I'm always collected."

Joel tilted his head and stared back at her, silently arguing with her self-assessment. "What happened? Exactly."

Ivy set her gloves on the desk and folded her hands. At least she was safe here. Safe. A pistol lay on the desk next to her gloves. There was some comfort in knowing Joel was armed.

"I went to the orphanage to make some inquiries."

"Ivy."

The disapproval on Joel's face told her he was far from pleased. He took a seat on the bed.

"On my return, and *after* a brief interlude with Mr. Foggerty, who walked away in the opposite direction," she continued in spite of his stern expression, "I saw movement in the woods. A man of medium build and height. He started toward me and I ran. I just ran."

Ivy swiped at her dripping hair and flipped it over her shoulder.

Joel's nostrils flared from the compressed fury that radiated from his eyes. "Did he speak to you? Was it Foggerty?"

"I told you, I didn't recognize him. It was hard to see through the rain." Ivy blinked rapidly. Tears threatened to fall but she never cried, and she wouldn't start now in front of Joel. "But he said, 'None to hear you. None to care.' "

Joel gave her an uncomprehending look. Ivy curled her fingers into her soaking wet dress. "It's what my attacker said before he threw me down the stairs at Foster Hill House."

With a muttered curse, Joel reached for the pistol. He stuck it into the waistband of his trousers at the small of his back.

"What are you doing?" Ivy caught the coverlet he snatched from the end of the bed and tossed toward her.

"I'm going out to look for him." Joel

marched across the room and pulled open the doors of a large wardrobe.

"He won't be there." Ivy wrapped the coverlet over her shoulders. She was shivering now.

Joel yanked a slicker from the wardrobe and shoved his arm into a sleeve. Ivy launched to her feet.

"Please, Joel." She cared. God help her, she cared. Ivy had visions of Joel charging through the rain and confronting the killer with the pistol. Ivy put her hand on his forearm.

Joel stilled. He looked at her hand.

"It's not worth going out in the rain when the man has most certainly vanished by now," Ivy said, trying to reason with him.

His eyes flashed. "Ivy, if he dared touch you again . . ."

She dropped her hand. That was why. *She* was the reason Joel wasn't acting rationally. The realization sent an unwelcome thrill through her.

Joel strode to the window and looked through the panes of glass as rain pelted against it. Ivy waited.

He took a deep breath and spun around. "Why did you visit the orphanage in the first place?"

Ivy faltered under his accusing glare. "It

doesn't matter why I was there, but —"

"It *does* matter, Ivy."

"You and Sheriff Dunst were so pre-occupied with organizing the search for Gabriella's baby, I thought I'd look at the orphanage. If it was as simple as she'd left it —"

Joel stared down his nose at her. "You think I didn't already ask there?"

Ivy swallowed and looked up at him.

If it were possible, Joel's blue eyes turned into ice. "That was the first place I went after we found out she'd even *had* a baby. Before you were attacked even." He dragged his fingers through his hair. "Blast it all, Ivy! I know you don't trust me, don't even *like* me anymore, but don't discredit me. Or Sheriff Dunst. We are as worried about this baby and the killer as you are."

Ivy swiped at a drop of water that ran from her hairline down her cheek. She realized her hand was shaking. "I just — Gabriella deserves justice, and her baby deserves life. I can't just sit by and not do anything."

Joel dropped the slicker to the floor and positioned his hands on the top of his head, his elbows sticking out. "Then care for someone *living*. Gabriella is dead and very possibly her child too. They're not worth your life."

Maybe he said it in the passion of his own fright for her safety, but his words revived her offense against him. Ivy turned her back on Joel and moved toward the door. She said over her shoulder, "If there's a chance that baby is alive, it *is* worth my life." Ivy whirled back to face him. "Just like Andrew was worth yours! But you didn't give it for him, did you? You let him die and then you left me alone. You never show passion for anyone, so how was I supposed to know you'd already been to the orphanage? I wouldn't think you'd ever want to go back there."

Furious, she reached for the door. Joel chased after her in a few long strides and grabbed her upper arm. "You really don't want to inquire about my *passion* for anything, Ivy Thorpe." He pulled her closer until Ivy's shoulder pressed against his chest.

She wriggled her arm to free herself.

"Don't discount my own investigation. Don't assume I don't care or that I didn't just get back to my room after twenty-four hours without sleep looking for the baby, wishing I could bring justice for Gabriella, and wanting to protect you."

His breath was warm on her face. Ivy turned away.

"And you know I tried to save Andrew." Joel's voice dropped. "You're an intelligent, beautiful woman, Ivy. Use that intelligence and stay home. Stay safe. I don't want to lose you again."

They searched each other's eyes. Lose her? He had left her! Ivy wondered if Joel could read her agony. Yet something pulled them together, even now, and the space between them lessened. She could sense Joel's face not far from hers, and the look in his eyes deepened. Unreadable but tumultuous.

Panic gripped her. The emotion that boiled inside needed sorting out, and she couldn't do that when he was too close, too intimate. Ivy pulled away and Joel let her go. She'd find an escort home. Someone, anyone other than Joel. Ivy twisted the doorknob and pulled, but the door slammed shut just as fast. Joel's hand spread on the door above her head, his arm stretching alongside her shoulder.

"Let me out," Ivy said.

Joel's breath moved a tendril of hair by her ear. She stiffened and stared at the door.

"Why do you do this to me, Ivy?"

She didn't answer.

"You assume the worst of me. Ever since Andrew died."

Ivy spoke at the door, her words ricocheting off the wood. "It's not an assumption when it's the truth." The quiver in her voice was evident.

Joel moved closer, the warmth from his body against her back, his hand still splayed across the door.

"But truth isn't based on theories. You must have all the facts, Ivy."

She stilled.

Joel's lips pressed against the back of her jaw just below her ear. Ivy shivered.

He whispered, "And assumptions can kill more than friendship." He kissed her jawline. Firm, brief, impactful. "I don't want to bury you too."

CHAPTER 18

Sunshine made the spring day even brighter. The day of a funeral should not be shrouded in beauty. At least Ivy didn't think so. Three onlookers gathered in addition to her father, the reverend, and Joel. The sheriff was one, Mr. Foggerty the other, and the third a curiosity seeker. There to gawk at the wooden casket of a murdered woman. Worst of all, the deep pit of earth that had no marker. Eventually, there would be a simple cross, but no name or specifics to remember Gabriella by.

Ivy glanced at Joel. His expression was indecipherable, although she noted him studying Mr. Foggerty from time to time. Andrew's gravestone stood three rows behind him and to the right. Her vision fell on it and caressed her brother's name. She didn't miss how Joel avoided looking at it. As well he should. He didn't deserve to mourn Andrew, not after he put the excla-

207

mation point on the tragedy by proving his loyalty did not run deep.

"Ashes to ashes . . ." The reverend's rote was unemotional. The young woman had felt the life squeezed from her, she'd been hidden in a rotting tree trunk, and no one was sincere in their grief over her. It was tradition to lay a soul to rest in peace, but how did that happen when her killer still ran free, she was nameless, and her infant had vanished?

The reverend bowed his head in prayer. Ivy closed her eyes. She should pray, but she couldn't. Ivy hadn't been able to since Andrew died. She wasn't angry with God. She had simply come to terms with the idea that God would do what He pleased, when He pleased, and she would be there when it happened. It saddened her father, whose faith was steady. But Ivy had a difficult time justifying why God, who supposedly loved His creations, would allow tragedy to strike. Andrew was her brother and, outside of Joel, her best friend.

She didn't have friends anymore.

Joel edged her way after the prayer ended. A robin chirruped from a tree above them, reminding them of spring, while the sun's rays cast a warm, comforting embrace over Gabriella's casket.

"I hope you can find closure today." He was distant, his tone impersonal.

Ivy didn't blink. The lace at her throat choked her. Closure? For whom? Gabriella? There was no closure, only a litany of unanswered questions. She stared down at the casket, then bent and placed a dried rose on the top of it. It reminded her of the dried roses on Andrew's casket, that cold, wintry day. The snowflakes had been large, soft, but as freezing as the ground into which they buried him. Joel's hand was the only thing that kept her warm, and later, even that slipped away. She had been cold ever since.

"Did you grieve Andrew's death?" Ivy whispered. Her question hung between them, hovering in the warmth of the sun but the starkness of death.

Joel took a deep breath through his nose. "Of course I did."

"You never came, Joel." Maybe she should listen, ask, and just listen. But it was so hard to hear Joel's version of those days. It meant reliving them, and she'd lived in her own interpretation for so long — it felt safer there, if not happier.

"Ivy . . ." Joel shifted his feet. "I was an orphan. I didn't have a family."

"*We* were your family. Andrew and I." Ivy

stepped backward as Joel's hand extended toward her. To take hers? To touch her arm? Regardless, he couldn't touch her. She couldn't let him. Her shoe sank into a soft, mossy patch of earth. She pulled it out.

What if she and Andrew had begged their father to adopt Joel? Would he have? With their mother's death at Ivy's birth, he'd fathered them well. But it was so much to care for two, let alone three children. They'd never asked. Their father had never offered.

Still, it was years ago. One couldn't change the past. Even if Joel gave her a more palatable explanation, it still wouldn't change the fact that Andrew had died, Joel had gone away, and she had been left behind.

Ivy sniffed back tears she refused with every ounce of her will. She gave Joel a sideways glance, but he was staring back down at the grave.

"We cannot let her go unremembered." Ivy's whisper covered the distance between them.

She didn't miss Joel's subtle nod of agreement. In this one small thing, they were unified. For now, it was enough.

The water poured from the pitcher into the washbasin, the sound a promise of refreshing and cleansing. Ivy plunged her hands into it and splashed it over her face. She allowed the drips to trail like tears down her cheeks as she lifted her face to the mirror. Her green eyes reflected back, filled with memories. Gabriella's funeral had sapped her of energy but not determination. The search party had not turned up a baby, nor had Joel or Sheriff Dunst found anyone who knew Gabriella. Sleep would be difficult to come by tonight, and now, with so much time passed, she could only pray someone had Gabriella's baby, or else it was most assuredly dead.

Drying her face, Ivy tied the ribbon at the neckline of her nightgown. She wandered across her room to a small desk and eased onto the chair, running her hand over a leather-covered journal. Her "death journal," as the town of Oakwood preferred to call it. They only knew of it because Ivy would take it with her to the examination room of her father's office or to the deathbed of the person who'd passed. They saw her writing in it, her pencil gliding across the page, and assumptions were made.

She opened it, flipping through the pages. Mrs. Templeton, her schoolteacher, died of consumption. Ivy had written her three favorite memories of the woman. Then there was George Clayborne, the town drunk.

She'd been the only person at his funeral outside of her father and the reverend. It was more difficult to find pleasant memories of the crotchety man, but eventually she did. Widow Bairns had supplied Ivy with tales of when she and George were younger and he'd been charming, flirtatious, even debonair, only changing after he lost his wife and newborn son in childbirth. Ivy turned the pages to a blank one. She picked up her pencil and in a fine script sketched *Gabriella* across the top. Her pencil moved to write *and child,* and then laid it down. No. She could not accept that. Not yet.

The *ping* of a stone against the upper panes of her open window captured Ivy's attention. Visions from years before invaded her mind. Joel, truant from the orphanage, sneaking to her window where he'd beckon her to come down. Nighttime jaunts in the moonlit woods, happy and soulful. Innocent and adventurous. So long ago.

Ivy pushed off the bed and lifted her heavy hair over her shoulder.

The shadows from the woods beyond the house were dark against the moonlit sky. The chill of the wind was more striking here, and Ivy grabbed a shawl from the back of the rocking chair in the corner.

Poking her head out the window, she

peered into the night.

Joel. Just like old times. He stood below, only now, instead of the lithe body of a sixteen-year-old boy, was the broad-shouldered version of a man. His hand was poised to toss another stone.

"Please don't. I'd prefer not to drop dead like Goliath." Ivy swallowed back the yearning for happier times. He'd caught her in the wake of her sentiment. When her guard was down.

"But I only wield my hand, not a slingshot." A hint of a smile touched Joel's mouth, then faded. "We need to have a chat."

Ivy tugged her shawl tighter around her shoulders. "I believe we've chatted quite enough."

Joel crossed his arms, and his black coat stretched over his shoulders. He chose to ignore her admonition. "I need to gain your promise that you will not put yourself in any further danger while we are investigating the murder."

A small thrill ran through Ivy as she allowed herself to read the protection written across Joel's face. "And you insist on chatting about this in the dead of night on the lawn below my window?"

"I don't trust you not to do something

addlebrained in the middle of the night."

"I rarely do anything without deep thought and contemplation." Ivy rested her elbows on the windowsill.

"Oh, really?" Joel's eyebrows rose in disbelief. "Recent events suggest otherwise. Come down and we'll talk."

"I politely decline." Ivy ducked inside and reached up to push the window shut.

"Ivy . . ." Joel's voice sounded hoarse, as if he were a beau trying to avoid a father's discovery. "Please, don't close that window," he insisted.

She brought it down a few more inches.

"I've said it before. You cannot insert yourself into this investigation."

Two more inches.

Joel grew agitated enough to make Ivy pause.

"Gabriella was murdered, Ivy. I don't want to see you end up in the same state."

Ivy's smile waned. She knew that in spite of her angst over Joel's return, he was wise in what he said. "I have no compulsion to wind up stuffed into a tree, if that's what concerns you."

"So you promise not to return to Foster Hill House?"

"Not alone, no."

"Not at all," Joel tried again.

"If you offer companionship, I will certainly oblige." She was feeling somewhat giddy, the emotion of the last week catching up with her.

"Don't be coy with me," Joel said, his tone adamant.

He was right, she knew, but his words stung all the same. Against his protests, Ivy slid the window closed, loosening the tie-backs on the white curtains. She let them fall into place, concealing Joel, and leaned against the wall, closing her eyes. There was a time when she believed Joel Cunningham would have done anything to protect her. But now he was only inspired because he was a duty-driven detective whose protectiveness was born out of his position.

Ivy had no desire to be the recipient of obligation.

CHAPTER 19

KAINE

The Oakwood Museum was about as inviting as a biker bar on a stretch of deserted highway. Kaine shot Grant a sideways look. No wonder Great-Great-Grandmother Ivy's quilt had been so easily stolen. If the museum was as ramshackle in 1963 as it was today, a toddler could break into the place. The old granary had been converted into a secured building only by the installation of basic stormproof windows and a front door lock that Kaine could break into with a credit card. Either the museum held little of monetary value or the crime rate in Oakwood, Wisconsin, had plummeted after Ivy's quilt was stolen.

A thud drew Kaine's attention back to the elderly man in faded blue overalls and a green plaid shirt. His wispy gray hair formed a sparse crown on his balding head. Mr. Mason, Grant had called him. The curator.

216

Curator of what? Some old photographs on the wall featuring a farmstead, a plow, three vintage people in Edwardian garb, and a dog? Oh, and the framed sequences of Foster Hill House at different stages of its hundred-plus years. Because it wasn't disturbing enough today, she had to see it back in the 1800s when it was even spookier-looking.

"This here is about all we have now." Mr. Mason handed Kaine an old leather journal. "The town calls it Ivy's 'death journal.' Would've probably been stolen back when the quilt was stolen, but it was locked up in a safe. Don't know why. It's not like it had monetary value."

"Death journal?" Kaine echoed. Could it get any weirder? Ivy's locket with hair in it lay in Kaine's purse, making her squirm. A book of death and potentially the hair of a dead person reminded her of a Gothic black-and-white movie.

Mr. Mason smiled, wrinkles reaching the corners of his eyes. He really was a sweet old man. "She was a self-appointed grave keeper of sorts. Made sure everyone who died had a memorial in her journal. Like an obituary, only more."

"A brief memoir," Grant offered.

"That's it." Mr. Mason nodded. "Stories

say the town didn't know her too well and all in all thought she was a bit crazy or maybe toyed with the otherworld."

"Doubtful." Kaine felt the need to defend her dead ancestor.

Mr. Mason tapped the book in her hand. "I tend to agree. It's really a nice collection of mem'ries."

Kaine opened the old book. Its pages were crumbling on the edges, and the script inside was small, cursive, and loopy.

"Look at this." Kaine motioned to the page, and Grant leaned over her shoulder. "She chronicles people who passed away under her father's medical care."

Grant tipped his head to look closer.

"It's touching." Kaine ran her finger along the script.

Marigold Farnsworth passed away at only twenty-two years of age. She has been married only one year, and the infant born to her this night will grow without the warmth of his mother's embrace. I remember Marigold as a gentle spirit. She was beautiful in life, and even in death a smile touches her lips. What I recall the most about Marigold is . . .

The entry continued, but Kaine stopped

and acknowledged Mr. Mason, who waited patiently for her to finish with the artifact. "This is amazing. It's a treasure. Think of the lives Ivy chronicled."

The wonder of the concept filtered into Kaine's voice, and Mr. Mason nodded in agreement. "She was just tryin' to keep the dead alive."

Kaine blinked against the sudden moisture in her eyes, and Mr. Mason swiped a Kleenex from its box on the counter. He handed it to her without comment about her tears.

"Other'n that journal," he continued, "there wasn't much else for memorabilia. Just her quilt stolen back in '63. I think we have a few doilies in the back storage that belonged to her. No one really cares anymore."

She cared. Now, especially, since she held the same book her great-great-grandmother held so many years before. Foster Hill House, the place where Ivy had been attacked, became suddenly more important. Kaine turned a page in the journal, its binding loose and fragile. She wanted to understand the details of what happened to Ivy, why she had been there and how the dead girl named Gabriella fit into the story.

"What do you have on record about the

murder that happened there?" Grant's blunt question sliced the nostalgia out of the air.

Murder. It was a shocking word that played in her memory on repeat since Danny's death. Tragic that both she and Ivy were linked by violence toward individuals they cared about.

Mr. Mason scratched behind his ear and shuffled into the back room. "Not much anymore." The open doorway allowed them to watch him as he dug around in a crate, then shoved it aside and opened a metal filing cabinet. Apparently, the museum was more of a hobby now than a place of historical archive.

"Patti?" His voice wobbled with age as he called. Kaine startled at the sound of footsteps coming down the back stairs. She glanced at Grant, who smiled.

"She's the town librarian who volunteers here sometimes," he explained.

Patti rounded the corner. Oh my. Kaine tried to steel herself. The librarian's shrewish expression skewered her with a dark gaze. "Yes, Mason?" she answered while keeping her stare locked on Kaine.

"Do you remember where you put those files on the murder at Foster Hill?"

Kaine tried not to flinch. Cataloguing historical archives digitally must not be top of the list here at the Oakwood Museum. Patti's lips pressed together. Still staring at Kaine, she said to Mr. Mason, "In the bottom filing cabinet."

"Ah!"

Patti crossed her arms. "So you're the one who bought Foster Hill House."

Kaine cast Grant a cautious glance. His eyes twinkled. She looked back to Patti. "Yes."

"Good luck with that." It wasn't nice sounding, not at all sincere, and almost sinister. Patti's pinched expression never wavered, and she spun on her loafer-clad heel and disappeared back to where she'd been.

Wow. Kaine mouthed the word to Grant.

He leaned closer and whispered in her ear. "Rumor has it Patti always wanted to buy Foster Hill House."

"I'd be glad to sell it to her!" Kaine whispered back.

"She's as poor as a church mouse. She gambles every weekend at the casino just north of here." Grant shrugged.

Bewildered by the unexpected interlude, Kaine's attention shifted as Mr. Mason shuffled back into the main room with the speed of a tortoise.

"Ooookay. I found some newspaper clippings from back then. Pretty crumbly, though. I should probably have Patti put them in plastic sleeves." Mr. Mason laid the folder on a wooden tabletop and opened it. He began thumbing through the browned sheaves of clippings, then stopped to lift one up to read it in the light. "Let's see here . . . 1906. That's the right year." He laid it down and thumbed some more.

Out of the corner of her eye, Kaine could see Grant wince at Mr. Mason's roughness with the material.

Finally, Mr. Mason cleared his throat, sounding like he was in the early stages of emphysema. "Okey-dokey. Here we go."

The newspaper he laid on the table had block letters identifying the *Oakwood Herald.* Beneath it, in letters almost as large, the headline *Murder on Foster Hill.*

"Probably Oakwood's most exciting paper ever printed." Mr. Mason's chuckle bounced his shoulders.

Kaine leaned forward, her shoulder brushing Grant's. He smiled, and Kaine dropped her gaze to the clipping. She scoured the article.

A foul murder was uncovered Monday afternoon on Foster Hill by Mr. Averil Foggerty. The victim is an unidentified young woman who was strangled, according to Dr. Matthew Thorpe's medical examination. Sheriff Dunst is investigating the case, and he claims the assault may have been perpetrated by a wandering vagrant. Detective Joel Cunningham has been commissioned to investigate the murder.

"There's nothing here about Ivy at all," Kaine murmured.

"Nope." Mr. Mason laid another newspaper clipping in front of them. Part of the corner tore off. "But look here." His finger rested on Ivy's name.

Though recent search parties have been unsuccessful, Ivy Thorpe has made the startling claim that the supposed infant of the murdered woman of Foster Hill House may still be alive. Inquiries at the Oakwood Orphanage indicate no orphan baby has been deposited there without a full account of parentage or history. Therefore, it is the opinion of this paper that Miss Thorpe's assertions of such claims may also prove to be that of a mystic.

Kaine stared at Grant. "A baby was involved?"

"There was a big search for it supposedly, but the baby was never found." Mr. Mason sagged onto a wooden chair. "Leastways not that we have record of."

Kaine ran her finger over the words, her heart feeling like it stretched across time and connected with Ivy's. It was an empty, dark place to be when you had an intuition about something and no one would take your word for it. Ivy was charged with being a mystic. Kaine was threatened with being charged with false claims. "Ivy wasn't a mystic. She must have known something the paper didn't expose."

Mr. Mason nodded. "Well, you can't deny that people were fascinated with death back then in a strange way. Today, we can go back and see that by looking at how they dressed the dead and propped open their eyes to take pictures of them postmortem as if they were still alive. Seems to me, Ivy's death journal wasn't much different, but folks just weren't comfortable with the idea. It was maybe easier to explain Ivy's claims away than deal with the fact a baby was never found. Speaking of weird, I even read of people who cut hair off the dead and saved it in books or jewelry."

Kaine exchanged glances with Grant. She didn't miss the subtle shake of his head. Pulling her hand from her purse where she'd instinctively plunged it to retrieve the locket, she diverted with another question.

"Why doesn't the newspaper say anything about Ivy's attack? Wouldn't that have given her credibility?"

"Maybe it did." Mr. Mason shrugged. "We don't have every paper, to be honest."

"And the *Oakwood Herald* doesn't have them?" Kaine asked. "Or in the library? Would Patti know?"

Grant said with a grimace, "The paper went under years ago. We don't have a local paper anymore. We get our news from the town over. The library has microfiche, but I don't think any of them go back much further than the twenties." He tapped the journal Kaine had set on the table. "Ivy does describe her attack in here, though."

"In this? But it's all memories of deceased people." Kaine searched his face.

"Until you get to Gabriella's entry at the end. She's the last one. Ivy's last memory entry. It turns into more of a diary than a memoir."

Kaine raised an eyebrow. "So you read this, Grant?"

"A couple years ago. Like I said, my dad —"

"Was a history professor," Kaine finished.

"That," Grant continued, "and Joy was the one who turned me on to it. She's always had a fascination with the story. Her grandmother was alive during the time of the murder, so Joy grew up hearing some of the stories. She's the one who said Ivy called the girl Gabriella, and Ivy's journal confirmed it. Joy's grandmother was the last one to pass away who lived during that time. She died sometime in the seventies."

"Shoot." Kaine would have loved to speak to Joy's grandmother. "Do you have any pictures?"

"Of Ivy?" Mr. Mason raised his brows and struggled from his chair. "Darn arthritis," he muttered. "Sure do."

As Mr. Mason once again disappeared into the back room, Kaine turned toward Grant. She tapped the locket in her pocket. "What if the hair in this locket belonged to the baby Ivy insisted was still alive?"

Grant wrinkled his face in doubt. "That's a stretch. There's no record it was ever found."

Kaine wanted to open the locket but didn't feel like answering any questions about it if Mr. Mason returned. "I don't understand why the locket was in Foster Hill House. If Gabriella did have a baby . . ." Her voice trailed off as a morbid thought entered her mind.

Grant frowned. "What is it?"

There it was, the familiar sense of dread that accompanied her every time she knew someone had been in her house. But this time it echoed back to decades before and touched today. "What if the baby was buried in Foster Hill House? Like in a wall, or the floor? I've seen that in movies. It could happen."

Grant's eyes widened.

Kaine pressed, "What if Ivy found it?"

"Then we would know, and it would have been buried by its mother in the Oakwood Cemetery." Grant's conclusion was logical. "I wouldn't start imagining dead bodies in the walls, Kaine."

"Okay. So maybe the baby didn't die, but if Ivy found it, what if she couldn't tell anyone?"

Grant shook his head. "Why wouldn't she be able to disclose finding a child? And how would she hide it from everyone?"

Kaine drew in a breath that reached into her soul. "Because maybe the same person who killed Gabriella posed a continued danger to Ivy's life too. And the baby's. Remember, my family tree in the old Bible did end with Ivy Thorpe. Maybe there was a reason no one kept it current. Maybe it was to keep them safe."

CHAPTER 20

Kaine shoved some empty cardboard boxes out of the way in search of a plastic tarp. She didn't miss the look Grant shot her. He still thought she was avoiding issues by starting demolition in an unimportant upstairs bedroom. But she needed to feel in control of something, especially after their trip to the museum. There was something too familiar with Ivy's story, and the story about the dead girl and a missing child. Kaine needed to attack something and work off some of her angst on the old, dilapidated house.

The trill of Kaine's phone interrupted her sweep of a plastic tarp as she spread it over the floor of bedroom three. She spun, looking for her phone.

"There." Grant pointed at the toolbox in the corner.

Kaine snatched up the glowing phone from among the tools Grant had been kind enough to bring.

"Hello?"

"So what's it like?"

The male voice made the hairs on Kaine's arms stand on end. She glanced at Grant as he finished stretching out the tarp. "Excuse me?"

"Being alone. What's it like?" An unnerving chuckle echoed through the phone.

"Who are you?" Kaine withdrew the phone from her ear and looked at the screen. The caller ID was blocked.

"Do you miss him?"

"I asked you who you are!" The sharpness in Kaine's voice caused Grant to look up. He frowned, and she pointed at the phone.

"It's hard being alone. People thinking you're crazy." The pause that followed was emphasized by his long sigh.

"I'm not crazy." Kaine's pulse pounded.

Grant crossed the room, a scowl on his face.

The stalker? he mouthed.

Kaine nodded and tapped the speakerphone icon.

"You should know. Your life is defined by the ones you've lost." The man stressed the words with an accent Kaine couldn't place. Or perhaps it was more of a slur. The influence of alcohol maybe? Or a cloth held over the phone's speaker to disguise the voice?

"Why are you calling me?" Kaine demanded. She fought the urge to throw her phone across the room.

"I asked if you liked being alone!" His voice rose, and Kaine clutched the phone tighter.

Grant waved his hand and shook his head. Kaine followed his cue and didn't answer. They could hear the man breathing on the other end of the line. Short, frustrated breaths, like he was agitated.

"You know I'll never leave you," he growled. "I'll make sure you are always reminded."

"Reminded of what?" Kaine shot Grant a frantic look.

Grant passed his hand across his throat. Did he mean no more questions or did he think Kaine should hang up?

Before Kaine could get clarification, the voice continued, "I want you to know what it is to be isolated, and the only presence with you is the one you hate the most. That person who haunts you, who ruined your life, who inhabits everything around you."

With that, Grant yanked the phone away and ended the call. He looked as if ready to jump into the phone and go all Darth Vader on the man. He swiped at the screen so that the number pad showed. Kaine grabbed the phone from him.

"No!"

"Kaine, you have to call the police."

"Not yet. Let me think." She stuffed the phone in her pocket and marched over to the tarp. She made a pretense of straightening it, as if it was critical to cover every square inch of the floor with the blue canvas. She finally had a witness, Grant. Going to the police would be smart, and if Detective Hanson from San Diego really had reopened her case, wouldn't that give her credence with Detective Carter here in Oakwood? Her mind spun. Or would it all backfire somehow?

Grant tugged the tarp from her grip. "Kaine, that man is mentally disturbed. Why aren't the police already involved?"

"The police *are* involved. They think I'm the one who's unstable. And if I make a habit of making unsubstantiated reports, then I'm in trouble." She could barely think. She steepled her fingers and pressed them to her mouth.

"But this isn't unsubstantiated. I was here. I heard it."

He was right. She needed to report it.

"How do people do this?" Kaine bit her lip.

"What do you mean?"

"I've spent years helping women escape men like this. And I . . . I can't even help myself. I sold my old car and bought the Jetta used from a private seller. I sold our condo. I pay cash for everything. My cellphone? It's prepaid under a Jane Doe account. How did he get my number? I did everything but change my name."

She had coached many women through this type of scenario and could hear her own voice in her head telling them what to do.

Have an emergency bag packed. Your vital documents, driver's license, orders of protection, passport, Social Security card.

The women's shelter helped women regain their safety, their financial independence, and their emotional security. But Kaine never wanted to be running from her own abuser. A man without a face, without a name. How did one escape a ghost?

"We need to go to the police and file a report." Grant was definitive, and his expression emphasized the urgency behind his statement.

Kaine stared out the bedroom doorway and locked eyes with the dead woman in the painting. Lines drew her face downward, as if circumstances had made her appear older and more worn than her age warranted. Had she fought through adversity, abuse, even fear? Kaine shook her head to clear her thoughts. It didn't matter who she was. What mattered was who Kaine was. She wasn't ready to give up the fight . . . not yet.

CHAPTER 21

IVY

Ivy curled her fingers around the edge of the church pew in front of her. Her starched dress of blue damask was as stiff as her back. She hadn't been fond of church or God since Andrew's death. Now, with her mounting passion to uncover the truth behind Gabriella's life and the fate of her baby, Ivy could hardly stand still. She glanced across the aisle at Joel. How could he be so focused on church when Gabriella's child could be out there somewhere?

The church organ droned out "Near to the Heart of God," and Ivy winced. She hadn't been near to God's heart for many years. The longer time marched on and stole more lives from the earth, the more it solidified Ivy's inability to find hope in the shadow of death. Her father had suggested many times that Ivy escape the life of his assistant so she could cease witnessing the passing of so many souls. Even under medical ministrations, and in spite of her father's expert care, the grave conquered souls. With death came the certainty that life would always be a mere breath of hopeful continuance. A hope that would be snuffed out in the end.

Turning away from her dismal thoughts, Ivy released a sigh of relief when the warbling of the congregation stopped and the reverend prayed the benediction. Her father preceded her in front of their pew and nodded at a few fellow churchgoers. Ivy met Joel in the aisle as they exited, the echo of their footsteps muffled by the green velvet carpet beneath their feet.

"I expect you'll be at home this afternoon?" Joel spoke with congeniality, but Ivy knew his question was laced with more than one meaning.

"My father prefers to take his afternoon naps in solitude." She avoided a direct answer and slipped her purse over her wrist, its gold cord wrapping around her white glove.

Joel nodded to a few community members, but commented out of the side of his mouth, "Perhaps a nap would suit you as well, considering your need to continue recovering from your attack."

"So true." Ivy smirked. "Were I a broken porcelain doll freshly glued back together."

They reached the reverend. He shook hands heartily with Ivy's father, who gave her a backward glance as he exited the church. Joel greeted the man of God with polite respect and a murmured, "Wonderful message." Ivy rested her gloved hand in the minister's briefly and dipped in a slight curtsy. She had no words of acknowledgment for him. She'd not been moved by his message at all, and her conscience pricked with guilt.

The cool air of the spring morning blew against her face. Ivy adjusted the pin in her hat, ensuring it wouldn't blow off in the March gusts, and wrapped her scarf around her neck.

"Ivy."

Oh goodness. Joel again.

"May I come calling this afternoon?"

"Calling?" Ivy's eyebrows lifted. Certainly not in a romantic sense? Her increased heartbeat betrayed her façade of indifference.

"Because you refused me your companionship last night? Beneath your window?"

They both noticed the sharp glance they garnered from a couple passing by. Red crept up his neck, and she was certain her cheeks matched.

Joel gripped her upper arm with a light grasp and leaned in to whisper in her ear, his breath warming her neck. "We've yet to turn up any clues to the baby's whereabouts or to Gabriella's killer, but I need to be certain you bite your tongue regarding the infant. No more inquiring at places like the orphanage or elsewhere. The last thing we need is for rumors to spread that Gabriella's baby is still alive, even if the odds are slight. You might endanger it if Gabriella's killer for some reason has the child. If they believe we are still searching, they could — hasten the baby's death."

Dread crept through Ivy. The kind of dread that paled her face and made her hands clammy inside her gloves. The idea had never crossed her mind — she'd never thought that maybe the person who had snatched Gabriella's life may have taken the baby. She jerked her arm away from Joel, averting her eyes.

"Ivy? What did you do?" Joel read the question on her mind. What *had* she done indeed!

Ivy lifted her chin, and felt it quiver with shame. "I was only inquiring in case there was something someone knew and they simply weren't speaking up. You know the newspaper is often privy to anonymous tips. I thought perhaps someone had found a baby, or had a clue, or —"

"You spoke to the *Herald* about the baby?" Joel's shoulders stiffened. A hint of disbelief tilted his mouth. "Have you considered the ramifications of that getting publicized? Did it not cross your mind there was a reason Sheriff Dunst and I had not taken the same question to the paper?"

Of course she had. The ramifications of it *not* being published could also cost the baby its life. It was a gamble either way. She caught the fury in Joel's eyes. It hadn't been her gamble to take.

"You must put some faith in Sheriff Dunst and myself! We are not inept." Joel snapped his mouth shut as a parishioner stopped to shake his hand. Ivy waited. Joel lowered his voice again after the man moved on. "Perhaps you should also consider, Ivy, that if you insist that baby is alive — who the sheriff and I are allowing the public to think is deceased — you will be branded as some superstitious spinster who thinks herself in touch with the dead."

"How is my reputation more important than the life of an infant?" Ivy really wasn't trying to challenge his reasoning so much as justify the urgency behind her actions. The nightmarish thoughts of Gabriella's missing baby consumed her, along with the ache that Gabriella had yet to be identified.

Joel waited as the reverend walked past with another couple. He watched them head off toward their carriage before turning his attention back to Ivy. His eyes snapped with fervor.

"You are linking yourself to Gabriella and her baby, and now, even more publicly. Whoever murdered the girl may have her baby and might be the man who already attacked you once and tried to a second time. He *will* come for you if he thinks you know who he is."

Ivy said nothing. Words escaped her along with her breath. The truth behind Joel's words sank deeper than anything he had said to this point. Her actions were potentially endangering the very child she was trying to rescue, and most assuredly putting herself directly in the eye of the killer himself.

"So, will you listen to me? Please?" Joel pleaded.

Ivy could only nod. Though she hadn't trusted Joel for twelve long years, it appeared she might have to begin again.

CHAPTER 22

KAINE

Their little work crew of four gathered to help Kaine on this sunny Saturday afternoon. Joy and Megan were downstairs stirring up some refreshments Joy had hauled in her car while Grant and Kaine were beginning demolition — of sorts. Kaine dug her crowbar into the floor to pry up a board.

She paused and stole a glance at Grant, who had already pried up three floorboards to her one. He caught her staring and offered her his signature crooked smile. "What's up?"

Kaine glanced back at the floor and winced. "I was just thinking, what if we find a body buried here? Under the floor."

Grant's chuckle filled the room. "Well, it'd be bones by now, if that happened."

"Let's hope," she said, prying up the board with her crowbar. "But I can't help but relate to Ivy — to Gabriella. I have this gut feeling there's way more to their story, and now here I am in a similar situation. I can't even be in my own home alone for fear I'll be attacked." The floorboard popped up with a loud *snap*. Kaine threw the board onto their newly started pile and turned to Grant. "I'm glad you're here, but . . . you can't always be with me."

"Here we are!" Joy's singsongy voice interrupted them. She lofted a tray of lemonade, her specialty. Hand-squeezed lemon and orange juice mixed with water and lots of sugar.

Kaine lowered her crowbar. Megan followed her mother in, her smile mimicking Joy's. Joy poured the drink and handed Kaine a cup. She took a long gulp.

"Wow." Kaine licked her lips after tasting the lemonade. "This is amazing." She drained the last of her lemonade, her mouth delighting in the mixture of citrus and sugar. Sweetness. She needed that in her life to overcome the sour.

"My grandmother's recipe." Joy tweaked Megan's nose, and the girl laughed. She ducked from her mother's affectionate play. "She taught it to me when I was little. I used to squeeze the oranges while she mangled the lemons into something sweet."

"More, Kaine?" Megan raised the pitcher

with a worshipful expression on her face.

"Absolutely, sweets." Kaine held out her red plastic cup.

Joy perched in a pink camouflage camp chair she'd brought with her. Her version of help was food, drinks, and chatter.

"Joy, did your grandmother grow up in Oakwood?" Kaine took a sip. She tossed Grant a quick look over the rim of her cup. Grant narrowed his eyes.

Joy blinked and her ruby earrings bobbed in a haphazard dance as she shook her head. "Her later years, yes. She was born in Canada actually, but other than that, she never talked much about her childhood."

"Did she know my great-great-grandmother?" Kaine sank into another camp chair, this one with the Green Bay Packers logo printed on its back.

Joy's laugh filled the room. "Oh, buttercup, you age me. My grandmother knowing your great-great-grandmother makes me realize just how old I am."

Megan patted her mother's hand as if Joy was experiencing authentic distress.

"Oh, honey, I'm teasing." Joy squeezed her daughter's hand. She turned back to Kaine. "My grandmother *did* know Ivy. She thought highly of her too, and Ivy's family."

Kaine set her cup on the floor. "Did she

share any memories of Ivy? Her family? Babies?"

"Babies?" Joy wrinkled her nose. "Funny you should ask. That's one thing my grandmother always brought up. How Ivy wasn't much for children or babies. She was very independent and private, and while she was kind toward children, she didn't gravitate to them like most women do. But she did have her own. Daughters, I believe."

"Daughters? One of them must have been my grandpa's mom, then."

"I thought there were three girls, but I don't recall exactly." Joy crossed her leg over her knee and bounced it up and down. "I suppose I could have my facts mixed up. It was my grandmother who made sure Ivy had a memorial in the museum. Along with Ivy's journal and the memory quilt that disappeared way back when."

Kaine shot Grant a look. She gave her head a little shake. She'd prefer he not reveal she had Ivy's quilt in her possession. She wasn't ready to try to explain how it ended up back in her family.

"Memory quilt?" Kaine evaded any explanation. She noticed Grant take a drink from his cup. Good. He wasn't going to say anything.

"Yep. She made a quilt with patches from

the clothes of her dead brother." Joy reached over and pulled Megan's camp chair closer to her.

"Her dead brother?"

"I think she said his name was . . . Adam? Andrew? Grandma said Ivy was an odd duck. She kept to herself most of the time. The town always figured that when her brother died, it traumatized Ivy."

"If your grandmother thought Ivy was so peculiar, why did she want to have her memory quilt and a story with such limited information kept at the museum?"

Joy shrugged, and her earrings dangled and caught the sunlight. "I always wondered that myself. Frankly, I have no idea."

Kaine caught Grant looking at her. He had been protective since the other night when she'd knocked on his door. She wasn't used to it. The way he took off work to help her, then went with her to the museum, and texted her at night to be sure she was all right. A part of her was thankful for his self-appointed guardianship, especially since they hadn't known each other that long. Another part of her worried she was just a psychological challenge to him. A case of grief with lots of baggage, which he wanted a shot at cracking.

Danny had been protective, but in a mild

way, not like the intense dedication that oozed from Grant. Danny was more longing, as if he would protect her but knew that, in reality, she was stronger than he was. It had worked — their marriage — but Kaine had found security in the fact Danny didn't probe into who she really was or into her memories. One look into Grant's eyes and she knew he was born to analyze, question, and diagnose. That was both comforting and disconcerting.

Her cellphone rang. Kaine reached into her pocket and pulled out the phone. She eyed it warily. It was a California number. Not Leah's or one of her long-ostracized friends or co-workers, but at least it was a number and not *Caller ID Unknown.* She tapped the green button on the screen.

"Kaine Prescott?"

It was a female voice. "Yes?"

"Sorry to call you on a Saturday, but this is Detective Tamara Hanson. I believe your sister spoke to you already?"

"Oh!" Kaine jumped to her feet and threw Grant a look to assure him everything was okay. Finally! She'd wanted a new phone since the suspicious call, but hadn't wanted to miss Detective Hanson's call. She hurried from the room and into the hallway. "Yes, Leah did. Thank you for looking into my husband's case again."

"I had questions about how thoroughly the case was investigated after your testimony."

Kaine wasn't sure what to say.

"Anyway," Detective Hanson continued, "I'd prefer to interview you here at the precinct. But since you're in Wisconsin, I'd rather not wait for you to fly back."

"Fly back?" Kaine leaned against the wall and looked up to meet the beady gaze of the woman in the ancient portrait hanging in the hallway.

"We may ask you to return if this case turns into something other than what was concluded. Not to mention your sister stated you suspect the perpetrator may have followed you there? I'd prefer to have you back in San Diego so we can offer protection. You're completely out of my jurisdiction right now."

Kaine pressed her fingers to the bridge of her nose. "I did receive a threatening call."

"You did?"

"Yes. I-I filed a report here with the local police department."

"And?"

"Well, they're looking into it, I guess. There wasn't much to go on, of course. The number was blocked."

"Good to know. I'll touch base with the precinct there and get a copy of the report," Detective Hanson assured her. There was no implication in her tone that she thought Kaine was crazy. "Miss Prescott?" The detective's voice broke through her musing.

"Yeah?"

"Do you have any idea who you believe may have killed your husband?" The detective's straightforward question caught her off guard.

"Of course not. If I did, I would have said so two years ago."

"I figured as much. Did Danny have any enemies?"

Kaine gave a wry laugh. "On World of Warcraft, sure. But in real life? He was . . . good." Her eyes burned. Too good.

"Do you have any enemies? I see you were a social worker?"

"Yes. I suppose I could have enemies. I mean, I helped a lot of women escape their abusers, even a few from sex trafficking. I suppose there could be a whole list of enemies." Kaine swallowed hard.

"Sure, sure. I see." Something clicked in the background, as if the detective was typing on a keyboard. "Okay. So the intrusions into your home. You stopped filing reports.

Didn't we have you install an alarm system?"

"No. I was told there wasn't any credible evidence of a break-in. No broken locks, windows, jimmied doors. A few times of my filing reports and their dispatching someone to check it out — they gave me a pretty strict warning to knock it off unless I had proof." Apparently, daffodils weren't considered threatening. "I did install my own alarm system, though."

"Was it ever triggered?"

"Once." And the police still found nothing. Everything in her had wanted to move in with Leah and her husband. But what if it became worse? More threatening? She couldn't endanger them.

"Had you been officially diagnosed with any type of anxiety disorder or depression?"

Kaine held back a growl. This wasn't the kind of help she was hoping for when it came to solving Danny's murder and arresting her stalker. Flying home was becoming less and less appealing. She would be returning to more questions about her own mental state. "It was insinuated that I should be seen."

"And did you ever visit a psychologist?"

Did Detective Hanson have a checklist? "I saw a counselor. I was not diagnosed with

PTSD." Depression, yes, but admitting that wasn't going to help her cause.

Grant peeked around the corner. *You okay?* he mouthed.

Kaine nodded. For now.

"All right." Detective Hanson's voice sounded like she was biting back a sigh. "It's been two years since your husband's death, but I want to revisit just a few facts."

Kaine gripped the phone tighter.

"You said your husband never took drugs of any kind?"

"That's right." Kaine squeezed her eyes shut. She'd been through this so many times.

"And yet drugs were found in his system."

Kaine was silent. She couldn't deny that, but then that had been her biggest argument for his murder. Danny would have never, *never* taken narcotics of any kind.

"So your statement said that you never knew Danny to use, and you were certain it had to have been slipped to him before he got in his vehicle to drive, therefore causing the accident?"

"Yes." Kaine had no proof. She never would.

"I went through the evidence. There was a disposable coffee cup found in the car."

Kaine smiled, tears filling her eyes. Yes.

The Bean and Brew. Danny loved that place.

"I pulled the cup and had it tested. It came back positive for drug residue. It's possible Danny's coffee was spiked with a narcotic. But in black coffee, it would be difficult for him to have known."

Detective Hanson's statement was a sucker punch to Kaine's stomach. "What would it have done to him?"

"Nausea, dizziness, poor coordination, even amnesia in some surviving cases." The list went on like a pharmaceutical warning label. "I have to apologize. It was sloppy that it was written off as drug use by the detective assigned to the case. It's obvious your husband wasn't using narcotics, and . . . well." Detective Hanson left it there, and Kaine understood the reason why. She probably couldn't say much about the detective who'd handled Danny's "accident." Unfortunately, Kaine could almost read between the lines. It was likely narcotics that had affected that detective as well, hindering his judgment and ultimately costing him his job.

A wave of realization surged through her. Someone believed her!

"I told them Danny was murdered." Kaine sagged against the wall, her shoulder brushing the vintage frame. She caught the dead stare of the Victorian-era woman and saw sadness in her eyes. As if somehow she could relate to tragedy caused by the hand of man. Unnatural and premature. "Why didn't anyone listen to me?"

Silence for a moment, followed by the clearing of a throat. "I'll be honest, Miss Prescott," Detective Hanson began. "The detective assigned to your husband's accident two years ago is no longer with the force. He ran into some . . . trouble. Lost his badge a few weeks ago. And I was assigned to look over a few of his past cases that had lingering question marks as to how thoroughly they were processed."

Kaine couldn't utter a response. Anger and anxiety warred within her, wanting to lash out at the department's inept ability to manage their investigations, and anxiety that two years was too long to go back and resolve Danny's death.

Detective Hanson was still talking.

". . . so I also need to check into the reports you filed. Do you still have your condo here in San Diego? Is there a possibility you'd give me access so I can try to gather forensic evidence, like fingerprints?"

Two months too late. "No. I don't own it anymore."

"Oh. And I see here that you've already

filed a similar report with the Oakwood police? Not in regard to the call you already mentioned but a break-in?"

Kaine closed her eyes. "I have."

"Did they find anything?"

"No." She wondered if her grimace could travel through the phone to San Diego.

"Okay." Kaine could imagine the detective's exasperation. Having to reopen the case already ruled an accident, then finding enough evidence to suggest murder, and at the end of it all a widow whose claims of being followed were substantiated by zero leads. "Well, I'll still be in touch with them. Maybe we can piece this whole thing together."

"That — would be great." Understatement of the year. "Thank you. For everything." And she meant it. Detective Hanson had risen to heroine status in Kaine's eyes. Validation. Someone who believed her.

"Thanks for your time, Miss Prescott. I'll do what I can."

Kaine ended the call and faced the dusty, moth-damaged painting. Grant said that Patti, the librarian, had found the portrait of Myrtle Foster, the original owner of the house, in the basement of the museum and insisted it be hung in the house. A few old photographs of Foster Hill House had shown them it originally hung in the hall-way. Patti's obsession with positioning it in an abandoned house had seemed odd to Grant, he'd said, but then she'd been transfixed by this place for years.

Kaine studied the portrait. The eyes of the woman came more alive the longer she stared. Was it possible that her expression mimicked the wasteland left behind in Kaine's soul? That burned-up blackness shadowed by the knowledge that the worst of the battle was still to come? She shook her head free of the hypnotic hold of the woman who couldn't have been much more than five or ten years her senior when it was painted. It was silly to believe, yet Kaine couldn't help it. This woman, whoever she was, knew what encompassed that awful stillness that fooled its victim into thinking peace had arrived, only to be stabbed by the wickedness lurking in the shadows.

Kaine's gaze traveled down the long hall toward the attic stairs and then in the other direction toward the stairwell that took its traveler downward into the daylight of the foyer.

Foster Hill House was already written in history as the place where two women had found mercy to be far from reach. One survived, one didn't. Kaine reached up and wiped her hand across the woman's face. It was like the soul of the house itself stared back, a soul imprisoned in these walls, hating the misery of it.

"Did this place bury you too?" And her unspoken question was even louder. *Will I be next?*

Chapter 23

Ivy

Ivy's steps through the graveyard were muted by wet leaves and grass now exposed to the air with the final melt of snow. The hem of her skirt where it dragged along the earth was soiled, and she'd long since given up trying to keep it clean. The warm air made her glad she'd traded her coat for a shawl. Many of the gravestones around her were familiar. She saw the names, recalled many of their faces, and treasured their stories. If no one else remembered them, she would, as would her children, and grandchildren, and great-grandchildren, and anyone else who would read her journal in years to come. Like the Thorpe family Bible, labeled with the names of generations, her journal recorded the memories of those who could no longer speak. Eternity had embraced them, leaving behind the chasm they once filled.

Eternity. Ivy hated the word.

She paused in front of Gabriella's grave, the ground mounded with dirt void of grass and life. A wooden cross marked it. No name. Just *Unknown.* But it was the two markers at the far corner of the yard that captured her attention. One, her mother's. Esther Mathilda Englewood-Thorpe was a memory inspired only by what her father told her. The stories of a mother who'd given her life to bring Ivy into the world. It was the stone next to her mother's that garnered Ivy's affection.

It had been too long since she'd visited her brother, but he was never far from her thoughts. Ivy came here every year, always one week after he died. The day of the second darkest moment in her life.

Andrew Matthew Thorpe
B. August 4, 1879–D. March 29, 1894
Always Remembered

Ivy unpinned her hat and set it on a wooden bench. She had used her own money to have the bench built and placed beside Andrew's grave. Some days she simply needed to sit and be near him. She liked to talk with Andrew as she always had and hoped he heard her — because it didn't seem that the Lord did. His ears had closed the day Andrew died.

She sank onto the bench beside her hat. A squirrel scampered a few yards away and cocked its head to study her. She stared back into the beady black eyes. What did the rodent see that Ivy couldn't? At night, when everyone was asleep. Did it witness Gabriella's death? Or was it as indifferent as God himself? The creature scurried away, chirruping a warning to other squirrels that there was an intruder in the cemetery.

Disenchanted by her thoughts, Ivy pulled her gloves from her hands and closed her eyes. She took a deep breath and memorized the scent of the musty woods, wet with the aged earth and fresh with the new growth on the trees.

"Your father told me I could find you here."

Ivy stiffened. She bit the inside of her bottom lip and fixed her eyes on Andrew's name etched in the gray granite. Joel lowered himself onto the bench beside her, his hat in his hands. His shirt was open at the collar, void of a necktie, its white crispness fresh and starched.

"You're late," she breathed.

Joel's head dipped, and he played with the brim of his black hat. He nodded without comment.

"One week and twelve years late," Ivy recited. "For reasons unknown."

"You never gave me an opportunity to explain." Joel's statement poked at Ivy.

"I know," Ivy whispered, a lump forming in her throat. She hadn't. She should have. She should have asked much sooner too, as soon as they'd had a moment to discuss more than just Gabriella and her missing child.

"Will you let me explain, Ivy?"

She refused to look at the man beside her who, in her eyes, was still so much the young man from years before.

"You made a promise, and you didn't fulfill it."

Joel nodded, his shoulders sagging with . . . regret? Hurt? Ivy couldn't tell.

"I was as much affected by that day — that missed graveyard visit — as you, Ivy. There were circumstances I had no control over."

"I came here all alone." The grief was as raw as that night, ripping at her soul, still hiding deep within. "You said you would meet me. That we would lay Andrew to rest together, the way it should have been. Not the showy funeral my father allowed the church to give him. Not the stares of the onlookers who made me feel like it was our fault Andrew died. We were going to tell him goodbye together." Ivy faced him, the way she'd wished she could have so many times before. "So I knelt in the mud and the cold and I waited. All night I waited. And in the morning, when I went to find you at the home, Mr. Casey said you were leaving on the morning train, that you were leaving on a grand adventure. It was as if you'd already forgotten Andrew."

"Forgotten him?" The pain in Joel's voice brought a twinge of guilt to Ivy. "Never."

Ivy moved from the bench and bent by Andrew's stone. She reached out and traced his name with her hand, the purple silk of her sleeve stark against the cold, gray stone. Green lichen was growing in the carved letters, melted ice formed tiny pools on the base, and last year's dead flowers were squashed into the ground. "Then it wasn't a grand adventure?"

Joel shook his head. "I spent three of those years begging for work, until I landed myself in jail after stealing one too many times. I was a bona fide street rat. If it weren't for the attention of a God-fearing police captain who whipped me into shape with some hard work and dragged me to church on Sundays, I'd probably be wearing metal bracelets about now." Joel leaned back against the bench. "If I learned anything in my 'grand adventure,' it was that without those you care about to urge you on in your life and in your faith, you shrivel into yourself."

Ivy raised her eyes to him. "And without those you care about in your life, you become alone." She was talking about herself now. Vulnerable. Admitting what Joel's absence had done to her, good reason for leaving or not. "I am alone."

"No." Joel squatted beside her. More explanation could come later, but for now, his fingers brushed hers. When she didn't pull away, he gripped her hand. "You're not alone," he whispered. "I came home."

CHAPTER 24

KAINE

Kaine wedged the crowbar beneath another floorboard and pulled with the collective force of her anger, her disappointment, and her guilt. Joy and Megan had left shortly after Detective Hanson's call, giving her looks of concern as Kaine fell into uncharacteristic silence. Grant lagged behind, but Kaine wasn't even sure where to begin to explain the call stating her husband's case had been categorized as sloppy police work. Part of her wanted to be grateful it was finally reopened, and another part, the one Kaine was warring with the most, wanted to send the crowbar flying through the window with a scream of pent-up emotion. After a few tense moments watching Kaine rip away at the floor, Grant excused himself to take Olive outside for a walk in the dusk. It was obvious he had no intention of leaving her alone in Foster Hill House. He would either see her back to her motel or she'd crash on his couch again.

To be honest, Kaine preferred that, yet sleeping on Grant's couch was asking for more trouble. Once her anger wore off, she knew herself well enough to know she'd be a puddled mess, and when Kaine was like that, she craved affection. That need had landed her in heaps of trouble before. Before Danny and before she'd had the sense to stand on her own two feet.

While working to remove a stubborn plank, the lightbulbs of the nearby floor lamp flickered. No doubt the house was poorly wired, yet another thing that needed updating. Kaine didn't even like the lamp, but it'd been cheap at Walmart and served the purpose — along with the construction-grade work light Grant had bought and plugged in. She was alone for a much-needed moment and there was nothing else to do but take out her frustration over Danny's case on the floor. Ripping up the floorboards was as effective at preserving Foster Hill House as Detective Hanson's questions were at solving Danny's death. Everything in Kaine's life was like a Band-Aid. It covered the wounds and their bleeding but did little to heal them. Not even the old wounds no one knew about.

The board released from the floor with a *snap* and a spray of dirt up her nose. Kaine buried her face in her elbow and sneezed.

"Drat." She dropped the crowbar to the floor and marched over to the box of face masks. Ripping it open, she tugged a white mask from inside. It tore from the force of her pull. "Drat!" Kaine threw it aside and yanked on another one. This time the rubber band for securing it around the wearer's head snapped from the side of the mask. "Are you kidding me?" she growled at the empty room. Kaine sent the second face mask to join the other on the floor.

This had to end. It all just needed to be over. As much as she hated the fact that Danny's death had been ruled an accident, she despised the idea of revisiting it over and over again if nothing was going to be resolved. But, until his killer was brought to justice, she'd need a bodyguard just to maintain her sanity. In the meantime, here she was ripping up floorboards in a house that had almost killed her great-great-grandmother and held dirty little secrets that seemed to want to be revived right alongside Danny's case file.

Kaine maneuvered a third mask from the box. This one was defective, and the hole in the front of it served as Kaine's undoing.

She crumpled to the floor, releasing a string of curses that made her cast a nervous glance toward the bedroom door for fear Grant had come up the stairs and witnessed her backslidden soul's darkness. Kaine pulled her knees up to her chin and buried her face in them.

She wouldn't cry. Not over stupid face masks. Not over a house so in ruins it was foolish for her to waste time ripping up this floor. Not over a case gone cold, or a man who toyed with her mind like a puppet master pulled strings. Tears were for those who couldn't handle tough times. She was a fighter. She could do this. She could *do* this!

"Why?" Kaine lifted her face to the ceiling as if her eyes could penetrate the cracked plaster and see into heaven. "Seriously?"

Through everything, she had been faithful. She had copied Job and not cursed God. Cursed, yes, but God? No. Sure, she hadn't buried herself in prayer or in Scripture, but she'd remained steadfast and pushed forward. Wasn't that why she'd come to Oakwood — to return to her family's roots, to honor her dead husband, to find hope to live again? So why would God thwart that now? There had to be some reward for her faithfulness.

Kaine kicked the box of masks with her foot.

Nothing.

No answer.

The heavens were silent.

Like always.

Forget it. Kaine scrambled to her feet. No mask then. She would breathe in the mold, the asbestos, and the hundred years' worth of dirt embedded in that floor. At worst, she would contract sarcoidosis and die from it. At least then God would have to answer her, because she would be face-to-face with Him.

Kaine snatched the crowbar from the floor, hooked it on the next floorboard, and tugged. A small chunk gave way. She snarled, leveled the bar at the floor, and lunged with a primal yell. Grant would probably come running now. Too bad she wasn't here at Foster Hill House alone and Danny's killer had come to confront her. She had a crowbar and was in the mood to use it on his face.

Two of the planks caved in as if made of styrofoam instead of wood. Another swipe with the crowbar demolished more. Surprised at how easily they cracked and the hollow beneath, Kaine took another hooking throw. The floor now had a hole the size of a small lockbox. The cavity she'd opened gaped at her with a century's worth of dust inside. She let the crowbar hang at her side, breathing heavily from the three angry swipes at the floor. She blinked, wiping dust from her eyes and second-guessing her suicidal mission to contract sarcoidosis.

Tossing the crowbar to the floor, Kaine slid the work light over so it could light up the gap. The floor's framing bordered the sides of the cavity. These floorboards had cracked so easily in comparison to the others she'd pried up earlier. Kaine reached down and pulled back the remnants of the boards that were still attached. She crouched to get a better look.

A bundle lay between the joists, wrapped in aged cotton material that was eaten away by bugs and time. Frowning, she reached in and carefully lifted it, hoping it wouldn't disintegrate from her touch. It didn't. The calico cloth was faded and worn, but dry. Her frustration ebbed away as she peeled back the layers of material.

Her eyes widened.

"No way."

Kaine ran her hand gently over the printed text on the sheaf of loose pages in her lap. The pages had been torn from their original binding and stacked. At the top of the musty typescript was the title *Great Expectations,* and in the margins, a woman's intricate penmanship. Her fingers tingled with the knowledge she was holding a page that matched the one she'd found in the library downstairs. She'd discovered more notes from the nameless, haunted soul.

Kaine focused on the top header of one of the pages: *Save me, oh God. Deliver me.*

These had to be the writings of Gabriella. They *had* to be!

The handwriting offered a familiar sentiment, echoing with her soul. She traced the letters with her index finger, her heart reaching through time and linking desperate hands with the writer.

I will not survive.

CHAPTER 25

IVY

Ivy slogged through the mud. Her visit with Maggie at the widow's house had been pleasant, and her conscience eased a bit from using the poor girl the other day on her jaunt to the orphanage. Maggie was still timid, but she seemed at home in her great-aunt's house, and Ivy was pleased she'd coaxed a smile from her more than once. Now, Ivy hurried across the road from the mercantile, dodging a wagon. She hopped onto the boardwalk, a slop of mud falling off her shoe. Ivy started at a black gloved hand that wrapped around her wrist. Foggerty stared at her through black eyes. His slouched hat covered his forehead and brushed his bushy eyebrows. He squeezed Ivy's arm.

"Time you leave the dead to rest, wouldn't you say?"

"Pardon me?" Ivy tugged her arm away.

The odd looks, the sidestepping, Ivy knew that Joel had been right. Since the paper published her claims that Gabriella's baby could still be alive, the entire town viewed her with even deeper curiosity than before. It didn't help that the paper insinuated she talked to the dead.

Mr. Foggerty's bony shoulders raised in a shrug. Ivy backed away a step. The old trapper unnerved her with his sharp gaze.

"A passin' fancy is one thing, but this witchery of claiming you see a dead child? Did ya see it in the afterlife?" He appeared far too curious, as if ghosts and spirits intrigued rather than frightened him.

"No!" Ivy adjusted her grip on her purse and eyed the man with suspicion. "I never claimed to see the baby." She stiffened. The rumors were becoming exaggerated. "I only —"

"The town knows all about your death journal. But your toyin' with the souls of the dead?"

"How do you know the baby is dead?" Ivy demanded. Either Mr. Foggerty was a nosy and bored old man or he knew more than he was saying.

He stared at her. "Stands to reason, don't it?"

Ivy spun on her heel and crossed the street

to the boardwalk on the opposite side. She glanced over her shoulder, but Mr. Foggerty was rambling down the road, muttering to himself. The man's assumption that the baby was dead only increased Ivy's determination. While she wasn't foolish enough to place herself in harm's way again, she would make sure the sheriff and Joel were held accountable — to find justice for Gabriella and to rescue her infant.

Ivy redirected her path toward the jailhouse. Didn't they at least owe her the courtesy of an update on the search? No. Ivy knew Joel believed they owed her nothing.

Ivy approached the jail, normally empty save for a drunk or two. She was reaching for the door when she heard voices filtering through the partially open window next to it.

". . . I want to kill him."

Joel's hard voice stunned Ivy. She peeked through the window, careful not to let the men see her. Joel was slouched in a chair, elbows on his knees, his fingers steepled under his chin.

"Settle down, Cunningham." The sheriff sat opposite him, behind his desk. "We don't need you personalizing this and becoming irrational."

"I don't like the fact Ivy was attacked at Foster Hill House, and then he followed her again at the orphanage. He's obviously made a connection that she recognizes him, or he's toying with her for some sadistic reason — maybe the same as why he killed Gabriella? And this baby has Ivy all out of sorts."

Sheriff Dunst shrugged. "It has me out of sorts too. There's been nothing to go on. If you hadn't found that cradle at the house, I'd say the baby wasn't a part of the equation and it was left wherever that girl came from. But the cradle with its obvious recent use definitely moves me."

Ivy watched Sheriff Dunst shove back in his chair, the legs scraping against the wood floor. "Talk. I need coffee." He stood and crossed the room to the potbelly stove and lifted the coffeepot. "Want any?"

Joel nodded. Ivy swallowed. She could use some as well, but she wasn't ready to interrupt the conversation, however awful it was that she was eavesdropping. Joel hadn't been forthcoming with her, and she wanted to know where the investigation was leading them.

Raking his fingers through his hair, Joel propped his hands behind his head. "The girl was killed and her body hidden at the base of Foster Hill House. Ivy was attacked inside. She claims to have seen a book with scribblings in it she attributes to Gabriella."

"Claims." Sheriff Dunst sipped his coffee, but his words didn't imply Ivy was crazy like the rest of the townspeople seemed to believe. She could tell he was challenging fact versus theory and respected him for it.

"The orphanage has no record of any young woman in her late teens who fits Gabriella's description, nor have they had any girl go missing. And, as you know, Ivy only reconfirmed what Mr. Casey told me, and that is that there has been no infant left there unaccounted for who could be related to our victim." Joel dropped his arms, agitated. Ivy could tell by his expression that whatever trip he'd taken to the orphanage to inquire about the case had been unsettling for him. His memories there took up a good portion of his childhood. Unpleasant memories.

The sheriff settled back in his chair after handing Joel his coffee. "There are really no solid clues to close this case. I was hoping you would find some for me, since I've not had a lick of help from anyone. No witnesses, nothing. It would have been nice to start your investigative services here in Oakwood with something that wasn't going to become an unsolved murder."

Joel frowned. "I wasn't looking for a boost in my career. But offering my services to the county seemed a way to earn a living. I was tired of Chicago."

Sheriff Dunst rested his coffee cup on his desk. "I understand that, and while I hate to admit failure, for either one of us, we're grasping at straws trying to figure this out."

"So you're calling it quits." Joel ignored the coffee cup in his hand, his statement rhetorical and chilling. Ivy lifted her hand to open the door with a flurry of protest, but the sheriff's response stopped her.

"Don't accuse me of that. I've had men canvassing the town and woods for anyone suspicious. I have ears in the saloons that will let me know if anyone dares to brag about the murder. I have a town to protect. A town that is unsettled, especially with Miss Thorpe's newspaper announcement of the missing baby. Half my time is spent assuaging them that we have this thing all under control."

Joel set his cup on the desk. "The murder was personal. The attack on Ivy was vicious. And there's no doubt the evidence points to someone being *in* that house for some time." Joel stood. Ivy backed away from the window for fear he'd turn and see her.

"What about the piano?"

"What about it?"

"There have been rumors for years that piano music has been heard coming from inside of Foster Hill House. The fact the piano was untouched by time suggests occupancy. I remember Andrew Thorpe telling me when we were kids that he heard the music himself."

Dunst heaved a sigh and shifted in his chair. "There have been ghost stories circulating about that place for decades, Joel. Piano music. Strange lights in the middle of the night. Some even say they've spied a ghost. Certainly you're not telling me that's all evidence for this case?"

Joel sank back down onto the chair, taking up his coffee again. "It's possible evidence to support the idea that the house hasn't been as deserted as we thought. Perhaps our victim stumbled there for sanctuary and disturbed whoever has been staying there."

Ivy peeked back in the window. Joel's back was to her.

"I find it difficult to believe someone has been living there for over a decade and passing themselves off as a ghost. They would need food, supplies. Someone would have seen them coming and going." Sheriff

Dunst gulped the last of his coffee, then slammed the cup down on the desktop.

"I understand it's farfetched." Joel gave the sheriff a nod of affirmation. "Who were the last people to live at Foster Hill House?"

"From what I'm aware, the Fosters themselves were the last people to live there. They were run out over forty years ago as Confederate sympathizers. I was just a toddler then. Ever since I can remember, it's been abandoned. The Fosters had two children, but they've never returned to Oakwood."

"The fact is," Joel said, "there are signs someone has been inhabiting the house for far longer than the last two weeks. If Gabriella had stumbled on someone who believed the place to be theirs, she paid with her life — and very possibly her child's too. And now that someone seems to be focusing his attention on Ivy. I don't like it. She needs to be protected."

"I agree. She never should have involved herself — even though her intentions were noble." Dunst rubbed his hands over his eyes.

"It's her good intentions that make me admire her, in spite of her idiosyncrasies. She has an empathetic heart and that's a rare gift." Joel rose to his feet and this time he reached for his hat. "Someone is hiding something — more than Gabriella's murder. If they weren't, they would have fled, not gone after Ivy over by the orphanage. Foster Hill House is holding secrets, and I'm going to find out what they are before they claim Ivy's life."

The pen dripped ink on the page of her journal, like the drop of blood that had dried at the corner of Gabriella's lip. It was a morbid memory. Ivy pulled her quilt closer around her shoulders, treasuring the feel of the cotton squares cut and sewn together from remnants of Andrew's clothes. It was all she had left of him. She dabbed the drip with an ink blotter and tried to redirect her thoughts to imagining what Gabriella had been like alive. She set the cloth aside and lifted her pen once again. The recent pages she had written in her memory book had evolved into a diary of sorts.

Ivy looped her *L* as she penned more thoughts. She could only imagine that Gabriella had felt abandoned by everyone, even God, in the end. Sometimes she grieved her own loss of faith almost as much as she did Andrew's death or Joel's abandonment. Maybe that was one reason why she could not release Gabriella to the grave.

They shared the commonality that God was indifferent to their pain.

She spun on the organ stool that served as her chair when a stone plunked against her window. Joel. Not again. She padded over to the window and moved the curtain aside just a bit to peek out. His frame was recognizable and distinct. Ivy let the curtain fall back into place and leaned her temple against the wall. Tonight she was vulnerable, and seeing Joel would only revive that longing for oneness of soul with another person . . . and with God. For the past twelve solitary years, her own mind had been her solace, and she had been content.

Joel had created the wound she bore the day he left her alone at Andrew's grave. He had reopened the wound the day he returned to Oakwood.

Ivy shoved her feet into slippers and shrugged on a coat over her nightgown. She tied the emerald green ribbon at the collar as another stone pinged against the glass. Opening her bedroom door, she glanced at her father's. It was closed. The darkness between the bottom of the door and the floor told her he'd retired for the night. She hurried down the familiar narrow stairway and crossed the braided rug that lay in the foyer. Ivy summoned her conviction. It was time to put an end to Joel's intrusion into her life.

The night air met her face with a gust of cool March air. Ivy buried her hands in her dressing coat pockets. The moon was hidden by the earth's rotation, yet an early sign of spring chirruped from the bushes as crickets awoke to the night. Ivy stalked around the corner of the house. Joel would be below her window with another pebble in his palm. She could easily imagine his chiseled face. The unwelcome yearning for the friendship they'd once shared was persistent.

A hand touched her arm. Regardless of the fact she'd expected to see Joel, the touch in the darkness startled her and Ivy screamed. Her scream was muffled as a hand clapped over her mouth to stifle it. She bit down as hard as she could into the soft part of the man's palm. The muffled cry of pain was followed by Joel's irritated hiss.

"Ivy! Have you lost control of your senses?" Joel shook the hand she'd bitten as an instinctive reaction. As he stepped closer to her, the light from her bedroom lamp filtered down onto his face.

"I panicked," Ivy countered, knowing how ridiculously she'd overreacted.

"I saw your curtain move. You knew it was me." Joel held his palm in front of him. "I think I need stitches."

"Balderdash," she muttered.

Joel shot her a surprised look mixed with irritation.

Ivy yanked his hand toward her and leaned over it. His skin was warm against hers. She fought against the desire to stroke his palm in apology. "I can't see it well enough. Come into the house." She knew she hadn't bit him hard enough to need stitches, but for some reason she wanted an excuse to be near him even though her original intent had been to send him away.

Once inside, Ivy led him to the left, through the door that connected to her father's office. She struck a match and lifted the mantle on a lamp near the examination table. The wick took and light burst into the room.

"Sit." She motioned to the examination table.

Joel was holding his hand to his chest, fingers curled.

Ivy lit another lamp on her father's desk, wishing absently that one day they would be wealthy enough to install gas lamps. She blew out the match and retrieved gauze and alcohol to cleanse the wound.

"Let me see your hand."

"Give me the gauze. I'll take care of it myself."

"And stitch it on your own too?" Ivy narrowed her eyes. "Don't be a child." She heard the sharpness in her voice and saw a flicker of hurt in Joel's face.

Ivy didn't apologize but took his hand gently this time. It was bleeding just a little where her teeth had broken the surface, but it was nowhere near needing a needle and thread. Shaking her head, she released Joel's hand and prepared the gauze to clean the wound.

Her murmured apology came two seconds before the first press of the alcohol-soaked gauze onto the bite.

Joel scrambled backward on the table. "Ouch, woman!"

"Oh, stop." Ivy tried to hide a smile as she yanked his arm down and continued dabbing the wound. He was quite whiny for such a strong, self-assured detective.

"At least apologize," Joel said through clenched teeth.

"I did."

"Words. Your harsh touch says otherwise."

"I'm being quite gentle. You, on the other hand, have a remarkably low tolerance for pain."

"You *bit* me!" Joel grimaced again as she gave the wound one final and unnecessarily firm blot.

"You startled me. What was I to do after being attacked at Foster Hill House and followed to the orphanage? I've no intentions of joining Gabriella in eternity. At least not this evening." Ivy couldn't help but chuckle. Relief, perhaps. Or maybe nervousness at the way his head bent so close to hers as she cleaned the bite mark she'd left on his hand.

"I was throwing pebbles at your window. You're supposed to *open* the window, not come outside." His pointed look made Ivy avert her eyes.

"So you attack me when I do?" Ivy bit the inside of her cheek. She had the choice to be furious or find the humor in the situation. There had been far too much darkness the past week.

Joel tilted his head, his expression one of exasperation. "I wouldn't exactly call touching your arm an 'attack.' Besides, aren't you a bit concerned about me? What if *you* were a nefarious murderer?"

She struggled to hide her grin. "A nefarious murderer in a nightdress? That should have been your first clue, Detective."

Ivy immediately regretted calling attention to her state of dress. Joel's eyes skimmed her body, from the green cotton dressing coat to the lacy hemline of her nightgown that peeked out beneath.

When he met her eyes, his were stormy. "Perhaps we should begin this conversation again."

"Perhaps you should cease throwing stones at my window as if I were fourteen."

"Perhaps you should open your window rather than wander through the night."

They were at an impasse. Mostly because Ivy was finishing the bandage on Joel's hand, but also because he had the audacity to slide his free hand up her arm to rest on her shoulder. His thumb stroked the base of her neck.

She stilled.

Joel leaned toward her.

Ivy stepped back, breaking the connection.

"Well then." She cleared her throat. "I believe your hand is cared for. You may be on your way, and I must beg of you to refrain from future visits in the night."

"My, so proper," Joel goaded, a teasing smile on his lips.

Ivy's insides turned to butter at his smile. The banter was almost like old times. Goading, teasing, flirtatious. She busied herself putting away the bandages. "Why did you come here, anyway?"

"Would you believe me if I said I missed you?"

Ivy froze as she returned clean gauze to its jar. She bit her bottom lip and closed her eyes. "I would believe you if you hadn't disappeared for twelve years."

Her mumbled words met with silence. She returned the lid to the jar.

"You're never going to forgive me, are you?"

She searched for words, but none came.

"It took me a long time to get over my own guilt of not being able to save Andrew." Joel's admission touched places in Ivy's heart she wished they wouldn't. "Once I left here, coming back felt like going before a judge and a jury all rolled into one. I knew you'd never forgive me."

"How would you have known that?" Ivy whispered, corking the bottle of alcohol.

"Because I know you."

Ivy turned. She searched his face, but it was shielded as he massaged his wrist below the wounded palm. He took a deep breath and then let it out, as if attempting to find the right words but instead, like her, he came up short. He slid off the examination table and leaned against it. They stared at each other, only a few feet between them, but with a history of broken trust separating them.

Joel's brows furrowed. An unspoken plea for her to give him understanding reflected in his eyes. "I was wrong to wait so long to come home," he said, then paused. "I knew you'd be furious. Then I got myself into my own spot of trouble. All that to say, I had some growing up to do. After I did, the years — they melded into each other as I learned my trade in Chicago. But I never forgot, I couldn't forget, and as time went on, I knew I needed to come back to Oakwood. To try to reconcile."

"Reconcile." It was a lot to ask. Perhaps Joel had reasons for being away so long. Immaturity, a penchant for trouble, his career. But with each passing year, the pain had only dulled into a tarnished memory for Ivy, fully awakened now with his presence.

"I need you — your help, Ivy." His tone seemed to release her from anything too personal. Yet Ivy's face warmed and she looked away.

He continued. "We know Gabriella's baby may still be out there, and you're the only one who's seen her killer."

"I hardly saw him — I could never identify him."

"I know. But I still need you to come with me — to Foster Hill House. Tomorrow morning."

My, my. Ivy drew in a shaky breath and blew it out through her lips. What a shift in conversation. From his painful absence to solving a murder. The man gave her conversational and emotional whiplash.

"What would returning to that house even accomplish?" she asked.

She caught a whiff of Joel's cologne as he closed the distance between them. It bothered Ivy that she hadn't the courage to look him in the eye when he took her hands. Their fingertips touched and formed peaks, like mountaintops. Mountains they had yet to climb since they had just found their balance on the tenuous ground of renewed friendship.

"I don't want you hurt, Ivy. I want to keep you safe, whether you believe it or not." Joel's voice lowered, resonating in her ears. "But, if there's a chance taking you back there just once more helps you remember something from the night you were attacked, that you couldn't recall the first time, then I need you."

He needed her. She needed him. She had for years. Ivy lifted her face, and their gazes met.

"Why didn't you at least write to me?" she whispered. Her fingertips tingled but she didn't pull away.

Joel closed the gap between their palms, his bandaged hand scratching against her skin. "I did. I wrote to you not long after I arrived in Chicago."

She shook her head. "I never received a letter."

Joel squeezed her hands. "I explained everything in the letter. Why I left, and why I had to stay away. To forgive myself before I could expect you to forgive me."

"Then the letter was lost. Somehow." Ivy stared at their fingers. "Or you're just saying that you wrote to convince me to help you now." There was instant regret as the words escaped her mouth. Joel's hands stiffened, but this time she sensed the frustration flowing through his grip.

Ivy searched his eyes. There was challenge in them.

"Do you really think I never loved Andrew, or you? That I would just leave here and only return to use you? You never returned correspondence, your father never came to look for me. It was as if, when Andrew died, the Thorpes severed ties with me. As if I were to blame. Coming back here to Oakwood has been one of the hardest things

I've ever done. I came back to say I'm sorry without knowing if you or your father would even listen to me. But I had to come back. To bring closure for myself, if not for you."

She dropped her hands. "How dare you," she whispered.

"I dare," Joel said, and tipped his head to the side, "because when it concerns me, you ignore the need to examine the evidence. Not what you *think* happened, but what *really* happened." He reached for his coat and stuffed his arms into the sleeves. "But then you've had twelve years to concoct a fictionalized version of the truth."

His words stung, like alcohol on an open wound. Joel stalked across the room, then turned on his heel, his face set. Ivy wrapped her arms around herself, bracing against the chill in his gaze.

"I'll be by in the morning. At least I know you care to find the actual truth for Gabriella and her baby. Which is more than I can ever hope for myself."

The door closed behind him, and Ivy was left alone once again. Only this time she knew it was all very much her own fault.

CHAPTER 26

KAINE

Here she was again in Grant Jesse's house. Olive lazed on the floor at the feet of the barstool Kaine was perched on. The night sky was black and moonless, yet Kaine fixated on it for a long moment, the kitchen window opened wide over the sink.

"I just can't believe it." She was still stunned over her discovery beneath the floorboards.

"I never expected to see that myself." Grant lifted dishes from the drying rack beside the sink and stacked them before putting them in the cupboard.

Kaine leaned on the granite top of the kitchen island. She stretched out her bare foot to scratch Sophie's broad pit-bull neck with her toes. Olive, unaffected by the other dog, only groaned in her relaxation. She liked it here. So did Kaine.

The image of the find was burned on

Kaine's mind. "*Great Expectations* pages. Like the one I found in the library downstairs. The scribblings in the margins. Lines so telling it's hard to breathe, as if a woman sat in that room day after day and wrote her thoughts on the only paper she could find. From a book! I just — I just can't get over it."

Grant shut the cupboard door with a smack and turned his back to the counter, bracing his hands against the sink. "Why hide them under the floor?"

Kaine waved her hands. "How would I know? Most women hide their journals, though. I hid my diary under my mattress."

Grant smiled. "That's original," he said wryly.

Kaine gave a sheepish grin in response. "I was only seven."

"Okay. Hold on." Grant pushed off the sink and slid his elbows onto the island, crossing his arms and leaning forward. "So Ivy's locket was upstairs in the attic. You have her quilt that was stolen from the museum back in the sixties. Now some buried treasure of *Great Expectations* turns into an antique, Facebook-style status bar? Could it be from Ivy?"

"I think it was the girl who was murdered at Foster Hill House."

289

The kitchen clock ticked. Olive's tail thudded on the floor once, then stopped. Sophie rounded the island to lick Grant's foot.

Grant frowned. "But how did they survive all this time?"

Kaine had already thought that through. "They were hidden in the floor, which blocked out sunlight and moist air."

"Crazy that no one has discovered them until now."

Kaine nodded, again prepared with another answer. Her brain had been spinning since she'd pulled the pages from beneath the floor. "I know. But those are the original floorboards, which means no one has ever seen the pages except for whoever put them there to begin with."

"That floor's one hundred years old — or more."

"Exactly," Kaine said.

"Still, why hide them? And how did Gabriella, supposing it was her, hide them under those floorboards? It's not like she took a crowbar to them like you did."

Good point. Kaine thought a moment, turning the facts over in her head. The faucet in the sink dripped onto the pan Grant had used to make his boxed macaroni-and-cheese dinner. "Probably one of them had been loose or something. I don't know. Regardless, the entries are distressing. Like whoever wrote them was being held against her will. Maybe she hid them — from him."

"From who?" Grant looked confused, as if in trying to follow Kaine's reasoning he'd been left behind.

"From the killer," Kaine supplied. "If he was threatening her, and she was being held captive, writing down her thoughts may have been her only outlet of relief. A cry for help."

Grant raised a doubtful brow. "That's way out there, Kaine."

Kaine gave a hissing sound through her teeth. "Yeah, well, you should see the stuff I've seen in San Diego. Jerks trying to cover their tracks after beating a woman within an inch of her life. I had one pimp who broke a girl's jaw and then had the audacity to paint the wall when he couldn't wash clean the bloodstains. In front of her. While she cried on the bed."

Kaine seethed with indignation as she said it, recalling the satisfaction she felt when the perp was finally locked up. One man put away and at least three girls freed. She remembered well her passion to find justice for those girls. Danny had called her "the crusader" in the first year of their marriage

— before it took a toll on their relationship. Before it took a toll on their love.

"All right." Grant rubbed his hand behind his neck. Kaine watched it drag down over his collarbone to his shoulder. "Let's assume you're right. What does it really tell us? I mean, we're not trying to solve a hundred-year-old cold case. Or are we?"

Kaine pursed her lips and shrugged, her eyes wide. "You tell me. It's all there. I sort of feel like I owe it to Ivy to finish what she started." Plus, it was another good distraction. From Detective Hanson reopening her case, from the creepy caller Detective Carter was looking into, and from the fact she still couldn't figure out how he'd gotten her anonymous cell number.

Grant searched her face, and Kaine met his eyes. "Why is it so important to you?"

Kaine blinked. "What do you mean?"

"Staying at Foster Hill House. Restoring it. The place isn't worth it, Kaine, and you know it. Now this? What's driving you, really?"

Kaine's insides went numb. She asked herself that question every day. She asked what motivated her when she drove away from Danny to rescue girls, she questioned her own memories buried so deep inside she wasn't sure she'd ever let them out, and she revisited it now as her ancestor's tale of mystery linked hands with her own tribulation.

"Hope," Kaine whispered around the lump in her throat. But then she said it again, louder. "Hope. I need to find the hope to live again. A reason to move on with my life. You didn't read what I read tonight, Grant. In the margins of a Dickens novel. They were pleas to God for escape and prayers of helplessness. And . . ." Kaine looked down at her hands and picked at a fingernail. Then, looking back at Grant, she said, "The girl was being held in that house against her will. The pages make it clear. She was abused. She was hunted. She was everything I've ever fought against, and everything I am now. I need to see this through. For Danny, for Ivy, for the girl Gabriella, and . . . and for me."

It was stupid to have assumed her motel key was lost in the bottom of her purse. More stupid to look for it there after leaving Grant's place and, not finding it, take a quick drive — alone — to Foster Hill House, thinking she may have left the key there.

Horror kept Kaine fixated on the window. Red dripped from the letters like blood from a knife. The wet paint glistened faintly with a tinge of bruised blue. A whippoorwill's mournful call echoed through the woods and matched Kaine's wild rush of alarm.

Danny.

The name of her murdered husband, painted across the front window of Foster Hill House, filled Kaine's vision. She stumbled backward down the stairs. Olive was busy sniffing the ground near the window. The wind picked up the oak leaves in the woods, rustling them like miniature handclaps to mock Kaine's fear.

There was no explaining this away. This was blatant. A message.

Kaine spun around, rushed back to the Jetta, and fumbled for the door handle. She yanked it open and scrambled inside, the car's interior offering a deceptive sense of security against the vast yard of Foster Hill House, bathed in midnight darkness.

Olive!

Kaine pushed the door open. "C'mon, girl!"

The dog jumped onto her lap, forcing the breath from Kaine's lungs. She slammed the door shut and pushed the lock button. Olive moved to the passenger seat, her ears perked, and gave a throaty whine. She sensed something amiss too.

Kaine grabbed her phone from where it was wedged between the driver's seat and the console. She cried out when she mis-dialed. How did one misdial 911 to 914? Fear, that's how. Handshaking, sense-numbing fear.

Maybe she should've taken Grant up on his offer to stay the night, but it hadn't felt healthy. Not that Grant would have taken advantage, but she couldn't guarantee she wouldn't have offered.

Stupid missing motel key! Now she questioned whether she'd left it in the house at all. It was disturbing that she couldn't re-member.

"Nine-one-one, what's your emergency?"

The voice was too cheerful.

"I need help. Someone painted my dead husband's name on my house."

"Are you in danger, ma'am?"

"Yes." Kaine squinted through the dark-ness but didn't need to. The wet paint ran from the window down the siding to the porch. The car, which at first seemed to of-fer protection, now felt exposed, with glass all around her. She slapped at her keys on the dashboard. If she'd just thought to hook the motel key to them, she wouldn't have discovered this tonight. She snatched up the key fob off the dash.

"Is there someone in your house?"

Kaine shook her head, clutching her phone tight to her ear. "I don't know. I'm in my car. With my dog."

Her keys slipped from her fingers, landing by the gas pedal.

"Ma'am, I've dispatched someone to assist you. Please, stay in your vehicle and on the phone."

"Okay." Kaine was grateful for the human connection. She bent, straining to reach the keychain.

A movement out of Kaine's peripheral vision caught her attention. Two large hands smacked against the rear window, and a man's body lunged over the trunk. A scream ripped from Kaine's throat. Olive's wild barking filled the car as the dog leaped over the seat toward the back window. Kaine pushed the locks repeatedly, making sure the car was secure. Her foot kicked her keys under the brake pedal. She shifted her reach and grabbed the can of bear spray from beneath her seat. The highly compressed pepper spray she'd bought from the local outfitters store was guaranteed to blind someone and was illegal to use on a human in the state of Wisconsin. Kaine didn't care.

The 911 operator's voice was calling to her.

Kaine twisted in her seat, catching sight of the man in her side mirror. Two blood-red handprints were impressed onto the Jetta's rear window. She screamed at the sight, causing Olive's barks to turn vicious.

The man's unidentifiable silhouette paused, then dashed away.

"Ma'am! Ma'am!" The operator's voice grew louder.

"I'm here," Kaine answered, straining to see out the window into the darkness where the man had disappeared. Olive continued her aggressive lunges at the back window.

Sirens sounded in the distance.

"Oh, thank you, Jesus," Kaine whimpered.

Olive returned to the front seat and nuzzled Kaine's shoulder, a whine coming from deep in her throat.

"Are the police there?" the operator asked.

"They're coming up the drive now. A man, he just jumped on my car. There's paint on my car's back window." Kaine looked in her rearview mirror. She hoped it was paint. *Oh God, please let it be the same paint as the house graffiti.*

Handprints, like bloody omens, streaked down the glass.

CHAPTER 27

There was never a more welcome sight than Grant pointing to Kaine as an officer stood between him and her car. Kaine wrapped her arms around herself, the fleece she wore failing to stop her shivers. Whatever Grant said made the officer step aside, and he sprinted over to Kaine. Without a word, he pulled her into his chest. She buried her face in his sweatshirt. The smell of his laundry detergent was mixed with woodsmoke from his stove and a comforting hint of dog.

"I heard the sirens. Why on earth are you here in the middle of the night?" Grant placed his hands on the sides of her face and searched her eyes.

"I couldn't find my motel key and thought I'd maybe left it here. I was just going to quick run in and grab it." Kaine turned her cheek so he would release her, and she rested it on his shoulder. Drawing a deep breath, she tried to stabilize her tremors and gather her wits. Grant's arms tightened. She shouldn't be so comfortable in his embrace.

"I told you to stay at my place," he murmured in her ear.

Still shivering, Kaine nodded against his shoulder. "I know, but . . ."

Her hesitation spoke louder than anything she might have said. Grant's fingers splayed across her back. "Yeah. Got it." He understood, and she felt his lips plant a light kiss on the top of her head.

Her body continued to tremble as a deep cold settled into her bones. She drew in a breath that shuddered audibly.

"You're going into shock." Grant rubbed her arms briskly.

Kaine offered up a shaky laugh. "I am?"

"Yes." Grant grew more assertive. "Did the paramedics check you out?" He led her to the ambulance.

Kaine shook her head. "They just got here. Literally. When you did."

Two paramedics were hurrying toward them. Grant recognized one and let his hand slip down and enfold Kaine's as he greeted him.

"Troy, she's going into shock."

"Got it," Troy acknowledged.

Before Kaine could respond, they'd urged

her onto a stretcher and wrapped her in blessedly warm blankets. Pillows were propped under her knees. Grant stepped back as the paramedics hoisted the stretcher into the parked ambulance.

Troy felt her pulse and then snapped his fingers at his partner. "Let's get her some O2."

Kaine tried to protest, but within seconds an oxygen mask was positioned over her nose and mouth. Awareness flooded into her, and her vision cleared.

"Just rest now. You'll be fine," Grant said, encouraging her from outside the ambulance.

The emergency vehicle was comforting. As Troy checked her blood pressure, she began to relax. But when she closed her eyes, the image of the handprints on the rear window of her car jerked her back to reality.

"Try to relax," Troy instructed. He felt her pulse again. "You're normalizing."

Minutes later, Troy helped Kaine sit up. The oxygen was removed, and her confusion lifted. He gave her a few more moments before helping her off the stretcher.

"Take it slow," Troy admonished.

Kaine did as she was told. She wasn't dizzy anymore, yet she had no desire to leave the safety of the ambulance. She bent down with Troy's help and sat on the back of the ambulance. The police were walking around Foster Hill House and taking samples for evidence. Someone had leashed Olive to a tree, where she nosed the ground but couldn't disrupt the scene. Grant returned and hoisted himself up next to Kaine.

"They want to ask you some questions." His voice was gentle.

Kaine tossed him a sheepish glance. "I'm not dying, Grant."

"I know." Still calm. Very much in his counselor mode. "But I don't need you going back into shock."

Kaine shook her head and pushed hair behind her ear, hoping Grant didn't see that her hand still trembled. He reached up and took it in his.

An officer approached, notepad in hand. The night sky exaggerated the shadows under his eyes, but she recognized him immediately. "How are you doing, Miss Prescott?"

Kaine offered Detective Carter a wobbly smile. "Sick of me yet?"

The detective shrugged and looked over his shoulder. "Not at all. But, this is unfortunate. For you."

Kaine leaned against Grant. "I never had this sort of evidence to back up my claims before." A daffodil certainly didn't hold the same type of ominous threat as blood-red graffiti.

"Well, after your report of that call you received, and then chatting with Detective Hanson from San Diego, I'd say this is a slap in the face of anyone who's ignored you."

Kaine appreciated his acknowledgment. She stared at the paint on the window of the house. *Danny.*

"I'd like to ask you a few questions, if that's all right?"

"Of course," Kaine said. Grant's arm tightened around her.

"Tell me exactly what you remember."

Kaine did so. With every recollection, she realized how close she had come to a physical altercation with Danny's killer.

A policewoman approached them. She carried a bundle in her hand and spoke into Detective Carter's ear. His eyebrows furrowed, and he took the bundle, turning back to them. Kaine's gaze dropped to his hands.

"Miss Prescott, were you aware that there was a stolen artifact in your vehicle?" There was no accusation in his voice, but his eyes were sharp and searching.

She nodded.

His frown deepened. "Obviously you didn't steal it, since you weren't born when it went missing. Do you have any idea of someone who may be interested in obtaining this quilt?"

Kaine matched his frown and exchanged glances with Grant. How was Ivy's quilt and tonight's attack connected? "No. I brought it with me from California. My great-great-grandmother was Ivy Thorpe, the one who originally owned the quilt. I thought it was just a family heirloom and" — she avoided looking at Grant — "I just recently found out it used to be a part of the Oakwood Museum."

The detective grunted. "I'm afraid we're going to have to take the quilt into evidence."

Grant cleared his throat. "Detective, are you implying the quilt is somehow tied to this?"

Carter paused, then gave a quick nod. "There was a note wedged between the cracks in the porch floor."

Kaine sucked in a breath. "What does it say?"

The detective's mouth tightened. He shook his head. "It's a cliché. It says, 'The apple doesn't fall far from the tree.' And there was a swatch of material stapled to it. We checked the quilt, and the material matches a missing section."

Instantly the warmth drained from Kaine, leaving her chilled inside and out. Hadn't Detective Hanson from back home implied that Danny's death was somehow related to her career? But this? Never in a million years would Kaine have thought her personal circumstances could be tied to Great-Great-Grandmother Ivy. To a woman who was remembered in Oakwood for her obsession with a dead girl.

CHAPTER 28

IVY

She breathed deep of the fresh air that poured through the window she'd just opened. Foster Hill House needed a good airing out. Ivy jumped when a gust of wind swung the door behind her, closing it with a resounding bang. While it ushered away the moldy smell of the barren library, the suction had caused the door to slam shut. She eyed every corner, as if at any moment the attacker would return to finish what he'd started the night he shoved her down the stairs. She'd had no compulsion to argue with Joel when he arrived that morning to bring her with him to the house. Enough had been said the night before. Words, feelings . . . so much better if just left alone. She would try to remember any detail she may have locked away inside from the night of the attack. For Gabriella, and maybe for Joel.

"Is everything all right? Have you found something?" The door opened, and Joel poked his head through. His hand still sported her neatly applied bandage, but the way he looked at her was distant and professional. It turned her cold, the chasm between them enlarged to insurmountable proportions.

Ivy shook her head. "No. No, I was just attempting to let in some fresh air."

"Has the window been disturbed in any way?"

"I didn't see anything." She knew enough to have checked first.

Joel stepped into the library. "So there were no handprints or fingerprints? Was the dust wiped away? Remember, we're looking for any clues that might help us understand what exactly happened in this house."

Certainly, she remembered that. "Nothing to make note of."

Joel rested his hands on his hips and blew out a breath of air. He shook his head as he scanned the room. Ivy followed his gaze. The bookshelves, the warped molding at the base of the shelves, and the faded, mouse-eaten wing chair in the corner. It was all so hollow and deserted.

"I'll remember something," she insisted before Joel could speak his mind. She had to. But her attacker's face was still dark and shadowed. Only the memory of the page from *Great Expectations* was vivid.

Ivy tugged at the cuffs of her goldenrod-yellow wool dress. It was soiled, on the hemline and the bodice. Even the piping on the bodice had taken on a tinge of gray. A poor choice of garments for today. Yet something in her had wanted to wear the color that suited her skin tone and dark hair, brought out flecks of yellow in her eyes, and made her more attractive than a twenty-six-year-old spinster could normally boast. It had done little to bring a flicker of admiration from Joel. He had retreated from her, probably for good now. It was what she'd orchestrated.

Joel ran his hand along a shelf. He passed his fingers over a few old hardbound books, then dropped his arm to rub the hand against his pant leg, brushing off the dust.

Feeling chilled, Ivy moved to close the window now that fresh air had invaded the room. "If I were Gabriella, I would have found the copy of *Great Expectations* here. In the library. Maybe even a writing instrument. One I would have kept hidden if I were being held captive."

"Stands to reason," Joel nodded.

"I would keep my infant somewhere as

warm as possible."

"The attic?" Joel said.

Ivy crossed her arms over her chest. "I thought so, at first, but where would she sleep? I think the cradle was moved, after Gabriella died. It only makes sense she stayed in the bedroom, where I found the book to begin with."

Joel wasn't convinced. "Its bedcover is old, moth-eaten, and dirty. No mother would wrap a baby in that."

Theoretically, Joel was correct. "But, to keep the baby warm, she would. She would do anything for the child." Ivy tried to put herself in Gabriella's shoes, imagining what she herself may have done had she been in the woman's predicament. "The nights are frigid, and there aren't any signs of recent fires in any of the fireplaces. Necessity takes priority over preference. We need to search the bedroom again," Ivy concluded.

It didn't seem Joel had any intention to argue. Rather, Ivy could sense he wanted her to take the lead, in case she remembered any detail, any smidgen of a clue that might bring life to this dead search. In a matter of seconds, they were climbing the familiar stairs to the bedrooms. Ivy shivered, reliving her tumble down them. She wrapped her right arm across her middle to where her ribs had been bruised. The skin was still yellow beneath her dress and corset.

Joel's footsteps echoed behind her on the stairs. Once in the hallway, she bypassed the first two bedrooms, so stark and empty. The portrait of the woman hung on the wall, only this time it was crooked. That's right. She had bumped it in her tussle with her attacker. Ivy paused and stared into the lifeless eyes of the lady. Her dark hair was capped with lace, and her black dress, obviously of rich silk, was typical of a widow in mourning.

"Mrs. Foster, I'd guess." Joel's voice in her ear made Ivy jump.

She stared at the matriarch of Foster Hill House. "I wonder what she was like."

"Crazy," Joel stated. "So I've heard, anyway," he added. Reaching out, he swiped at a cobweb from the corner of the frame. "She was originally from Georgia and relocated here when she married Billy Foster."

"And that's why she was sympathetic to the Confederacy?"

"I would assume." Joel wrinkled his nose at the woman. "She looks like a shrew."

Ivy tipped her head to stare into the woman's painted eyes. Something in them moved her. It touched that part of Ivy that always connected with people, where others just saw the surface. "She seems haunted. As if grief and trouble defined her life."

Joel and Ivy gazed at the painting a while longer before Joel turned and entered the third bedroom. Ivy reached up and touched Myrtle Foster's face, drawing a deep breath. Yes. The woman had not been happy. There was no joy in this painting.

Ivy followed Joel into the room. Memories assailed her. Joel watched her carefully, as if at any moment something would come back to her in a rush and she would identify Gabriella's killer and her attacker. But, there was nothing. No further recollections beyond the last ones she shared when they'd stood in this bedroom over a week ago. Ivy went to the bedside, looking down at the moth-eaten coverlet.

Ivy knelt by the bed and bent to peer under it. Nothing.

Joel spoke from above her. "There has always been something amiss with this house. I am beginning to fear Gabriella stumbled upon the truth of whatever it is."

She ignored propriety and sat on her rear, lying down with her back against the wood floor.

"Ivy, let me." Joel's offer to scoot under the bed for a better look was chivalrous, but

Ivy had already pushed her feet against the floor so that her head and shoulders moved beneath the bed's shadows.

"I used to hide my diary between the slats and the mattress." Her voice echoed around her like she was in a tunnel. Dust tickled Ivy's nose. Her dress would be ruined after this. "I figured you and Andrew would try to find it."

"We did." Joel's chuckle was distant, muffled by the bed that she had squeezed under.

"You did?" She hoped not.

"Unfortunately for you."

Ivy stopped her scoot and looked up at the dusty slats of the bed frame. Her mind raced with her childhood scrawling. They had mostly been about Joel, how she would marry him one day, and Andrew would live on their property, and the three of them would be blissful in their adulthood. She coughed from the dust. Oh, how dreams were thwarted by tragedy.

Her attention was snagged by a piece of paper wedged between the mattress and a slat that stretched across the frame. She gripped the paper and pulled it free.

There wasn't enough room between the bed and her arms to maneuver the paper to where she could see it. Sliding out from

311

beneath her confines and staying decent was going to prove difficult.

"Turn your back, please." Ivy instructed, clutching the paper in her hand. She fought the urge to scurry out from under the bed, regardless of propriety, so she could see what it was she'd found. "Am I safe?"

"Yes."

She hoped he was telling the truth. Ivy pushed herself from beneath the bed, then sat up and righted her skirts. Joel's back was turned in a gentlemanly fashion, his hands in his trouser pockets. He stared through the open doorway toward the hall where Myrtle Foster watched over them.

"I found something," Ivy announced. She twisted onto her knees by the bed in the position of prayer and laid the paper on the mattress.

"May I look?" Joel still had his back to her.

"Yes." She unfolded the paper gently, her heart pounding. The words on the page were typeset. It was a page torn from a book.

"What is that?" Joel crouched next to her.

"I knew it," Ivy breathed.

Only God. He brings me hope. Where darkness swallows and death nips at my heels.

"It's written on a page from *Great Expectations,*" Ivy whispered, the moment too surreal to speak in a normal tone. "See? I told you."

Joel took the page and turned it over. There was another line of handwriting.

Lord, save my baby from this pit that hints of hell.

His jaw tightened. Ivy watched his mouth contort with some unspoken thought or emotion, then he tossed the page onto the bed. Joel cleared his throat and sniffed, running his finger under his nose. The words distressed him as much as they had Ivy. Neither of them spoke as they stared at the page on the bed as if it would begin to speak and Gabriella's story would start to unfold. But there was nothing. No words. Just the silence of Foster Hill House screaming Gabriella's cries.

Joel marched past Myrtle Foster's portrait.

"Where are you going?" Ivy's dress rustled as she hurried after him.

"The orphanage."

"Whatever for? Mr. Casey said there were no unaccounted-for babies."

He didn't respond but hurried down the

stairs. Ivy gathered her skirts to hurry after him.

"We're not going to find anything at the orphanage that we haven't already heard from Mr. Casey." She couldn't follow Joel's line of reasoning, nor his urgency.

Joel yanked the front door open, then stilled, his shoulders drawing upward in a heave of his breath. He turned, and his eyes drilled into Ivy. "But he has orphans there. A baby was left there, remember? What if we've allowed ourselves to overlook something just because Mr. Casey's description of the girl who left it there doesn't match Gabriella?"

Ivy lifted her hand to reach for him, but dropped it as he glared at it. The situation was becoming even more personal to Joel. Something inside him was warring against his past, just as she was.

"But the baby at the orphanage wasn't Gabriella's. It was her own mother who left her there. She told Mr. Casey the baby was hers."

"I'm no longer convinced, Ivy." Joel charged out of the house, leaving her to trail behind in a flurry of skirts.

"Joel, wait!" She rushed after him. He arrived at the carriage they had brought to the house and untied the reins. Ivy helped herself into the carriage. Joel hoisted himself up and onto the seat next to her.

The horse responded to the slap of the reins on its back. With a toss of its head, the gelding snorted and started forward. Joel eyed the hollow oak tree at the bottom of the hill. They rolled by it, and he pulled back on the reins.

"What are you doing?" Ivy glanced over and noticed the white knuckles and how the reins were gripped in his fists. His jaw clenched, and a muscle in his cheek twitched.

"Gabriella." Joel's voice was hoarse as he stared at the tree, the girl's tomb. "I've never felt so helpless, Ivy." He paused, then added, "Not since Andrew, and not since I was a kid."

Ivy looked away from Joel's tortured expression. She knew being orphaned hadn't been something he talked about much as a boy, but at times he revealed his questions of who his own mother had been, if she had cried for him or merely passed him along with indifference. He had come into his own and found his place in his faith and himself. But Ivy could tell that Gabriella's ache resonated with Joel. More than theories and pieces of evidence, Gabriella was a human being who had experienced the kind of torment no one ever should. Her infant needed rescuing, something no one had ever done for Joel.

"We need to visit the orphanage. I need to go deeper, not just accept what Mr. Casey says at face value." Joel flicked the reins against the horse's back. In an impulsive gesture, he reached for Ivy as he threaded the reins through the fingers of his left hand. Her fingers interlaced with his, and Ivy swallowed hard at her concession. She was accustomed to pulling away from him, but she knew, in spite of their own adversity, he needed that connection. In this moment, whatever held them at odds was overshadowed by Gabriella's circumstances and Joel's own pain. No woman should have to endure such terrifying conditions, and then to bear a child? For that child's life to be cut short or to be abandoned? From the moment she'd read Gabriella's writings about her babe, Ivy knew Joel imagined himself as that child. Orphaned. Alone. Maybe even left for dead. He understood the babe's circumstances. He had been alone for far too long.

She'd let him hold her hand. Ivy sat in the wing chair across from the orphanage director's desk, but her eyes were on her left hand. Bare skin. Her fingers had intertwined with Joel's like when they were children and she was racing ahead of him on the path and dragging him along behind. He'd often teased her that her feet had wings and she flew without thinking. She always told him thinking was too painful and one day he would learn to fly ahead of her.

Joel shifted in his own seat as Mr. Casey entered his office. The director's walrus mustache bounced as he wrinkled his nose a few times. Perturbed or an itch? Ivy wasn't sure, but he did narrow his eyes when he saw her. Perhaps it would have been better for her to wait in the carriage or even the sitting room. She had no desire to sabotage Joel's inquiry.

"Miss Thorpe. Joel." Mr. Casey eased onto his desk chair and tipped his head.

"*Detective* Cunningham."

Ivy didn't miss the inflection in Joel's voice as he corrected his old guardian.

Mr. Casey cleared his throat. "What brings you both here? Again."

Joel shifted in his chair. "I have more questions about the infant that was left here at the orphanage."

The director's face remained placid. He folded his hands on the desktop, a tarnished silver ring on his middle finger. "Very well."

"You stated its mother was the one to leave it here?"

Ivy glanced between Joel and Mr. Casey. They eyed each other with distrust, or maybe dislike. She wasn't certain. Either way, an invisible thread of discord stretched between them.

"She was." Mr. Casey tapped his index fingers together. "I've already discussed this with both of you at separate times. I am not certain what more you think I can provide. This is not connected to the recent murder or to Miss Thorpe's fascination with the victim."

Ivy bit her tongue and adjusted her attention to pull at a thread on the cuff of her sleeve, grime on its cuff from rifling through Foster Hill House looking for remnants and clues.

Joel moved to the edge of his seat, his hair wavier than usual due to the moisture in the air. Ivy fought a smile. It gave him an especially rakish and impressive profile.

"The mother's name. I would like it please."

The addition of the word *please* was merely a formality. Ivy could easily read the demand disguised by the cool courtesy in Joel's tone of voice. The glower of Mr.

318

Casey's expression indicated he heard it as well.

The director leaned back in his chair, the wood creaking beneath his weight. He ran his hands down his coat lapels, worn at the seams. "As I told you on your last visit, I'm afraid I don't have a name, *Detective.* But even if I did, that isn't something I would merely hand over to you. We do attempt to protect the anonymity of parentage here at Oakwood's Home for Orphans and Waifs."

"Of course you do." Joel's knee bounced now, evidence of growing impatience. Ivy resisted the urge to reach out and rest her hand on it.

Mr. Casey raised a bushy eyebrow. "What are you implying?"

"I would like to see my own records." Joel's knee bounced faster.

"Your own?" Mr. Casey unfolded his hands with such a flourish it caused papers to fly to the floor. "Why ever would you want to see those?"

"My own history. My parentage. I'm certain you require more than the mere disposal of a child here at your premises."

"No, we do not. Most parents who leave a child with us have no care for them, or perhaps do not have the wherewithal to provide for them. Sometimes they prefer anonymity." Mr. Casey bent and retrieved the papers from the floor. "Whatever the circumstances, your implications are insulting. We have never hidden anything from you since the day you arrived here."

"As a toddler," Joel stated.

Ivy couldn't resist any longer. Her hand landed softly on his knee. Joel stiffened and stared at it before raising his gaze to meet hers.

This isn't about you, Joel. She hoped her thoughts communicated through her look. He blinked and drew in a deep breath.

"Mr. Casey, every child should have an opportunity to know their lineage. If the baby left here was not left by its own mother, then there are further pieces that must be investigated. I, of all people, know what it is like to travel through life with no evidence to support who I am. Is my last name even truly my own or did you simply make one up for me?"

Oh goodness. Ivy had never contemplated such a thing. The idea that Joel Cunningham wasn't his given name stunned her, bringing with it an understanding of why he was so insistent on having proof instead of assumption. His life was based on theory. It must be a miserable thing to bear.

Mr. Casey cleared his throat. Then he

cleared it once more, louder. He launched into the answers Joel was digging for while giving them a cold look. "The girl left with us was less than two weeks old. As for the woman who left her here, I truly have no evidence if she was the mother, outside of the fact that she claimed to be. She left no name. I did not require one. Her only message was that the girl was to remain anonymous. Only her given first name was offered."

"Which is?"

Joel's hand slid over Ivy's where it still rested on his knee.

Mr. Casey glanced between them. "Hallie."

Hallie. Gabriella's daughter's name was Hallie. Assuming it was her baby, and if so, how would they prove it?

"Did the woman who left Hallie here give you any indication of where she was headed?" Joel voiced the question that bounced in Ivy's mind.

The director sniffed and swiped at his nose with a handkerchief he'd pulled from his vest pocket. He crumpled it and stuffed it back in the pocket as he gave an agitated shake of his head. "No. No, she did not. But I suppose next you would like a description of her? I already gave it to Miss Thorpe.

Brunette. Brown eyes. Shorter than Miss Thorpe, and round. Homely, really."

Ivy searched her memory. The description seemed familiar. While vague, something pricked in the back of her mind, as if she had known the woman in the past.

"Were there any other identifiers?" Joel's interrogation turned the annoyed glint in Mr. Casey's eye to outright frustration.

"No!" He slammed his palms on the desk. An exasperated snort escaped him. "I did not make a sketch of her either. I wasn't expecting it to be of such interest that a wanted poster would be required."

"Why are you so defensive, Mr. Casey?" Joel's knee bounced beneath Ivy's hand again, and his fingers gripped hers painfully.

"Because, my boy," Mr. Casey said, shoving his chair back and rising to his feet, "you have been assertive and nosy since you were a lad. I wearied of you then and am still weary of you now."

"Are you hiding something?" Ivy interrupted, hoping to spare Joel the verbal knives Mr. Casey threw at him.

"Of course not," the director sputtered. "Except for a complete dislike of Joel Cunningham. And in answer to your *other* question, and in hopes that it will satiate your curiosity and end these confounded inquiries, I *did* give you your surname. Actually, Nurse Josephine requested you bear her name. She'd wanted to adopt you, but as an unmarried woman it was simply not possible."

Joel's face paled. His jaw worked back and forth. Ivy's fingers hurt within his iron grasp.

"Nurse Josephine was the only one here who ever cared for me."

Ivy's breath caught. Someone had once wanted Joel and been denied. He had been refused a family, a home, a mother.

Mr. Casey made pretense of stacking paper work. "Well, we aren't an institution of affection. We're an institution of necessity within proper reason."

"You're called a *home,*" Ivy said. She couldn't help but insert herself again. The old feelings of defensiveness for Joel rose up inside her. That young man who threw pebbles at her window, who had made her laugh, and who went on grand adventures with her.

"Home is a figurative word, Miss Thorpe, for house."

Joel stood, pulling Ivy up with him. "Mr. Casey, I would like to see the babe."

"Absolutely not."

"Why?"

Mr. Casey stalked past them and yanked his office door open, a clear invitation to leave. "Because you severed all ties here when you left our good graces, Mr. Cunningham."

Joel sniffed in disdain as he met Mr. Casey at the door. Ivy followed, glad to have retrieved her hand back from Joel's desperate grip. The two men stood nose to nose. Joel's mouth was set in a tight line, contempt exuding from his glare.

"*You* severed my ties here when you loaded me on the train and shipped me off to Chicago to fend for myself with only five dollars to my name and not a soul to greet me."

Ivy froze. Mr. Casey had sent Joel away?

A vein throbbed in Mr. Casey's neck. "You were of age."

"My best friend had just drowned in an icy lake." Joel's voice lowered into a deep growl. Ivy looked between the men, pieces she'd not invited Joel to share falling into place. Mr. Casey sent Joel away! A chilling realization spread through her.

"Perhaps your friend wouldn't have drowned in that lake had you obeyed the rules of the house and not led the boy on your ridiculous, adolescent escapades."

Joel grabbed the director's coat lapels and

pulled him forward. "How dare you," he growled.

"Joel!" Ivy put a restraining hand on Joel's arm.

"You were nothing but a troubled young man with a frank disregard for the rules," Mr. Casey continued, his face turning red. "When I discovered that you were sneaking from the house day and night, you left me with no choice but to be rid of you."

Ivy's hand slipped from Joel's arm. Joel had just said it, but now, hearing it from Mr. Casey, it seemed so much more irrefutable. Joel had been sent away. Under the worst circumstances imaginable. And she'd accused him of even worse.

Mr. Casey snarled in Joel's face, Joel's grip on the man's shirtfront still firm. "I don't know why you returned to Oakwood."

Ivy stared in disbelief at the director, the man who had sent Joel away in his most desperate moment. The man who had only just now proven that Joel had not made excuses to justify his absence that night at the grave. He had never intended to betray her, nor had he deserted her.

Joel gave the man a shove and released him. "I don't know why you run a home for orphans when you have the empathy of an ogre."

With a tug on his coat, Joel straightened it. "I will return to see the babe, and I will bring the sheriff with me so you cannot deny me that right."

Mr. Casey glowered at him. "I don't know why this girl is important anyway. It's not as if she's worth anything to you."

Ivy never felt such satisfaction as when Joel's knuckles rammed into the man's nose.

CHAPTER 29

KAINE

Kaine stood in the bedroom doorway and stared at the pink-carnation-colored walls of Megan's bedroom.

"You're welcome to stay here until this whole kerfuffle is sorted out." Joy's musical lilt drifted down the hall. Kaine turned and almost slammed into Grant, who'd snuck up behind her. Joy peeked over his shoulder, her red-lipped smile inviting. Grant's brows were bent with concern.

"Thank you." Kaine took the extra blanket Joy had shoved over Grant's shoulder. "But I really would be fine at the motel." Not really. She had no desire to spend another night alone ever.

"No." The rebuttal was in unison. Joy's smile dislocated to a half slouch on her face. Grant scowled and speared her with a hazel glare.

Kaine caught Grant's eyes. The warmth in

them tripped down into her soul. Safe. *He* was safe. But he didn't live with Joy. "I'm scared I'll endanger you and Megan." She directed her words to Joy.

Joy squeezed past Grant through the doorway and went over to the twin bed that matched Megan's on the opposite side of the room. Gaudy and bold flowers decorated the pillowcase Joy fluffed up as she attempted to reassure Kaine. "You belong here until everything gets figured out."

"Or you could stay at my place." Grant offered her a wink that made warmth seep into Kaine's face. There, right there. *That* was the reason she shouldn't stay with Grant. She had a weakness for the man, who counseled the grieving and had seen inside her the instant they collided at the gas station. She didn't want her weakness to lead to temptation.

Joy tossed a pillow back at Grant. "Stay on my couch. We'll all sleep better having a man around. And bring your dog. Besides, you won't have to lie awake texting Kaine every five seconds to see if she's all right. The girl won't get a wink of sleep."

"I'll bring my shotgun too." Grant's lopsided grin brought a touch of levity into a tense situation, relaxing Kaine even further. The idea of Grant camped out just yards from the bedroom in which she slept brought comfort. He wasn't exactly the Navy SEAL type, but he was tougher than Joy.

Joy propped her hands on her hips. A gray curl flipped upward, like a horn on the side of her head. "I have my own pistol, and my husband was a sharpshooter. Call me Annie Oakley. So, whether you're here or not, I'll make sure no one lays a hand on your Kaine."

Your Kaine?

Kaine stole a glance at Grant. A few red splotches appeared on his neck. She wasn't sure if she was flattered, intrigued, or terrified at the thought that, in such a short period of time, she was already considered Grant's. Actually, she wasn't sure she was ready for a relationship with a man ever again.

"So." Joy plopped onto the bed while Kaine and Grant lingered by the door. "What's the game plan?" She pointed a long red fingernail at them. "Sounds like it's time for Foster Hill House to unveil its history of mystery." She giggled at her clever rhyme.

Kaine managed a smile.

Joy rolled her eyes and waved her hand at Kaine in dismissal. "Smile, girl. I've never found any sense in not seeing the humor when going through a trial. But if you're both going to act mopey, I'll be serious."

Kaine went over and sank onto Megan's bed next to Joy, gaining some distance from Grant. His presence, so close to her, was a distraction at the moment.

Grant leaned against the doorjamb and crossed his arms. "I just want to know what Ivy's quilt has to do with Kaine's past in San Diego."

"You and me both," Kaine said, and picked at a thread on the comforter. "I had the quilt at the motel for the last few days and just yesterday put it in my car." She gave Grant a sheepish look. "I figured maybe it was time to take it to the Oakwood police. It *was* stolen after all."

"So how on God's green earth did anyone get a chance to slice off a piece of that beautiful antique?" Joy asked. Then she looked at Kaine. "How long *have* you been missing your motel key?"

The question sent a chill down Kaine's spine. The motel had issued her two keys at check-in. Since they weren't cards, and it was just a cheap motel, Kaine remembered dropping the spare key in the room's ashtray and keeping the other one with her.

Kaine looked up at her friends. "I was given two keys," she began. "I misplaced

330

one of them, and the key I lost tonight was the spare. I think. I thought maybe I'd left it at the house, so I grabbed the extra key and have been using that — until it went missing tonight too." She jumped from the bed and snatched her purse from her pile of belongings on the floor. Dumping out the contents on the bed, she rifled through them. "The police found a key at Foster Hill tonight in the entryway, on the windowsill. I remember setting it there today. That must be the spare key, which means I'm still missing one. I figured it was just lost in my mess of junk, but then I couldn't remember which key I put where." She tossed a handful of receipts into the wastebasket and then took stock of what remained: lip gloss, Kleenex pack, wallet, gum, a few more receipts, the charger for her phone. "Well, it's definitely not in my purse."

"I'm not sure I'm following," Joy said, looking confused.

"Sorry." Kaine swallowed and drew a deep breath. "The police found one motel key tonight at Foster Hill House, and there isn't a second one in my purse or in the ashtray where I left it in my room at the motel. Which means —"

"The first key went missing a few days ago," Grant supplied.

"Oh my . . ." Joy's eyes widened.

"Which also means someone got ahold of the key somehow and broke into my motel room — I'm thinking to cut off the piece of the quilt — while I was out." Did they search her things? Touch her pillow? Pick up her toothbrush, then set it back on the vanity? Kaine's skin crawled. This was San Diego all over again — times one hundred!

Joy leaned back against the wall alongside the bed. "I declare, we will *not* be swayed by this." Her charismatic tone wasn't something Kaine was accustomed to, but Joy's confidence was inspiring, if not comforting. "The Lord brought you here. To us. You're ours now, not just Grant's. And I declare that this freak of nature isn't going to haunt you anymore."

Grant cleared his throat and kicked at one of Megan's shoes on the floor.

Kaine appreciated their protectiveness and even Joy's reference to God. Maybe He had brought her here. But then, she had no clue what He was thinking. That had been her original intention of moving here in the first place — uncover what the Lord had for her. Find a reason to move on in life. Instead, trouble followed her. Or found her. Or smashed into her California trouble and it all got muddled.

"The police will check out your motel room. For prints, if nothing else," Grant said.

Kaine shook her head. "They won't find anything. They never have." *This guy is too careful, too smart.*

"Still," Grant persisted, "it's worth a try. Anyone can make a mistake."

"I can't figure it out," Kaine went on, ignoring him, though she knew he was right. "Danny was killed two years ago. Since then, it's been subtle things. Like I knew someone was in my house, but it wasn't overt. When I moved here, I assumed it would all go away. There are no ties between what happened in California, my husband's suspicious death, and Foster Hill House. Zero. And yet now Danny's killer is here. Or it's someone else and not the killer. Or . . . I just don't get it." She finished with a frustrated flourish of her hands. Thank goodness, Grant and Joy were willing to let her talk it through. If left to her own devices, Kaine would probably end up on the next plane for New Zealand in the hopes her stalker didn't care for international travel and horrible jet lag.

"Okay." Thank goodness. Grant, the voice of reason. "We need to work our way backward. Foster Hill House. How does it connect to you, Kaine, and to your great-great-grandmother? If we can piece that together, maybe we'll find a commonality, because whoever left the piece of quilt there wants us to connect the dots."

Joy drummed her fingers on the yellow nightstand beside the bed. "I think you need to go even further back. To the Fosters. The original builders of the house. There's history there that has never been resolved. Sort of like a puzzle put together without the edges."

"The Fosters?" Kaine drew her leg up under her knee. The bed bounced with her movement.

Joy waggled her drawn-on eyebrows. "They may have nothing to do with you, or your genealogy, and I have no possible idea how it'd tie to your dear husband, but I'm still saying. Foster Hill House has been a point of mystery in this town since the history books started recording it. And, we know Patti, our jealous little librarian, hung Myrtle Foster's picture back in the hallway upstairs across from the bedrooms after she found it in the museum's storage room."

"Jealous?" Grant's eyes widened. "She is, isn't she?"

Kaine read his thoughts. "My stalker is male. A muffled, disguised voice based on

334

the phone call, but definitely male."

Grant shrugged. "Well, Patti has always wanted Foster Hill House."

"Word has it," Joy continued, "the picture goes with the house, so I can see why Patti felt it should be there. She certainly didn't expect Kaine to buy Foster Hill, but then she never held out much hope of purchasing it with that gambling problem of hers. Meanwhile, Patti and Mr. Mason have done what they could to preserve things, even if it was a losing battle."

"So, Myrtle Foster's painting was left behind in the house originally?" Kaine asked. "I mean, where did it come from before it got put in storage in the museum for Patti to find?"

Joy tipped her head, thinking. "I'm not sure. But, keep in mind, Myrtle Foster and her children were run out of town when they found out she was loyal to the South. Story goes, they left everything behind. No one lived in the house until about forty years later, when a family bought the place from the town of Oakwood, moved in and made it their own."

"Who bought the house?" Kaine frowned. "Wouldn't that be about the same time as when the girl was found murdered on Foster Hill?"

Joy nodded. "Maybe that's your missing link."

"Maybe." Kaine swallowed the ball of anxiety that had yet to leave her stomach since the attack the previous night.

Nothing computed. That was the problem. Nothing tied together, and now even Grant and Joy could offer no real answers, only an endless amount of ancient stories with unanswered questions trailing behind them.

Kaine scrubbed at the paint on the window. Useless. She threw the brush into the soapy pail of water.

"Soap won't remove paint, Kaine. You'll probably first have to scrape it off with a razor blade. Or use paint remover." Grant climbed the porch stairs and rested his hands on her shoulders. Kaine pulled away from him. Danny's name screamed at her in blood red.

"I need a new window, that's what." She kicked the pail of water and stalked into the house.

Grant had helped her replace the front door earlier in the day. The make-do modern design was like a blatant scar on the face of the historical architecture. Detective Carter had recommended that with the suspicion of a break-in at her motel, plus the recent attack, an alarm system should be installed for her own safety. One that would alert the police of an intruder. But to do that, the house needed to be secured, which meant putting in a sturdy front door and repairing or replacing several broken windows.

Kaine climbed the stairs with Grant close behind her. She passed Myrtle Foster's portrait, slapping her hand on the woman's face and accidentally sending a piece of canvas floating to the floor. The painting was crumbling, much like Kaine's life, though she was past caring. She was boiling mad now, mad that she was back at this evil, horrific house that was stealing the last vestiges of hope she had left. Taking out her anger on the woman's image was minor compared with how she felt after seeing Danny's name in the light of day.

"Kaine." Grant tried to get her attention.

Ignoring him, Kaine went to her backpack in the corner and pulled from it the pages she'd found under the floorboards. She thumbed through them again, kneeling on the floor and spreading the pages around her like a map of another damaged life. Page after page of scribbling.

Weary and worn, yet God has not deserted me.

God.

I will hope in what I cannot see. For these walls close around me like a prison.

Faith.

He will come soon. I cannot bear this much longer. Oh, Lord, as David cried, "Please deliver me." Even in death, I welcome your presence and your rescue.

"What did she mean?" Kaine pressed her palms on the pages. "What did you mean?" she whispered once more, as if Gabriella could hear her on the other side of death.

The room was silent. Kaine ran her fingers down a page. Grant came and knelt beside her.

"How did she find hope?" Kaine blinked several times, willing away the cloud of tears that made reading Gabriella's handwriting impossible. Ivy's locket dangled from her neck, and she grasped it. "Even Ivy — she was here. What if she wrote all this?"

Grant's voice was calm beside her. "Doubtful. Outside of Ivy's attack, she isn't

338

linked to Foster Hill House as having been held captive here."

Kaine picked up a page. "Then it must be that girl, Gabriella. The one who mothered the child Ivy was so determined to find. It's obvious, whoever it was, that her life was horrific. She was held here in the house by someone. And yet here she is, writing promises to herself that God will rescue her."

"He will." Grant's quiet statement of faith irked Kaine.

"He didn't. She was *murdered*! And only God knows what happened to my great-great-grandmother. My whole life is filled with women treated as if they're nothing. But we are valuable human beings. Intelligent. Strong. Independent. I can't believe God would allow Gabriella to be held here, against her will, or whatever her circumstances were. And now, I'm imprisoned by some monster who probably murdered my husband and thinks he can play mind games with me. I can't do this anymore! I'm so done!"

Kaine jumped to her feet, and Grant followed suit. She shoved past him and marched to the window overlooking the field and woods beyond. She bit her lip. Great. Now she was making an emotional display of herself.

"What happened to you, Kaine?"

Grant's words sliced through her with the sharp edge of honest insight.

Lord, no. Please. Not that. Not now.

Kaine shook her head. Not even Danny knew. Or her sister, Leah. No one knew. It had always been her secret.

"Kaine . . ." Grant's footsteps echoed in the empty room. She could feel his presence behind her.

Go away. But she couldn't say the words out loud, because a part of her screamed for him to stay.

"This is deeper than Foster Hill House. Than even Danny's death. Why did you become a crusader for abused women? Why did you put your own safety on the line, your marriage or so it seems, to stand between those women and the ones who hurt them?"

Kaine swallowed back a lump the size of California. She wrapped her arms around her body and bit the inside of her lip so hard she could taste blood. The grasses in the field outside were turning green, and she focused her gaze on them. New growth. New life, and yet she related to the dead oak tree in the distance. Not the one that had been Gabriella's coffin at the turn of the century, but another. Another stark reminder that death always triumphed. It was the hunter, and man was its prey.

"Was it a relative who hurt you?" Grant pressed.

Lord have mercy! Kaine squeezed her eyes shut. How did he know? He was a counselor, that's how. He could read people, read their faces, and Kaine knew she would be the first one out in a poker game.

"No." She shook her head. The whisper hurt her throat.

"Danny?"

"No." Kaine's voice rose, vehement. No. Danny had done nothing but love her, and she had held him at arm's length.

Grant didn't press anymore. A tear trickled from the corner of her eye, betraying the truth she'd locked deep inside. She'd kept it buried for so long, she'd grown used to locking it away. Like it filled a place all its own. Every other secret had a way of slipping out, but this one was buried in such a way she'd need to excavate her soul to reveal it.

"It was my boyfriend in college. Freshman year." It should have been Danny she told, not a man she'd known less than a month.

"There's no shame in it." Grant's reassurance made another tear trace down her cheek.

Kaine swiped it away. "I know. Believe me. I preached that to every woman I've ever fought for."

Grant nodded, the movement dancing on the edge of her peripheral vision.

"It wasn't sexual." Kaine had thanked God for that day after day. "But he was jealous. Possessive. If I even looked at another guy, he'd get jealous and shove me around later. Then he'd make me feel guilty, as if he was a victim and I'd ignored him, or hurt him by not being true."

"That's more common than people realize," Grant said.

Kaine turned, but kept her arms wrapped tightly around her torso. She lifted her shoulders in a shrug. "My sister and I were practically raised by my grandpa. He was kind but indifferent. I struggled in high school. I wanted to be safe. In college, it was as if . . . well, my boyfriend gave me that security. I didn't want to jeopardize it, and I thought if I lost him, I'd never make it."

"What happened?"

Kaine looked at Gabriella's pages spread out on the floor. She took strength from the young woman's handwriting. "One night I smiled at a waiter when he poured my coffee. Just a smile. When we got in the car later, as I was buckling my seat belt, my boyfriend lost it. He was in my face, yelling at me. Telling me I was cheating on him. That he was going to leave me and no man would ever want me because I was a —" she stopped then and let out a sigh — "I can't repeat the word he used, not out loud."

A muscle in Grant's jaw clenched. He jammed his hands in his jean pockets.

Kaine continued, "The seat belt trapped me. I ended up in the hospital with two broken ribs, a black eye, and a few other bruises and scrapes. To this day, my sister, Leah, thinks I wiped out on my bicycle that I rode to class every day."

"What ended it?" Grant shifted his weight to his other foot.

Kaine licked her lips, recalling the taste of blood on them after her boyfriend beat her. She remembered clawing at her seat belt, at his face. She was a fighter, she always had been. And that night she'd awakened to what she had settled for.

"I got a restraining order and I broke up with him. He moved out of town shortly after that. I found out a few years later that he died of a drug overdose. I fought back," Kaine whispered, "and I won."

A proud smile tilted Grant's mouth. "Good girl."

Kaine lifted her face to the ceiling and blinked fast to push away more tears. "No. I stuffed it all inside. It hurt my marriage to Danny. I couldn't trust him. I buried myself in fighting for other women and teaching them to be strong, but in doing so I ostracized the one person who loved me the most."

Annnnnnd here comes the tears. Kaine pressed the heels of her hands to her eyes, hoping to stop the flow.

"And now, this. Everywhere. A reminder. I can't get away from it. It seems every woman I know is affected by it and I can't see God's light, or this hope that believers preach about. I mean, I believe. In Jesus. In faith. But, I can't see His promise of a future — a good future." Kaine waved her hand at Gabriella's pages. "But she could. How? How, Grant?"

When she spoke his name, Grant pulled his hands from his pockets and reached for her, one hand closing tenderly around hers. "Look at this." With gentleness, he bent and lifted a page from the floor. "I don't think you saw this one."

He showed her page 113 of *Great Expectations,* hidden under the floor by a young woman whose identity had never been discovered. The ink had faded but was still legible. Its words reached deep into Kaine's soul, gripped it, and she knew they would never let go.

My eyes see beyond today, beyond my circumstances in a world jaded and scarred by sin. I see into Heaven. And it is beautiful. And it is good. It is my future. There is no despair in eternity, in God's presence, in His perfection. There is only hope. He is my hope.

CHAPTER 30

Kaine palmed Ivy's locket, thumbing the tarnished gold and the engraved initials. She nestled cross-legged on the bed in Megan's brightly colored bedroom, cozy in her pajamas, with Olive resting on the floor between the beds. Megan sat at her desk, colored markers strewn around her. Occasionally, she lifted her head to give Kaine a lopsided smile. Megan was so innocent, kind, and untainted. She was the most pleasant roommate Kaine ever recalled having. A fierce protectiveness overcame her. Kaine would hurt anyone who tried to steal that perfection from Megan.

Her new cellphone with her new number pealed. She glanced at the caller's number, her heart beating faster. Detective Hanson. Thank God. She'd already given the detective her new number, so if her stalker had somehow retrieved this number, she would probably lose her mind. The fact that Grant was in the living room, crashed on the couch and watching ESPN was comforting. If she needed him, he'd be there, along with Sophie the pit bull. She'd hardly talked to Grant since her emotional breakdown earlier in the day and her confession that left her feeling like a limp dishrag.

"Hello?" Kaine waited for Detective Hanson to reply.

"Miss Prescott?"

"Yes."

"I know it's a bit late there in Wisconsin, but I didn't want to wait until tomorrow to call you."

There was something in the detective's voice that made Kaine sit straighter. She let Ivy's locket slip from her hand into her lap. "Yes?"

"We found him."

Visions of the blood-colored handprints and Danny's name on Foster Hill House's window flashed through Kaine's mind. "Found who?" She didn't mean to be obtuse, but if her stalker from San Diego had followed her to Wisconsin, she wasn't quite certain who Detective Hanson might have found.

"The man who took your husband's life."

Kaine's stomach twisted into a knot, and she lost her breath for a moment, though not in relief. A thousand questions swirled in her mind. "That's . . . not possible," she protested weakly.

Megan looked up from her Strawberry Shortcake coloring page with a concerned expression. Kaine mustered a confident smile. The girl didn't deserve to be touched by Kaine's messy life.

She considered carefully her next words. "How? I don't understand. Who is it?"

"I've been in communication with the Oakwood police, so I know you've had a recent string of very unfortunate incidents there. But they appear to be unrelated. We have taken a Jason Fullgate into custody. I have a complete confession. He also came clean about breaking and entering at your condo, and leaving the daffodils."

The San Diego police knew about the first daffodil, but not the subsequent ones that continued over the months. The ones Kaine never reported because she'd been threatened with filing fraudulent reports. This Jason Fullgate had made a confession. Was it authentic? Kaine's breaths grew shallow. Was it possible to have *two* stalkers? What bad luck was that?

Anxiety increased the tremor in her hands as her brain struggled to process the latest occurrences at Foster Hill House and reconcile them with Danny's murder two years before.

"Who is Jason Fullgate?" Kaine asked. She reached for Olive as the dog sensed her angst and nosed Kaine's hand.

"Do you recall a woman named Susan?"

Kaine had worked with several Susans at the shelter, although one in particular did stand out.

"Well, Susan is a young woman you helped get a fresh start. You helped her find a job, an apartment. She changed her last name to Gregson."

Susan Gregson. Yes. Susan. The petite redhead had the fight and tenacity of a beat-up kitten. She'd arrived at the shelter one night with a broken wrist and so many bruises on her chest and legs, Kaine had contemplated enacting her own vigilante justice. Susan's condition brought back memories of Kaine's abusive experience, and she had taken Susan under her wing.

"Fullgate was her husband," Detective Hanson explained. "When he couldn't find Susan after you helped her relocate, he traced Susan as far as you. He confessed to spending time following you, learning who you were, your relationship with Danny, where you lived, even that your favorite flower was daffodils . . . all to see if he could find Susan."

"But he never did." Kaine knew where Detective Hanson was taking the story. She had replaced Susan in the abuser's mind, because she became the obstacle to his twisted, abusive love.

"As fate would have it," the detective went on, her voice dropping a bit, "your husband visited a particular coffee shop frequently, so Jason got a job there and eventually slipped the drug into Danny's coffee. It resulted in his accident and subsequent death. Jason insists he didn't mean to kill Danny, only to carry out some retribution for what you'd taken from him."

Revenge.

Kaine slumped back against her pillows and drew her knees up to her chest. She squelched any tears for fear of upsetting Megan. How obsessive could one man be? To taint Danny's coffee, to get a job at Danny's favorite coffee shop and follow her, all out of love for a woman he'd beaten so many times? Were women merely belongings to him? Kaine rubbed her eyes with her fingertips. Yes. They were. It was a pattern that had traveled through history. If there was any link between Foster Hill House and Danny, it was that. Abuse. And it followed Kaine like a cancer.

One thing at a time, Prescott, she coached herself. Her body began to shiver. She pulled a blanket over her legs, and Olive hopped onto the bed and lay across her lap.

"And after Danny died?" Kaine asked. "What was his excuse then?"

"Fullgate is schizophrenic. He was diagnosed four years ago, and that's probably what started the abuse against Susan. He was — *is* — still obsessed with her and how she disappeared. To his mixed-up way of thinking, you were to blame. He transferred that obsession to you. He was convinced you needed to feel as he did. Alone. Helpless. With your husband dead, he wanted you at his mercy, and in his mind the best way to do that was to instill fear."

"Well, it worked. For two whole years." Kaine dug her fingers into Olive's fur. The dog twisted her head and licked Kaine's wrist. "How did you find him?"

"I went through old evidence. There was a receipt for the coffee shop, and once we found evidence of Danny's coffee being laced, we pulled the employee records to see if there was any connection to Danny or cases you had worked with. That's when the dots began to line up. When we brought Fullgate in for questioning, he caved."

The reminder of the photograph of Danny

positioned in the middle of the floor in the third bedroom skittered through Kaine's mind. Along with the weird phone call from the anonymous caller.

"When did you take Mr. Fullgate into custody?"

"I know where you're going with this, and I hate to say it, but it was two days ago. The interesting thing is, he just recently started up on his meds. It wasn't hard to get a confession out of him. The man's completely broken."

Kaine had little sympathy for the man who killed her husband, intentional or not.

The detective cleared her throat. "I have to close the case, Miss Prescott. Obviously, it'll go to trial and we'll need you back in San Diego at some point. I've contacted the Oakwood Police Department as well, and I know — you're involved in your own new set of circumstances."

Circumstances. That was a gentle way of stating it. Kaine looked up and met Megan's eyes. The adorable slant of them and her rounded face created a stark contrast to the frightening realization that clenched her gut.

Detective Hanson voiced Kaine's fears. "The incidents there in Wisconsin are unrelated to Jason Fullgate. There isn't anything I can do to help with your investigation there."

Kaine could hear the hesitation in the detective's voice. "Yeah." Kaine grimaced into the phone. "I know what you're thinking, and I have no idea how this sort of luck followed me here."

The detective chuckled, then coughed to cover it. "Well, I wish you the best of luck and safety. It sounds like the department there is well qualified and you're in good hands."

Good hands.

It didn't leave Kaine with any sort of comfort. She had thought that, once Danny's killer was found, there would be resolution, that life would settle down, a new normal. Even if there was a forthcoming trial and a revisiting of her grief, at least the terror would be behind her. But it wasn't. Not at all.

Kaine hung up with the detective and dialed Leah. She'd avoided calling her sister, not wanting to bring her into the current events. Having Leah panic all the way across the country wasn't going to help quell Kaine's fear in any way. But Leah needed to know Danny's killer had been caught. At least it was one book they could close.

After saying goodbye to Leah, Kaine

leaned back against the pillows again and watched Megan, whose coloring page really was a work of art. Blended colors, bright pinks and yellows, oranges and purples, created a beautiful kaleidoscope of happiness. It matched the joy in Leah's voice when Kaine told her Danny could finally rest in peace. But it didn't match Kaine's heart, or the fact that her world was still as tumultuous as a puddle of gray-and-black ink.

"So everything is okay now, right?" Leah had asked.

"It will be," Kaine replied, and left it there. She decided not to burden her sister anymore. Besides, being so far away, Leah could do little to help her. The reassurance she gave was interpreted by her sister as Kaine needing time to heal. Kaine let her believe that was the case. And it was — among other, far more intimidating factors.

Kaine fixed her stare on Megan's sweep of a blue pen, but her mind was consumed by the events of the evening. Danny's killer was in custody. *Danny.* She drew a shaky breath. In the end, it *had* been her fault, in a roundabout way. He'd suffered, for her. The truth was both startling and brutal. Tears burned her eyes. Who else would end up suffering because of her, caught up in the whirlpool trap of abuse that was her life, surging forth from the past and whipping its way into the present?

Chapter 31

IVY

She knew where to find Joel. It was the same place that called to Ivy in the dark cavern of her own sorrow. A mist floated just above the ground, embracing the bases of the tombstones. Some of the markers were tilted from time and the earth settling the graves deeper into their eternal beds.

Joel's broad shoulders were covered in a gray cotton shirt, with darker gray stripes that raced down his back to his trim waist. His shirtsleeves were rolled and cuffed, exposing his forearms. The trees that draped over the cemetery rustled as a light breeze awakened them. Joel dragged his hand across tired eyes.

Ivy's heart twisted, the truth seeping into her conscience with the brutal sting of how wrong she had been. In her grief, she had drawn conclusions without understanding events. The years of harboring her defiant offense against Joel Cunningham, her dearest friend and the only one who knew her as well as Andrew, had taken its toll. But not only on her.

She watched as Joel squatted in front of Andrew's simple white stone, reaching out to rest a palm on its top. A strange cough emitted from his throat, the kind someone made when fighting back tears. Ivy couldn't fathom a man like Joel weeping. He would hold his grief deep inside and expose it to no one. He would do what needed to be done. He would exist and he would survive. He was strong, as evidenced by his broad shoulders that bore the weight of time and pain, that had borne abandonment, rejection, and her own bitter accusations. Yet, he was here. He had returned home, to her and to Andrew.

Joel rocked forward, his knees sinking into the moist ground. He rested his other hand on Andrew's grave marker and bowed his head. Ivy hesitated as she approached him, as if to speak would break the reverent silence. Her foot snapped a twig, and Joel raised his head to look over his shoulder. The rims of his eyes were red as if he hadn't slept. She hadn't either. The debacle at the orphanage, ending in a visit and stern warning from Sheriff Dunst, was enough to put them both on edge. Beyond that, Mr. Casey's revelation regarding the night of Andrew's funeral exposed Joel's vulnerability and Ivy's ill-placed defiance. Sleep was a friend to no one in times such as these.

There was much unspoken emotion as Joel's blue eyes bore into hers. He was obviously in pain, holding it deep inside, just as he had always done.

"I still miss him." Weariness tainted Joel's voice.

Ivy stood over his crouched form.

"Do you doubt that?" His eyes were half accusing and half begging her to believe him.

"No." Ivy's whisper squeezed around the lump in her throat.

Joel drew his hand back from Andrew's marker and stood. "I'll never forget that day."

Neither would Ivy. That spring day long ago when the three of them laughed and coaxed one another out onto the ice that covered Wilkes Pond. The moment the ice cracked and then gave way beneath Andrew's feet, his six-foot frame, so strong and athletic, becoming helpless against the elements. Ivy could still hear herself screaming Andrew's name, could still picture Joel sliding across the ice and launching to his belly, reaching for his friend Andrew. She had screamed at Joel to save her brother, waited for him to dive into the frigid water, to do what must be done to bring Andrew back to them. But Joel hadn't. He'd remained sprawled on his stomach, arms plunged into the water toward Andrew. A horrific silence followed, a nothingness that would forever echo around the pond.

Ivy had slipped and slid across the ice in her own frantic dash to get to her brother. Joel vaulted to his feet, the ice continuing to crack beneath their weight as he wrapped his arms around her. Ivy wrestled against his grip; her screams filled the air. Dragging her away from where Andrew had disappeared, he saved her from dying along with her brother. But all these years later — Ivy clenched her teeth against the memory — all these years she had seen it so differently. Joel had kept her from saving Andrew, and Joel had left him in the pond to die.

"That night? Here? I wanted to be with you at the grave." Joel's words ripped into her past and present agony. But he hadn't been here.

"Why didn't you come? Why didn't you fight Mr. Casey?" She lifted her eyes to the man she had loved so fervently as a younger version of herself.

"Ivy," Joel whispered and shook his head in regret. "Every time I left the orphanage at night to meet you and Andrew, I was never caught. We were free, Ivy." He reached out and took her hands, tightening his grip. His calluses reminded her of his strength. The strength she'd so desperately needed the day of Andrew's burial.

"So what changed? That night?" Ivy stared at their clasped hands, thinking how she'd wished they'd been able to grab hold of Andrew like this and pull him to safety.

"When we'd made plans to meet here, after the funeral, to say goodbye to Andrew together, Mr. Casey had already received word I was with you that afternoon. That I'd been on the ice and not helping the other boys cut wood for heating the orphanage. Mr. Casey stopped me that night, detained me. I couldn't get away, Ivy. I couldn't be with you." Agony reflected in Joel's face, the kind that must have eaten at his soul for years and left behind a pain he couldn't verbalize.

"But you tried. . . ."

"You were worth the risk to me," he said, searching her eyes. "You were always worth the risk to me."

"Why did you leave?" Ivy asked, even

though she knew the truth.

Joel gave a short laugh of disbelief. "I didn't have a choice. Mr. Casey made sure I was on that train and it pulled out of the station without me jumping off."

All night she had wept over her brother's cold grave, shivering and waiting in the damp snow. In the morning, Ivy returned home only to be told by her father that Joel had left Oakwood.

"I hated you for leaving." Ivy swallowed a shuddering breath.

Joel winced, the corners of his eyes squinting with hurt. "I know."

"But you didn't have a choice." Resignation laced her voice. Ivy saw surprise flicker in his eyes. He didn't say anything, but his fingers gripped hers tighter. "I blamed you. I said it was your fault. I didn't realize Mr. Casey was sending you away, that you were being shipped off to fend for yourself in Chicago. I didn't know you'd tried to come to me, I just — assumed. I jumped to conclusions that you let Andrew die and that you were just selfish, that you didn't care about us."

About me.

"I'm so sorry." Ivy leaned into Joel's chest, her forehead against his shirtfront, the spicy smell of him warming her senses.

The ache — it never went away. No matter how much she'd hated Joel. No matter the silence, and even if his letter seeking reconciliation was lost, Ivy had buried herself with Andrew that night. She had ceased to live.

"Why did you write only one letter? Why not more? Hundreds of them, until I answered you?"

Joel sniffed and, even as his hands rose to cup her arms, looked beyond her to Andrew's grave. "One letter with no answers? I couldn't abide not hearing back from you. Wondering — no — *knowing* you hated me. The silence was your answer."

"But I never received it," Ivy argued.

Joel shrugged. "How was I to know that?"

"Why did you come home?" Ivy spoke into his chest, but Joel's hand came up and brushed her cheek with the backs of his fingers. She looked up at him. "Besides needing resolution for yourself, why did you come home, really?"

"For you, Ivy. I came home for you."

CHAPTER 32

Ivy sat opposite the Widow Bairns, balancing a teacup in her hands. The parlor was stifling hot, with the fire in the fireplace blazing to warm the spring chill from the older woman's bones. Her father had wanted her to deliver the latest round of medicines to the widow's home, but after her interlude with Joel at the cemetery, Ivy wanted only to escape to her room. She needed her journal, she needed to revisit the night of Andrew's burial and to reconcile the anger she had harbored for so many years. But first, the Widow Bairns needed her medications. She hadn't anticipated the elderly woman to be chatty and desiring company. She had Maggie, didn't she? Her great-niece?

Ivy managed a wobbly smile as she lifted the teacup and sipped.

". . . And so that's what I did with that flower patch." The widow smiled, her wrinkles deepening. Ivy had drifted away in her thoughts. Apparently, they were discussing gardens. She nodded.

"Mm-hmm." Ivy tried to sound interested.

Widow Bairns raised her eyebrows. "More tea?"

Ivy glanced into her cup. It was almost full. "No, no. I'm fine, thank you. I must be on my way shortly."

Widow Bairns snapped her fingers at Maggie, who sat unobtrusively in a corner chair. Maggie leaped to her feet.

"More tea for Miss Thorpe," the widow demanded, not unkindly but with significant importance.

"Yes, ma'am."

Ma'am? Ivy squelched a frown. The relationship between great-aunt and niece seemed odd. Formal. Too formal. More of a servant and mistress than old family.

Maggie lifted the teapot from its place on the table. Ivy offered her cup out of politeness. Reaching forward, Maggie began to fill the cup. Her sleeves stretched up her arms, revealing her wrists.

Ivy frowned. "Maggie, what happened?"

Bruises around Maggie's wrists were faded and so pale, Ivy almost didn't see them. Maggie set the teapot on the table and yanked down on her sleeves. "N-nothing, miss. I —"

Ivy didn't miss the look she exchanged with the widow.

"She slipped and took a tumble a few weeks ago," Widow Bairns interjected.

"I see." Ivy sipped her tea out of pretense now, suspicion taking over. The markings were similar — no — *identical* to Gabriella's. As if Maggie had been bound. No fall would result in bruising such as that. "My father would be willing to help, if you're still in pain."

"No, I'm quite well, thank you." Maggie's hands shook as she clasped them behind her back.

Ivy met Widow Bairns's eyes. For an old woman, they were sharp and knowing. She narrowed them. Protective. The widow was protecting Maggie from something — or someone.

Another sip, another exchanged look with the widow and Ivy changed the topic strategically. "So, how do you enjoy living here in Oakwood with your aunt?"

Maggie plopped back onto her corner chair and twisted her hands in her apron. "It's very nice." There was a question in her eyes. They'd had a similar conversation before, Ivy knew, and repeating the former, rather introductory, questions was redundant. But she needed to watch Maggie's reactions this time.

"And you came from . . . ?"

"Milwaukee."

"Madison."

Both Maggie and Widow Bairns spoke at the same time. Ivy raised an eyebrow at the contradiction. Maggie ducked her head, and the older woman pursed her lips.

"Maggie hails from Milwaukee but came by way of the Madison train station."

"I see." Ivy was suddenly thankful for her tea and the distraction of sipping it. That made absolutely no sense. The train didn't route through Madison to get to Oakwood. "How long are you staying, Maggie?"

This time Maggie didn't respond. Widow Bairns set her teacup on its saucer with a nervous clatter. "As long as she needs."

Ivy glanced between the two women. *As long as she needs?* She frowned, then quickly softened her expression into something less direct. Staying with Widow Bairns or *hiding* at Widow Bairns's? Ivy recounted the clues and ties to Foster Hill House. She remembered Mr. Casey's description of the woman who had left baby Hallie at the orphanage, claiming parentage. There was no doubt Maggie fit the description, however generic and vague it was.

Another sip.

Silence.

The widow sniffed into her handkerchief.

Maggie played with her apron strings.

Ivy knew. Maggie had left the baby at the orphanage. Baby Hallie *had* to be Gabriella's, which meant . . . Ivy met Maggie's eyes once more, and this time the truth radiated from them whether Maggie wished it to or not. Maggie knew who Gabriella was, as well as the terrible secret Foster Hill House harbored.

She wanted to launch into a thousand questions, but she knew in an instant that Maggie would flee, taking the answers with her. No. It was best to leave it to Joel and Sheriff Dunst and feign a lack of interest. They would need to question Maggie, to find out what had happened and why Maggie had chosen to stay in Oakwood with Widow Bairns. Until then . . .

Ivy sipped her tea, now almost gone. "It's delightful that you're here, Maggie." She mustered a warm, inviting smile intended to put the two women at ease. "Nothing is more wonderful than being surrounded by family."

Maggie returned Ivy's smile with hesitancy, and the widow's shoulders relaxed under the crocheted shawl.

There was one more stop Ivy must make before she returned to her home to revisit her own tumultuous emotions. She must find Joel again, but for entirely different reasons than reconciliation.

CHAPTER 33

KAINE

"We don't have those records, ma'am." Small eyes blinked back at Kaine through glasses at least a half inch thick. Kaine shot a glance at Grant. No. She would not accept another dead end. With Jason Fullgate behind bars, and Gabriella's written prayers replaying in Kaine's mind like a broken record of unseen hope, Kaine wanted to fight. Only this time for herself, not because she owed something to Danny.

Kaine rested her palms on the countertop at the County Records Office. The older woman blinked again, unyielding. "How do you not have the property records for a house that was the home of a founding family of Oakwood?"

The woman tipped her head to the side, and her glasses tilted. The red turtleneck she wore made Kaine's neck claustrophobic. As if whoever was following her had their hands around Kaine's throat and was squeezing.

"Well, there was a fire." The records keeper was as intimidating and unreadable as Gandalf the wizard.

"Of course there was a fire," Kaine said, lifting her eyes to the ceiling. Could she not catch a break? She turned to Grant, whose mouth was pulled into an ironic smile.

Grant leaned against the counter that separated them from the female Gandalf. "How far back do your records go?"

"Well . . ." The woman ran her finger around her turtleneck. Maybe she was tired of her clothes strangling her. "The last deed was filed in 1978 by the Davidson family. They owned Foster Hill House until the bank foreclosed nine years later. They weren't able to resell the place. That's why it's been abandoned ever since."

"Wonder of wonders." Kaine turned her back to the woman, but Grant shot her a warning look.

"Your records only go back to the seventies?"

"No. They go as far back as the sixties. The fire burned down the courthouse in 1958 and took everything with it. But there's no record of Foster Hill House between the sixties and 1978. It went abandoned for a time. It seems to be a thing with that house."

"Then who sold the place to Kaine?" Grant reached for a pad of paper, and the woman handed him a pen.

"The city." She pushed her glasses up her nose. "Oakwood took possession of it after the bank shut its doors in the nineties. Recession and all that, you know. Anyway, they put it on the market and it didn't sell. The county just reviewed futile properties this year and decided to try again — short sale. Find someone impulsive and willing to mess with the place. The land was worth nothing to the county as it stood, and they couldn't use it for bartering with anyone for property more conducive to road expansion or county buildings."

"So Kaine purchased it from Oakwood."

"Yes."

Kaine grimaced. No wonder the sale had been so sketchy. Throw it online, have a realtor take amateur pictures of the rooms where repairs were more cosmetic, a few creative angles from the outside avoiding the worst sections, and *voilà,* a not-so-bad historical home. One an "impulsive" person would buy.

Grant set the pen down. His paper was blank. Kaine knew he was as frustrated as she was, only he showed it by jamming his hands in jeans pockets and heaving a huge sigh. "Well, I guess that's that."

The courthouse records keeper blinked. She blinked a lot. Kaine would have wanted to buy her some eye drops — if she'd liked her. Which she didn't.

"You might try the museum," the woman suggested. "Mr. Mason has much of Foster Hill House's history recorded there. Not the deeds, mind you, but genealogies and the like." She sniffed and glowered at Kaine. "It *is* a place of historical significance."

"Then why didn't Oakwood register it as a historical landmark?" Kaine couldn't help one last question.

The woman raised a thin eyebrow and stared at Kaine from beneath half-lidded eyes. "I don't know. Ask the city. No one likes Foster Hill House."

"Thank you." Grant offered a charming smile, and the woman's eyes brightened. She returned the smile, and Kaine tried not to chuckle at the subtle flirtation from the older woman.

As they passed through the doorway onto the open street, Kaine leveled a look of derision on Grant. "A fire? Really. What more can happen in this town's history? The place is a cesspool of circumstantial factors. I'm beginning to think there was some big cover-up."

"Maybe there was." Grant took her hand as they crossed the street toward his pickup. "It's worth investigating." Olive's nose poked through the four-inch gap where they'd left the window rolled down. When Grant opened the driver's-side door, the lab licked him in greeting.

Kaine pulled her hand from Grant's and circled the truck, opening the door to climb up into the cab. She settled into the seat as Grant turned the key in the ignition.

"So."

"So."

They spoke in unison. Grant chuckled and reached for Kaine's hand again. Kaine contemplated drawing back. She probably should, but she didn't want to.

"All right." Grant cleared his throat. "We have a few options."

"Really? I only heard one. And have you seen that museum? The man doesn't even own a desktop computer, let alone a tablet and digital archives."

"Kaine, don't give up hope. Remember Gabriella's words? C'mon, hon."

Grant's endearment appeared to surprise him as much as it did Kaine. He looked away and watched a white Suburban drive past them.

Kaine tried to relieve his discomfort by responding as if she hadn't noticed. "I *am* hoping. I'm hoping to put this whole thing to bed and shut the door on it. Before I have to return to San Diego for the hearing against my husband's killer, and before whatever nutcase here in Wisconsin decides to make good on his bloody handprints."

Grant's thumb moved back and forth over her fingers. Kaine didn't think he even realized he was doing it.

"That call from the detective in San Diego didn't bring you any resolution, did it?" Grant was too perceptive. That was the problem with collaborating with a psychologist.

"How could it? Not too many women can claim being stalked by two psychos in her lifetime." Kaine turned her face to Olive, who nosed her from the back seat.

"Do you think this is somehow your fault, Kaine?"

She turned and stared out the window. The grocery store parking lot wasn't much to look at, but it beat Grant's discerning gaze.

"Kaine?"

He didn't let up, did he?

"No. I mean, not the circumstances. But,

the guilt. I pushed Danny away. All the time. I wasn't the wife he needed. I feel as if I owe it to him, to live out his dream and fix up an old house and do the things he had on his bucket list, because he didn't get a chance to. Because *my job,* which I was so dedicated to, cost him his life."

Grant was so casual yet so strategic in how he dug into her emotions. It was unfair. She had no defense against him.

"You pushed him away because of your boyfriend in college?"

Kaine nodded. "Yeah. That. And also because I was always the one who had to take care of Leah after Mom died. Grandpa tried. He loved us. But he was old, you know? It was self-preservation, survival of the fittest. I had to be strong all the time. Put myself out there for Leah, for myself, even for Danny."

"You're the protector in your family. Like Ivy was."

Kaine frowned. She didn't see the correlation.

"Her memory book at the museum. The stories she logged of people whose lives she believed merited preservation. She protected their legacies. She empathized with them. She fought for Gabriella."

"She did," Kaine acknowledged.

Grant nodded. "And whoever this creep is that's still out there, he sees what we don't. That quilt piece he left behind was a direct message. If the apple doesn't fall far from the tree, then that means you must be like your great-great-grandmother in some significant way."

Kaine bit her lip. "There isn't a soul alive who would be able to draw the conclusion that I resembled her."

Grant squeezed her hand, then released it to put the truck into drive. "If I can draw that conclusion, someone else certainly can. And we're going to find out how. Then we're going to find out *who.*"

CHAPTER 34

Kaine clawed at the piece of material positioned between her car's windshield and wiper blade. Morning mist dotted the glass with tiny pinpricks of moisture. She looked over her shoulder at Joy's modest ranch house. The windows were dark. Joy and Megan still slept on this Saturday morning. Kaine scanned the short blacktop driveway, the street in front of the house, and the line of neighboring yards.

The quilt that had brought a smile to her face when Leah told her of it now served as a reminder of one thing: She wasn't alone. Apparently, more than one piece of the quilt had been cut from it. She wouldn't know. The police had kept it as evidence.

Danny's face flashed in her memory, and Kaine blinked her eyes fast to clear it. His killer had been caught. Her hunter had been put behind bars and yet there was another one. A copycat. Someone who knew far too much about her life in San Diego, her life here, and her vulnerability. Kaine crumpled the quilt scrap in her hand, her breaths coming rapidly in short gasps.

"What do you want!" She yelled into the morning's emptiness. A pickup truck and a work van drove past the house, oblivious to her shout.

Kaine spun in a circle. Olive barked from inside the car where she waited. "If you're there, show yourself. Let's have this out!"

A mourning dove cooed. Another car drove by, the woman at the wheel focused on the road, her red hair so red that Kaine had the fleeting thought the poor driver had overdyed it.

"Fine." She jammed the material into her pocket. "Be a coward." She yanked open the car door and slid into the driver's seat. Olive nosed the back of her head, and Kaine scratched the dog's chin before turning the key. The Jetta hummed. She cast a disconcerted glance at the rear window. No red handprints.

She put the car in gear and headed toward downtown Oakwood. Filing another police report was a must, but she needed to meet Grant first. He'd told her the night before that he'd be heading out early to his office at his house but then would meet her at a little coffee shop. It beat Joy's burnt gas-station coffee — the woman brought home the leftovers.

Her phone trilled, and Kaine snatched it from the passenger seat.

"Hello?"

Expecting Grant, the whispered voice in her ear made Kaine let off the gas.

"Are you still lonely?"

"Who are you?" Kaine demanded. How on earth had he gotten her replacement cell number? She steered the car off the street into the Walmart parking lot, her knuckles white from gripping the wheel.

"I've been lonely my entire life." The man's voice was so soft, so muffled, it was like he'd covered the mic of his phone with a thick towel.

"Well, stinks to be you." She was goading him. It felt good. She felt strong — and maybe reckless.

"No, no. I'll be fine."

As if she was concerned with his welfare.

"How dare you stalk me? Why did you paint my husband's name on my porch? Put my great-great-grandmother's quilt piece there?"

"Why did you come to Oakwood?"

"That's cryptic." Kaine fumbled for paper in her purse. A pen. She had to write down snippets of what he was saying. To remember. To tell Grant later. To report to the Oakwood authorities. He wanted her to believe this was still tied to Danny's murder, but she knew better. And if she wasn't mistaken, he would too in a matter of days. When news of Danny's case hit the online world, her stalker would know the jig was up. He would be exposed as a sole entity with an entirely different agenda. But what was it? And how did it link Kaine, Ivy, and Foster Hill House?

"Do you love him?" The question took Kaine off guard.

"Who?" Danny was dead. He knew that. Kaine jotted down the question.

"Grant Jesse."

Kaine's breath halted. "I haven't even known Grant for more than a month." Why had she answered? The creep didn't deserve one word.

But he would capitalize on it. "Mmm, you do. I see."

"No." Kaine's hand shook as she pushed her straight hair behind her ear. "I don't." And even if she did have feelings for the man, she would never admit it. Not to this pathetic piece of humanity.

Olive jumped from the back seat onto the passenger seat. Her paw crinkled the paper

Kaine was writing on. She pushed on the dog, and Olive readjusted but whined deep in her throat.

"I saw Grant at the coffee shop."

Okay, that was it. Kaine was now determined to jump-start her prayer life. How in the world did this man know where Grant was? *Please, God . . .* "You leave him alone."

"Ooooh." The dry chuckle riveted Kaine to the phone. His words were slurred, the voice undiscernible. "It's so hard when what you love is threatened, isn't it? Sort of consumes you."

"What do you want from me?"

"I want you to stop gripping your steering wheel so hard. I want you to hang up the phone and drive yourself home. To San Diego. You never should have left, you know. It wasn't wise. It wasn't smart. Foster Hill House should be left alone, as it has been for years."

Stop gripping her wheel? Kaine pulled her hand from the black steering wheel. He was *watching* her! She scanned the parking lot of Walmart. Cars. Empty. Another car drove down aisle four. Female. With two little children in car seats.

Kaine turned her attention to the narrow two-lane street with its one stoplight at the Walmart intersection. A few cars drove by, the 25 mph speed limit allowing her to see the occupants. A blue sedan. A tan minivan. A Dodge Neon from the late nineties. A jalopy that should have been retired in 1982. A white Suburban.

The stoplight turned red. The driver slowed the Suburban. A hat was pulled low over his eyes. A baseball cap with a white *M* on the brim. She couldn't make out his features as his hand lifted in a wave.

"Now go home where you belong."

Then the light switched to green and he drove away. The phone went silent. The Suburban's taillights blinked three times as if in a final message. Kaine squinted, trying to read the license plate — except there was none to be read. The huge vehicle turned the corner and disappeared, taking with it the answers to the hundred questions that riddled Kaine's mind.

They'd interrogated her at the station for over an hour. Did she have the piece of the quilt left on her windshield? Yes? They'd need it for evidence. Had she left her new cellphone number with anyone? No. Was she positive? Well, she'd given it to Detective Hanson, Leah, to Grant, and to Joy. Had she let anyone use her phone? No. Maybe. There was the lady at the grocery store the other night who had a dead battery in her car and needed to call her husband to come jump it. Kaine had let her borrow it but only for a call. Who was the lady? She didn't know. Did her husband come? Kaine hadn't stayed to find out.

By the time she was through, the police were fairly convinced the only plausible way Kaine's number had been obtained was that the mystery woman had stolen her number off the phone. But finding out who she was and how she was connected to a male caller was a shot in the dark. They would try to trace the call back to the originator, but odds were high it'd come back as a burner phone.

Kaine held the bridge of her nose between her finger and thumb, squeezing away the headache. It was calming to see Grant waiting for her in the lobby of the station. He took her by the arm and led her outside. She opened the passenger-side door to his truck, and Olive met her with a few friendly licks.

"Hey, girl." She rubbed her neck, then urged her to the back seat with a tug on her hot-pink collar. Settling into the passenger seat, Kaine slammed the truck door shut. With a deep sigh, her head rested back against the seat and she closed her eyes. She fiddled with a button on her purple flannel shirt. Tylenol. She needed Tylenol.

"What's next?" Grant waited.

Kaine kept her eyes shut. So much for coffee this morning. She had to admit, she'd hoped it'd be more like a first date and less like another traumatic layer in their relationship.

"Same as usual. They'll investigate. The alarm at the house hasn't been tripped since they installed it. I was stupid and gave my phone to a stranger to use, trying to be helpful. They probably stole my number from there."

"We'll figure this out." Grant's assurance fell flat. She'd thought the same thing with Danny's death. Two years later, that resolution had collided with an entirely new case.

Kaine ran her fingers through her dark hair. Finally, she turned her head, and her gaze fell on the books in his lap.

"What are those?"

Grant furrowed his brow at the swift change in subject, but he followed where she was looking. "Oh, those. They're books on the Fosters. I checked them out at the library." He chuckled. "Patti begrudgingly showed them to me. I think she'd gladly trade places with you if it meant she could own Oakwood's Foster Hill House."

Kaine rolled her eyes. "She wouldn't if she had to deal with filing endless police reports and running for her life."

Grant smiled at the sarcasm. "Anyway, according to Patti, the books were self-published about thirty years ago by a local historian who passed away in the nineties. I thought maybe they'd give us some insight into the house's history."

Kaine reached over and picked up the top book, a paperback. It was square, more like a coffee-table book, its cover including a photograph of the faded portrait of Myrtle Foster from the hallway. She eyed the author's name. "Who's Levi Foggerty?"

"A descendent of the man who used to trap animals in the woods around Oakwood." Grant grabbed another book and thumbed through it. "Patti told me it was his grandfather who first discovered the body of the woman in the oak tree." He showed Kaine a black-and-white photograph taken in 1906 of a hollowed oak tree, its bark gone from its skeletal form. "But Levi Foggerty traces the history further back into who Myrtle Foster was, her children, and even some weird things that happened while they were living in the house. It seems Oakwood thought Myrtle Foster was a bit crazy before she left town."

"Interesting. Oakwood has a history of accusing women of lacking intelligence." Kaine set the book back onto Grant's lap, remembering how the town had labeled Ivy as a mystic. "I think we need to let it rest. The whole thing. Just let it be." After the phone call today with the veiled threat toward Grant, Kaine couldn't even fathom seeing another person she cared about hurt or killed in the cross fire of her choices. Panic replaced her earlier sarcasm, and she tried to swallow it. When she couldn't, she turned away and stared out the window at the trees, the birds, the city park, anything but Grant. "Just let it be," she repeated.

"Oooookay." He put the books in the back seat.

"Okay?" Kaine pulled back. "Just like that? Okay?"

"I'm not going to force you to go somewhere or do something you don't want to." Grant was too understanding, but Kaine could see disappointment in his eyes. He wanted to uncover how she was tied to Ivy and in turn to the dead girl, Gabriella. He wanted to see resolution to her fear. So did she. But not at the cost of his safety. Or Joy's or Megan's. Her choices had already killed Danny. She couldn't bear a repeat of that.

"When he called me . . ." Kaine paused.

Grant deserved to know. He needed to know. "The man knew you were at the coffee shop waiting for me." She pulled a strand of hair to her mouth and chewed on it.

Grant reached over and pulled it from her fingers. "Don't, Kaine."

She grimaced and sighed. "Grant, you don't understand. He *knew* you were at the coffee shop."

"I heard you." Grant's hazel eyes drilled into hers. They held a stormy kind of strength. "But I'm not going to overreact, and I'm not going to put myself in lockdown mode."

Kaine leaned into the middle part of the front seat, her eyes wide. "C'mon, Grant. He's studied me. Now he's studying you. He even asked —" Whoa. She didn't want to go there.

"Asked what?" Grant pressed. He leaned over the center console toward her, filling the remaining space between them. He let his hand rest against hers, the sides of their palms touching. She didn't respond, but she didn't pull away. She glanced at their hands before she looked out the truck window again.

"What did he ask?" Grant asked again.

Kaine turned back and pulled her hand

away. "He asked if I . . . cared for you."

"What did you say?" Grant looked out the front window. Whether to give her emotional distance or because he was uncomfortable, Kaine couldn't tell.

"What could I say?" Kaine's brows dipped in frustration. "Yes, I care for you? Have him kill you like that other creep in San Diego killed Danny?"

"No one is going to kill me, Kaine."

"Said the man before he died," Kaine muttered.

"C'mere." Grant grabbed her hand and tugged. "Listen. Don't let him win. We're obviously getting close to the truth."

"I know, and that's basically why he threatened me. When he called, he told me he wanted me to stay away from Foster Hill House. That I shouldn't have left San Diego."

"So it all comes back to Foster Hill House."

Kaine glanced back at the books. Myrtle Foster stared at her. Her dead eyes seemed to come alive, to plead with them to keep investigating.

"I think you're right." Grant interrupted her link to the woman on the book cover.

Kaine lifted her face to his.

"Think about it," he continued. "Two

women, both rumored to be crazy, both drawn to Foster Hill House, and yet no historical records kept to complete either of their stories. There had to be a cover-up of something. It's obvious Gabriella had been held there."

"That's a pretty difficult thing to cover up." Kaine reached back and grabbed the book. "Erasing history?"

"Even you said Ivy's genealogy in your family Bible stops with her. Why?"

Kaine met Grant's frank stare. She grimaced. "I don't know."

"Get this." Grant snagged the book from her hands and flipped a few pages into it. "Gabriella's body and Ivy's attack and subsequent suspicions around Foster Hill House took place forty years *after* Myrtle Foster claimed she'd seen strange women wandering the halls of her home in the middle of the night."

"What?" Kaine leaned forward and stared down at the words on the page.

Grant nodded. "I was reading while you were in the station. Myrtle claimed she would awaken periodically in the night only to see figures that were never accounted for. It says that to go back to sleep, Myrtle played piano into the wee hours of the morning. Beethoven. She was partial to Bee-

389

thoven."

"Piano music and ghosts? In the middle of the night?" Kaine shook her head slowly. "This gets more farfetched the deeper we dig."

Grant reached up and tucked a strand of hair behind her ear. He gave her his quirky smile, the sideways one that hinted of mischief and daring at the same time. "Then let's keep digging."

CHAPTER 35

Kaine's mouth watered when Joy set the bowl of green beans in the middle of her dining room table. Megan grinned. "I love green beans! But I need butter, please."

She pointed to the butter plate, and Grant handed it to her. "Go easy and leave some for me."

Megan laughed. She was so full of glee. Precious. Hopeful. Her twenty-two years hadn't scarred her like the other women Kaine knew.

Joy passed Kaine the platter of lasagna. While green beans and lasagna was an odd combination, Kaine was hungry. The pasta tickled her nose with scents of garlic and oregano, and cheese — lots of Wisconsin mozzarella cheese. She noted the bright red of the sauce from a jar. Danny's mother was Italian and made her marinara sauce from scratch. Kaine took a bite and savored it. From a jar or not, it was delicious.

"The police called today." Joy's announcement stilled Kaine's fork on its journey to her mouth. She had intentionally tried to leave Joy out of her situation. It was bad enough she was presuming upon the woman's hospitality, but if the man decided to threaten Joy, or God help her, Megan, in any way, Kaine might lose her mind.

Joy smiled. "Don't worry. They just wanted to verify that you were staying with me. Apparently, they're going to send a squad car around at different intervals, for your protection."

Her protection. *Their* protection. The message was very clear.

Grant met her eyes across the table. "That's a good thing, Kaine."

"And you won't have to sleep on the couch, Mr. Jesse, with your loaded shotgun. You can go home." Joy chuckled, and Kaine shot Grant a sharp look.

He grinned. "You want to get rid of me?"

"Never," Joy replied.

"You keep the gun loaded?" Concern edged into Kaine's voice. She was quickly losing her appetite.

Grant waved his empty fork between her and Joy. "I protect my women," he mumbled around a mouthful of lasagna. "And I'm not going home. Sophie and I are staying put.

On the couch."

Kaine rested her fork on her plate without eating the bite stabbed on its prongs. She knew Joy and Grant were trying to add levity to a dire situation, but she was nauseated all the same. "I hate putting you all in the middle of this mess. I thought that one day, when the police found Danny's killer, it would all subside and I could just keep building my virtual assistant consulting job and make enough money to paint rooms in my new house and buy vintage furniture at estate sales."

The wrinkles at the corners of Joy's eyes deepened with sincerity. "Well, I say we stop ruminating on what could be and discuss what *is*. You both like to leave me out of the discussion as if I were some old gooney."

"That's not true," Grant said, and winked at Kaine. But she still wasn't feeling the humor.

"Joy, I want to protect you. I don't know who this guy is, but he doesn't seem to discriminate who he targets. He's even set his sights on Grant."

"Well, don't that beat all!" Joy took a drink of water, then plunked down the glass. "Listen here, I've got at least thirty years on you both, and I was born and raised in Oakwood. Why don't you lay out all you've found so far and see if I can fill in any gaps?"

It was a nice thought. But Joy wasn't a historian. Even Patti, with her fixation on Foster Hill House, couldn't fill in the gaps when Grant questioned her at the library. Joy was just a loving eccentric who worked at a gas station to provide for her special-needs daughter.

Grant didn't seem to care, though, and he launched into a recap.

"Gabriella was definitely held at that house against her will, based on what we've read in her writings that we found at the house," Grant finished. "The amazing thing is, whoever she was, she had faith that could move mountains. She saw hope where most women would see abandonment."

"See?" Joy poked her fork in Kaine's direction. "Hope isn't a waste of time, sweetie. You've got to cling to those promises, and the Lord will provide the rest."

Kaine didn't fully believe it. "He provided for Gabriella by allowing her to be murdered and stuffed in a tree." She shot a wary look at Megan. She didn't want to upset the girl, but Megan met her eyes and smiled.

She nodded. "It's okay, Kaine, I'm fine."

Smart as a whip, that Megan.

"Kaine Prescott." Joy's voice had an edge to it and turned mother hen on her. Kaine had no choice but to listen. "You're looking at things backward. As if this life and all it has to offer is all there is. It sounds as if this Gabriella could teach us all a thing or two about seeing beyond this world and setting our eyes on Jesus instead."

Kaine's bite of lasagna went down in a hard swallow. Jesus. Not just God, but Jesus. Joy was as blatantly evangelical as they came.

Joy shifted her attention back to Grant. "I'd be curious to read what Gabriella wrote. Especially since my grandmother knew Ivy." She folded her hands and rested her elbows on the table. "She said Ivy never discovered who Gabriella was, why she was murdered, or what happened."

Grant gave a nod. "That's pretty much what Mr. Mason indicated, and Patti affirmed. Ivy's memory journal was never completed and there was no record of how it all ended."

"Were Gabriella's writings in a journal also?" Joy glanced between Grant and Kaine.

"Not exactly," Grant said.

"That's the really creepy part," Kaine inserted.

"They were pages, buried beneath the

floorboards in the third bedroom," Grant added.

Kaine pushed her plate away. "She wrote her thoughts in the margins of an old book. *Great Expectations.*"

Joy's face blanched. Her elbows slid from the table, and her hands bumped the edge. Her plate jumped from the force, clinking against the wood when it landed. Megan stopped chewing and stared at her mother.

"Did you say *Great Expectations?*" Joy whispered.

"Yes." Grant reached out to touch Joy's hand. "Are you all right?"

Joy shook her head. Color returned to her face, but her hands shook. "Just a moment." She pushed up from her chair and disappeared down the carpeted hallway.

"What was that all about?" Grant said.

Megan smiled and wiped up some of the water that had splashed from her mother's glass. "Momma has *Great Expectations* in her room. It was Grandma's favorite book."

Kaine cocked an eyebrow at Grant.

He speared a green bean with his fork. "That can't be a coincidence."

Joy returned with a shoe box. She pushed her plate out of the way, set the box on the table and removed its cover. "This was my grandmother's." She pulled out a lace doily.

Then a hardback book. The title was embossed in gold. "She cherished it, but never let anyone read it."

Kaine tried to calm her excitement. Because *Great Expectations* was a popular classic and still in print, there was nothing strange about a family having an old copy stored on a bookshelf. Or in Joy's case, in a shoe box. But, like Grant said, it couldn't be just coincidence.

Joy ran her hand over the book's front cover. "I remember one day — I was maybe eight or nine at the time — I saw it in a drawer in her bedroom. I pulled the book out and was going to open it, but my grandmother found me with it." She looked up at Kaine, her eyes reflective with unshed tears. "It's the only time I ever remember her raising her voice to me. She propped it up on a high shelf and I never touched it again. Not until after she died."

"You believe her book relates to Ivy somehow?" Grant spoke Kaine's thoughts.

Joy took a deep breath and tapped the book with a long fingernail. "You just wait and see, young man." Opening the book, she rotated it so they could see. A beautiful, cursive script filled the margins. She turned the page and then another, and another. Almost every page included handwriting surrounding the text. "This isn't just a novel — it was my grandmother's *diary*. She wouldn't let anyone read it because it held her private thoughts. After she died, and I found it, that's when I saw it was her diary and I knew why she wanted no one to read the book."

Kaine leaned forward in anticipation. "Just like Gabriella." The image of Gabriella's pages popped into her head. "Your grandmother chose the same book and the same style of diary entries. That cannot be chance."

After helping Megan to another piece of lasagna, Grant looked at Joy and the book in her hands. "Do her writings explain anything?"

Joy blanched. She shut the book. "I don't know. I never read it."

Grant folded his arms on the table. "Why?"

The older woman sagged onto her chair, staring at the book for a long, silent moment. "I couldn't. I can't. I keep remembering her face that day she discovered me with it. She wasn't just stern, she was . . . panicked. Anxious. It upset her very much."

Kaine wanted to ask if she could read it. After all, the book might hold the answers she'd been searching for. But Joy had the appearance of someone guarding a treasure chest, someone with no intention of unlocking it anytime soon.

"You can't tell me my grandmother didn't get the idea to write in the margins from someone. Who writes their diary in an old book? And there's this." Joy reached into the shoe box and pulled out a page taken from the novel. "I always thought this was my grandmother's. Now I wonder." She opened her grandmother's copy of *Great Expectations* and compared the page to it. "Just as I thought: The typeset doesn't match. This page isn't from the same copy."

Grant reached for the page and studied it a moment. He looked up at Kaine. "I think this matches Gabriella's copy. Remember the little fleur-de-lis printed at the top corners of each page? This one has it."

Kaine took the page Grant offered her. He was right. "How is this possible?"

Joy shook her head and held the book to her chest. "This has to prove one thing I'd never considered and my grandmother never implied." For the first time, Kaine saw Joy as fragile. "My grandmother didn't just know Ivy Thorpe; she knew the dead girl of Foster Hill when she was alive."

Chapter 36

IVY

Darkness swamped Ivy's vision, and her scream was muffled as a hand pushed a rough cloth into her mouth, pressing her head into her pillow. Dazed from being woken from her sleep, she kicked at her mattress, clawing her attacker's arms. The memory journal she'd been writing in before she fell asleep dropped to the floor with a thud. Ivy cast a wild glance over the man's shoulder to her open window. She'd only wanted to enjoy the warm nighttime air of spring. Instead, she had opened the way for Gabriella's killer to find her.

"You didn't die." The voice grated in her ears. She squirmed in his grasp, but he tied the gag behind her head as she twisted, her bedcovers tangling around her feet.

Hear me, Papa. Her inner cries for help had no effect on awakening her father. Ivy's attacker dragged her from the bed as Ivy thrashed. Her foot kicked the organ stool at her desk, but it was too solid and heavy to tip over. This time the intruder was prepared for her fight and yanked her arms behind her, wrapping bindings around her wrists. The coarse fibers of rope rubbed her wrists raw as he tugged it tight. Like Gabriella's bruises, and the yellowed bruises of Maggie. She'd told Joel of her suspicions about Maggie several hours ago, before retreating to her room and her memories. Now, the fear she'd seen in Maggie's eyes clawed at Ivy.

She whimpered around her gag and kicked at her attacker as he threw her back on her bed and grabbed at her feet. She caught a glimpse of peppery dark hair and a craggy face, but within seconds he had overpowered her and bound her legs at the ankles. Mr. Foggerty? Or no. No, it wasn't him. Her brain was still cloudy from being startled from her sleep, and her breath was knocked from her when he slung her over his shoulder like a bag of flour. Ivy squirmed against him, her bedroom door opening under his free hand. Her muted cries were futile. She knew her father was a heavy sleeper. It was how she and Andrew had snuck from the house night after night for their midnight escapades.

The man moved like a thief, silent and strong. His grip around her was impressive, as Ivy was no lightweight. But by the time they reached the bottom of the stairs, she could tell he was breathing heavily.

She was dumped into the back of a wagon, which jolted and rolled away, bruising her with every bounce along the road.

Of all the risks she'd taken, the lectures from Joel for being reckless, and now she had been taken from her own home. Her own bed! When the wagon finally stopped, Ivy kicked to brace herself so she could twist onto her knees. She raked her face against the wagon floor, working her jaw back and forth to attempt to free herself of the gag. Her captor flung open the back of the wagon and grabbed Ivy's bound ankles, pulling her toward him. As he did, her gag finally freed.

"Let go of me!" she screamed.

"Shut up." He dragged Ivy from the wagon, and her shoulder slammed against the earth. Pain shot through the shoulder and down her arm, taking her breath away.

"Stand up," the older man demanded. He yanked her to her feet, then reached down to slice free the ankle binding. "Now walk." He shoved her forward, her wrists tied in front of her like a jailed prisoner. She tripped and stumbled along.

The man's dark silhouette was unmistakable. Instinctively, Ivy knew all along where they were going. Foster Hill rose above her, mocking her with its ominous shadows. Like Gabriella, it appeared this place was there to consume Ivy's life.

She was forced up the porch stairs and over a threshold. Her captor shoved Ivy in front of him. "Go." He pushed again, and Ivy contemplated running. If she bolted past the stairs toward the rear of the house, could she make it through the back door before being caught? She wiggled her wrists in the rope that tied them. Her skin was already raw. Now was her chance, for there wouldn't be another.

Ivy catapulted forward, her shoulder catching on the banister of the stairs as she ran. A shout. Pounding of footsteps behind her and then her abductor slammed Ivy into a wall. His furious black eyes drove into her, along with the full length of his body. He pinned her against the wall, and Ivy's skin crawled beneath the pressure of him against her. She may have at one time suspected Mr. Foggerty of being involved somehow, but now he would have been a welcome relief.

Her abductor glared at her. "Never run

again," he hissed, running his finger down the length of her neck and along the top of her nightgown. He eased back and, with a grunt, hoisted her over his shoulder again. Ivy struggled to regain her breath as his shoulder drove into her belly.

His boots pounded on the stairs. The hallway floor passed below her, the shadows never ending, his footsteps echoing in the empty house.

Why would he bring her here? Why not just kill her as he'd tried to the first night here when he shoved her down the stairs? He had to know the house was one of the first places Joel and Sheriff Dunst would look when they found out she'd been taken.

They stopped in the middle of the third bedroom. Ivy saw the familiar bed, and fear like she'd never known flooded her body.

"No. No!" She beat against the man's back. He swore and dumped her on the bed, straddling her as he did so. The soiled linens smelled moldy, but Ivy turned her face into them and away from his.

"None to hear you, none to care," he whispered into her ear as his hands trailed down her side. Ivy lurched with her shoulders to fight him off. Her head collided with his nose, and he flung himself away from her with a growl, holding his face.

He pulled a knife from where it was tucked into a sheath that hung from his belt. He sliced at her restraints, freeing her hands. She surged forward, but he was prepared.

"Oh no you don't." The man's grip bit into her arm, leaving blood from his nose on her sleeve. "In here." He opened the closet door with Ivy struggling against him.

"Let me go!" she demanded. Ivy attempted a scream, but he clapped his hand over her mouth. The empty closet proved only to be a gateway. Her attacker worked at the back wall and slid open a loose panel to reveal a small space behind it.

No. Good Lord in heaven, no. Ivy's eyes widened at the secret compartment. She knew instinctively that more women had been hidden behind this wall. She wasn't the first. Perhaps even *he* had hidden here, watching them during the times she and Joel had searched the house.

Ivy dug her feet into the floor as he pushed her toward it. She wrestled against his grip, but he shoved her with a force she couldn't match. She plowed into the back wall of the compartment and fell to the floor. She put her hands out to feel the confines of the space. There was barely enough room for her to turn around.

She looked up and locked eyes with him. Black eyes. A scruffy face that might have been handsome were it not for the voluminous beard and long hair tied back with a leather cord. He was at least fifty years of age. Ivy had never seen him before.

Evil shone in his eyes. "Go ahead and scream. It doesn't matter."

"What do you want from me?"

His lips tightened. "You surprised me the first time. I didn't expect you in my house and I wanted you dead. In a way, I'm glad you didn't die after all. I'm down two girls, so you'll have to do as a replacement — for *all* my needs."

Ivy launched forward as he slid the panel across the opening. Her hands slammed into the wall as it sealed her in. She pounded on it with her palms.

"Let me go!" It was a futile plea against the wickedness she'd seen on the man's face.

Ivy closed her eyes, even though the darkness of the tomb-like space had effectively blinded her. She slumped against the wall, telling herself to breathe, to remain calm. But remaining calm was near to impossible as she began to understand how it felt to be buried alive in a place that threatened to steal a woman's soul.

Chapter 37

Kaine

"We want to see the family trees of my great-great-grandmother Ivy and of Joy Wilson, as well as the family tree of Myrtle Foster."

Mr. Mason, museum curator, blinked. He looked nonplussed, as if the museum was there merely to provide entertainment for the few tourists who were historically inclined. Certainly not as an archive for research. But he was adorable, in a curator sort of way, and Kaine felt sympathy toward the man for his looking like a deer in the headlights. His wispy gray hair perked on top of his head with more interest in life than he seemed to possess.

He took a sip of coffee from a green thermos. "I'll see what we have," he said, then ambled off toward the back room.

Kaine suppressed a smile. "I think we should've gone with my suggestion. Online databases are more thorough now. Haven't you watched those TV shows that trace celebrities' ancestors back to the Tudors?"

Grant's expression scolded her mildly. "I have. But sometimes I prefer paper."

Kaine slugged his arm. "Traditionalist."

He smiled. "Let's start here and then we'll pull up whatever else we need online."

"If there is anything." Kaine figured the way Oakwood went about protecting records, they probably wouldn't have a thing submitted to any online database.

Mr. Mason shuffled back into the room. He laid a manila folder on the counter that stood between them. "That's all I could find." He scratched his head. "I know we had more at one time, but Patti probably put them somewhere. That woman and her infernal filing. Not to mention there was that break-in back in the sixties. I think some stuff got swiped along with Ivy's quilt."

"Did you work here then?" Grant asked.

Mr. Mason chuckled. "I was in my early twenties. Rather than volunteering my time at a museum, I went to go fight in Nam."

"Oh." Kaine nodded. *Vietnam War.*

"I didn't know you were there," Grant said with a quizzical look.

Mr. Mason nodded as he flipped open the

folder but said nothing more on the subject.

Kaine and Grant exchanged glances and decided to let it drop.

"Here." Mr. Mason tapped a copy of old scribblings. "This is Joy's family tree. Wilson is her married name, so most of this will show you the line of the Slaskis, Joy's maiden name."

"What about Ivy's family tree?" Grant said.

"We all know there's not much on her," Mr. Mason muttered. He began thumbing through some loose papers. "Must've got stolen too or something. Here. An old Wisconsin census from 1915."

"Nine years after the dead girl was found," Kaine mused. She ran her index finger down the paper. She could barely read the handwriting.

Grant peered over her shoulder. "Obviously Ivy married, so what was her married name?"

Kaine looked closer at the census. "I don't know for sure. My grandfather's name was Prescott, and my mom had us take that name instead of my father's. But my grandfather's mom was from Ivy's line. I don't even know what her maiden name was."

Grant shifted back to the genealogy Mr. Mason handed him. He scanned it until he came to Joy's name.

"And the Foster family?" Kaine set aside the census records. She didn't even know what she was looking for. The census was line after line of names, households, occupations, and so forth. She'd have to call Leah later to see if she recalled Grandpa Prescott's mother's maiden name.

Mr. Mason heaved a sigh. Apology filtered through his eyes as he met hers. "I have some of the Fosters' family tree here." He handed her two sheets of paper, again copies. "But it only goes up to 1909."

"Why did it stop? I mean, why didn't anyone continue writing it down?" Kaine noted Myrtle Foster's name in the genealogy.

Grant took a break from surveying Joy's genealogy to look over Kaine's shoulder again. "Well, they did move out of Oakwood in the late 1840s. I'm surprised anyone kept track of them at all after that."

"Myrtle Foster was married to Billy. He was born in Alabama and transplanted to Wisconsin. They had a son and daughter born in the early 1850s. So they would've not been quite teenagers when the Civil War started."

"What happened to her husband?" Grant frowned, leaning closer to read the copy. "I

410

always heard Myrtle was run out of town, but not much about him."

"He left Oakwood to join a vigilante group for the South." Mr. Mason pointed to a line of text. "Left his family behind and was killed by Union soldiers."

"So Oakwood ostracized his family too." Grant nodded, his lips puckered in concentration.

Kaine's eyes rested on his lips. She quickly looked away as Grant spoke again, his sideways glance making her blush. "I bet they didn't send vigilantes home for special honors and burial."

" 'Course not." Mr. Mason took the genealogy sheet from them and surveyed it with a squint of his faded blue eyes. "Looks like the records stopped with the death of the Fosters' son, Arnold."

"Who recorded this family tree?" Kaine asked.

He shrugged. "Don't know."

"Whoa." Grant's exclamation drew their attention to Joy's family tree. "Check this out." He pointed to a branch, and Kaine leaned into him.

"What is it?" she said.

"Joy's grandmother. She didn't die until the late 1960s."

"So?"

"So she was only sixteen when all this went down with Gabriella and Ivy."

"How old was Ivy when it happened?" Kaine lifted her eyes to the museum curator.

"Her mid-twenties," Mr. Mason answered.

Grant winked at Kaine. "Like you."

"I'm thirty." She ducked her head and stared at the paper. "What if Joy's grandmother and Gabriella were held captive together in Foster Hill House?"

Mr. Mason shook his head. "I never heard of women being held at the house. Just the story of the murdered girl."

"Well," Kaine went on, "we know Gabriella was kept there — for some reason, somehow. If Joy's grandmother knew her, that's the only feasible way they could have been connected."

"What makes you think they knew each other?" Mr. Mason set the Fosters' genealogy back in the manila folder.

"Joy. Some stories she remembers her grandmother telling her," Grant said with a quick look at Kaine. She bit her tongue. He was right. They needed to sort out all the clues before they broadcast Gabriella's letters and Maggie's diary to Oakwood.

Mr. Mason cleared his throat. "Sounds like you're leveling some pretty hefty ac-

cusations on Foster Hill House." He chuckled. "Patti won't like it."

Patti. Always Patti. Kaine raised an eyebrow at Grant, but he didn't seem to follow
her suspicion. Of course not. Her mysterious caller and the handprints on the window
of her car had all been from a man. Patti
couldn't be behind any of it.

Kaine's pulse was racing. "It's not an accusation, Mr. Mason. We're just trying to
find out what happened there so many years
ago. My great-great-grandmother almost
gave her life to uncover what happened to
these women. To Gabriella, to Joy's grandmother . . ." Kaine looked down at Joy's
family tree. "Maggie." She put her finger
under the name. "This woman probably
knew everything." Kaine turned to Grant.
"Why would she know what happened and
take her story to the grave? She never let on
that she alone could solve the entire mystery
surrounding Foster Hill House. Why?"

Mr. Mason broke into Kaine's string of
questions. "Maybe she didn't want to upset
her future."

"Huh?" Kaine couldn't help the perplexed
curl of her upper lip.

Mr. Mason shrugged. "Sometimes the
only way you can silence the bad being done
and protect the ones you love is to hold it

all inside and never breathe a word."

The plush carpet was soft beneath Kaine's bare feet. She sat cross-legged in the middle of Joy's living room floor, Grant beside her. Midnight's arrival had sent Joy and Megan to bed. Kaine picked a piece of fuzz off the leg of her bright pink lounge pants as Grant pushed a copy of a newspaper clipping toward her. She took it from him and their fingertips grazed. Kaine froze and looked at the man across from her, but he was engrossed in a library book on the history of Oakwood, comparing it with another page in his hand. She studied his hair that stuck up in ruffled places, the straight line of his nose, his carved lips, and his jaw. His arms were strong beneath a long-sleeved blue United States Navy T-shirt, and he wore his own pair of sweats that made Kaine wonder what it would be like to snuggle up with him. Instead, here they were dissecting incomplete town documents with copies afforded them by Mr. Mason and library resources.

Grant leaned forward and picked up his iPad. "I'm going to see if I can pull up that census that Mr. Mason had. I bet we can find Ivy Thorpe if we look hard enough."

Kaine had called her sister, but Leah

hadn't come through with Ivy's married name. She didn't ever remember hearing it, and outside of Prescott, all they recognized was *Thorpe,* the name Ivy had seemed to hand down. As if she had never married yet mothered the future genealogy.

Kaine didn't respond but instead reached for a book. Somewhere in all these documents and books, the puzzle pieces had to fit together. Tomorrow, she was going to read every single diary entry Gabriella had penned on the pages Kaine had carefully placed in a shoe box and slid under the bed in Megan's room. Joy had finally acquiesced to reading her grandmother Maggie's diary. Kaine longed to read it herself, but what for her was a puzzle piece to her situation, to Joy was an emotional journey into her grandmother's tumultuous past. Perhaps, with those previously unknown pieces, the links would connect.

"Hey."

Kaine looked up.

Grant was studying her, the tablet propped in his lap. "You okay?"

"Yeah," Kaine breathed. "Yeah, I'm fine." And she was. For the moment.

Grant shoved the tablet from his lap and reached for her. Without considering any consequences, Kaine followed his lead and nestled into his side as he tucked her there. She was right. He *was* nice to snuggle into.

He bent his neck to look into her face, and Kaine tipped her head back.

"I'm not going anywhere." Grant traced his finger down her cheek.

Kaine's skin tingled along the trail his finger made. "I know."

Grant's eyes smiled back at her. Kaine might consider drowning in them someday, if she could only get past her fear.

"We'll get through this," he reassured her.

"We?" Kaine baited him. Maybe it was wrong to, but she couldn't help herself.

"*We* sounds good to me."

Kaine couldn't argue. But it had only been a month since she'd come to Oakwood. It was so soon, so early in knowing him, so —

His lips were soft. Gentle. Confident. Kaine closed her eyes. Maybe God *did* speak, but through circumstances and not words. Maybe He had led her here not to uncover something tragic but to answer her prayer for hope. Kaine leaned into Grant's caress. Maybe Grant was part of that hopeful equation.

He kissed her again, never increasing in passion, his kiss merely expressing the beginning of their tenuous relationship. Grant pulled back and leaned his forehead against hers.

Kaine was thankful he'd kept the kiss light. Her insides were dancing with the thrill of the moment and also the fear of what was to come.

Grant twisted and reached for one of the library books. His movement, casual and sure, assuaged her trepidation. He was a genius when it came to squelching her anxiety. He was taking things slowly, and Kaine might be beginning to love him just a little for that.

"Can I show you something?" he asked.

Grant held out a book opened to a page with a glossy black-and-white photo of Ivy. Kaine met Ivy's eyes. They were alive in the photograph, filled with spirit, and there was a small quirk to her upper lip as if she was smiling. Not in humor, but as if she knew something the photographer didn't and was satisfied to take her secrets to the grave.

"Why does she look like she's hiding something?" Kaine said.

Grant bent over the book. "She does, doesn't she?"

"I wonder if . . ."

"If what?" Grant's voice lowered.

"If she knew the truth after all. Like Maggie."

"You mean, what if Ivy *did* solve the

417

mystery of Foster Hill House?" Grant's eyebrows flexed upward.

"Yes. But, she never told anyone."

Grant's eyes dropped to her lips, then raised back to her eyes. He offered a lazy smile, and Kaine tried to make sense of her frazzled and fragmented thoughts. "I suppose that's a possibility."

Kaine avoided Grant's smoldering gaze and instead studied Ivy's face. Her mouth, her cheekbones, her hair swooped into a haphazard pile on the top of her head, dress with puffed sleeves, and a locket.

"Grant!" Kaine's finger landed on the locket with a flash of her red chipped fingernail polish.

Grant slid Kaine's finger aside. "So it *is* Ivy's locket."

"That's the one we found in the attic!" Kaine straightened on the floor to face Grant, but her finger pounded Ivy's face.

Grant scooped up his iPad. He flicked his fingers in opposite directions on the screen, enlarging the scrolling handwriting. "I have the census here. Okay. We need to find out about what happened to Ivy *after* all this."

Kaine peered over his shoulder. "I don't know her by anything other than Ivy Thorpe."

Grant nodded. "I know. But what about

her father? Let's look for the name Thorpe and just see what we find."

Was it wrong that she rested her chin against his shoulder just so she could smell his spicy scent? He didn't seem to mind as he worked the tablet.

"Wait." Kaine lifted her head. She pointed. "There. Matthew Thorpe. I remember that name now — from the family Bible my grandpa had. It was Ivy's father."

"Ah ha!" Grant grinned. "Now we're getting somewhere."

"Matthew Thorpe resides with Joe Cold-ham and wife, Ivy, ages thirty-five and thirty-one. Daughters, ages ten, five, and two." Kaine finished deciphering the script.

"The census was taken nine years after the dead girl was found at Foster Hill House," Grant added.

"I know my great-great-grandmother was married in —" Kaine pulled the library book back onto her lap and skimmed over Ivy's picture to a brief description of her — "1906."

Grant didn't answer, and Kaine lifted her head to study him. His brows were furrowed as he stared at the tablet.

"What is it?" Kaine couldn't help the feeling of familiar unease that resurfaced inside her.

Grant's mouth contorted in contemplation. "The census was taken in 1915. Ivy married Joe Coldham in 1906. That's nine years later."

"So?"

"So their eldest daughter? She's ten years old, not nine, or even younger. Which means Ivy's daughter was born before Ivy married."

"But . . ." Kaine leaned back with her shoulders slouched. Kaine snatched the tablet from Grant's hand. "She can't . . . she can't have . . ." The pit in her stomach grew and erased the warm peace of just moments before.

"If Gabriella and Maggie were both held in Foster Hill House, and Ivy was attacked and almost killed there, what if the killer did to Ivy whatever it was he did to Gabriella and Maggie?"

Kaine removed Ivy's locket from where it hung around her neck beneath her T-shirt. She unlatched it to reveal the lock of hair. "This. It's like baby hair. What if . . . ?" She let her sentence hang. She couldn't speak it, couldn't voice the horrible abuse she was terrified had been visited on Ivy.

"You're thinking Ivy was raped?" When Grant said the words, it made Kaine snap the locket shut. She'd seen it so many times before. The abused, the victims of sexual violence, pregnant, the aftereffects of an abortion, or raising a child that resembled their abusers. It was horrific. It was worth never speaking of again. Of wiping from the pages of history. Kaine recalled the Bible whose family tree ended with Ivy's name.

She cleared her throat and fought back tears. "What if Ivy's daughter was the result of whatever she endured at Foster Hill House? What if it was the same horror Maggie never wished to talk about and Ivy took to the grave?"

Grant's scowled. "Wait. Are you talking about sex trafficking?"

Kaine laid her palm over the photograph of Ivy in the library book. "People think the concept of the sex trade is modern day." She closed the book on Ivy's face. "But it's been around since man decided that the value of women was the same as their livestock."

"It would explain a lot about the comings and goings at Foster Hill House through the years." Grant nodded. "Even the women Myrtle Foster claimed to have seen."

Kaine didn't want to contemplate it further, but all the facts were pointing toward the horrors she'd worked with her entire career.

"But why Foster Hill House? In small-town Oakwood? It's not like this is Chicago where you'd find a hub or a network."

Grant's question was valid, but to Kaine it made sense. "Canada." She pointed to the iPad. "Pull up a map."

Grant took a few seconds, but soon the tablet had loaded a map of Wisconsin, Illinois, the Great Lakes to the east, and Lake Superior and Canada to the north. Kaine studied it for a long moment, then pointed.

"See? Traffickers have routes, sort of like the Underground Railroad did. If women were abducted in Canada, they would need to bring them south, toward Chicago, or to logging and mining camps along the way. They were known to transport women from Canada and the Upper Peninsula of Michigan in ships on the Great Lakes. More likely than not, Chicago was the hub where women could be transported via rail out west."

"How do you know all this?" Grant interrupted.

Kaine grimaced. "You learn how this stuff works after you're immersed in helping to save these women. It wasn't much different in Victorian times or the early 1900s. Mail-order brides?"

"Really?"

Kaine nodded and continued. "Some mail-order bride advertisements weren't really that. There was a sex-trafficking ring in Chicago way back when, and they'd advertise for brides to transport them out west. But instead of finding husbands, they were sold to brothels."

"Man, that's sick." Disgusted, Grant shook his head. "So you think Foster Hill House was a stop-off point between Canada and Chicago?"

Kaine drew in a deep breath as she reached up to unclasp Ivy's locket from her neck. "I think Foster Hill House was the perfect hiding place. It was obscure, out of the way, off the map. An abandoned house no one cared about. A midway point." She set the locket on the floor by the books. The very idea of it hanging around her neck made her skin burn with the memories it held.

Silence enveloped them until Grant cleared his throat. "But Ivy wasn't sold. She survived."

"So did Maggie," Kaine nodded.

"Then why did they stay in Oakwood? After all the horror, why not flee from the memories?"

Kaine met Grant's eyes. "I need to find out."

"*We* need to find out," Grant stated.

Kaine nodded her agreement. Abuse had followed her family for generations. Abuse had scarred her, affected her marriage, and the side effects of abuse had taken Danny's life. Now it reared its ugly existence again, only from the pages of her own history. It had followed Kaine, since 1906.

"It's time we lay Gabriella to rest forever," Kaine murmured. "It's what Ivy tried to do before she fell victim too."

Grant reached for Kaine and tugged her once more into the comforting circle of his embrace. He rested his chin on the top of her head. "Crazy, but it seems that over a hundred years later, someone still doesn't want us to exhume the truth."

"But we will," Kaine whispered. "For Ivy, for Gabriella, for Maggie . . . For me."

CHAPTER 38

IVY

Something crawled over her hand, and Ivy snatched it back. A spider probably, or a cockroach perhaps. God only knew what dwelt in this claustrophobic pocket behind the wall. Darkness enveloped her, and she had only enough room to sit with her knees curled to her chest. A tiny strip of light poked through the seam where the panel met the wall. Ivy had tried to move the panel, but it had to be latched on the outside somehow. She wasn't the first to try. She could feel the indentations where other fingernails had scraped the wall.

It was becoming horribly clear as time ticked by that this secret in the walls of Foster Hill House stretched beyond Gabriella. Maggie must know that secret. Ivy had seen the fear in the girl's eyes when she'd visited Widow Bairns and she remembered that fear long after she had gone to

Joel and Sheriff Dunst to communicate her suspicions.

Ivy's breaths began to come in shorter gasps, but she forced herself to pause and draw in a long one. She couldn't afford to panic, even though hundreds of scenarios played through her mind. Her father would notice her missing the moment he made coffee for breakfast and she didn't appear. Or he would notice her door open and that she was gone. Either way, he would go to Joel, and Joel would know where to come looking, wouldn't he? Although, Ivy leaned her head against the wall, he likely would not consider the possibility of secret spaces behind closet walls. She could scream and pound on the wall, but eventually her voice would give out, and how would she know when or if Joel had even arrived? It was obvious her abductor would move his horse and wagon since there was never any evidence of one being near Foster Hill House before. He was well practiced, this man, and very, *very* organized.

Ivy shifted as her leg cramped beneath her. She couldn't wait for Joel, or her father, or even Sheriff Dunst. Her survival and well-being were in her own hands. The captor would return, and Ivy cringed at the reminder of his hands on her sides. The motives in his hands was evil, with intent to rob Ivy of everything precious.

She flinched when the panel scraped open.

"Haven't gone anywhere, eh?" The dark eye of her captor winked at her.

Ivy took the opportunity to memorize his face. She would need to be able to describe him to Joel and Sheriff Dunst when she escaped.

"Here." He shoved a tin plate at her. Ivy took it. A biscuit, beans, a small piece of cheese.

Please, God. Not now. Not that. She tried not to flinch under the man's leering expression. The longer she could keep him chatting, the more she could see beyond him into the closet and the bedroom to see if he was alone. The next time he opened the door, she wanted to be prepared to escape.

"Do you have any honey for my biscuit?" Ivy couldn't help baiting him, even though inside she was trembling.

"Cheeky thing." He snatched the biscuit from her plate and tossed it over his shoulder. "Now eat up. Don't need you fainting away from starvation." The man moved to close the door.

"What do you plan to do with me?" Ivy's question made him stop.

His eyebrows shot upward and disappeared behind a shock of graying hair. His mustache twitched as his mouth twisted into a snarl. "What I do with all the girls." He reached out, and Ivy regretted her question immediately. His hand pulled at her hair that tumbled down around her shoulders, in disarray from sleep and her struggle. He rolled a lock of it between his first finger and thumb, then plunged his fingers into her hair with force, pulling her face closer to his. "You'll fetch a pretty penny."

"You intend to sell me?" The words turned her mouth sour.

"I sell them all. But you? Only when I'm finished with you."

Disgust gripped her, but Ivy leaned forward. "She almost bested you, didn't she? Is that what happened?"

"Who?" He squinted, lines stretching from the corners of his eyes into the wrinkles on either side of his nose.

"The girl you killed and disposed of in the hollowed-out oak tree."

Without pause, he shoved her backward. The panel slammed back into place. Ivy kicked at it, then again for good measure.

Her leg cramped again in the confined space. Ivy longed to stand up and stretch. Had it been an hour or twelve? It was impossible to gauge time in her prison. She flexed her fingers and arms, unbuttoning another pearl button on her nightgown's collar. The compartment was suffocating, and Ivy's lungs ached for fresh air.

She shifted, reaching out in the darkness for the thousandth time, as if feeling the wall would reveal a magical doorknob to open and provide an escape. Giving up, Ivy dropped her hands to her lap and leaned her head against the wall.

This place was a grave. Ivy's throat clenched. In some ways, it wasn't much different from how she had felt since burying Andrew. Boxed into a dark tomb of routine, living day by day trapped in the memories that stopped collecting the moment Andrew died. Her father had his medical practice and people to pour his life into. He had his faith in God and a quiet, resigned peace that God knew best. God knew best? Ivy always spurned such clichés. God hadn't righted a broken world yet. He could stop injustice and yet He didn't. By recording memories, honoring the lives of those who had passed, and refusing to allow legacies to float away on the winds of time, Ivy had chosen to do what God had seen fit not to. In her own way, Ivy kept them alive.

She stiffened, alert and wary, as scuffling

sounded on the other side of the secret panel. Ivy scrambled to curl her legs beneath her so she could crouch with her feet firmly planted on the floor. The moment her captor opened the panel, she'd launch herself forward. Foolhardy perhaps, but it was her only option. She had no intention of waiting to see what he did with her. If Gabriella's untold story was any indication, Ivy had best succeed in her efforts to escape or she would not survive.

A sliver of light peeked through. Ivy caught a glimpse into the closet and the room beyond. Daylight. Thank God, it wasn't nighttime when she would need to flee into darkness. The panel snagged, then jerked all the way open as the man pushed it aside. Without hesitation, Ivy leaped forward, her hands extended in front of her. She rammed them into her captor's chest, and he toppled backward. His curse and yell followed Ivy as she hurried to her feet. Her toe caught on the hem of her gown and she tripped, grabbing at the bed frame to right herself.

"What in blazes!" The man had already righted himself. She couldn't waste time looking back. She sprinted from the bedroom, catching the eye of Myrtle Foster as she fled past the portrait. It seemed the matriarch's expression had somehow changed. Urgent, concerned, as if she begged Ivy to hurry, to run faster.

Fingers curled around the collar of Ivy's nightgown, yanking her backward. She slammed into the wall, and the man flipped her around to face him. He slapped her across the face with the back of his hand. Ivy cried out, her head jerking to the side, but she turned it back in time to level a fiery glare at her captor. She would not give up, she would not die. Not like Gabriella had. She clawed at his wrists as his hands closed around her throat and began to squeeze.

"You're just like the other one. You won't be reasonable."

Ivy opened her mouth but she couldn't breathe. She pried at the fingers around her throat, trying to loosen them. Her cries were muffled. Ivy lifted her hands to his face, but he loosened his grip around her throat to trap her against the wall. Once again the full length of his body pressed into hers, his face so close Ivy could smell tobacco on his breath and the tiniest hint of liquor.

"Stop fighting!" he shouted. She squirmed beneath him, but it only seemed to bring a strange light into his eyes. A light Ivy didn't want to interpret. She calmed beneath his weight, allowing herself a moment to draw deep breaths as her mind raced with the limited options left to free herself.

Locking eyes with her attacker, Ivy snarled, "You're a monster."

He didn't even flinch. The corner of his mouth lifted in a wicked smile.

"They're coming for me." Ivy prayed they were. She prayed that her father had alerted Joel and that even now he was on his way. But she couldn't rely on rescue. It hadn't come for Gabriella, and she had died, maybe with Maggie watching in horror. "I know what you did to her."

"To who?" His growling tone implied he knew exactly whom Ivy referred to.

"Was she the only one?" Ivy didn't mention Maggie. Something told her to protect the girl who still lived in the shelter of Widow Bairns's home.

His hands snaked up her sides toward her neck. Ivy's skin crawled at his rough and greedy caress. His fingers closed around her throat once again. "You ask too many questions. You're just like my mother."

Ivy frowned, but she watched as his attention shifted from her face to the portrait behind her. The portrait of Myrtle Foster. Realization dawned then.

"Are you her son?" Ivy managed to ask around his stranglehold.

He looked back at her, eyes narrowed, and pressed his lips against her ear. " 'Save the girls,' my mother prayed. She failed. All those years, she failed."

In his moment of distraction, Ivy raised her foot and rammed it into his kneecap. The man Foster buckled and hollered in pain, collapsing to the floor. She ran a few steps, but his hand shot out and caught her around the ankle. Ivy fell, her chin hitting the floorboards. Her teeth bit into her tongue, and the taste of blood filled her mouth.

"Let go of me!" Ivy kicked at him, yet he dragged her toward him and then lunged on top of her. As they wrestled, she raked at his face with her fingernails. A vile name escaped his mouth. The sting of his hand across her face blinded her for a moment, and then rage filled her. Rage for Gabriella. She had fought for her life. The evidence of her self-defense was left on her body, and Ivy recalled vividly every bruise and scrape Gabriella had been given by this man.

A cry rose in Ivy, pushing up from the depths of her own tired and hope-lost soul. She shoved her arms upward and dug her thumbs into the man's throat. He wheezed, and she dug harder.

"You killed her." Every ounce of hatred

dripped from her accusation.

Myrtle Foster's son gagged, but he tightened his knees around her waist.

Ivy rolled, catching him by surprise. He fell to the side, and she grabbed for the wall, bracing herself as she stumbled to her feet. She ran toward the stairs and sped down them, her hands hoisting her nightgown high. She could hear Foster tramping down the stairs behind her. His shouts filled her ears, though his words were indiscernible.

She yanked the front door open, the daylight blinding her. Blinking rapidly, she charged down the porch steps onto the lawn and ran. Ivy sprinted down Foster Hill, as if following the footsteps Gabriella had laid before her. Her panicked vision skimmed the hollow oak tree. Gabriella's grave. She tripped on a root in the path and skidded across the ground. Ivy fought to catch her breath, her chest heaving.

Foster yelled at her, and she scrambled to her feet, her gaze still fixed on the tree. Ivy could almost hear Gabriella, urging her on across the breeze.

Run, Ivy, run! Hope is waiting.
So she did.

CHAPTER 39

Ivy paid no attention to the patter of rain as it dripped from the infant spring leaves in the woods that bordered the road to Foster Hill House. There had been an early morning rain and even now it continued to fall lightly, striking the top of her head. Her lungs threatened to explode as she gasped for air, but she couldn't afford to stop. Not even for a moment. Ivy knew that the tiny room in that closet had imprisoned enough girls over the years to imply something far more devious and wretched. Foster Hill House was a stopover point for girls. Girls who would be sold to abusers like Foster.

The whinny of a horse captured Ivy's attention. She squinted as she hurried over ruts in the road. Pushing back her damp hair, she couldn't hold back the cry of hope that escaped her throat. Joel. She watched his masculine form jump down from the back of his chestnut gelding even before it stopped prancing at the sudden pull of the reins.

"Joel!" Ivy stumbled.

He sprinted toward her. She righted herself and crashed into him. Burying her face in his shoulder, sucking in deep breaths, she tried to coax air into exhausted lungs. His hands framed her face as he held her away from him. She could feel his icy blue appraisal of her face. Ivy licked her split lip, tasting dried blood where Foster had hit her. Joel's thumb brushed across her scuffed chin and over what had to be a bruise forming on her left cheekbone.

"*Who* did this to you?" Joel asked, anger in his eyes. He touched her mouth, then gripped her shoulders as the sheriff rode up beside them and swung down from the saddle. Ivy glanced at the lawman, who cocked the gun already in his hand.

"What happened?" Sheriff Dunst demanded.

Ivy pointed down the road toward Foster Hill House. "It's him." Her gasps made her words barely understandable. She tried to collect herself, but her strength was depleted.

Joel's fingers combed the hair back from her face, and his hands pressed warmth into her cheeks while looking her in the eye.

"Who, Ivy?"

"Myrtle Foster's son." Ivy pulled back from Joel and cast a glance in the sheriff's direction. "He held me in a secret room in the house. He all but admitted to doing the same to Gabriella and Maggie and God knows how many others."

"Why?" Sheriff Dunst barked.

"He sells them!" Ivy waved her arm toward Foster Hill. "You must stop him. You have to arrest him."

Sheriff Dunst swung back into the saddle. "Joel, stay here with Miss Thorpe," he ordered. Then he spurred his horse into a run. As the sheriff headed toward Foster Hill, Ivy shoved away from Joel.

"We need to go. We need to get Foster, once and for all." She marched with determination for Joel's gelding, reaching up to grip the saddle and shoving her foot into the stirrup.

Joel grabbed her around the waist and pulled her down. Ivy spun and slapped him across the face. The instant after her hand connected with his face, it flew to cover her mouth. What had she done? The shock of inflicting pain on Joel was enough to give Ivy pause. He didn't react, only pulled her toward him, his hands gripping her upper arms.

A gunshot echoed. Birds scattered from the treetops into the sky. Joel eyed them, then looked up the road to where Sheriff Dunst had disappeared, then back to Ivy.

"I have to go, Ivy." His expression was torn. Wanting to stay to protect her, but the obvious need of assisting the sheriff heavy on his conscience.

"I'll be all right," Ivy reassured him. But something was off, a dizzy, spinning feeling. Her sight went dark, then cleared, and then Joel's face blurred.

"Ivy," he said and gave her a small shake. Her skin felt sickeningly cold. "Ivy."

Her body started to tremble. No. Not now. Ivy urged her physical reaction of shock away. This wasn't the time to become a hindrance and detract from the chance to bring Gabriella's killer to justice.

She jolted as she heard Joel curse under his breath. But as her eyes met his, his face blurred again. Ivy blinked rapidly as it seemed the wind had turned into an icy breath. Shock. She knew her body was reacting to the increase of adrenaline and the sudden reality of being within the grip of safety. Joel's face cleared again as Ivy squeezed her eyes shut and then opened them.

"I'll be fine. Please —" she faltered —

"go." Blackness once again crowded her vision, and her knees turned to jelly. She remained standing only by sheer force of her will to push herself up against Joel's grip on her.

She heard Joel whisper, "Forgive me." And then his mouth claimed hers in a fierce caress. At her whimper, Joel plunged his fingers through her hair, hungry, as if the years between them had stored his need and now it'd been loosed. Ivy gripped his shirt, knowing in her head he was trying to bring her out of her shock, but in her heart she understood that this moment had been cultivated from years of loss.

Warmth returned to her skin, and for the first time she held on to him.

"Ivy . . ." Joel's eyes looked haunted, filled with the need for vengeance but also the necessity to be with the one he loved.

Ivy stepped away from him, her legs stable again. "Go, Joel. Get him. For me." She blinked back tears that hadn't pooled in her eyes since Andrew's death. "For Gabriella."

CHAPTER 40

KAINE

"Foster!" Grant slammed the book in front of Kaine. She jumped, her coffee sloshing over the rim of the styrofoam cup. Patti, the librarian across the room, cleared her throat.

"Look." Grant pushed the book closer to Kaine.

She grabbed a Kleenex from her purse and dabbed the coffee drips before the librarian could see the mess. "Shh. Patti is giving us dirty looks."

He slid his chair closer to Kaine and ran his index finger along the image of a newspaper clipping's headline inserted between paragraphs in a book about Oakwood's history. "Read this."

Kaine squeezed the bridge of her nose. Grant was a bloodhound when it came to trying to figure out Ivy's and Gabriella's stories. She released her nose and read.

Kaine frowned. "I don't get it."

"Keep reading." Grant rested his elbow on the table, and she caught a whiff of his cinnamon latte as he took a sip.

Yesterday, Sheriff Patrick Dunst, with the aid of Detective Joel Cunningham, apprehended Arnold Foster, member of the founding family and son of Billy and Myrtle Foster. Mr. Foster is being held in question for the murder of the unknown girl found at the base of Foster Hill. No additional details have been provided.

Kaine read the paragraph again. "Arnold Foster was the son of the family run out of town at the end of the Civil War?"

"Mm-hmm." Grant leaned back in his chair and stretched his arms over his head. "Which means the Fosters came back to Oakwood. At least Arnold did."

"I wonder how they caught him." Kaine lowered her voice as she caught Patti's eye. The woman was a gargoyle. "Did he really kill Gabriella?"

Grant lowered his arms, and one of them came to rest on the back of Kaine's chair. "Therein lies the question."

"How come no one saw this before?" She found it hard to believe that Gabriella's death at Foster Hill House had been so cloaked in mystery when a newspaper clipping in an Oakwood historical volume was practically emblazoned with the culprit. "It doesn't seem as though anyone ever brought up the Fosters as being a part of the mystery."

Grant checked the book's copyright date. "This was compiled in the early sixties. Part of a collaborative effort of the town historians to preserve Oakwood's history."

"Preserve." Kaine nodded. "Was it compiled before 1963?"

"Yeah, 1961."

"Shortly before Ivy's quilt was stolen from the museum. Remember how Mr. Mason said other items went missing then too? Clippings and such? Our theory of a cover-up? It seems as though people *did* know a fuller story, but then decades later someone tried to strike it from the books. As if, when this book was published, it stirred up someone who didn't want the Fosters' past to come to light."

"Sounds like a conspiracy theory." He flipped through the book again, focusing on the pages of photographs. There were no more news clippings, and the pictures were of random items that used to be in Foster Hill House.

Kaine leaned in over the book. "Someone doesn't want the truth told. They have never wanted it told. And now, my being here is bringing it all back into the light."

Grant stilled and reached for her hand. "Whatever the reason, we're going to figure this out."

Kaine tossed him a doubtful roll of her eyes and pulled her hand back. She was tired. She pushed her chair back and stood, reaching for her purse. "I need some air." She caught Grant's concerned expression as she hurried away, avoiding Patti at the main desk by weaving through the maze of library tables and shelves.

She pushed open one of the double doors to the library, and a blast of fresh air met her. Kaine skipped down the flight of stairs and across the sidewalk to a small flower garden with a park bench. The flowers were mere sprouts pushing up from the earth. Kaine set her purse down on the walkway next to them as she plopped onto the bench. She leaned forward with her elbows on her knees, breathing deeply of the fresh air. So much lost history. Scribbled censuses, incomplete family trees . . . Kaine knew that many people attempted to trace their roots back in time and many historical documents were incorrect, illegible, or confusing. But did the results of that family history carry the same weight that it did in Kaine's life?

A whiff of cinnamon and coffee met Kaine's nostrils, and she glanced up to see Grant approaching her. She stared down at her hands, picking some old fingernail polish off her thumbnail.

"When I was kid, I used to come here." Grant eased onto the bench beside her. He mimicked her position, folding his hands in front of him. "I loved the library."

"Like you love the animal shelter, and broken hearts." Kaine didn't appreciate the way her words came out in a muted, cracked tone. The tears in her throat clogged her voice.

"Well," he chuckled, "maybe God was sort of setting me up to be the more sensitive type." Grant smiled, and it reached his eyes, saturating his face with warmth. "But a *manly* sensitive," he clarified with an exaggerated flex of his left bicep.

Kaine gave a weak smile. It was that empathy in him that she was coming to rely on. A trait that caused her to open up and see her emotional bruises and scars. Even before Danny's death, she'd been suffering wounds. The wounds of abuse, of her father's abandonment, and of her mother's death.

"Where is God in all of this?" The question escaped her. Kaine let it rest between them.

Grant pursed his lips and stared ahead at the garden. She was thankful he didn't leap into an answer. Kaine knew God was here. She never doubted it. But the existence of evil was something mankind would wrestle with until God righted the world.

Kaine twisted on the bench to face Grant. "Do you know why I love daffodils?"

"Why?" Grant looked deep into her eyes, listening with focused intent.

"Because they have simple layers. Tulips don't seem real. They're like wax flowers with five or six petals all wrapped around a center. Roses make no sense. They have so many elements to them, it's chaotic. But daffodils? Their layers are in order, simple and consistent from flower to flower. Their yellow cheers me and makes me believe in beauty."

Grant nodded but said nothing. He knew when to listen, and she was glad of that.

"I want to see beauty. Not darkness. Not death. But life and promise."

Her breath caught as Grant's eyes softened and his brows drew together in a look so

445

tender she thought for a moment she might become lost in it.

"Our promise of life is so much larger than this moment, Kaine." His hand came up, and his fingers trailed down her cheek. "God promises that this world will have trouble. And a lot of it. But He also promises that He has overcome it."

"How?" Kaine whispered, blinking furiously against tears.

Grant threaded his fingers through hers. "He gives us glimpses now, but His plan for us is so much greater than what we see. That's the pitfall of humanity. We look at our present circumstances, our trials, even our joys, and believe that this is all there is. But the Lord's vision is so much broader and stretches into eternity. We limit ourselves by looking at the here and now when hope, real hope, is found in our relationship with Him and the future that Christ went ahead to prepare for."

"And He will come again . . ." Kaine whispered.

"Until then" — Grant kept his hand interlocked with hers but looked back at the garden and its tiny promises of life — "we live on His promises. We hope."

"Like Gabriella," Kaine murmured.

"Like Gabriella," Grant echoed.

■ ■ ■ ■

The musty smell of Foster Hill House greeted her nose as Kaine climbed the stairs after disarming the security alarm system. Their intimate chat at the library helped Kaine to regain the gumption to continue to piece together the puzzle. She and Grant drove in silence to the house, Kaine staring at the trees whizzing by. The road, paved and curved, was probably the same road Ivy had walked once, so many years before. Grant had parked the truck outside, stating he needed to catch up on some voicemails from work before he followed her in. Kaine didn't mind. Sometimes, even as an extrovert, she needed time alone.

Now she paused by Myrtle Foster's portrait. Warped and torn, it had more than seen its last day on display, yet Kaine was loath to take it down. She had witnessed everything in her silent sentinel. Myrtle Foster knew the secrets of this house, had witnessed the night Gabriella was murdered, understood why Ivy's locket had been hiding in the attic, and somehow her face reflected the grief that the horrors demanded.

"You hated what you saw, didn't you?"

Kaine whispered, adjusting the shoulder strap of her backpack laden with books from the library. Of course, Myrtle Foster didn't respond. But her tiny black eyes stared back, empty and sorrowful. "And they called you crazy, just like Ivy."

She backed away, turning toward the third bedroom. Kaine stared at the half-torn-up floor and the empty chasm where Gabriella had hid her pages. If she'd been held captive, she must have hidden a pencil stub there too. How she'd ever gotten her hands on something to write with would probably always be a mystery, but Kaine was thankful she had.

Kaine slipped the backpack from her shoulder and unzipped it, pulling out an accordion folder with the loose pages of Gabriella's makeshift diary. Sifting through the papers, she paused on page forty-two of *Great Expectations.* The ink in the margins was faded. Kaine held up a flashlight even though daylight streamed through the window.

I choose to believe.

Kaine lowered the flashlight to the next line.

I know God's presence here. Even in darkness, He is here. He awaits.

Kaine moved to the next page.

I am glad Maggie remains with me. She
will be here when my baby is born. God
provides.

Kaine released a shuddering breath. It was
evidence that Joy's grandmother had indeed
been held at Foster Hill House. So why
hadn't they run? If Gabriella was free to
write on the pages of a book, to hide them
beneath the floor or in the library, what had
kept them within the walls of the house?
And why, after Gabriella had been killed,
did Maggie stay in Oakwood?
Another line captured Kaine's attention.

Someday I will see His face and all of this
will wash away. What will I leave behind?
What will my legacy be? I choose hope.

Kaine clicked off the flashlight.
That was why Gabriella was so compelling. Her story had sucked Kaine in. Gabriella was someone who truly grabbed hold
of God's hand when life threw curveballs.
No. Not even curveballs. Fireballs, really.

What life attempted to destroy, God only made stronger. Gabriella's strength reflected in her story.

And they didn't even know her real name.

A door banged and Kaine started. She needed to show Grant the reference to Joy's grandmother. Jumping to her feet, Kaine tightened the laces on her red Converse tennis shoes and scooped up Gabriella's pages.

She hurried down the stairs, straightening the stack of pages as she spoke.

"You need to see this page, Grant. Gabriella names Maggie in it. We were right about Joy's grandmother. She did know who Gabriella was." Kaine landed at the bottom of the stairs and lifted her eyes. That was weird. Her gaze swept the entryway. She was certain she'd heard Grant enter, but the door was left open. She'd disarmed the alarm system when they arrived, so that didn't help calm the nagging sense of wariness that drifted over her.

Kaine went to the open front door and looked around on the porch and the yard. Grant's pickup truck was there, the front seat empty. Fear pinged in Kaine's mind. She scanned the tree line. Stepping out onto the porch, she caught a flash along the side of the house. The sight of the white Suburban sent panic through her. The sun's reflection off the windshield blinded Kaine.

"Grant?" Kaine's voice wobbled as she yelled for him. She spun on her heel, sprinting for the door as she fumbled in her jeans pocket for her phone. Swiping the screen, she tapped Phone and then Grant's name. She stopped just inside the front door when he answered.

"Grant. Where are you?" she hissed into the phone.

"I'm in the woods. Somehow Sophie got out after I left her in her kennel this morning when I had that session at the house with my client. I saw her running in the field just down Foster Hill."

"Someone's here, Grant." Kaine held her hand around the mouthpiece of her phone. She canvassed the entryway. Empty. "The Suburban. It's outside." She rushed to the bottom of the stairs and looked up toward the second floor.

"Kaine, get outside and into my truck. Lock the doors. I'll be right there. I have a feeling Sophie escaping my place wasn't an accident."

Kaine slipped on the wood floor as she spun to leave. She righted herself by grabbing hold of the banister.

"I'm going to hang up and call the cops," Grant said.

She nodded, even though Grant couldn't see her. The line went dead. Kaine took a step toward the front door and the safety of Grant's truck, but movement caught her eye. She froze.

He stood in the doorway of the parlor. His overalls stretched over his shoulders and hung baggily on his thin frame.

Perplexed, Kaine had a momentary wave of relief, followed by a disturbing surge of alarm.

"Mr. Mason?"

The museum curator stepped into the foyer, his hands nonchalantly tucked in the pockets of his overalls. Oddly, the old man didn't seem quite so fragile now or clueless.

Kaine backed up a step, putting the banister between her and the curator.

Mr. Mason sniffed and looked around the room as if seeing it for the first time. "This place always feels so ghostly."

Kaine watched him warily. "Can I help you with something?" It couldn't be co-incidence that Mr. Mason drove a white Suburban, could it?

"It's not good being alone. Is it, Miss Prescott?"

His words. She hadn't tied the muffled, disguised voice from the phone calls to the elderly man, but the words were too coincidental to be happenstance.

"I'm not alone," Kaine ventured.

"Oh, that's right." He snapped his fingers and pointed. "You have Grant. Chasing after a silly dog that somehow got loose."

Kaine stared at him. Was this really the cute old museum curator? Even his faded blue eyes had sharpened and taken on a more savvy expression.

"Why are you here?" Kaine eyed the doorway, but she'd have to get past Mr. Mason first. While he didn't seem remarkably threatening, she hesitated when he answered.

"You were supposed to get scared off. Silly girl. But you just kept digging."

Kaine blinked. It was like watching a really bad television crime show.

"You called me, didn't you? You're the one."

Mr. Mason crossed the room and looked out the window. He spoke into the glass. "I did. But you don't take hints very well. So, now I'm here, with everything blown wide open. I can't hide any of it anymore, thanks to you."

Hide what? Kaine swallowed hard. Foster Hill's secrets? Its history? Or something more?

Mr. Mason scratched the spot on his head

453

that was covered by wisps of gray hair. He furrowed his brows as if genuinely confused — or totally insane. "I'm just so disappointed in you. In everything. All these years, and it comes to this. Me. You. Foster Hill House. The tail end of a long line of family."

Now he was downright chilling. Kaine took a step, but he stiffened, his eyes boring into her. She tried a different approach. "How'd you get my phone numbers?" Kaine peered over his shoulder and out the window. Where was Grant? Where were the police?

Mr. Mason smiled as he hooked his thumbs on his overall straps. "The first time you left your phone on the table at the museum, and it wasn't hard to get the number off it when you weren't paying attention. You really should set a passcode on your phone."

"And the second phone number?" Kaine was stalling.

"My daughter-in-law. She likes to help me sometimes. It's a nice feeling, I suppose, helping out a pathetic old man."

Kaine scowled. He was a stellar actor. "You manipulated her. She faked a dead car battery and got in my good graces just to use my cellphone and steal the number?

She's okay with that?"

Mr. Mason shrugged. "She knows what it means to protect family."

Kaine shifted, hoping she could edge her way to the front door. "And Ivy's quilt? You painted Danny's name on the house and left the quilt piece here and on my windshield. How did you get in my motel room?"

"Easy," he laughed. "You left your motel key with your phone on the table at the museum. It was simple enough to distract you from noticing as I slipped it from you."

Kaine chided herself for being so sloppy. There was something in Mr. Mason's eyes that cautioned her not to respond.

"Your husband was murdered. Funny how much you can find about another person on the internet."

Kaine was taken aback. With the archaic system at the museum, she hadn't pictured Mr. Mason searching the internet, knowing how to find his way around on a computer. Or maybe it had all been part of his act, part of his plan. Unassuming old Mr. Mason with his manila folders and haphazard methods of historical preservation. It was the perfect way to rid a town of its history.

"You researched me?" A slow anger boiled inside her.

Mr. Mason nodded, his hands still in his pockets. "I look out for Foster Hill House. They've tried to dump this place many times. And then all of a sudden they sell it to some girl from California? Sight unseen? Leave it to Patti to spill the beans on you. She always wanted this place, and a little background check on its buyer and she had your name. 'Course then I had to research you, and it was a pretty quick connection — if you know where to look and why."

Kaine took a few steps to the right. She eyed the front door again, calculating the distance between Mr. Mason and escape. "Did you leave the picture of Danny upstairs to frighten me away?"

Mr. Mason pushed his wire-framed glasses up his nose again. "It seemed fitting to, seeing as you forgot what was most important to you by coming here."

"What is that?" Kaine took another small step. Soon Grant would arrive, along with his pit bull Sophie and the police.

Mr. Mason faced her again, the sunlight from the window beyond turning him into a silhouette. "Family. Family is most important." He lifted his index finger and wagged it at her. "I read how you fought to have your husband's case reopened. I was impressed. But then you gave up, and you came here."

"I had good reason to." Like another freak who wouldn't leave her alone. The same horrid man who had taken Danny from her in revenge for her attempt to help the man's abused wife.

Mr. Mason nodded. "I know you reported a stalker. Again, it's horrible to be alone. You should always stay faithful to your family."

Kaine eased back a step. "I am faithful to Danny. To my family."

Mr. Mason scowled. "By giving up on your husband's death? Running from your stalker and leaving your sister behind? Pursuing Grant Jesse?"

Good grief! "Why do you care? Why would you terrorize me here?"

The old man grimaced and blew a sigh threw his nose. "Because young folk these days don't understand legacy. It's important. It passes from generation to generation. Family should be protected, preserved."

"But Ivy Thorpe was my family too. This place, Oakwood, is the legacy my family left behind. Maybe I came here to preserve my roots and in turn bring some closure to my husband's death?"

"Oh, but you didn't, did you?" Mr. Mason

stalked toward her. Kaine backed up. The front door got farther away as he pressed toward her, leaving little space between them. He raised an accusing finger.

"You ran away because you were scared. Scared of being alone. And you came here and disrupted everything. Digging your nose into Foster Hill House, into the dead woman, into Ivy's tale of woe. Always the martyrs, dead souls that they are. Well, not anymore. I have spent years guarding this history, even the ugly side. But I didn't run from it. I faced it. For my family."

Kaine watched a strange light spring into Mr. Mason's eyes and glisten behind his spectacles. She had no clue what he was rambling about, but then she didn't want to stick around to find out. With a twist of her body, Kaine sprang toward the door.

A shout from behind alerted her. She heard the *click* of a gun an instant before the shot echoed through Foster Hill House.

CHAPTER 41

IVY

A second gunshot's reverberations sent a flurry of wings into the air as more birds fluttered from the treetops.

Joel

Ivy broke into a run, only this time she ran back toward Foster Hill House. Her foot slipped on a patch of ice, but she quickly regained her balance before careening forward into the mud. She grabbed at her ribs, sore from her collision down the stairs and now exacerbated by her struggle with Myrtle Foster's son.

The sound of crashing in the woods to her right caused her to whirl around. A man leaped over a log and sprinted through the trees, slapping at branches that attempted to break his attempt to flee. *Foster.*

The compulsion to get away from the threat only a few hundred yards from her collided with her instinct to protect those she loved. Regardless of everything, regardless of the unresolved, there had been a time she and Joel stood beside each other. Tragedy ripped them apart, but now Ivy recognized the truth. The one who had allowed their loyalty to be severed wasn't Joel at all, it had been her.

Ivy veered into the woods toward the sound of snapping twigs and the shouts of the men. She scurried over a fallen tree, wincing as her body argued against the movement, and swiped away a cobweb that stretched between branches. Raindrops that dripped from the foliage soaked her dress. Ivy recognized the path Foster had taken. He was headed toward the pond. The same pond where they had swum, fished, and where Andrew died.

Several yards ahead, Joel's form cut her off as he dodged a tree. He was all right. Relief only urged Ivy forward. Where was the sheriff? Had he fired the initial shot that had sent Joel on a mission to back him up, and was he the one who'd fired the second shot as well? Ivy hesitated, not wanting to get caught in any cross fire. She grabbed a small sapling to stabilize herself when she saw Joel and Foster, facing off at the bottom of the hill.

"Foster!" Joel shouted.

The older man tossed him a glance. The intensity of Foster's look was so different from the Foster she had seen at the house. Even from a distance, Ivy could see he was panicked.

Foster turned and ran toward the pond, mud spraying his pants as his feet slipped on the soft ground. Joel dashed after him as Ivy watched, frozen. She could do nothing. There was no way she could catch up, no way she could intercede. It was the same helpless feeling she experienced when she'd watched Andrew plunge beneath the ice. Only this time it was Joel whose life hung precariously in the balance. Prayer could give Joel the strength he needed, but she had prayed once before, so many years ago and almost in this very spot. That prayer had ended in the event that forever steered their lives onto different paths.

Joel's steps were sure, cutting a straight line through the muck toward Foster. Ivy squelched a cry as he jumped and Foster crumpled beneath him. Together they crashed to the earth. Foster grunted and wrestled beneath Joel. He got his arm out from beneath Joel's clutch and pushed Joel to the side.

Ivy released the tree and scrambled down the hillside, stopping only when she heard

Joel grunt after Foster's fist drove into his gut.

"Get away from me!" Foster yelled, drawing his arm back to aim his fist at Joel's face. Joel twisted to the side, and Foster's hand pummeled the ground. Joel shoved his arm under Foster's armpit and wrapped his forearm around the man's neck, pushing backward. Foster yelled and punched at Joel's stomach again. Joel absorbed the blow as he pushed Foster off him.

Ivy winced, her breaths coming in gasps, watching as the men wrestled each other. Foster came back at Joel, his hands reaching for Joel's neck. A third gunshot echoed through the woods, and Ivy ducked as if she could avoid the bullet.

Sheriff Dunst burst from the woods into the clearing by the pond and behind Foster. His rifle was jammed against his shoulder and poised to take another shot, this time at Foster instead of the sky. Foster froze in place. Joel panted, trying to catch his breath.

"On your knees, Foster!" Sheriff Dunst commanded. His eyes showed recognition when he looked beyond Joel and saw Ivy. She stayed low to the ground.

Foster dropped to his knees. Joel sprang forward and drew the man's arms behind his back. He gave a sharp yank, and Foster hollered out in pain.

"That's for Ivy," she heard Joel say between gritted teeth. It almost hurt to hear him defend her. This was the Joel she had always wanted and was so certain no longer existed. She could tell he had no qualms about the way he locked the handcuffs Sheriff Dunst tossed him painfully tight around Foster's wrists.

"Who?" Foster snarled.

"Don't play ignorant with me." Joel jerked Foster to his feet.

"I had plans for her," Foster argued, struggling against Joel's hold.

"Try it and I'll shoot. I mean it." Sheriff Dunst leveled the gun on Foster.

"It's my house. I have a right to be there," Foster went on. "You all chased my mother away, but I came back."

"How long have you been funneling women through that house?" Sheriff Dunst demanded. He glanced to where Ivy had sunk to the ground, the wet earth soaking through her dress.

"Longer than you've been alive." Foster spat at the ground in a defiant move against the lawman.

"That's impossible," Sheriff Dunst said.

"There's *big* business in it," Foster laughed, and the sound resonated inside

463

Ivy's head. "The people of Oakwood have been too stupid to see it since my father before me. I don't owe you anything."

Joel shoved Foster, and the man tripped and stumbled to the ground. He stared up at Joel, mud spattered on his face. "Hey!"

"What have you done with the women?" Joel said. His back was still to Ivy, but the expression on Sheriff Dunst's face told her he was none too pleased that she'd followed them into the woods.

Foster snarled, "We sold them. Just like my father used to do."

"To who?" Sheriff Dunst demanded.

Foster glanced at him. "Whoever wanted them. I don't know. We're just a midway point. I'm a runner is all."

Sheriff Dunst shook his head in disgust. "And your father was a part of this?"

"Right under my mother's nose." Foster laughed again. "My father made her believe she was crazy. She would catch a glimpse of one of them girls sometimes when he snuck them from the secret room and down the hall to hand off to the next carrier. He told her she was insane and that she was lucky he didn't put her in an institution. Crazies run in my mother's family, you know."

"Not just your mother's." Joel yanked him to his feet and slammed him against the trunk of a pine tree. "Why did you kill Gabriella?"

Foster frowned. "Who?"

Ivy stiffened, leaning forward to catch every word.

"The girl you stuffed in the hollow oak tree." Joel gave Foster a shake.

"Her?" Foster sniffed. "She deserved it."

"Why'd you put her body in the tree when you knew someone would find her?" Sheriff Dunst interjected.

"I didn't think anyone would find her until later. I didn't have much of a choice. The ground was still half frozen."

Ivy clapped her hand over her mouth as Joel slammed his fist into Foster's stomach. The man doubled over.

Joel stood over him. "Where's her baby?"

Foster coughed, trying to catch his breath. He didn't answer. Joel reached down and clutched the man's neck, his face inches from Foster's. "*Where* is the baby?"

Foster glared at Joel, then his eyes lifted and he caught sight of Ivy. Her body went cold at the fury that emanated from the man fighting against Joel's hold.

"Where!" Joel's hand tightened around Foster's throat. Foster kept staring at Ivy. She couldn't blink. She couldn't breathe. She had to know.

"Find it yourself," Foster finally said.

Sheriff Dunst's stern shout didn't stop Joel from plowing his fist into Foster's gut one more time.

Silence emphasized every tiny sound as Ivy's father stitched a cut above her eyebrow from where Foster had backhanded her. She avoided his eyes, but the ministrations of his hands were soothing to both her body and spirit. There had been moments when she wondered if she would ever see him again. The memory of the hidden space in Foster Hill House and the hints of the evil that happened there humbled Ivy. She could have been killed. She had always promised herself she'd be prepared for death, but now that she had faced its sincere possibility, she realized how much her life meant to her, even with its dark edges and painful moments.

The examination room door burst open.

"Joel!" Her father's face brightened at the sight of him, as if Ivy telling him that Joel was all right had not been enough to appease his worry.

Ivy twisted on the table to see him. He was still covered in mud, his hair matted, his shirt torn and his trouser pocket ripped. Disbelief shone in his eyes as he locked gazes with her.

"Why did you follow us? You weren't thinking at all! You could've been killed!" The accusation in his voice did not match the worried expression in his eyes.

"Because she has always done what she wants." Dr. Thorpe muttered under his breath as he pulled the thread through her skin.

Ivy winced. Both at the truth in her father's words and the sting of the stitching.

Joel dropped onto a chair, his elbows on his knees, and rested his forehead on his palms. "If something had happened to you . . ."

"It didn't." Ivy bit her lip as her father tied off the stitch. How did she tell him she had followed because she thought something terrible might have happened to Joel? The kiss they had shared in the woods only hours before seemed a distant memory now.

"Ivy, you should've let Joel do his job."

Ivy met her father's reprimand with shock. Her father snipped the last stitch and stepped back.

"Dr. Thorpe." Joel lifted his head from his hands. A muscle twitched in his jaw. "May I speak with Ivy?"

Ivy's father glanced between them.

"Alone," Joel added.

Dr. Thorpe walked to a basin of water to wash his hands. "All right then." He sloshed water on his forearms, shook his hands, and reached for a towel. When he turned, he leveled a fatherly gaze on Ivy. She squirmed. She always hated it when he looked at her that way. She didn't know if she should feel criticized or loved.

"Ivy, you took years off my life when you disappeared." He rolled down his sleeves. "I lost Andrew —" the doctor's voice cracked — "and most of you with him. I don't know what I would've done had I lost what little of you I have left."

Her father brushed a kiss on Ivy's cheek. His mustache tickled her skin, and Ivy remembered his kissing her as a child. There was nostalgia behind her father's peck, an unspoken plea. Like her, he needed resolution too. Andrew was buried. Gabriella was buried. Many more would be buried. She could not continue to hold on to the grave.

The door closed behind him, leaving her alone with Joel.

"You're absolutely filthy." She slid off the examination table. A glimpse of her reflection in a mirror on the wall showed Ivy how bruised her face really was. As for cleanliness, she wasn't in much better condition and still in her soiled nightgown, covered only by the blanket she pulled tighter around her.

Joel brushed at the dried mud on his sleeve, oblivious to the dirt that crumbled to the wood floor.

"Did Foster give up where Gabriella's baby is?" She hugged herself as Joel's gaze skimmed her neck where her gown was torn. She squirmed beneath his observation.

Joel cleared his throat. "He won't talk. I think he's miffed he gave up as much as he did."

"We can't quit. We need to find —"

"I have no intention of quitting. Now that you're back and safe, we'll be interviewing Maggie to see what she knows. Maybe she'll talk now that Foster has been detained." The inflection in Joel's voice was clear. She was to leave it to him.

"At least there's no more danger." Ivy's observation was met with a dark glower.

"You heard what Foster said. Foster Hill House has been siphoning women to Chicago for decades. God only knows who else is out there. Foster is only a small part of a much bigger circle."

Ivy crossed the room to the window, next to the chair where Joel sat. She rubbed her arms as she stared through the glass at the front walk. Her breath was shaky and she let it out, the trauma from the last twenty-four hours settling in her muscles. She startled when Joel's hands rested on her shoulders. His body was behind her, his grip firm but making her skin tingle beneath its warmth.

"You knew I'd come for you, didn't you?" he said.

Ivy turned, and Joel dropped his hands. "With God's providence, I saved myself."

She didn't mean for it to hurt him, but hurt flashed across Joel's face anyway. "I wish," she started, "I wish things had been different. I wish your letter hadn't been lost in the mail. I wish I hadn't created inaccurate conclusions about why you left." Ivy toyed with her sleeve. "I wish . . ." She paused, then met Joel's eyes. "I wish you had saved Andrew."

"I wish I'd saved him too," Joel whispered. "I tried, Ivy."

"I know you did."

"It killed me not to be there with you, that night at Andrew's grave." Joel rested his palm gently over her bruised cheek. "I knew you were there, alone, waiting for me, and I didn't come. I failed you. I failed Andrew."

She couldn't speak. The emotion lodged in Ivy's throat defied her desire to say something, anything, to relieve Joel of the pain of responsibility for the events of that day and the night of Andrew's funeral.

Joel dropped his hand, and the absence of warmth from his fingers on her face was stark. "I miss Andrew as much as you do. I have had to think about that day over and over and ask the Lord to still the questions of what I could have done differently to save Andrew and to be there for you. And now, I'm home and I watched you bury yourself alongside a dead woman you don't even know. You live in her death. You have risked your life for a woman's child, and that woman never earned your allegiance, nor has she betrayed it. Didn't you hear your father? When will you learn to live again, Ivy? To see the people around you who love you instead of dwelling in grief and death?"

His question hung between them, unanswered but poignant. It begged her to forgive, to trust. It pleaded with her to release him from the guilt of that day and from the loss of that night. Joel's hand lifted again, hesitated, then reached out to swipe at her cheek. He pulled it away and on his fingertip glistened her tear.

For the first time since Andrew's death, Ivy allowed herself to feel something other than betrayal and determination. For the first time, Ivy wept.

CHAPTER 42

KAINE

Kaine fell to the floor, as if dropping would provide her cover from a flying bullet. The sound of the gunshot ricocheted in the room. Mr. Mason aimed the pistol at her.

"What do you want from me?" she gasped as she rolled onto her back, unwilling to stand for fear any significant movement would cause him to fire again, this time directly at her.

The vast foyer seemed cavernous as Mr. Mason took a few steps toward her.

"I wanted you to go away." His hands were shaking, and the gun wobbled. Kaine bent her knee and planted her foot on the wood floor. He lowered the gun toward her leg, and Kaine stopped. "I knew I needed to come here today. You've involved Grant, and Joy now . . . it's Pandora's box. You should have gone away."

"You're crazy," she whispered.

"I tried to steer you away. I've tried to steer people away from the history of this place for decades." Mr. Mason raised his eyes and gave the vaulted ceiling a cursory once-over. He dropped his gaze back to Kaine. "When Maggie robbed the museum in '63, I knew then — one day a Prescott would show up at Foster Hill House. It's karma. But I wanted to stop it."

"What are you talking about? Maggie, Joy's grandmother?" Kaine raised her other knee. Slowly. So he wouldn't notice.

Mr. Mason removed one hand from the gun to scratch his nose. "Funny old lady, she was. Eighty-three years old and robbing the museum. She took Ivy Thorpe's quilt, a few pictures, but she didn't find Ivy's death journal. No, she didn't. And I knew all along it was her, though no one else figured it out. Who would suspect a doddering old woman of trying to keep mementos for herself?"

Kaine had to agree, but then she hadn't expected this of Mr. Mason either. And, if Maggie was anything like her granddaughter Joy, she could totally picture it.

Mr. Mason stared beyond Kaine toward the window where dust particles danced in the light. It was as if his mind had taken him elsewhere, distracting him. Kaine braced her palm against the floor. The only thing left to do now was shove upward and jump to her feet. But how could she keep the fidgety old man from popping off a random shot? In the distance, Kaine heard the police siren. Grant had succeeded in his 911 call. But where was he now? She had to keep Mr. Mason chatting and pray Grant didn't get shot barreling through the door.

"Why would Maggie steal my great-great-grandmother's quilt?"

Mr. Mason turned in surprise. "Because she was a sentimental old fool who thought it should stay in the family. She wanted to spite the Fosters, to spite me. And what do you mean your 'great-great-grandmother'? It was Ivy Thorpe's quilt."

"She *is* my great-great-grandmother," Kaine insisted. The man was crazy.

"No, no." Mr. Mason's smile was almost sad, as if he pitied Kaine. "Your great-great-grandmother was *not* Ivy Thorpe."

Kaine pictured the family tree. How Ivy had a child listed before her marriage. If what Mr. Mason said was true, then Ivy *hadn't* been assaulted and borne a child? But whose child was it, and how had it become a part of the census under Joe Coldham and Ivy's home?

"Then who was my great-great-grandmother?"

Mr. Mason squatted, his elderly knees cracking, and he circled the barrel of his pistol in the air. "You haven't figured that out yet? It seems obvious to me. Your great-great-grandmother was the infamous Gabriella. The dead woman found at the bottom of Foster Hill. Her baby was the one Ivy Thorpe and Joel Cunningham, the detective, tried so hard to save."

He might as well have thrown a bucket of ice water in Kaine's face. She hadn't predicted that, but it made sense. Far too much sense. The mysterious dead woman, the trafficking of women, the abuse . . . it had followed her through generations. And somehow Ivy must have found Gabriella's child, a daughter. The hair in the locket had to have been hers.

Mr. Mason read the shock on Kaine's face, and he tipped his head to the side and winced. The wince deepened the wrinkles at his eyes. "I'm sorry. See? This is why family should be protected, not put on display for all to see. It becomes such a tragic mess."

"But Maggie is not Gabriella's family. So her stealing the quilt to preserve it for the family . . . it still makes no sense. Why did she care?" Kaine's mind raced. She could see the outline of the puzzle, but the inner

476

pieces were still in disarray.

"I asked her the same thing when I confronted her. Told her I knew it was her who broke in. She said it was none of my business. Maggie said Gabriella's descendents should have it so they could remember Ivy, the woman who saved Gabriella's legacy, her child. An unspoken hero, Maggie implied. Sort of sickened me, really."

Tears sprang to Kaine's eyes, and she blinked them back. Joy's grandmother had repaid Ivy's devotion by robbing the museum at eighty-three years old. It would almost be funny if it weren't so desperately bittersweet.

"Did she steal the missing records too?" Kaine started to push off the floor, but he noticed and his eyes sharpened. She stopped.

"No. I did. I disposed of anything else that would incriminate our family without being too obvious. It was easy to do. I could blame it all on the break-in."

"Incriminate our family?" Kaine searched her memory, trying to piece together what Mr. Mason was saying. *Our* insinuated Kaine was tied to Mr. Mason. That was not an equation she was able to add up.

He filled in the gap for her. "My family. Your family. The Fosters. The ones who trafficked women through this place. Do you think that's a legacy that should be preserved? No. It should be lost in the annals of history to protect our family name. But just like Ivy Thorpe, you had to come to Foster Hill House and unearth the family's secrets I've worked so hard to bury with them."

Kaine braced herself against her palm. The barrel of the gun was pointing toward the floor now, the conversation distracting Mr. Mason. "What do you mean 'our family'? I'm Gabriella's great-great-granddaughter. Not a Foster."

His head snapped up. The gun lifted. "Oh, but you *are* a Foster. You are. Who do you think fathered Gabriella's child?"

CHAPTER 43

IVY

Maggie cowered in the corner of the parlor. Ivy had insisted they meet Maggie at Widow Bairns's in an attempt to make her more comfortable. What would be peaceful about being questioned in the jail? With Arnold Foster in a cell in the next room? The poor girl would be miserable. Of course, there really was nothing tranquil about the situation in totality, but maybe the comfort of a house would seem less intimidating.

Ivy inserted herself as hostess as she poured tea into a cup painted with green ivy and lavender violets. Widow Bairns perched by Maggie, clutching the girl's hand and tilting her chin forward. The old woman had a stubborn spirit, and for a brief moment, Ivy hoped she was like the widow someday when she was old. She handed the cup to Maggie, who took it with delicate hands that shook. Their eyes met. In them

Ivy saw the same fear she had been enveloped with in the closet of Foster Hill House. Dare Ivy hope that Gabriella's child was the only reason Maggie had stayed in Oakwood and not fled as far away as she could?

Sheriff Dunst shifted on the blue velvet settee. He was as uncomfortable in the Bairns parlor as Ivy would have been in the jailhouse. They had agreed to let Ivy begin asking the questions. Sheriff Dunst had suggested that Maggie might trust someone with feminine sensibilities, but it was evident by the expression on Joel's face that he'd prefer to commandeer the questioning.

Ivy settled into a wing chair with scrolled wooden arms. She cleared her throat gently. It captured Maggie's attention, and the girl lifted her head. Ivy was struck even more by the youth still in the face of this young woman. She was barely beyond her sixteenth year.

"Maggie," Ivy started softly, "thank you for being willing to speak with us."

Maggie glanced anxiously at the two men, then nodded. Widow Bairns patted the girl's hand in comfort.

Ivy took a sip of her own tea, and Maggie followed suit. "Will you tell me about Foster Hill House? How did you come to be there?"

Maggie looked down at the floor. She was silent for a long time. Sheriff Dunst coughed, and Ivy held her hand up to stop him from saying anything. Poor Maggie needed time. Time to summon courage. Time to open up the memories. She finally spoke, in a voice barely above a whisper.

"My parents died last year. There was an advertisement in the paper for housemaids, so I applied. When I met the man who was to help place me, he took me and I was helpless to fight him off. I was loaded on a steamer along with some other girls, and we crossed Lake Superior into Wisconsin. That's where Foster met us."

"What happened to the other girls? Was Gabriella with you?" Sheriff Dunst interrupted.

"Gabriella?" Confusion filtered across Maggie's face.

"The dead girl," Joel supplied before Ivy could say it more tactfully.

"Oh." Something akin to grief and resignation changed Maggie's posture. Her shoulders sagged. "She was with Foster and some other girls he already had with him." Maggie nodded her head. "We traveled south, and Foster left all of us girls at a brothel outside a logging camp in northern Wisconsin." Her face blanched, and Maggie shut her eyes as if closing away memories, locking them tight and refusing to revisit those moments.

Ivy could only imagine. She didn't *want* to imagine, but the leering look she'd seen in Foster's eyes made the intent of selfish men far too obvious. Ivy swallowed back emotion. Poor Maggie. She was a child. A *child.* Maggie began to speak again, and Ivy shoved down the inner rage that rose as she pictured Foster sitting less than a mile away in his cell. God forgive her, but Ivy hoped he rotted there — painfully.

Maggie looked between the two men sitting in the parlor and then at Widow Bairns as she spoke. The widow rested her wrinkled hand on Maggie's shoulder. Maggie continued.

"*Gabriella* was expecting and she told me it was Foster's baby. She was having difficulties carrying it and needed someone to assist her. Foster was more invested in Gabriella, as you call her, than the baby." A shudder visibly shook Maggie. She picked at a fingernail, her eyes focused on it. "So he brought me here, with her."

"Why you and not one of the other girls?" Joel asked. Ivy cast him a stern look. If they kept interrupting, Maggie might completely withdraw.

"I thought he chose me by chance." Maggie met Joel's eyes briefly. "But Gabriella said it was by providence. She wasn't well. She almost lost the baby on the way to Foster Hill." Her voice turned watery.

"And Foster cared?" Sheriff Dunst snorted.

Ivy gritted her teeth. There was no hope in silencing the overzealous men.

Maggie's hands twisted in the folds of her calico dress. "Not for the baby, no. Like I said, he thought Gabriella belonged to him." She focused on Ivy, and Ivy gave her a nod of encouragement. "Gabriella was his possession."

Ivy saw Maggie's eyes fill with tears, reminding Ivy of her own terrifying moments at the mercy of Arnold Foster. "Maggie, what happened when you arrived at Foster Hill House?"

Maggie blinked and took a nervous sip of her tea. She swallowed. "He said he would take me south to Chicago once Gabriella was well enough to travel. We were at the house for maybe two weeks. We were told to stay inside and not go out, and at night we could use a candle only if we were upstairs in the bedroom. If he left the house, he locked us in the . . . there's a secret space."

"Yes. I know." Ivy remembered — all too well.

"Why didn't you run?" Joel sat on the edge of his chair, leaning forward. "If you weren't always locked away, what made you obey him?"

"How could we run?" Maggie pleaded for understanding. "She . . . *Gabriella,* she could barely walk. Even then h-he came for her sometimes." Tears escaped the corners of Maggie's eyes. "I wasn't going to leave her alone. She kept me safe from him. I owed her that."

Ivy nodded. She hurt for Maggie, agonized for Gabriella, but she had to bite her tongue not to scream out the question that plagued her. Where was Gabriella's baby?

Maggie's expression grew distant. She fiddled with a button on the sleeve of her brown calico. "Gabriella found a pencil stub and hid it away in a bedroom upstairs. She would write prayers. She would pray out loud. She had a book, *Great Expectations,* that Foster must have let her have from his library. She would write in it and rip out the pages and hide them. 'To remember,' she said. 'To remember who I am. I belong to the Lord, not to him.' "

"But you finally did run away, didn't you?" Widow Bairns took Maggie's hand in hers. The elderly woman reached up and brushed aside the brown hair from the pitiful girl's face.

Maggie nodded. "I helped her give birth. Gabriella called her little girl Hallie. Screaming little baby. She had to give birth while Foster was playing that piano downstairs to drown out the sound. He always played it, late at night, when he thought no one would pass by the house. One song, over and over again. He said his mama used to play it, and Gabriella said it was the only thing that seemed to calm the crazy in him."

Ivy glanced at Joel. He gave her a short, meaningful nod. Andrew had heard it once. Even then, while they were innocent children having adventures in the woods, the horrors were taking place in Foster Hill House. They had played in its shadows.

"What happened, Maggie?" Ivy tightened her grip on her teacup. "What happened the night Gabriella died?"

Maggie's eyes instantly glossed over. She swiped at them, to strike away the tears that came unwanted. "It was awful. Two nights after Hallie was born, Gabriella pulled me aside and said she saw a note Foster had written to his contact saying he was going to pack up his 'things' and meet this person. She said that we were Foster's 'things' and she was frightened for Hallie, but also for me. Now that her girl was born, sick or not, Gabriella planned on running that night, to get the baby away from Foster. She made me promise, if anything happened, I'd take Hallie. I'd take her and act as her mama so no one knew where she came from."

Stunned, Sheriff Dunst fell back against the settee.

"Maggie. You never told me," Widow Bairns gasped, holding her hand over her mouth.

Maggie wiped more tears from her cheeks. "We ran. But, Hallie started crying, and it woke up Foster. He chased us down that hill. Gabriella . . . she was weak. Oh, Lord have mercy." Maggie's voice caught in a sob. She covered her mouth with her hands.

"Shh." Ivy reached over and rested her hand on Maggie's knee. She wanted to march down to the jailhouse and slap Foster across the face. Hard. Or worse.

Maggie's eyes were huge in her face. "Plain and simple, she pushed Hallie into my arms and told me to run and not look back. She told me she would be all right. That the good Lord had much bigger places for her to be, but she wanted Hallie to live. Free of her pa. Free of that legacy. So I ran."

"And then you left Hallie at the orphanage? Why didn't you just take her with you and leave Oakwood forever?" Ivy bit her cheek. She couldn't press Maggie too hard, but hope welled within her at the idea that Gabriella's baby was well and alive.

"I hadn't eaten in a few days." Maggie glanced at the widow for support, then turned her attention back to Ivy. "And, I didn't think I could make it very far. The orphanage was there, in my path, it seemed. As if God — and Gabriella — led me to it." A slight smile touched Maggie's lips. "And then I met the widow here, and she took me in."

"She was hiding in my garden shed," Widow Bairns inserted. "Poor child told me most of this, and I had no intention of turning her out."

"And you had no intention of involving the authorities?" Joel said. Sheriff Dunst must have had a similar frame of mind because he sat on the edge of his seat, skewering the elderly benefactress with a glare.

Widow Bairns scowled protectively and waved her lace-glove-covered hand in the air as if to dismiss them. "Intentions, yes! Gumption, absolutely! But you look into this poor face, Sheriff Dunst, and tell me that bringing in burly males from all over to rain justice down on that empty old house's owner wouldn't upset her more."

"Or save more girls' lives?" Sheriff Dunst barked.

Widow Bairns's white eyebrows rose as if speaking to an obstinate child. "All in due time, Sheriff. We thought Foster had moved on to Chicago and the house was empty for now. Maggie needed some time before this —" the widow swept her arm through the air — "this interrogation was to happen!"

Apparently, the widow had no recognition that perhaps Foster hadn't returned to Chicago, and perhaps he could have been waylaid sooner. Ivy couldn't hold such naiveté against the old woman. Widow Bairns was a heroine in Ivy's opinion, whether her choices and methods had been properly vetted or not.

Maggie's eyes widened in earnest determination to defend her benefactress's decisions. "I begged her not to say anything yet. I can't — couldn't — speak of it." Tears ran down the girl's face as she pleaded with the sheriff to understand. "I'm not like Gabriella. I'm not brave," she ended in a whisper.

Ivy opened her mouth to argue but was surprised when Joel pushed himself off his chair and knelt before the girl. He didn't touch her or reach out, but his eyes searched her face earnestly until Maggie met them.

"You are brave, Maggie. You saved Gabriella's baby."

"I left her in an orphanage!" Guilt stretched over Maggie's face. "I couldn't leave Oakwood — I had to stay for Gabriella. I made a promise I'd watch over her girl. She watched over me, kept Foster from touching me — she kept me safe! I owe her my life. But I deserted her baby."

"No." Joel sat back on his heels, and Ivy found herself blinking fast to avoid matching tears to Maggie's. "No. You are Hallie's guardian, just as Widow Bairns is yours. Hallie will forever thank you for that."

Maggie swiped at her tears with her arm, wiping them on her sleeve. She nodded, seeming only to half believe what Joel stated.

Silence pervaded the room. After a moment, Joel cleared his throat. "Maggie, what was Gabriella's real name?"

Maggie raised her head, spearing him with a determined expression. "I'll never tell." Her voice was hard. "Her daddy sold her to Foster. Plain out sold his daughter for money. I won't have him coming for his granddaughter so he can do it all over again. That's one secret you will leave with me and I will take to my grave. I swear it — on my body and my soul."

CHAPTER 44

KAINE

Kaine heard the sound of footsteps on the porch and the sirens screaming up the road. Mr. Mason heard it too. She launched to her feet the moment his gun rose, and the front door flew open as Grant charged through.

"He's got a gun!" Kaine screamed. It was all happening as if someone had stilled the moment. She saw Mr. Mason pointing his pistol at Grant. Without hesitation, Grant hurtled toward Mr. Mason, putting his body in front of Kaine's. Tackling an elderly man brought no remorse to Grant as he straddled Mr. Mason. Gripping the older man's wrist, Grant slammed it against the floor twice until Mr. Mason released the pistol. Kaine sprung forward and snagged it, holding it by the grip with both hands and aiming it at the man who claimed to be her distant relative via the Foster line.

"Kaine. Better set that down. I've got him." Grant shot her a sideways glance.

She looked at the pistol that shook erratically in her hands. Adrenaline was seeping from her, leaving behind a horrible quake.

"Just lay it down," Grant said again.

Surprised by the firmness in his voice, Kaine laid the pistol on the floor by the window. She wrapped her arms around her body. No way was she stepping away from the gun.

"There's no use holding me down. I'm not fighting anymore." Mr. Mason's personality seemed to morph back into the aged, weaker man of the museum. Grant moved off him, then yanked him off the floor with little gentleness. He shoved him onto the bottom step of the staircase and waved his fingers at Kaine.

"The gun."

Kaine bent and retrieved the pistol, placing it in Grant's outstretched hand. He stuffed the gun in the back of his jeans. Any other day, in any other setting, Kaine would have no problem admitting that Grant looked remarkably sexy just now. But physical attraction was quite low on the bullet list of importance at the moment.

Grant reached for Kaine. She backed away, shaking her head. She didn't want to be near Mr. Mason. She didn't want to hear his ridiculous tales of ancestry, the idea that she'd descended from the Fosters. That the very people Kaine had spent her entire career working against were the sort Mr. Mason claimed she came from.

"He's crazy." Kaine reached behind her head and tightened her loosened ponytail, more for something to do with her hands than anything. Grant stood over the elderly man, even as he cast a glance out the window at the police pulling to a stop outside the house.

"He told me that Gabriella, not Ivy, was my great-great-grandmother, and that her baby's father was Myrtle Foster's son! I mean, he's nuts, right?"

Grant's jaw clenched.

"What is it, Grant?"

He let out a sigh. "He's not crazy, Kaine. He's right."

"He's right?" Kaine repeated in disbelief.

Grant nodded. "The voicemails I needed to check when we got here earlier?"

"Yeah?"

His jaw muscle twitched again. Grant continued to grip Mr. Mason's shoulder, even as the cops exited their cars. "One of them was from Joy. She was so excited, she called me instead of you. Force of habit, I guess. She found more of the story in Maggie's book. It's all true. Right down to the fact that Gabriella saved Maggie's life."

Kaine drew in a shuddered breath. "So I'm a descendent of the Fosters? The ones who trafficked women?"

They were interrupted as the police took over. Mr. Mason was whipped around to face the wall, his hands cuffed, with one of the officers quoting the man his rights. Grant turned over Mr. Mason's gun to another cop, and the next several minutes were chaos.

"We'll need you down at the station." Detective Carter shook his head in disbelief as the other cops led Mr. Mason from Foster Hill House. "We need a statement with your account of what happened here. I just can't believe it, that Mason would do this."

Kaine couldn't either, but neither could she speak. The sick feeling was growing in her stomach. The story — *her* story — was unfolding in an ugly tale. Maybe the old man was right and it should have been buried and kept dead in the annals of history. Who wanted to be remembered as the offspring of rape? A result of an antiquated ring of trafficking?

"Hey." Grant took hold of her arm, and

Kaine realized she was still shaking.

She looked up at him. "I can't, Grant. I just — can't fathom."

He led her out of Foster Hill House. Kaine paused on the porch, turning back toward the place. Detective Carter stood in the middle of the doorway, watching her, but Kaine looked beyond him — toward the stairwell that led up to the third bedroom. The stairwell that was guarded by the portrait of her own grandmother, three times removed. Myrtle Foster.

"Myrtle Foster knew, didn't she?" Kaine swallowed hard. Her throat throbbed with emotion.

Grant cleared his own throat. "I called Joy, before I saw Sophie in the field. I was going to come. I was going to tell you. Maggie recounted in her diary that when Oakwood ran Myrtle and her children out of town, Arnold had already seen his father sneaking women through Foster Hill House. After the war, he came back to Oakwood and used the house, now abandoned, as a place to stop off as they transported women to and from the North."

Kaine turned her back to Foster Hill House and walked with Grant down the porch stairs toward his truck. Sophie danced around in the bed of the pickup, her tongue lolling out, oblivious to her role as a pawn in Mr. Mason's attempt to distract Grant and get Kaine alone. It had worked.

"We need to go, Kaine. They need your statement." Grant's hand at her elbow urged her forward.

"I know." Kaine grimaced. Memories of previous statements she'd given in San Diego washed over her. "I've done this before." With her husband's murder. By a man furious that Kaine had helped his abused wife to leave him. What was one more statement? One that would summarize a hundred years' worth of terror and the lives of women whose horrors were finally going to be brought into the light.

Chapter 45

Ivy

The baby's mouth opened wide in a yawn. Her red lips puckered and kissed the air a few times. Hallie turned her face into Ivy's chest and nestled her cheek above her breast, sleep claiming her.

"She's so tiny." Hallie's fingers curled around Ivy's index finger. Her thick white-blond hair was so like her mother's.

"I apologize," Mr. Casey said. Joel stood in front of his old director's desk, his arms crossed over his chest. The man ran his hand over his sideburns and down his cheek. "I had no idea. No idea."

"Perhaps in the future, Mr. Casey, you'll be more cooperative in an investigation." Joel's admonition was met with silence from the director.

"What's to be done with Hallie?" Ivy had never considered herself maternal, but her protective nature encircled the baby as if loving and shielding her could redeem Gabriella from the grave itself. Hallie was a part of her. A part of the horrible Foster family too. But it was Gabriella's faith, her hope, her courage that should live on in Hallie.

Ivy's memory journal was nothing compared with a breathing legacy.

"We're more than happy to care for her here." Mr. Casey rounded his desk. "We will give the child the best of care. Perhaps we can place her with a family."

Ivy gave Joel a look. A family? If what Maggie said was true, they had a small possibility, but still a possibility that Hallie's extended family might look for her should they learn of her existence. Foster was being shipped away to a larger city to stand trial on several charges. What might be printed in the papers about Foster Hill House could expose Hallie to the world from which Maggie had rescued her. They needed to keep Hallie disconnected from Foster Hill House. For now, and in the future.

"I will be checking in on Hallie's care," Joel stated. Mr. Casey nodded nervously. How the tables had turned.

Mr. Casey rang a bell on his desk, and a nursemaid entered. Ivy regretfully relinquished the baby girl into the nursemaid's arms. She watched them leave the room, Hallie's little head resting in the crook of the woman's arm.

"Ivy?" Joel waited at the door.

"Yes." Ivy held herself back from chasing after the nursemaid. It wasn't her place, regardless of what she'd been through, or what she *and* Joel had been through. Hallie wasn't her child, even if she found herself invested in her life more than she had been invested in anyone's death.

She tugged at her jacket that was tailored to her waist and followed Joel from the orphanage. As they walked down the path, Ivy placed her hand around his offered elbow. They'd spoken little since the day Foster had been captured. Ivy's bruises were healing slowly. Maggie seemed to have found a place of permanence with Widow Bairns. Her life would continue, blessed because of Gabriella's sacrifice.

"Maggie said Gabriella wrote often on the pages of *Great Expectations* and hid them. I wonder where? I saw her book that night I was attacked, but if she ripped pages out, like the one we found beneath the bed . . . where are the others?"

Joel gave her a sideways look as they walked. "Foster said he burned the book after he threw you down the stairs."

"Oh." Of course he had. Foster destroyed everything that was Gabriella. Everything but Hallie. "I wish I could have read all of what she wrote."

"I suppose her words are lost forever."

Ivy nodded. She watched a squirrel scamper across the dirt road. A robin swooped overhead. Her eyes alighted on a small patch of buttercups. Spring was here. Warmth was in the air. Something sparked inside Ivy. She wanted to hope again. Like Gabriella.

CHAPTER 46

KAINE

Kaine tapped End on her iPhone after calling Leah on their way back to Joy's house from the police station. It was good to be able to tell her sister that everything was fine, and this time truly mean it. Joy flew at her when they entered the house, and Kaine welcomed Joy's embrace. Megan threw her arms around her as well. Kaine couldn't help the bubble of laughter that escaped. She was never much of a hugger and yet she felt so at home here.

"Oh, honey, I'm so glad you're safe!" Joy pulled back. "Did they take that man into custody?"

Grant nodded and dropped onto Joy's sofa. "For a man who stirred up so much trouble, he was a mess and ready to give himself up by the time the police arrived."

"I think everything caught up to him," Kaine said, leaning back against the wall.

"The years of trying to cover up the Foster family history. Then when I showed up, it consumed him."

"What I still don't get —" Grant frowned, then straightened on the sofa and rested his elbows on his knees — "is how Foster could be so involved in the museum during the time Maggie broke into it. I mean, didn't he say he was in Vietnam when it happened? His timeline doesn't match up."

"Vietnam?" Joy was repositioning Megan's ponytail. "He wasn't in Vietnam. He's been curator of that museum since he graduated from college in '61. Rumor has it he dodged the draft, and like I said, my grandmother Maggie wasn't afraid to make known she was going to protect Ivy and her family."

"Another Mr. Mason cover-up." Kaine raised her brows knowingly in Grant's direction. "He was trying to throw us off the trail, one that would lead back to him."

"Makes sense, I guess," Grant said.

Olive got up from where she lay on the floor and hobbled over to Grant. Sophie followed. Kaine smiled at the two dogs, so comfortable with each other. Sort of like her and Grant.

"Hmm . . . I question one major detail," he added.

"What's that, Grant?" Joy planted a kiss

on Megan's cheek. Megan hurried away down the hall toward her bedroom.

"If Foster was part of a prostitution ring, how come it didn't hit the papers and make more of a splash? Wouldn't it have been all over Oakwood?"

Kaine shrugged. "This is what I fought all the time in San Diego and why human trafficking is so prevalent still today. It's next to impossible to bring down an entire network. You catch the little guys mostly, and Foster was a little guy. If it made the papers wherever he was tried, maybe the story did get linked back to Oakwood. Who knows? Not to mention, Ivy and Maggie certainly weren't going to offer any explanations. And remember, the courthouse burned down — the records were probably all lost years ago. So, what to us has become mysterious, maybe wasn't so much back in the early 1900s."

"Ah, I forgot about that," Grant nodded.

"And," Joy inserted, "Mr. Mason would have swept whatever he could under the rug and probably his parents did the same before him, and so on. Like my grandmother did, only for different reasons."

"He must be a descendent of Arnold Foster's sister, then," Kaine reasoned. "It's not as if Foster went on to have a family.

Gabriella's baby would have been his only offspring . . . then my grandpa Prescott, my mother, Leah and myself."

The image of her shifting family tree drew itself in Kaine's mind. Ivy shifted into a surrogate position, and Gabriella's name took her place as great-great-grandmother.

Grant shook his head. "I wonder what will happen to Mr. Mason? I sort of pity him. All these years he's been obsessed with his family name and their legacy. Meanwhile, he's shriveled into a deceitful old man with no purpose."

"He's the antithesis of Ivy," Joy said, and clucked her tongue.

"No, of what Ivy became," Grant corrected. "Before Gabriella, it seemed Ivy was on the same path. Consumed with preserving the stories of those who had died instead of living the life God blessed her with."

Kaine let Grant's words penetrate her soul. Silence invaded the living room. She watched Grant as he toyed with a leather string tied around his wrist. He had been so faithful to her, so strong when she needed him to be, and had cracked through the walls of protection she'd built around her memories. Kaine moved to the sofa and sank into its cushions, her leg brushed up against Grant's. He glanced at her in surprise. Kaine met his gaze squarely, purpose in her soul.

"I want to be like Ivy," she said.

Grant lifted his arm and curled it around her shoulders. She leaned into him, breathing deeply, drinking in one of the first moments of peace she'd had in . . . well, in years.

Joy settled into a chair across from them. "You can, honey. You can begin to heal now," the older woman comforted. "It's all over."

Kaine didn't want to cry, but the tears burned behind her eyes. Only this time they were healing tears. She blinked. "I've never really cried for Danny or for me. I've just been running. And now I'm here."

Grant ran his fingers through her hair. "You're here. Where you belong. Where your roots are."

"Where my faith can grow," Kaine nodded.

"Yeah. Where a lot of things can grow." Grant thumbed her bottom lip.

Butterflies danced inside her, and a wave of anticipation — of hope — brought a smile to her lips. "For sure," she promised and relaxed into him, knowing that his friendship and probably more would be a part of her future.

"So what happened to Ivy? After all of this?" Kaine looked between Grant and Joy. "Did she adopt Gabriella's baby after all? We found that locket in Foster Hill House. Why was it there?"

Joy bit her lip, and when she let up, red lipstick coated her front tooth. "My grandmother told Ivy's story in her book." Joy wagged her finger. "Now, none of those doubtful looks. She wrote tiny, and there are extra blank pages in the back. Who knew I was sitting on the answers all these years?"

"And?" Kaine leaned forward. "What did she write?"

Grant tugged her closer, and Kaine yielded. It was so nice to be held, to be cherished, to be safe.

Joy smiled. "You'll never believe it, but Ivy's father, Dr. Thorpe, bought Foster Hill House shortly afterward."

"Why would he want to do that?" Grant shook his head in disbelief. Kaine couldn't help but agree, although she didn't say anything.

Joy shifted in her chair. "Well, I should just give you the diary to read, I suppose. But Maggie said it was his way of ensuring the house wasn't used for evil anymore. Ivy married, and they adopted Gabriella's baby, Hallie, and Dr. Thorpe lived with them until he died."

"Hallie!" Kaine straightened. "My sister's middle name is Hallie."

"Wow." Grant raised an eyebrow.

"Yeah," Kaine said. "The generational connections are becoming clear now." Finally, the pieces of the puzzle fell into place. "Hallie, Gabriella's baby, was my great-grandmother."

"I would bet you anything that hair in Ivy's locket is Hallie's," Grant concluded. "It's symbolic of Gabriella's memory and Ivy's love for Gabriella's child."

"And I betcha her locket got lost among the belongings up there in the attic," Joy added.

"If Ivy lived in a house owned by her father, then that's why we found her under the Thorpe name in the census," Grant realized aloud. "Which makes sense, since Ivy wanted to protect Hallie. That's probably why they ended the family tree in your family Bible. Strike her from as many records as possible. Why let that legacy follow Hallie around? In a way, it's the same reasoning as what was behind Mr. Mason's actions."

"Hmmm, could be," Kaine nodded. "The census states that Ivy was married to a Joe Coldham, yet Oakwood recorded her as Ivy Thorpe." On second thought, Kaine hadn't quite connected the dots of her family tree.

"That's what her name was when the events took place," Grant said. "Her married name sort of got lost in your family with the lineage being primarily female. So names would be lost as marriages occurred."

Kaine sighed. Names, genealogies, with over a hundred years in between? It was easy to get muddled by it all.

Grant adjusted his position on the sofa and reached out to scratch Sophie's nose as the dog laid it on his knee.

Kaine buried her fingers in Olive's fur. The black lab had followed her counterpart's move and rested her muzzle in Kaine's lap. "Funny," she murmured, "but I'm tempted to investigate Ivy's husband's lineage now. Coldham. It's a new name to me."

"Who?" Joy's drawn-on eyebrows shot up.

"Joe Coldham. He was listed in the census we researched."

Joy licked the lipstick from her front tooth. "Well, my grandmother's writing says something totally different. Ivy didn't marry a Joe Coldham."

"But that's what the census says," Kaine argued.

"Which would you believe, that census or my grandmother's memory?" Joy waved her hand wildly in dismissal. "You know those old documents with all the scrolly writing? Well, I saw on TV once how last names were often spelled about eight different ways in family trees and government records. Guess that's one plus for the digital age. Maybe we'll get things right going forward."

"Joy is totally right," Grant agreed. "Some people have careers just interpreting old script."

"Well then, who does *Maggie* say Ivy Thorpe married? Who became father to Gabriella's daughter?"

Joy's grin was infectious, and Kaine sensed that she wasn't the only one who had found hope in the shadows of Foster Hill House.

"Oh, Kaine," Joy breathed, "you'll never guess. It just might be the most romantic part of this whole sordid business!"

"So tell me!" Kaine said, sharing a curious smile with Grant.

"The detective." Joy spread her arms wide, as if somehow Kaine should have drawn the conclusion herself. "Joel Cunningham!"

Grant nodded slowly in consideration. "I suppose. Joe Coldham, Joel Cunningham. Yeah, that type of variation wouldn't be out of the norm for a census."

"Joel Cunningham?" Kaine frowned, remembering. "Wasn't he the one who captured Arnold Foster? What made them marry so quickly? Was it just for Hallie?"

"Oh, honey, you have no idea!" Joy leaped to her feet. She did a little hop from foot to foot, her purple tunic top swaying over her yellow polka-dot leggings. "Hold on. I'm going to get Maggie's diary and read it to ya. But first I need some coffee." She swept from the room in a flourish of excitement and left a flowery perfume scent in her wake.

Grant and Kaine sat in silence, until finally his arm slid around her waist and pulled her closer. He leaned over and pressed his lips to her temple.

"I have a feeling there's a whole other part of Ivy's story we're about to find out." His lips moved against Kaine's hair and she shivered, this time from pleasure.

She laid her head on his shoulder. "Me too."

"Do you mind? Not having all the answers?"

Kaine considered Grant's question for a bit, closing her eyes as she pictured Gabriella shoving Hallie into Maggie's arms and giving her life to save them both . . . and changing Ivy's life as well. "Family history may not always be complete, and some of it becomes foggy over time, but one thing I know." She looked up, and Grant gazed down into her eyes.

He waited.

Kaine smiled. "I know that I come from a line of strong women, who fought for their families, fought for those they loved, and saw hope in their future. And I know . . ." She breathed deep in the realization of it. "I know I am one of them."

IVY

Leaves from the previous autumn blanketed the ground and softened Ivy's footsteps as she wove between headstones. Old names, old friends, a place that felt like home. But today was different. The sun warmed the earth and made the dew on the grass glisten like diamonds. The gauzy hemline of her pale blue dress caressed the earth as she passed. She brushed her fingertips over the healing wounds on her face. Healing.

It was why her father was a physician. It was why Ivy had written the stories of those who were buried here. To heal. To survive. But now, Ivy examined herself. She stilled in front of Gabriella's grave. She had set out to find her name, and Maggie made it clear Ivy would never know it. But still, Ivy had been earnest in her journey to unveil Gabriella's story, and there was satisfaction in knowing that Gabriella would be remembered, if not by her name, then by her daughter. By the generations that would come from Hallie and Maggie, the two people Gabriella had given her life to save. And because she wasn't afraid of the grave, she had hope of what would come next.

Ivy ran her hand over Gabriella's cross. Hope was the one thing she had missed in her healing. Hope not only healed, it lessened the scars. She had grown used to loss. She expected it. She expected failure from those around her. But Gabriella, in the brutality of her circumstances, had found hope in Someone greater. Her faith reached into Ivy's soul.

She inhaled a deep breath of warm spring air filled with the freshness of rain. She wanted that hope. To cling to God as Gabriella had. To hold Him so close that this world became an interlude before life truly began.

Ivy trailed her fingers over the marker and turned her face to her brother's stone. She'd expected Joel to meet her here, in the early morning hours. He had promised he would. This time no one would stop him from keeping that promise.

His head was bent as he stood with his back to her. Andrew's resting place was illuminated by a shaft of the morning sun. Joel's shoulders were broad, encased in a white shirt, and relaxed. He looked up at her when she approached, and Ivy offered him a small smile as she noted the gentleness in his eyes. She had seen it there so often many years before. Andrew had told her once that she would marry Joel one day. Joel was one half of her heart, and Andrew the other.

Joel reached for Ivy's hand. She lifted it willingly and wrapped her fingers around his. They both stood in silence over Andrew's grave.

"I'm here," Joel murmured.

Ivy smiled, though her contentment was seasoned with sorrow. "Thank you."

Joel's grip tightened. A mourning dove cooed in a bush beyond the grave. Ivy closed her eyes. She could almost hear the words as they entered her heart.

" 'For in thee, O Lord, do I hope: thou wilt hear, O Lord my God.' " Ivy's whisper floated over the cemetery.

She turned to Joel, and he searched her eyes.

"Gabriella had written that Scripture on the page I found under the bed at Foster Hill House. It was a promise she clung to."

"He heard her," Joel affirmed.

"He did. But it is difficult to accept that promise is fulfilled in spite of our circumstances, not *instead* of our circumstances." The admission pained Ivy. If she accepted Gabriella's death as God's promise of new life, then she must believe the same for Andrew, whose faith was equally strong.

Joel reached for her other hand. Ivy stared down at their interlocked fingers.

"Ivy, it's time."

She looked down at Andrew's grave. "To say goodbye? I know."

Ivy knelt and pressed her lips against the cold stone. But Andrew wasn't there. Not really. And therein lay her hope.

"Farewell, my brother," she whispered. A hot tear trickled down her cheek. Saying goodbye did not mean the ache of emptiness would leave. But, it was time to live again. Andrew would want that. She could see it now.

Joel helped her stand, and Ivy leaned into him.

"We need to protect Hallie and Maggie," she said with firm determination. "And we need to keep the story of Foster Hill House as quiet as we can, for their sake."

"I know." Joel wrapped his arm around her waist. He spoke into her temple, his breath warm and comforting. "It is possible to do that . . . together."

Ivy pulled back a bit and allowed herself

to look deep into his eyes. There was promise there, maturity, and strength that had grown since he was young. She loved him. She always had.

"I would like that," Ivy murmured.

Joel's smile cloaked her in its warmth. "Ivy." His finger trailed softly down her face to her chin. "You were always my Ivy."

She had no bitterness now, no doubts, no questions. Joel's kiss was gentle, slow, but claimed her with purpose. When he pulled back, he seemed thoughtful but very much at peace.

"So we'll make Hallie our own?" Ivy had to ask, searching his face. To be sure.

Joel's mouth tipped up at the corner. He pressed a kiss to her forehead. "Yes. Definitely."

She laid her head against his shoulder as the sun rose above the treetops, shining down on them. A witness to the hope that was rising inside her.

Ivy closed her eyes. She wanted to remember this moment. For it was in this moment that she breathed in life.

"What do we do now?" she whispered into the morning light.

Joel's words brushed her ear with promise. "We do what Gabriella would have wanted us to. We live, right on into eternity."

QUESTIONS FOR DISCUSSION

1. Kaine decides to renovate a house over a century old. Is this a project you would tackle, and if so, what secrets would you hope to find in its architecture?

2. Ivy has a memory book in which she records the lives of those who have passed away. How do you record and remember loved ones who have impacted your own life?

3. Of the two heroes, Joel and Grant, what about them attracted you? Why?

4. What plot twists did you think might happen, but didn't? Or what plot twist surprised you the most?

5. What do you know of your own family ancestry? Are there any lingering questions you'd love to find the answers to?

6. Both Ivy and Kaine have a personal journey to trudge through. Whose journey do you most relate to? What personal journey do you feel you are on at this time in your life?

7. As Ivy and Kaine uncover who Gabriella was and the circumstances surrounding her life and death, they also realize that Gabriella had hope in spite of her circumstances. Where did Gabriella's hope come from and how might you incorporate this same perspective in your life?

8. Were you aware that human trafficking was alive and flourishing at the turn of the century? In what ways do you think it's different today from then? In what ways has society's attitude toward trafficking changed?

9. When you consider human trafficking, what can you do to fight this horrific trade?

Human trafficking is not new to the twenty-first century. It is alive and flourishing. If you or anyone you know are potential victims, please contact the National Human Trafficking Hotline 1-888-373-7888, or visit www.humantraffickinghotline.org.

ACKNOWLEDGMENTS

This book was made possible by Dad, who told me that my first story was dripping with natural talent. While I believe he may have overstated the fact, it helped that he didn't chainsaw down my manuscript and leave me with different aspirations, like becoming an accountant. Because that would have been an epic fail.

It was also made possible by Mom, who didn't force me to learn to cook, so I could learn to write instead. I thank you. My family, on the other hand, does not.

This novel was launched by a swift kick in the pants by Colleen Coble. When Colleen sends you a challenge, you do it. Because she's cool, and making her smile is a great reward.

And, of course, my razor-sharp agent, Mary Keeley, who knows everything. It's true. She does. She's amazing.

Thank you to Becky Germany, who was

the first editor to take a risk on me. She sits high on the shelf of trophy editors. Not literally. That would be creepy. But, seriously, I am in her debt.

Massive thanks go to my stellar Bethany House editor and, more importantly, my friend, Raela Schoenherr. Thank you for Twitter-stalking me. I'm sorry I thought you were a scammer.

Oh, my sisters. Anne Love, Laurie Tomlinson, Kara Isaac, and Sarah Varland. You all help to chart my path. Without you, I am a wanderer. I love you all so very much.

Thank you, my Coffee Clutch peeps! You all are THE best. Ever. Always.

Heaps of gratitude to Julie Baker, my Admin. She keeps me alive. Fed. Hydrated. Organized. Even if she is a tad more obsessed with her dogs than with me. Thank you for giving me the pleasure of bringing your Sophie to life on the page. I love you.

Special thanks to veteran law enforcement officer Dave Edwards, for Facebooking with me to discuss logistics of crimes. I still owe you coffee.

Of course, I will never not mention Peter Pan and CoCo (my Tinker Bell). You will always and forever be the little people who keep me in Neverland. Let's play and never grow up, even though Cap'n Hook seems to think we should be responsible humans.

Cap'n Hook. We are unconventional. I love us for that. Thanks for being my person.

Finally, the most influential person in the creation of this book was my sister, Halee Matthews. Her intuitive editing skills, natural ability to plot and scheme all things dark, and her belief in this book infused spirit into my words. But more importantly, her belief in me and her devoted love in spite of disagreements, annoyances, emotional ups-and-downs (by me!) has changed my life. It has been proven we are bound by soul. Forever. I love you.

ABOUT THE AUTHOR

Jaime Jo Wright is the *Publishers Weekly* and ECPA bestselling author of two novellas, and a human resources director by trade. She lives in Wisconsin with her husband and two children. *The House on Foster Hill* is her debut novel. To learn more, visit jaimewrightbooks.com.